JACKDAWS

ALSO BY KEN FOLLETT

JACK

DAWS

KEN FOLLETT

BOOKSPAN LARGE PRINT EDITION

DUTTON

This Large Print Edition, prepared especially for Bookspan, Inc., contains the complete, unabridged text of the original Publisher's Edition.

DUTTON
Published by the Penguin Group
Penguin Putnam Inc., 375 Hudson Street, New York,
New York 10014, U.S.A.
Penguin Books Ltd, 80 Strand, London WC2R ORL, England
Penguin Books Australia Ltd, Ringwood, Victoria, Australia
Penguin Books Canada Ltd, 10 Alcorn Avenue, Toronto,
Ontario, Canada M4V 3B2
Penguin Books (N.Z.) Ltd, 182-190 Wairau Road, Auckland 10,
New Zealand

Penguin Books Ltd, Registered Offices: Harmondsworth,
Middlesex, England

Published by Dutton, a member of Penguin Putnam Inc.

 REGISTERED TRADEMARK-MARCA REGISTRADA

ISBN 0-7394-2299-5
Printed in the United States of America

**This Large Print Book carries the
Seal of Approval of N.A.V.H.**

Exactly fifty women were sent into France as secret agents by the Special Operations Executive during the Second World War.
Of those, thirty-six survived the war.
The other fourteen gave their lives.

This book is dedicated to all of them.

THE FIRST DAY
Sunday, May 28, 1944

CHAPTER 1

One minute before the explosion, the square at Sainte-Cécile was at peace. The evening was warm, and a layer of still air covered the town like a blanket. The church bell tolled a lazy beat, calling worshipers to the service with little enthusiasm. To Felicity Clairet it sounded like a countdown.

The square was dominated by the seventeenth-century château. A small version of Versailles, it had a grand projecting front entrance, and wings on both sides that turned right angles and tailed off rearwards. There was a basement and two main floors topped by a tall roof with arched dormer windows.

Felicity, who was always called Flick, loved France. She enjoyed its graceful buildings, its mild weather, its leisurely lunches, its cultured people. She liked French paintings, French literature, and stylish French clothes. Visitors often found the French people unfriendly, but Flick had been speaking the language since she was six years old, and no one could tell she was a foreigner.

It angered her that the France she loved no longer existed. There was not enough food for leisurely lunches, the paintings had all been stolen by the Nazis, and only the whores had pretty clothes. Like most women, Flick was wearing a shapeless dress whose colors had long ago been washed to dullness. Her heart's desire was that the real France would come back. It might return soon, if she and people like her did what they were supposed to.

She might not live to see it—indeed, she might not survive the next few minutes. She was no fatalist; she wanted to live. There were a hundred things she planned to do after the war: finish her doctorate, have a baby, see New York, own a sports car, drink champagne on the beach at Cannes. But if she was about to die, she was glad to be spending her last few moments in a sunlit square, looking at a beautiful old house, with the lilting sounds of the French language soft in her ears.

The château had been built as a home for the local aristocracy, but the last Comte de Sainte-Cécile had lost his head on the guillotine in 1793. The ornamental gardens had long ago been turned into vineyards, for this was wine country, the heart of the Champagne district. The building now housed an important telephone exchange, sited here because the government minister responsible had been born in Sainte-Cécile.

When the Germans came they enlarged the exchange to provide connections between the French system and the new cable route to Germany. They also sited a Gestapo regional headquarters in the building, with offices on the upper floors and cells in the basement.

Four weeks ago the château had been bombed by the Allies. Such precision bombing was new. The heavy four-engined Lancasters and Flying Fortresses that roared high over Europe every night were inaccurate—they sometimes missed an entire *city*—but the latest generation of fighter-bombers, the Lightnings and Thunderbolts, could sneak in by day and hit a small target, a bridge or a railway station. Much of the west wing of the château was now a heap of irregular seventeenth-century red bricks and square white stones.

But the air raid had failed. Repairs were made quickly, and the phone service had been disrupted only as long as it took the Germans to install replacement switchboards. All the automatic telephone equipment and the vital amplifiers for the long-distance lines were in the basement, which had escaped serious damage.

That was why Flick was here.

The château was on the north side of the square, surrounded by a high wall of stone pillars and iron railings, guarded by uniformed sentries. To the east was a small medieval church, its ancient wooden doors wide open to the summer air and the arriving congregation. Opposite the church, on the west side of the square, was the town hall, run by an ultraconservative mayor who had few disagreements with the occupying Nazi rulers. The south side was a row of shops and a bar called Café des Sports. Flick sat outside the bar, waiting for the church bell to stop. On the table in front of her was a glass of the local white wine, thin and light. She had not drunk any.

She was a British officer with the rank of

major. Officially, she belonged to the First Aid Nursing Yeomanry, the all-female service that was inevitably called the FANYs. But that was a cover story. In fact, she worked for a secret organization, the Special Operations Executive, responsible for sabotage behind enemy lines. At twenty-eight, she was one of the most senior agents. This was not the first time she had felt herself close to death. She had learned to live with the threat, and manage her fear, but all the same she felt the touch of a cold hand on her heart when she looked at the steel helmets and powerful rifles of the château guards.

Three years ago, her greatest ambition had been to become a professor of French literature in a British university, teaching students to enjoy the vigor of Hugo, the wit of Flaubert, the passion of Zola. She had been working in the War Office, translating French documents, when she had been summoned to a mysterious interview in a hotel room and asked if she was willing to do something dangerous.

She had said yes without thinking much. There was a war on, and all the boys she had been at Oxford with were risking their lives every day, so why shouldn't she do the same? Two days after Christmas 1941 she had started her SOE training.

Six months later she was a courier, carrying messages from SOE headquarters, at 64 Baker Street in London, to Resistance groups in occupied France, in the days when wireless sets were scarce and trained operators even fewer. She would parachute in, move around with her false identity papers, contact the Resistance, give them their orders, and note their replies, complaints, and requests for guns and ammunition. For the return journey she would rendezvous with a pickup plane, usually a three-seater Westland Lysander, small enough to land on six hundred yards of grass.

From courier work she had graduated to organizing sabotage. Most SOE agents were officers, the theory being that their "men" were the local Resistance. In practice, the Resistance were not under military discipline, and an agent had to win their cooperation by being tough, knowledgeable, and authoritative.

The work was dangerous. Six men and three women had finished the training course with Flick, and she was the only one still operating two years later. Two were known to be dead: one shot by the Milice, the hated French security police, and the second killed when his parachute failed to open. The other six had been captured, interrogated, and tortured, and had then disappeared into prison camps in Germany. Flick had survived because she was ruthless, she had quick reactions, and she was careful about security to the point of paranoia.

Beside her sat her husband, Michel, leader of the Resistance circuit codenamed Bollinger, which was based in the cathedral city of Reims, ten miles from here. Although about to risk his life, Michel was sitting back in his chair, his right ankle resting on his left knee, holding a tall glass of pale, watery wartime beer. His careless grin had won her heart when she was a student at the Sorbonne, writing a thesis on Molière's ethics that she had abandoned at the outbreak of war. He had been a disheveled young philosophy lecturer with a legion of adoring students.

He was still the sexiest man she had ever met. He was tall, and he dressed with careless elegance in rumpled suits and faded blue shirts. His hair was always a little too long. He had a come-to-bed voice and an intense blue-eyed gaze that made a girl feel she was the only woman in the world.

This mission had given Flick a welcome chance to spend a few days with her husband, but it had not been a happy time. They had not quarreled, exactly, but Michel's affection had seemed halfhearted, as if he were going through the motions. She had felt hurt. Her instinct told her he was interested in someone else. He was only thirty-five, and his unkempt charm still worked on young women. It did not help that since their wedding they had been apart more than together, because of the war. And there were plenty of willing French girls, she thought sourly, in the Resistance and out of it.

She still loved him. Not in the same way: she no longer worshiped him as she had on their honeymoon, no longer yearned to devote her life to making him happy. The morning mists of romantic love had lifted, and in the clear daylight of married life she could see that he was vain, self-absorbed, and unreliable. But when he chose to focus his attention on her, he could still make her feel unique and beautiful and cherished.

His charm worked on men, too, and he was a great leader, courageous and charismatic. He and Flick had figured out the battle plan together. They would attack the château in two places, dividing the defenders, then regroup inside to form a single force that would penetrate the basement, find the main equipment room, and blow it up.

They had a floor plan of the building supplied by Antoinette Dupert, supervisor of the group of local women who cleaned the château every evening. She was also Michel's aunt. The cleaners started work at seven o'clock, the same time as vespers, and Flick could see some of them now, presenting their special passes to the guard at the wrought-iron gate. Antoinette's sketch showed the entrance to the basement but no further details, for it was a restricted area, open to Germans only, and cleaned by soldiers.

Michel's attack plan was based on reports from MI6, the British intelligence service, which said the château was guarded by a Waffen SS detachment working in three shifts, each of twelve men. The Gestapo personnel in the building were not fighting troops, and most would not even be armed. The Bollinger circuit had been able to muster fifteen fighters for the attack, and they were now deployed, either among the worshipers in the church, or posing as Sunday idlers around the square, concealing their weapons under their clothing or in satchels and duffel bags. If MI6 was right, the Resistance would outnumber the guards.

But a worry nagged at Flick's brain and made her heart heavy with apprehension. When she had told Antoinette of MI6's estimate, Antoinette had frowned and said, "It seems to me there are more." Antoinette was no fool—she had been secretary to Joseph Laperrière, the head of a champagne house, until the occupation reduced his profits and his wife became his secretary—and she might be right.

Michel had been unable to resolve the contradiction between the MI6 estimate and Antoinette's guess. He lived in Reims, and neither he nor any of his group was familiar with Sainte-Cécile. There had been no time for further reconnaissance. If the Resistance were outnumbered, Flick thought with dread, they were not likely to prevail against disciplined German troops.

She looked around the square, picking out the people she knew, apparently innocent strollers who were in fact waiting to kill or be killed. Outside the haberdashery, studying a bolt of dull green cloth in the window, stood Geneviève, a tall girl of twenty with a Sten gun under her light summer coat. The Sten was a submachine gun much favored by the Resistance because it could be broken into three parts and carried in a small bag. Geneviève might well be the girl Michel had his eye on, but all the same Flick felt a shudder of horror at the thought that she might be mowed down by gunfire in a few seconds' time. Crossing the cobbled square, heading for the church, was Bertrand, even younger at seventeen, a blond boy with an eager face and a .45 caliber Colt automatic hidden in a folded newspaper under his arm. The Allies had dropped thousands of Colts by parachute. Flick had at first forbidden Bertrand from the team because of his age, but he had pleaded to be included, and she had needed every available man, so she had given in. She hoped his youthful bravado would survive once the shooting started. Loitering on the church porch, apparently finishing his cigarette before going in, was Albert, whose wife had given birth to their first child this morning, a girl. Albert had an extra reason to stay alive today. He carried a cloth bag that looked full of potatoes, but they were No.36 Mark I Mills hand grenades.

The scene in the square looked normal but for one element. Beside the church was parked an enormous, powerful sports car. It was a French-built Hispano-Suiza type 68-*bis,* with a V12 aeroengine, one of the fastest cars in the world. It had a tall, arrogant-looking silver radiator topped by the flying-stork mascot, and it was painted sky blue.

It had arrived half an hour ago. The driver, a handsome man of about forty, was wearing an elegant civilian suit, but he had to be a German officer—no one else would have the nerve to flaunt such a car. His companion, a tall, striking redhead in a green silk dress and high-heeled suede shoes, was too perfectly chic to be anything but French. The man had set up a camera on a tripod and was taking photographs of the château. The woman wore a defiant look, as if she knew that the shabby townspeople who stared at her on their way to church were calling her *whore* in their minds.

A few minutes ago, the man had scared Flick by asking her to take a picture of him and his lady friend against the background of the château. He had spoken courteously, with an engaging smile, and only the trace of a German accent. The distraction at a crucial moment was absolutely maddening, but Flick had felt it might have caused trouble to refuse, especially as she was pretending to be a local resident who had nothing better to do than lounge around at a pavement café. So she had responded as most French people would have in the circumstances: she had put on an expression of cold indifference and complied with the German's request.

It had been a farcically frightening moment: the British secret agent standing behind the camera; the German officer and his tart smiling at her, and the church bell tolling the seconds until the explosion. Then the officer had thanked her and offered to buy her a drink. She had refused very firmly: no French girl could drink with a German unless she was prepared to be called a whore. He had nodded understandingly, and she had returned to her husband.

The officer was obviously off-duty and did not appear to be armed, so he presented no danger, but all the same he bothered Flick. She puzzled over this feeling in the last few seconds of calm and finally realized that she did not really believe he was a tourist. There was a watchful alertness in his manner that was not appropriate for soaking up the beauty of old architecture. His woman might be exactly what she seemed, but he was something else.

Before Flick could figure out what, the bell ceased to toll.

Michel drained his glass, then wiped his mouth with the back of his hand.

Flick and Michel stood up. Trying to look casual, they strolled to the café entrance and stood in the doorway, inconspicuously taking cover.

CHAPTER 2

Dieter Franck had noticed the girl at the café table the moment he drove into the square. He always noticed beautiful women. This one struck him as a tiny bundle of sex appeal. She was a pale blonde with light green eyes, and she probably had German blood—it was not unusual here in the northeast of France, so close to the border. Her small, slim body was wrapped in a dress like a sack, but she had added a bright yellow scarf of cheap cotton, with a flair for style that he thought enchantingly French. When he spoke to her, he had observed the initial flash of fear usual in a French person on being approached by one of the German occupiers; but then, immediately afterwards, he had seen on her pretty face a look of ill-concealed defiance that had piqued his interest.

She was with an attractive man who was not very interested in her—probably her husband. Dieter had asked her to take a photo only because he wanted to talk to her. He had a wife and two pretty children in Cologne, and he shared his Paris apartment with Stéphanie, but that would not stop him making a play for another girl. Beautiful women were like the gorgeous French impressionist paintings he collected: having one did not stop you wanting another.

French women were the most beautiful in the world. But everything French was beautiful: their bridges, their boulevards, their furniture, even their china tableware. Dieter loved Paris nightclubs, champagne, foie gras, and warm baguettes. He enjoyed buying shirts and ties at Charvet, the legendary *chemisier* opposite the Ritz hotel. He could happily have lived in Paris forever.

He did not know where he had acquired such tastes. His father was a professor of music—the one art form of which the Germans, not the French, were the undisputed masters. But to Dieter, the dry academic life his father led seemed unbearably dull, and he had horrified his parents by becoming a policeman, one of the first university graduates in Germany so to do. By 1939, he was head of the criminal intelligence department of the Cologne police. In May 1940, when General Heinz Guderian's panzer tanks crossed the river Meuse at Sedan and swept triumphantly through France to the English Channel in a week, Dieter impulsively applied for a commission in the army. Because of his police experience, he was given an intelligence posting immediately. He spoke fluent French and adequate English, so he was put to work interrogating captured prisoners. He had a talent for the work, and it gave him profound satisfaction to extract information that could help his side win battles. In North Africa his results had been noticed by Rommel himself.

He was always willing to use torture when necessary, but he liked to persuade people by subtler means. That was how he had got Stéphanie. Poised, sensual, and shrewd, she had been the owner of a Paris store selling ladies' hats that were devastatingly chic and obscenely expensive. But she had a Jewish grandmother. She had lost the store and spent six months in a French prison, and she had been on her way to a camp in Germany when Dieter rescued her.

He could have raped her. She had certainly expected that. No one would have raised a protest, let alone punished him. But instead, he had fed her, given her new clothes, installed her in the spare bedroom in his apartment, and treated her with gentle affection until one evening, after a dinner of *foie de veau* and a bottle of La Tache, he had seduced her deliciously on the couch in front of a blazing coal fire.

Today, though, she was part of his camouflage. He was working with Rommel again. Field Marshal Erwin Rommel, the "Desert Fox," was now Commander of Army Group B, defending northern France. German intelligence expected an Allied invasion this summer. Rommel did not have enough men to guard the hundreds of miles of vulnerable coastline, so he had adopted a daring strategy of flexible response: his battalions were miles inland, ready to be swiftly deployed wherever needed.

The British knew this—they had intelligence, too. Their counterplan was to slow Rommel's response by disrupting his communications. Night and day, British and American bombers pounded roads and railways, bridges and tunnels, stations and marshaling yards. And the Resistance blew up power stations and factories, derailed trains, cut telephone lines, and sent teenage girls to pour grit into the oil reservoirs of trucks and tanks.

Dieter's brief was to identify key communications targets and assess the ability of the Resistance to attack them. In the last few months, from his base in Paris, he had ranged all over northern France, barking at sleepy sentries and putting the fear of God into lazy captains, tightening up security at railway signal boxes, train sheds, vehicle parks, and airfield control towers. Today he was paying a surprise visit to a telephone exchange of enormous strategic importance. Through this building passed all telephone traffic from the High Command in Berlin to German forces in northern France. That included teleprinter messages, the means by which most orders were sent nowadays. If the exchange was destroyed, German communications would be crippled.

The Allies obviously knew that and had tried to bomb the place, with limited success. It was the perfect candidate for a Resistance attack. Yet security was infuriatingly lax, by

Dieter's standards. That was probably due to the influence of the Gestapo, who had a post in the same building. The *Geheime Staatspolizei* was the state security service, and men were often promoted by reason of loyalty to Hitler and enthusiasm for Fascism rather than because of their brains or ability. Dieter had been here for half an hour, taking photographs, his anger mounting as the men responsible for guarding the place continued to ignore him.

However, as the church bell stopped ringing, a Gestapo officer in major's uniform came strutting through the tall iron gates of the château and headed straight for Dieter. In bad French he shouted, "Give me that camera!"

Dieter turned away, pretending not to hear.

"It is forbidden to take photographs of the château, imbecile!" the man yelled. "Can't you see this is a military installation?"

Dieter turned to him and replied quietly in German, "You took a damn long time to notice me."

The man was taken aback. People in civilian clothing were usually frightened of the

Gestapo. "What are you talking about?" he said less aggressively.

Dieter checked his watch. "I've been here for thirty-two minutes. I could have taken a dozen photographs and driven away long ago. Are you in charge of security?"

"Who are you?"

"Major Dieter Franck, from Field Marshal Rommel's personal staff."

"Franck!" said the man. "I remember you."

Dieter looked harder at him. "My God," he said as recognition dawned. "Willi Weber."

"*Sturmbannführer* Weber, at your service." Like most senior Gestapo men, Weber held an SS rank, which he felt was more prestigious than his ordinary police rank.

"Well, I'm damned," Dieter said. No wonder security was slack.

Weber and Dieter had been young policemen together in Cologne in the twenties. Dieter had been a high flyer, Weber a failure. Weber resented Dieter's success and attributed it to his privileged background. (Dieter's background was not extraordinarily privileged, but it seemed so to Weber, the son of a stevedore.)

In the end, Weber had been fired. The details began to come back to Dieter: there had been a road accident, a crowd had gathered, Weber had panicked and fired his weapon, and a rubbernecking bystander had been killed.

Dieter had not seen the man for fifteen years, but he could guess the course of Weber's career: he had joined the Nazi party, become a volunteer organizer, applied for a job with the Gestapo citing his police training, and risen swiftly in that community of embittered second-raters.

Weber said, "What are you doing here?"

"Checking your security, on behalf of the Field Marshal."

Weber bristled. "Our security is good."

"Good enough for a sausage factory. Look around you." Dieter waved a hand, indicating the town square. "What if these people belonged to the Resistance? They could pick off your guards in a few seconds." He pointed to a tall girl wearing a light summer coat over her dress. "What if she had a gun under her coat? What if . . ."

He stopped.

This was not just a fantasy he was weaving to illustrate a point, he realized. His unconscious mind had seen the people in the square deploying in battle formation. The tiny blonde and her husband had taken cover in the bar. The two men in the church doorway had moved behind pillars. The tall girl in the summer coat, who had been staring into a shop window until a moment ago, was now standing in the shadow of Dieter's car. As Dieter looked, her coat flapped open, and to his astonishment he saw that his imagination had been prophetic: under the coat she had a submachine gun with a skeleton-frame butt, exactly the type favored by the Resistance. "My God!" he said.

He reached inside his suit jacket and remembered he was not carrying a gun.

Where was Stéphanie? He looked around, momentarily shocked into a state close to panic, but she was standing behind him, waiting patiently for him to finish his conversation with Weber. "Get down!" he yelled.

Then there was a bang.

CHAPTER 3

Flick was in the doorway of the Café des Sports, behind Michel, standing on tiptoe to look over his shoulder. She was alert, her heart pounding, her muscles tensed for action, but in her brain the blood flowed like ice water, and she watched and calculated with cool detachment.

There were eight guards in sight: two at the gate checking passes, two just inside the gate, two patrolling the grounds behind the iron railings, and two at the top of the short flight of steps leading to the château's grand doorway. But Michel's main force would bypass the gate.

The long north side of the church building formed part of the wall surrounding the château's grounds. The north transept jutted a few feet into the parking lot that had once been part of the ornamental garden. In the days of the *ancien régime,* the comte had had his own personal entrance to the church, a little door in the transept wall. The doorway had been boarded up and plastered over more than a hundred years ago, and had remained that way until today.

An hour ago, a retired quarryman called Gaston had entered the empty church and carefully placed four half-pound sticks of yellow plastic explosive at the foot of the blocked doorway. He had inserted detonators, connected them together so that they would all go off at the same instant, and added a five-second fuse ignited by a thumb plunger. Then he had smeared everything with ash from his kitchen fire to make it inconspicuous and moved an old wooden bench in front of the doorway for additional concealment. Satisfied with his handiwork, he had knelt down to pray.

When the church bell had stopped ringing a few seconds ago, Gaston had got up from his pew, walked a few paces from the nave into the transept, depressed the plunger, and ducked quickly back around the corner. The blast must have shaken centuries of dust from the Gothic arches. But the transept was not occupied during services, so no one would have been injured.

After the boom of the explosion, there was a long moment of silence in the square. Everyone froze: the guards at the château gate, the sentries patrolling the fence, the Gestapo major, and the well-dressed German with the glamorous mistress. Flick, taut with apprehension, looked across the square and through the iron railings into the grounds. In the parking lot was a relic of the seventeenth-century garden, a stone fountain with three mossy cherubs sporting where jets of water had once flowed. Around the dry marble bowl were parked a truck, an armored car, a Mercedes sedan painted the gray-green of the German army, and two black Citroëns of the Traction Avant type favored by the Gestapo in France. A soldier was filling the tank of one of the Citroëns, using a gas pump that stood incongruously in front of a tall château window. For a few seconds, nothing moved. Flick waited, holding her breath.

Among the congregation in the church were ten armed men. The priest, who was not a sympathizer and therefore had no warning, must have been pleased that so many people had shown up for the evening service, which was not normally very popular. He might have wondered why some of them wore topcoats, despite the warm weather, but after four years of austerity lots of people wore odd clothes, and a man might wear a raincoat to church because he had no jacket. By now, Flick hoped, the priest understood it all. At this moment, the ten would be leaping from their seats, pulling out their guns, and rushing through the brand-new hole in the wall.

At last they came into view around the end of the church. Flick's heart leaped with pride and fear when she saw them, a motley army in old caps and worn-out shoes, running across the parking lot toward the grand entrance of the château, feet pounding the dusty soil, clutching their assorted weapons—pistols, revolvers, rifles, and one submachine gun. They had not yet begun firing them, for they were trying to get as close as possible to the building before the shooting started.

Michel saw them at the same time. He made a noise between a grunt and a sigh, and Flick knew he felt the same mixture of pride at their bravery and fear for their lives.

Now was the moment to distract the guards. Michel raised his rifle, a Lee-Enfield No.4 Mark I, the kind the Resistance called a Canadian Rifle, because many of them were made in Canada. He drew a bead, took up the slack of the two-stage trigger, then fired. He worked the bolt action with a practiced movement so that the weapon was immediately ready to be fired again.

The crash of the rifle ended the moment of shocked silence in the square. At the gate, one of the guards cried out and fell, and Flick felt a savage moment of satisfaction: there was one less man to shoot at her comrades. Michel's shot was the signal for everyone else to open fire. In the church porch, young Bertrand squeezed off two shots that sounded like firecrackers. He was too far from the guards for accuracy with a pistol, and he did not hit anyone. Beside him, Albert pulled the ring of a grenade and hurled it high over the railing, to land inside the grounds, where it exploded in the vineyard, uselessly scattering vegetation in the air. Flick wanted to yell angrily at them, "Don't fire for the sake of the noise, you'll just reveal your position!" But only the best and most highly trained troops could exercise restraint once the shooting started. From behind the parked sports car, Geneviève opened up, and the deafening rattle of her Sten gun filled Flick's ears. Her shooting was more effective, and another guard fell.

At last the Germans began to act. The guards took cover behind the stone pillars, or lay flat, and brought their rifles to bear. The Gestapo major fumbled his pistol out of its holster. The redhead turned and ran, but her sexy shoes slipped on the cobblestones, and she fell. Her man lay on top of her, protecting her with his body, and Flick decided she had been right to suppose he was a soldier, for a civilian would not know that it was safer to lie down than to run.

The sentries opened fire. Almost immediately, Albert was hit. Flick saw him stagger and clutch his throat. A hand grenade he had been about to throw dropped from his grasp. Then a second round hit him, this time in the forehead. He fell like a stone, and Flick thought with sudden grief of the baby girl born this morning who now had no father. Beside Albert, Bertrand saw the turtleshell grenade roll across the age-worn stone step of the church porch. He hurled himself through the doorway as the grenade exploded. Flick waited for him to reappear, but he did not, and she thought with anguished uncertainty that he could be dead, wounded, or just stunned.

In the parking lot, the team from the church stopped running, turned on the remaining six sentries, and opened up. The four guards near the gate were caught in a crossfire, between those inside the grounds and those outside in the square, and they were wiped out in seconds, leaving only the two on the château steps. Michel's plan was working, Flick thought with a surge of hope.

But the enemy troops inside the building had now had time to seize their weapons and rush to the doors and windows, and they began to shoot, changing the odds again. Everything depended on how many of them there were.

For a few moments the bullets poured like rain, and Flick stopped counting. Then she realized with dismay that there were many more guns in the château than she had expected. Fire seemed to be coming from at least twelve doors and windows. The men from the church, who should by now be inside the building, retreated to take cover behind the vehicles in the parking lot.

Antoinette had been right, and MI6 wrong, about the number of troops stationed here. Twelve was the MI6 estimate, yet the Resistance had downed six for certain and there were at least fourteen still firing.

Flick cursed passionately. In a fight like this, the Resistance could win only by sudden, overwhelming violence. If they did not crush the enemy right away, they were in trouble. As the seconds ticked by, army training and discipline began to tell. In the end, regular troops would always prevail in a drawn-out conflict.

On the upper floor of the château, a tall seventeenth-century window was smashed open, and a machine gun began to fire. Because of its high position, it caused horrible carnage among the Resistance in the parking lot. Flick was sickened as, one after another, the men there fell and lay bleeding beside the dry fountain, until there were only two or three still shooting.

It was all over, Flick realized in despair. They were outnumbered and they had failed. The sour taste of defeat rose in her throat.

Michel had been shooting at the machine-gun position. "We can't take out that machine gunner from the ground!" he said. He looked around the square, his gaze flying to the tops of the buildings, the bell tower of the church, and the upper floor of the town hall. "If I could get into the mayor's office, I'd have a clear shot."

"Wait." Flick's mouth was dry. She could not stop him risking his life, much as she wanted to. But she could improve the odds. She yelled at the top of her voice, "Geneviève!"

Geneviève turned to look at her.

"Cover Michel!"

Geneviève nodded vigorously, then dashed out from behind the sports car, spraying bullets at the château windows.

"Thanks," Michel said to Flick. Then he broke cover and sprinted across the square, heading for the town hall.

Geneviève ran on, heading for the church porch. Her fire distracted the men in the château, giving Michel a chance of crossing the square unscathed. But then there was a flash on Flick's left. She glanced that way and saw the Gestapo major, flattened against the wall of the town hall, aiming his pistol at Michel.

It was hard to hit a moving target with a

handgun at anything but close range—but the major might be lucky, Flick thought fearfully. She was under orders to observe and report back, and not to join the fighting under any circumstances, but now she thought: To hell with that. In her shoulder bag she carried her personal weapon, a Browning nine-millimeter automatic, which she preferred to the SOE standard Colt because it had thirteen rounds in the clip instead of seven, and because she could load it with the same nine-millimeter Parabellum rounds used in the Sten submachine gun. She snatched it out of the bag. She released the safety catch, cocked the hammer, extended her arm, and fired two hasty shots at the major.

She missed him, but her bullets chipped fragments of stone from the wall near his face, and he ducked.

Michel ran on.

The major recovered quickly and raised his weapon again.

As Michel approached his destination, he also came closer to the major, shortening the range. Michel fired his rifle in the major's direction, but the shot went wild, and the major kept his head and fired back. This time, Michel went down, and Flick let out a yell of fear.

Michel hit the ground, tried to get up, and collapsed. Flick calmed herself and thought fast. Michel was still alive. Geneviève had reached the church porch, and her submachine gun fire continued to draw the attention of the enemy inside the château. Flick had a chance of rescuing Michel. It was against her orders, but no orders could make her leave her husband bleeding on the ground. Besides, if she left him there, he would be captured and interrogated. As leader of the Bollinger circuit, Michel knew every name, every address, every code word. His capture would be a catastrophe.

There was no choice.

She shot at the major again. Again she missed, but she pulled the trigger repeatedly, and the steady fire forced the man to retreat along the wall, looking for cover.

She ran out of the bar into the square. From the corner of her eye she saw the owner of the sports car, still protecting his mistress from gunfire by lying on top of her. Flick had forgotten him, she realized with sudden fear. Was he armed? If so, he could shoot her easily. But no bullets came.

She reached the supine Michel and went down on one knee. She turned toward the town hall and fired two wild shots to keep the major busy. Then she looked at her husband.

To her relief she saw that his eyes were open and he was breathing. He seemed to be bleeding from his left buttock. Her fear receded a little. "You got a bullet in your bum," she said in English.

He replied in French, "It hurts like hell."

She turned again to the town hall. The major had retreated twenty meters and crossed the narrow street to a shop doorway. This time Flick took a few seconds to aim carefully. She squeezed off four shots. The shop window exploded in a storm of glass, and the major staggered back and fell to the ground.

Flick spoke to Michel in French. "Try to get up," she said. He rolled over, groaning in pain, and got to one knee, but he could not move his injured leg. "Come on," she said harshly. "If you stay here, you'll be killed." She grabbed him by the front of his shirt and heaved him upright with a mighty effort. He stood on his good leg, but he could not bear his own weight, and leaned heavily against her. She realized that he was not going to be able to walk, and she groaned in despair.

She glanced over to the side of the town hall. The major was getting up. He had blood on his face, but he did not seem badly injured. She guessed that he had been cut superficially by flying glass but might still be capable of shooting.

There was only one thing for it: she would have to pick Michel up and carry him to safety.

She bent in front of him, grasped him around the thighs, and eased him on to her shoulder in the classic fireman's lift. He was tall but thin—most French people were thin, these days. All the same, she thought she would collapse under his weight. She staggered, and felt dizzy for a second, but she stayed upright.

After a moment, she took a step forward.

She lumbered across the cobblestones. She thought the major was shooting at her, but she could not be sure as there was so much gunfire from the château, from Geneviève, and from the Resistance fighters still alive in the parking lot. The fear that a bullet might hit her at any second gave her strength, and she broke into a lurching run. She made for the road leading out of the square to the south, the nearest exit. She passed the German lying on top of the red-head, and for a startled moment she met his eye and saw an expression of surprise and wry admiration. Then she crashed into a café table, sending it flying, and she almost fell, but managed to right herself and run on. A bullet hit the window of the bar, and she saw a cobweb of fracture lines craze the glass. A moment later, she was around the corner and out of the major's line of sight. Alive, she thought gratefully; both of us—for a few more minutes, at least.

Until now she had not thought where to go once she was clear of the battlefield. Two getaway vehicles were waiting a couple of streets away, but she could not carry Michel that far. However, Antoinette Dupert lived on this street, just a few steps farther. Antoinette was not in the Resistance, but she was sympathetic enough to have provided Michel with a plan of the château. And Michel was her nephew, so she surely would not turn him away.

Anyway, Flick had no alternative.

Antoinette had a ground-floor apartment

in a building with a courtyard. Flick came to the open gateway, a few yards along the street from the square, and staggered under the archway. She pushed open a door and lowered Michel to the tiles.

She hammered on Antoinette's door, panting with effort. She heard a frightened voice say, "What is it?" Antoinette had been scared by the gunfire and did not want to open the door.

Breathlessly, Flick said, "Quickly, quickly!" She tried to keep her voice low. Some of the neighbors might be Nazi sympathizers.

The door did not open, but Antoinette's voice came nearer. "Who's there?"

Flick instinctively avoided speaking a name aloud. She replied, "Your nephew is wounded."

The door opened. Antoinette was a straight-backed woman of fifty wearing a cotton dress that had once been chic and was now faded but crisply pressed. She was pale with fear. "Michel!" she said. She knelt beside him. "Is it serious?"

"It hurts, but I'm not dying," Michel said through clenched teeth.

"You poor thing." She brushed his hair off

his sweaty forehead with a gesture like a caress.

Flick said impatiently, "Let's get him inside."

She took Michel's arms and Antoinette lifted him by the knees. He grunted with pain. Together they carried him into the living room and put him down on a faded velvet sofa.

"Take care of him while I fetch the car," Flick said. She ran back into the street.

The gunfire was dying down. She did not have long. She raced along the street and turned two corners.

Outside a closed bakery, two vehicles were parked with their engines running: one a rusty Renault, the other a van with a faded sign on the side that had once read *Blanchisserie Bisset*—Bisset's Laundry. The van was borrowed from the father of Bertrand, who was able to get fuel because he washed sheets for hotels used by the Germans. The Renault had been stolen this morning in Châlons, and Michel had changed its license plates. Flick decided to take the car, leaving the van for any survivors who might get away from the carnage in the château grounds.

She spoke briefly to the driver of the van. "Wait here for five minutes, then leave." She ran to the car, jumped into the passenger seat, and said, "Let's go, quickly!"

At the wheel of the Renault was Gilberte, a nineteen-year-old girl with long dark hair, pretty but stupid. Flick did not know why she was in the Resistance—she was not the usual type. Instead of pulling away, Gilberte said, "Where to?"

"I'll direct you—for the love of Christ, move!"

Gilberte put the car in gear and drove off.

"Left, then right," Flick said.

In the two minutes of inaction that followed, the full realization of her failure hit her. Most of the Bollinger circuit was wiped out. Albert and others had died. Geneviève, Bertrand, and any others who survived would probably be tortured.

And it was all for nothing. The telephone exchange was undamaged, and German communications were intact. Flick felt worthless. She tried to think what she had done wrong. Had it been a mistake to try a frontal attack on a guarded military installation? Not necessarily—the plan might have worked but for the inaccurate intelligence supplied by MI6. However, it would have been safer, she now thought, to get inside the building by some clandestine means. That would have given the Resistance a better chance of getting to the crucial equipment.

Gilberte pulled up at the courtyard entrance. "Turn the car around," Flick said, and jumped out.

Michel was lying facedown on Antoinette's sofa, trousers pulled down, looking undignified. Antoinette knelt beside him, holding a bloodstained towel, a pair of glasses perched on her nose, peering at his backside. "The bleeding has slowed, but the bullet is still in there," she said.

On the floor beside the sofa was her handbag. She had emptied the contents onto a small table, presumably while hurriedly searching for her spectacles. Flick's eye was caught by a sheet of paper, typed on and stamped, with a small photograph of Antoinette pasted to it, the whole thing in a little cardboard folder. It was the pass that permitted her to enter the château. In that moment, Flick had the glimmer of an idea.

"I've got a car outside," Flick said.

Antoinette continued to study the wound. "He shouldn't be moved."

"If he stays here, the Boche will kill him." Flick casually picked up Antoinette's pass. As she did so she asked Michel, "How do you feel?"

"I might be able to walk now," he said. "The pain is easing."

Flick slipped the pass into her shoulder bag. Antoinette did not notice. Flick said to her, "Help me get him up."

The two women raised Michel to his feet. Antoinette pulled up his blue canvas trousers and fastened his worn leather belt.

"Stay inside," Flick said to Antoinette. "I don't want anyone to see you with us." She had not yet begun to work out her idea, but she already knew it would be blighted if any suspicion were to fall on Antoinette and her cleaners.

Michel put his arm around Flick's shoulders and leaned heavily on her. She took his weight, and he hobbled out of the building into the street. By the time they reached the car, he was white with pain. Gilberte stared through the window at them, looking terrified. Flick hissed at her, "Get out and open the fucking door, dimwit!" Gilberte leaped out of the car and threw open the rear door. With her help, Flick bundled Michel onto the backseat.

The two women jumped in the front. "Let's get out of here," said Flick.

CHAPTER 4

Dieter was dismayed and appalled. As the shooting began to peter out, and his heartbeat returned to normal, he started to reflect on what he had seen. He had not thought the Resistance capable of such a well-planned and carefully executed attack. From everything he had learned in the last few months, he believed their raids were normally hit-and-run affairs. But this had been his first sight of them in action. They had been bristling with guns and obviously not short of ammunition—unlike the German army! Worst of all, they had been courageous. Dieter had been impressed by the rifleman who had dashed across the square, by the girl with the Sten gun who had given him covering fire, and most of all by the little blonde who had picked up the wounded rifleman and had carried him—a man six inches taller than she—out of the square to safety. Such people could not fail to be a profound threat to the occupying military force. These were not like the criminals Dieter had dealt with as a cop in Cologne before the war. Criminals were stupid, lazy, cowardly, and brutish. These French Resistance people were fighters.

But their defeat gave him a rare opportunity.

When he was sure the shooting had stopped, he got to his feet and helped Stéphanie up. Her cheeks were flushed, and she was breathing hard. She held his hands and looked into his face. "You protected me," she said. Tears came to her eyes. "You made yourself a shield for me."

He brushed dirt from her hip. He was surprised by his own gallantry. The action had been instinctive. When he thought about it, he was not at all sure he would really be willing to give his life to save Stéphanie. He tried to pass over it lightly. "No harm should come to this perfect body," he said.

She began to cry.

He took her hand and led her across the square to the gates. "Let's go inside," he said. "You can sit down for a while." They entered the grounds. Dieter saw a hole in the wall of the church. That explained how the main force had got inside.

The Waffen-SS troops had come out of the building and were disarming the attackers. Dieter looked keenly at the Resistance fighters. Most were dead, but some were only wounded, and one or two appeared to have surrendered unhurt. There should be several for him to interrogate.

Until now, his work had been defensive. The most he had been able to do was fortify key installations against the Resistance by beefing up security. The occasional prisoner had yielded little information. But having several prisoners, all from one large and evidently well-organized circuit, was a different matter. This might be his chance of going on the attack, he thought eagerly.

He shouted at a sergeant, "You—get a doctor for these prisoners. I want to interrogate them. Don't let any die."

Although Dieter was not in uniform, the sergeant assumed from his manner that he was a superior officer, and said, "Very good, sir."

Dieter took Stéphanie up the steps and

through the stately doorway into the wide hall. It was a breathtaking sight: a pink marble floor, tall windows with elaborate curtains, walls with Etruscan motifs in plaster picked out in dusty shades of pink and green, and a ceiling painted with fading cherubs. Once, Dieter assumed, the room had been filled with gorgeous furniture: pier tables under high mirrors, sideboards encrusted with ormolu, dainty chairs with gilded legs, oil paintings, huge vases, little marble statuettes. All that was gone now, of course. Instead there were rows of switchboards, each with its chair, and a snake's nest of cables on the floor.

The telephone operators seemed to have fled into the grounds at the rear but, now that the shooting had stopped, a few of them were standing at the glazed doors, still wearing their headsets and breast microphones, wondering if it was safe to come back inside. Dieter sat Stéphanie at one of the switchboards, then beckoned a middle-aged woman telephonist. "Madame," he said in a polite but commanding voice. He spoke French. "Please bring a cup of hot coffee for this lady."

The woman came forward, shooting a

look of hatred at Stéphanie. "Very good, monsieur."

"And some cognac. She's had a shock."

"We have no cognac."

They had cognac, but she did not want to give it to the mistress of a German. Dieter did not argue the point. "Just coffee, then, but be quick, or there will be trouble."

He patted Stéphanie's shoulder and left her. He passed through double doors into the east wing. The château was laid out as a series of reception rooms, one leading into the next on the Versailles pattern, he found. The rooms were full of switchboards, but these had a more permanent look, the cables bundled into neatly made wooden trunking that disappeared through the floor into the cellar beneath. Dieter guessed the hall looked messy only because it had been brought into service as an emergency measure after the west wing had been bombed. Some of the windows were permanently blacked out, no doubt as an air-raid precaution, but others had heavy curtains drawn open, and Dieter supposed the women did not like to work in permanent night.

At the end of the east wing was a stairwell. Dieter went down. At the foot of the staircase he passed through a steel door. A small desk and a chair stood just inside, and Dieter assumed a guard normally sat there. The man on duty had presumably left his post to join in the fighting. Dieter entered unchallenged and made a mental note of a security breach.

This was a different environment from that of the grand principal floors. Designed as kitchens, storage, and accommodation for the dozens of staff who would have serviced this house three hundred years ago, it had low ceilings, bare walls, and floors of stone, or even, in some rooms, beaten earth. Dieter walked along a broad corridor. Every door was clearly labeled in neat German signwriting, but Dieter looked inside anyway. On his left, at the front of the building, was the complex equipment of a major telephone exchange: a generator, enormous batteries, and rooms full of tangled cables. On his right, toward the back of the house, were the Gestapo's facilities: a photo lab, a large wireless listening room for eavesdropping on the Resistance, and prison cells with peepholes in the doors. The basement had been bombproofed: all windows were blocked, the walls were sandbagged, and the ceilings had been reinforced with steel girders and poured concrete. Obviously that was to prevent Allied bombers from putting the phone system out of action.

At the end of the corridor was a door marked Interrogation Center. He went inside. The first room had bare white walls, bright lights, and the standard furniture of a simple interview room: a cheap table, hard chairs, and an ashtray. Dieter went through to the next room. Here the lights were less bright and the walls bare brick. There was a bloodstained pillar with hooks for tying people up; an umbrella stand holding a selection of wooden clubs and steel bars; a hospital operating table with a head clamp and straps for the wrists and ankles; an electric shock machine; and a locked cabinet that probably contained drugs and hypodermic syringes. It was a torture chamber. Dieter had been in many similar, but still they sickened him. He had to remind himself that intelligence gathered in places such as this helped save the lives of decent young German soldiers so that they could eventually go home to their wives and children instead of dying on battlefields. All the same, the place gave him the creeps.

There was a noise behind him, startling him. He spun around. When he saw what was in the doorway he took a frightened step back. "Christ!" he said. He was looking at a squat figure, its face thrown into shadow by the strong light from the next room. "Who are you?" he said, and he could hear the fear in his own voice.

The figure stepped into the light and turned into a man in the uniform shirt of a Gestapo sergeant. He was short and pudgy, with a fleshy face and ash-blond hair cropped so short that he looked bald. "What are you doing here?" he said in a Frankfurt accent.

Dieter recovered his composure. The torture chamber had unnerved him, but he regained his habitual tone of authority and said, "I am Major Franck. Your name?"

The sergeant became deferential at once. "Becker, sir, at your service."

"Get the prisoners down here as soon as possible, Becker," said Dieter. "Those who can walk should be brought immediately, the others when they have been seen by a doctor."

"Very good, Major."

Becker went away. Dieter returned to the

interview room and sat in the hard chair. He wondered how much information he would get out of the prisoners. Their knowledge might be limited to their own town. If his luck was bad, and their security good, each individual might know only a little about what went on in their own circuit. On the other hand, there was no such thing as perfect security. A few individuals inevitably amassed a wide knowledge of their own and other Resistance circuits. His dream was that one circuit might lead him to another in a chain, and he might be able to inflict enormous damage on the Resistance in the weeks remaining before the Allied invasion.

He heard footsteps in the corridor and looked out. The prisoners were being brought in. The first was the woman who had concealed a Sten gun beneath her coat. Dieter was pleased. It was so useful to have a woman among the prisoners. Under interrogation, women could be as tough as men, but often the way to make a man talk was to beat a woman in front of him. This one was tall and sexy, which was all the better. She seemed to be uninjured. Dieter held up a hand to the soldier escorting her and spoke to the woman in French. "What is your name?" he said in a friendly tone.

She looked at him with haughty eyes. "Why should I tell you?"

He shrugged. This level of opposition was easy to overcome. He used an answer that had served him well a hundred times. "Your relatives may inquire whether you are in custody. If we know your name, we may tell them."

"I am Geneviève Delys."

"A beautiful name for a beautiful woman." He waved her on.

Next came a man in his sixties, bleeding from a head injury and limping too. Dieter said, "You're a little old for this sort of thing, aren't you?"

The man looked proud. "I set the charges," he said defiantly.

"Name?"

"Gaston Lefèvre."

"Just remember one thing, Gaston," Dieter said in a kindly voice. "The pain lasts as long as you choose. When you decide to end it, it will stop."

Fear came into the man's eyes as he contemplated what faced him.

Dieter nodded, satisfied. "Carry on."

A youngster was next, no more than seventeen, Dieter guessed, a good-looking boy who was absolutely terrified. "Name?"

He hesitated, seeming dazed by shock. After thinking, he said, "Bertrand Bisset."

"Good evening, Bertrand," Dieter said pleasantly. "Welcome to Hell."

The boy looked as if he had been slapped.

Dieter pushed him on.

Willi Weber appeared, with Becker pacing behind him like a dangerous dog on a chain. "How did you get in here?" Weber said rudely to Dieter.

"I walked in," Dieter said. "Your security stinks."

"Ridiculous! You've just seen us beat off a major attack!"

"By a dozen men and some girls!"

"We defeated them, that's all that counts."

"Think about it, Willi," Dieter said reasonably. "They were able to assemble close by, quite unnoticed by you, then force their way into the grounds and kill at least six good German soldiers. I suspect the only reason you defeated them was that they had underestimated the numbers against them.

And I entered this basement unchallenged because the guard had left his post."

"He's a brave German, he wanted to join the fighting."

"God give me strength," Dieter said in despair. "A soldier in battle doesn't leave his post to join the fighting, he follows orders!"

"I don't need a lecture from you on military discipline."

Dieter gave up, for now. "And I have no desire to give one."

"What *do* you want?"

"I'm going to interview the prisoners."

"That's the Gestapo's job."

"Don't be idiotic. Field Marshal Rommel has asked me, not the Gestapo, to limit the capacity of the Resistance to damage his communications in the event of an invasion. These prisoners can give me priceless information. I intend to question them."

"Not while they're in my custody," Weber said stubbornly. "I shall interrogate them myself and send the results to the Field Marshal."

"The Allies are probably going to invade this summer—isn't it time to stop fighting turf wars?"

"It is never time to abandon efficient organization."

Dieter could have screamed. In desperation, he swallowed his pride and tried for a compromise. "Let's interrogate them together."

Weber smiled, sensing victory. "Absolutely not."

"This means I'll have to go over your head."

"If you can."

"Of course I can. All you will achieve is a delay."

"So you say."

"You damned fool," Dieter said savagely. "God preserve the fatherland from patriots such as you." He turned on his heel and stalked out.

CHAPTER 5

Gilberte and Flick left the town of Sainte-Cécile behind, heading for the city of Reims on a country back road. Gilberte drove as fast as she could along the narrow lane. Flick's eyes apprehensively raked the road ahead. It rose and fell over low hills and wound through vineyards as it made its leisurely way from village to village. Their progress was slowed by many crossroads, but the number of junctions made it impossible for the Gestapo to block every route away from Sainte-Cécile. All the same, Flick gnawed her lip, worrying about the chance of being stopped at random by a patrol. She could not explain away a man in the backseat bleeding from a bullet wound.

Thinking ahead, she realized she could not take Michel to his home. After France

surrendered in 1940, and Michel was demo-
bilized, he had not returned to his lecture-
ship at the Sorbonne but had come back to
his hometown, to be deputy head of a high
school, and—his real motive—to organize a
Resistance circuit. He had moved into the
home of his late parents, a charming town
house near the cathedral. But, Flick decided, he could not go there now. It was
known to too many people. Although Resistance members often did not know one another's addresses—for the sake of security,
they revealed them only if necessary for a
delivery or rendezvous—Michel was leader,
and most people knew where he lived.

Back in Sainte-Cécile, some of the team
must have been taken alive. Before long
they would be under interrogation. Unlike
British agents, the French Resistance did
not carry suicide pills. The only reliable rule
of interrogation was that everybody would
talk in the long run. Sometimes the Gestapo
ran out of patience, and sometimes they
killed their subjects by overenthusiasm but,
if they were careful and determined, they
could make the strongest personality betray
his or her dearest comrades. No one could
bear agony forever.

So Flick had to treat Michel's house as known to the enemy. Where could she take him instead?

"How is he?" said Gilberte anxiously.

Flick glanced into the backseat. His eyes were closed, but he was breathing normally. He had fallen into a sleep, the best thing for him. She looked at him fondly. He needed someone to take care of him, at least for a day or two. She turned to Gilberte. Young and single, she was probably still with her parents. "Where do you live?" Flick asked her.

"On the outskirts of town, on the Route de Cernay."

"On your own?"

For some reason, Gilberte looked scared. "Yes, of course on my own."

"A house, an apartment, a bedsitting room?"

"An apartment, two rooms."

"We'll go there."

"No!"

"Why not? Are you scared?"

She looked injured. "No, not scared."

"What, then?"

"I don't trust the neighbors."

"Is there a back entrance?"

Reluctantly, Gilberte said, "Yes, an alley that runs along the side of a little factory."

"It sounds ideal."

"Okay, you're right, we should go to my place. I just . . . You surprised me, that's all."

"I'm sorry."

Flick was scheduled to return to London tonight. She was to rendezvous with a plane in a meadow outside the village of Chatelle, five miles north of Reims. She wondered if the plane would make it. Navigating by the stars, it was extraordinarily difficult to find a specific field near a small village. Pilots often went astray—in fact, it was a miracle they ever arrived where they were supposed to. She looked at the weather. A clear sky was darkening to the deep blue of evening. There would be moonlight, provided the weather held.

If not tonight, then tomorrow, she thought, as always.

Her mind went to the comrades she had left behind. Was young Bertrand dead or alive? What about Geneviève? They might be better off dead. Alive, they faced the agony of torture. Flick's heart seemed to convulse with grief as she thought again that she had led them to defeat. Bertrand had a crush on her, she guessed. He was young enough to feel guilty about secretly loving the wife of his commander. She wished she had ordered him to stay at home. It would have made no difference to the outcome, and he would have remained a bright, likeable youth for a little longer, instead of a corpse, or worse.

No one could succeed every time, and war meant that when leaders failed, people died. It was a hard fact, but still she cast about for consolation. She longed for a way to make sure their suffering was not in vain. Perhaps she could build on their sacrifice and get some kind of victory out of it after all.

She thought about the pass she had stolen from Antoinette and the possibility of getting into the château clandestinely. A team could enter disguised as civilian employees. She swiftly dismissed the idea of having them pose as telephone operators: it was a skilled job that took time to learn. But anyone could use a broom.

Would the Germans notice if the cleaners were strangers? They probably paid no attention to the women who mopped the floor. What about the French telephonists—would they give the game away? It might be a risk worth taking.

SOE had a remarkable forgery department that could copy any kind of document, sometimes even making their own paper to match the original, in a couple of days. They could soon produce counterfeits of Antoinette's pass.

Flick suffered a guilty pang at having stolen it. At this moment, Antoinette might be looking for it frantically, searching under the couch and in all her pockets, going out into the courtyard with a flashlight. When she told the Gestapo she had lost it, she would be in trouble. But in the end they would just give her a replacement. And this way she was not guilty of helping the Resistance. If interrogated, she could steadfastly maintain that she had mislaid it, for she believed that to be the truth. Besides, Flick thought grimly, if she had asked permission to borrow the thing, Antoinette might have said no.

Of course, there was one major snag with this plan. All the cleaners were women. The Resistance team that went in disguised as cleaners would have to be all-female.

But then, Flick thought, why not?

They were entering the suburbs of Reims. It was dark when Gilberte pulled up near a low industrial building surrounded by a high wire fence. She killed the engine. Flick spoke sharply to Michel. "Wake up! We have to get you indoors." He groaned. "We must be quick," she added. "We're breaking the curfew."

The two women got him out of the car. Gilberte pointed to the narrow alley that led along the back of the factory. Michel put his arms over their shoulders, and they helped him along the alley. Gilberte opened a door in a wall that led to the backyard of a small apartment building. They crossed the yard and went in through a back door.

It was a block of cheap flats with five floors and no lift. Unfortunately, Gilberte's rooms were on the attic floor. Flick showed her how to make a carrying chair. Crossing their arms, they linked hands under Michel's thighs and took his weight. He put an arm around the shoulders of each woman to steady himself. That way they carried him up four flights. Luckily, they met no one on the stairs.

They were blowing hard by the time they reached Gilberte's door. They stood Michel on his feet and he managed to limp inside, where he collapsed into an armchair.

Flick looked around. It was a girl's place, pretty and neat and clean. More importantly, it was not overlooked. That was the advantage of the top floor: no one could see in. Michel should be safe.

Gilberte fussed about Michel, trying to make him comfortable with cushions, wiping his face gently with a towel, offering him aspirins. She was tender but impractical, as Antoinette had been. Michel had that effect on women, though not on Flick—which was partly why he had fallen for her: he could not resist a challenge. "You need a doctor," Flick said brusquely. "What about Claude Bouler? He used to help us, but last time I spoke to him, he didn't want to know me. I thought he was going to run away, he was so nervous."

"He's become scared since he got married," Michel replied. "But he'll come for me."

Flick nodded. Lots of people would make exceptions for Michel. "Gilberte, go and fetch Dr. Bouler."

"I'd rather stay with Michel."

Flick groaned inwardly. Someone like Gilberte was no good for anything but carrying messages, yet she could make difficulties about that. "Please do as I ask," Flick said firmly. "I need time alone with Michel before I return to London."

"What about the curfew?"

"If you're stopped, say you're fetching a doctor. It's an accepted excuse. They may accompany you to Claude's house to make sure you're telling the truth. But they won't come here."

Gilberte looked troubled, but she pulled on a cardigan and went out.

Flick sat on the arm of Michel's chair and kissed him. "That was a catastrophe," she said.

"I know." He grunted with disgust. "So much for MI6. There must have been double the number of men they told us."

"I'll never trust those clowns again."

"We lost Albert. I'll have to tell his wife."

"I'm going back tonight. I'll get London to send you another radio operator."

"Thanks."

"You'll have to find out who else is dead, and who's alive."

"If I can." He sighed.

She held his hand. "How are you feeling?"

"Foolish. It's an undignified place for a
bullet wound."

"But physically?"

"A little giddy."

"You need something to drink. I wonder
what she has."

"Scotch would be nice." Flick's friends in
London had taught Michel to like whisky,
before the war.

"That's a little strong." The kitchen was
in a corner of the living room. Flick opened
a cupboard. To her surprise, she saw a bottle of Dewar's White Label. Agents from Britain often brought whisky with them, for their
own use or for their comrades-in-arms, but
it seemed an unlikely drink for a French girl.
There was also an opened bottle of red
wine, much more suitable for a wounded
man. She poured half a glass and topped it
up with water from the tap. Michel drank
greedily: loss of blood had made him thirsty.
He emptied the glass, then leaned back and
closed his eyes.

Flick would have liked some of the
scotch, but it seemed unkind to deny it to
Michel, then drink it herself. Besides, she

still needed her wits about her. She would have a drink when she was back on British soil.

She looked around the room. There were a couple of sentimental pictures on the wall, a stack of old fashion magazines, no books. She poked her nose into the bedroom. Michel said sharply, "Where are you going?"

"Just looking around."

"Don't you think it's a little rude, when she's not here?"

Flick shrugged. "Not really. Anyway, I need the bathroom."

"It's outside. Down the stairs and along the corridor to the end. If I remember rightly."

She followed his instructions. While she was in the bathroom she realized that something was bothering her, something about Gilberte's apartment. She thought hard. She never ignored her instincts: they had saved her life more than once. When she returned, she said to Michel, "Something's wrong here. What is it?"

He shrugged, looking uncomfortable. "I don't know."

"You seem edgy."

"Perhaps it's because I've just been wounded in a gunfight."

"No, it's not that. It's the apartment." It had something to do with Gilberte's unease, something to do with Michel's knowing where the bathroom was, something to do with the whisky. She went into the bedroom, exploring. This time Michel did not reprove her. She looked around. On the bedside table stood a photograph of a man with Gilberte's big eyes and black eyebrows, perhaps her father. There was a doll on the counterpane. In the corner was a washbasin with a mirrored cabinet over. Flick opened the cabinet door. Inside was a man's razor, bowl, and shaving brush. Gilberte was not so innocent: some man stayed overnight often enough to leave his shaving tackle here.

Flick looked more closely. The razor and brush were a set, with polished bone handles. She recognized them. She had given the set to Michel for his thirty-second birthday.

So that was it.

She was so shocked that for a moment she could not move.

She had suspected him of being interested in someone else, but she had not imagined it had gone this far. Yet here was the proof, in front of her eyes.

Shock turned to hurt. How could he cuddle up to another woman when Flick was lying in bed alone in London? She turned and looked at the bed. They had done it right here, in this room. It was unbearable.

Then she became angry. She had been loyal and faithful, she had borne the loneliness—but he had not. He had cheated. She was so furious she felt she would explode.

She strode into the other room and stood in front of him. "You bastard," she said in English. "You lousy rotten bastard."

Michel replied in the same language. "Don't angry yourself at me."

He knew that she found his fractured English endearing, but it was not going to work this time. She switched to French. "How could you betray me for a nineteen-year-old nitwit?"

"It doesn't mean anything, she's just a pretty girl."

"Do you think that makes it better?" Flick knew she had originally attracted Michel's attention, back in the days when she was a student and he a lecturer, by challenging

him in class—French students were deferential by comparison with their English
counterparts, and on top of that Flick was
by nature disrespectful of authority. If someone similar had seduced Michel—perhaps
Geneviève, a woman who would have been
his equal—she could have borne it better. It
was more hurtful that he had chosen Gilberte, a girl with nothing on her mind more
interesting than nail polish.

"I was lonely," Michel said pathetically.

"Spare me the sob story. You weren't
lonely—you were weak, dishonest, and
faithless."

"Flick, my darling, let's not quarrel. Half
our friends have just been killed. You're going back to England. We could both die
soon. Don't go away angry."

"How can I not be angry? I'm leaving you
in the arms of your floozie!"

"She's not a floozie—"

"Skip the technicalities. I'm your wife, but
you're sharing her bed."

Michel moved in his chair and winced
with pain, then he fixed Flick with his intense
blue eyes. "I plead guilty," he said. "I'm a
louse. But I'm a louse who loves you, and

I'm just asking you to forgive me, this once, in case I never see you again."

It was hard to resist. Flick weighed five years of marriage against a fling with a popsie and gave in. She moved a step toward him. He put his arms around her legs and pressed his face into the worn cotton of her dress. She stroked his hair. "All right," she said. "All right."

"I'm so sorry," he said. "I feel awful. You're the most wonderful woman I ever met, or even heard of. I won't do it any more, I promise."

The door opened, and Gilberte came in with Claude. Flick gave a guilty start and released Michel's head from her embrace. Then she felt stupid. He was *her* husband, not Gilberte's. Why should she feel guilty about hugging him, even in Gilberte's apartment? She was angry with herself.

Gilberte looked shocked to see her lover embracing his wife here, but she swiftly recovered her composure, and her face assumed a frozen expression of indifference.

Claude, a handsome young doctor, followed her in, looking anxious.

Flick went to Claude and kissed him on

both cheeks. "Thank you for coming," she said. "We're truly grateful."

Claude looked at Michel. "How do you feel, old buddy?"

"I've got a bullet in my arse."

"Then I'd better take it out." He lost his worried air and became briskly professional. Turning to Flick, he said, "Put some towels on the bed to soak up the blood, then get his trousers off and lie him facedown. I'll wash my hands."

Gilberte put old magazines on her bed and towels over the paper while Flick got Michel up and helped him hobble to the bed. As he lay down, she could not help wondering how many other times he had lain here.

Claude inserted a metal instrument into the wound and felt around for the slug. Michel cried out with pain.

"I'm sorry, old friend," Claude said solicitously.

Flick almost took pleasure in the sight of Michel in agony on the bed where he had formerly cried out with guilty pleasure. She hoped he would always remember Gilberte's bedroom this way.

Michel said, "Just get it over with."

Flick's vengeful feeling passed quickly, and she felt sorry for Michel. She moved the pillow closer to his face, saying, "Bite on this, it will help."

Michel stuffed the pillow into his mouth.

Claude probed again, and this time got the bullet out. Blood flowed freely for a few seconds, then slowed, and Claude put a dressing on.

"Keep as still as you can for a few days," he advised Michel. That meant Michel would have to stay at Gilberte's place. However, he would be too sore for sex, Flick thought with grim satisfaction.

"Thank you, Claude," she said.

"Glad to be able to help."

"I have another request."

Claude looked scared. "What?"

"I'm meeting a plane at a quarter to midnight. I need you to drive me to Chatelle."

"Why can't Gilberte take you, in the car she used to come to my place?"

"Because of the curfew. But we'll be safe with you, you're a doctor."

"Why would I have two people with me?"

"Three. We need Michel to hold a torch."

There was an unvarying procedure for pickups: four Resistance people held flashlights in the shape of a giant letter "L," indicating the direction of the wind and where the plane should come down. The small battery-operated torches needed to be directed at the aircraft to make sure the pilot saw them. They could simply be placed in position on the ground, but that was less sure, and if the pilot did not see what he expected he might suspect a trap and decide not to land. It was better to have four people if at all possible.

Claude said, "How would I explain you all to the police? A doctor on emergency call doesn't travel with three people in his car."

"We'll think of some story."

"It's too dangerous!"

"It will take only a few minutes, at this time of night."

"Marie-Jeanne will kill me. She says I have to think of the children."

"You don't have any."

"She's pregnant."

Flick nodded. That would explain why he had become so jumpy.

Michel rolled over and sat upright. He reached out and grasped Claude's arm. "Claude, I'm begging you, this is really important. Do it for me, will you?"

It was hard to say no to Michel. Claude sighed. "When?"

Flick looked at her watch. It was almost eleven. "Now."

Claude looked at Michel. "His wound may reopen."

"I know," Flick said. "Let it bleed."

The village of Chatelle consisted of a few buildings clustered around a crossroads: three farmhouses, a strip of laborers' cottages, and a bakery that served the surrounding farms and hamlets. Flick stood in a cow pasture a mile from the crossroads, holding in her hand a flashlight about the size of a pack of cigarettes.

She had been on a weeklong course, run by the pilots of 161 Squadron, to train her for the task of guiding an aircraft in. This location fitted the specifications they had given her. The field was almost a kilometer long—a Lysander needed six hundred meters to land and take off. The ground beneath her feet was firm, and there was no slope. A nearby pond was clearly visible from the air in the moonlight, providing a useful landmark for pilots.

Michel and Gilberte stood upwind of Flick in a straight line, also holding flashlights, and Claude stood a few yards to one side of Gilberte, making a flare path in the shape of an upside-down "L" to guide the pilot. In remote areas, bonfires could be used instead of electric lights, but here, close to a village, it was too dangerous to leave the telltale burn mark on the ground.

The four people formed what the agents called a reception committee. Flick's were always silent and disciplined, but less-well-organized groups sometimes turned the landing into a party, with groups of men shouting jokes and smoking cigarettes, and spectators from nearby villages turning up to watch. This was dangerous. If the pilot suspected that the landing had been betrayed to the Germans, and thought the Gestapo might be lying in wait, he had to react quickly. The instructions to reception committees warned that anyone approaching the plane from the wrong angle was liable to be shot by the pilot. This had never actually happened, but on one occasion a spectator had been run over by a Hudson bomber and killed.

Waiting for the plane was always hell. If

it did not arrive, Flick would face another twenty-four hours of unremitting tension and danger before the next opportunity. But an agent never knew whether a plane would show up. This was not because the RAF was unreliable. Rather, as the pilots of 161 Squadron had explained to Flick, the task of navigating a plane by moonlight across hundreds of miles of country was monumentally difficult. The pilot used dead reckoning—calculating his position by direction, speed, and elapsed time—and tried to verify the result by landmarks such as rivers, towns, railway lines, and forests. The problem with dead reckoning was that it was impossible to make an exact adjustment for the drift caused by wind. And the trouble with landmarks was that one river looked very much like another by moonlight. Getting to roughly the right area was difficult enough, but these pilots had to find an individual field.

If there was cloud hiding the moon it was impossible, and the plane would not even take off.

However, this was a fine night, and Flick was hopeful. Sure enough, a couple of minutes before midnight, she heard the unmistakable sound of a single-engined plane, faint at first, then rapidly growing louder, like a burst of applause, and she felt a home-going thrill. She began to flash her light in the Morse letter "X." If she flashed the wrong letter, the pilot would suspect a trap and go away without landing.

The plane circled once, then came down steeply. It touched down on Flick's right, braked, turned between Michel and Claude, taxied back to Flick, and turned into the wind again, completing a long oval and finishing up ready for takeoff.

The aircraft was a Westland Lysander, a small, high-winged monoplane, painted matte black. It was flown by a crew of one. It had two seats for passengers, but Flick had known a "Lizzie" to carry four, one on the floor and one on the parcel shelf.

The pilot did not stop the engine. His aim was to remain on the ground no more than a few seconds.

Flick wanted to hug Michel and wish him well, but she also wanted to slap his face and tell him to keep his hands off other women. Perhaps it was just as well that she had no time for either.

With a brief wave, Flick scrambled up the

metal ladder, threw open the hatch, and climbed aboard. She closed the glazed dome over her head.

The pilot glanced behind, and Flick gave him the thumbs-up. The little plane jerked forward and picked up speed, then rose into the air and climbed steeply.

Flick could see one or two lights in the village: country people were careless about the blackout. When Flick had flown in, perilously late at four in the morning, she had been able to see from the air the red glare of the baker's oven, and driving through the village she had smelled the new bread, the essence of France.

The plane banked to turn, and Flick saw the moonlit faces of Michel, Gilberte, and Claude as three white smears on the black background of the pasture. As the plane leveled and headed for England, she realized with a sudden surge of grief that she might never see them again.

THE SECOND DAY

Monday, May 29, 1944

CHAPTER 6

Dieter Franck drove through the night in the big Hispano-Suiza, accompanied by his young assistant, Lieutenant Hans Hesse. The car was ten years old, but its massive eleven-liter engine was tireless. Yesterday evening, Dieter had found a neat row of bullet holes stitched in the generous curve of its offside fender, a souvenir of the skirmish in the square at Sainte-Cécile, but there was no mechanical damage, and he felt the holes added to the car's glamour, like a dueling scar on the cheek of a Prussian officer.

Lieutenant Hesse masked the headlights to drive through the blacked-out streets of Paris, then removed the covers when they got on the road to Normandy. They took turns at the wheel, two hours each, though Hesse, who adored the car and hero-worshiped its owner, would gladly have driven the whole way.

Half asleep in the passenger seat, mesmerized by the country roads unwinding in the headlights, Dieter tried to picture his future. Would the Allies reconquer France, driving the occupying forces out? The thought of Germany defeated was dismal. Perhaps there would be some kind of peace settlement, with Germany surrendering France and Poland but keeping Austria and Czechoslovakia. That seemed not much better. He found it hard to imagine everyday life back in Cologne, with his wife and family, after the excitement and sensual indulgence of Paris and Stéphanie. The only happy ending, for Dieter and for Germany, would be for Rommel's army to push the invaders back into the sea.

Before dawn on a damp morning Hesse drove into the small medieval village of La Roche-Guyon, on the Seine river between Paris and Rouen. He stopped at the roadblock at the edge of the village, but they were expected, and were quickly waved on. They went past silent, shuttered houses to another checkpoint at the gates of the ancient castle. At last they parked in the great cobbled courtyard. Dieter left Hesse with the car and went into the building.

The German commander in chief [West] was Field Marshal Gerd von Runstedt, a reliable senior general from the old officer class. Under him, charged with the defense of the French coast, was Field Marshal Erwin Rommel. The castle of La Roche-Guyon was Rommel's headquarters.

Dieter Franck felt an affinity with Rommel. Both were the sons of teachers—Rommel's father had been a headmaster—and consequently both had felt the icy breath of German military snobbery from such men as von Runstedt. But otherwise they were very different. Dieter was a sybarite, enjoying all the cultural and sensual pleasures France had to offer. Rommel was an obsessive worker who did not smoke or drink and often forgot to eat. He had married the only girlfriend he had ever had, and he wrote to her three times a day.

In the hall, Dieter met Rommel's aide-de-camp, Major Walter Goedel, a cold personality with a formidable brain. Dieter respected him but could never like him. They had spoken on the phone late last night. Dieter had outlined the problem he was having with the Gestapo and said he wanted to see Rommel as soon as possible. "Be here at four a.m.," Goedel had said. Rommel was always at his desk by four o'clock in the morning.

Now Dieter wondered if he had done the right thing. Rommel might say, "How dare you bother me with trivial details?" Dieter thought not. Commanders liked to feel they were on top of the details. Rommel would almost certainly give Dieter the support he was asking for. But you could never be sure, especially when the commander was under strain.

Goedel nodded a curt greeting and said, "He wants to see you right now. Come this way."

As they walked along the hallway, Dieter said, "What do you hear from Italy?"

"Nothing but bad news," Goedel said. "We're withdrawing from Arce."

Dieter gave a resigned nod. The Germans were fighting fiercely, but they had been depressingly unable to halt the northward advance of the enemy.

A moment later Dieter entered Rommel's office. It was a grand room on the ground floor. Dieter noticed with envy a priceless seventeenth-century Gobelin tapestry on one wall. There was little furniture but for a few chairs and a huge antique desk that looked, to Dieter, as if it might be the same age as the tapestry. On the desk stood a single lamp. Behind the desk sat a small man with receding sandy hair.

Goedel said, "Major Franck is here, Field Marshal."

Dieter waited nervously. Rommel continued reading for a few seconds, then made a mark on the sheet of paper. He might have been a bank manager reviewing the accounts of his more important customers—until he looked up. Dieter had seen the face before, but it never failed to make him feel threatened. It was a boxer's face, with a flat nose and a broad chin and close-set eyes, and it was suffused with the naked aggression that had made Rommel a legendary commander. Dieter recalled the story of Rommel's first military engagement, during the First World War. Leading an advance guard of three men, Rommel had come upon a group of twenty French troops. Instead of retreating and calling for reinforcements, Rommel had opened fire and dashed at the enemy. He had been lucky to survive—but Dieter recalled Napoleon's dictum: "Send me lucky generals." Since then, Rommel had always favored the sudden bold assault over the cautious planned advance. In that he was the polar opposite of his desert opponent, Montgomery, whose philosophy was never to attack until you were certain of victory.

"Sit down, Franck," said Rommel briskly. "What's on your mind?"

Dieter had rehearsed this. "On your instructions, I've been visiting key installations that might be vulnerable to attack by the Resistance and upgrading their security."

"Good."

"I've also been trying to assess the potential of the Resistance to inflict serious damage. Can they really hamper our response to an invasion?"

"And your conclusion?"

"The situation is worse than we imagined."

Rommel grunted with distaste, as if an unpleasant suspicion had been confirmed. "Reasons?"

Rommel was not going to bite his head off. Dieter relaxed a little. He recounted yesterday's attack at Sainte-Cécile: the imaginative planning, the plentiful weaponry, and most of all the bravery of the fighters. The only detail he left out was the beauty of the blonde girl.

Rommel stood up and walked across to the tapestry. He stared at it, but Dieter was sure he did not see it. "I was afraid of this," Rommel said. He spoke quietly, almost to himself. "I can beat off an invasion, even with the few troops I have, if only I can remain mobile and flexible—but if my communications fail, I'm lost."

Goedel nodded agreement.

Dieter said, "I believe we can turn the attack on the telephone exchange into an opportunity."

Rommel turned to him with a wry smile. "By God, I wish all my officers were like you. Go on, how will you do this?"

Dieter began to feel the meeting was going his way. "If I can interrogate the captured prisoners, they may lead me to other groups. With luck, we might inflict a lot of damage on the Resistance before the invasion."

Rommel looked skeptical. "That sounds like bragging." Dieter's heart sank. Then Rommel went on. "If anyone else said it, I might send him packing. But I remember your work in the desert. You got men to tell you things they hardly realized they knew."

Dieter was pleased. Seizing his advantage, he said, "Unfortunately, the Gestapo is refusing me access to the prisoners."

"They are such imbeciles."

"I need you to intervene."

"Of course." Rommel looked at Goedel. "Call avenue Foch." The Gestapo's French headquarters was at 84 avenue Foch in Paris. "Tell them that Major Franck will interrogate the prisoners today, or their next phone call will come from Berchtesgaden." He was referring to Hitler's Bavarian fortress. Rommel never hesitated to use the Field Marshal's privilege of direct access to Hitler.

"Very good," said Goedel.

Rommel walked around his seventeenth-century desk and sat down again. "Keep me informed, please, Franck," he said, and returned his attention to his papers.

Dieter and Goedel left the room.

Goedel walked Dieter to the main door of the castle.

Outside, it was still dark.

CHAPTER 7

Flick landed at RAF Tempsford, an airstrip fifty miles north of London, near the village of Sandy in Bedfordshire. She would have known, just from the cool, damp taste of the night air in her mouth, that she was back in England. She loved France, but this was home.

Walking across the airfield, she remembered coming back from holidays as a child. Her mother would always say the same thing as the house came into view: "It's nice to go away, but it's nice to come home." The things her mother said came back to her at the oddest moments.

A young woman in the uniform of a FANY corporal was waiting with a powerful Jaguar to drive her to London. "This is luxurious,"

Flick said as she settled into the leather seat.

"I'm to take you directly to Orchard Court," the driver said. "They're waiting to debrief you."

Flick rubbed her eyes. "Christ," she said feelingly. "Do they think we don't need sleep?"

The driver did not respond to that. Instead she said, "I hope the mission went well, Major."

"It was a snafu."

"I beg pardon?"

"Snafu," Flick repeated. "It's an acronym. It stands for Situation Normal All Fucked Up."

The woman fell silent. Flick guessed she was embarrassed. It was nice, she thought ruefully, that there were still girls to whom the language of the barracks was shocking.

Dawn broke as the fast car sped through the Hertfordshire villages of Stevenage and Knebworth. Flick looked out at the modest houses with vegetables growing in the front gardens, the country post offices where grumpy postmistresses resentfully doled out penny stamps, and the assorted pubs with their warm beer and battered pianos, and she felt profoundly grateful that the Nazis had not got this far.

The feeling made her all the more determined to return to France. She wanted another chance to attack the château. She pictured the people she had left behind at Sainte-Cécile: Albert, young Bertrand, beautiful Geneviève, and the others dead or captured. She thought of their families, distraught with worry or stunned by grief. She resolved that their sacrifice should not have been fruitless.

She would have to start right away. It was a good thing she was to be debriefed immediately: she would have a chance to propose her new plan today. The men who ran SOE would be wary at first, for no one had ever sent an all-female team on such a mission. There were all sorts of snags. But there were always snags.

By the time they reached the north London suburbs it was full daylight, and the special people of the early morning were out and about: postmen and milkmen making their deliveries, train drivers and bus conductors walking to work. The signs of war were everywhere: a poster warning against waste, a notice in a butcher's window saying

No Meat Today, a woman driving a rubbish cart, a whole row of small houses bombed into rubble. But no one here would stop Flick, and demand to see her papers, and put her in a cell, and torture her for information, then send her in a cattle truck to a camp where she would starve. She felt the high-voltage tension of living undercover drain slowly out of her, and she slumped in the car seat and closed her eyes.

She woke up when the car turned into Baker Street. It went past No. 64: agents were kept out of the headquarters building so that they could not reveal its secrets under interrogation. Indeed, many agents did not know its address. The car turned into Portman Square and stopped outside Orchard Court, an apartment building. The driver sprang out to hold the door open.

Flick went inside and made her way to SOE's flat. Her spirits lifted when she saw Percy Thwaite. A balding man of fifty with a toothbrush moustache, he was paternally fond of Flick. He wore civilian clothing, and neither of them saluted, for SOE was impatient of military formalities.

"I can tell by your face that it went badly," Percy said.

His sympathetic tone of voice was too much for Flick to bear. The tragedy of what had happened overwhelmed her suddenly, and she burst into tears. Percy put his arms around her and patted her back. She buried her face in his old tweed jacket. "All right," he said. "I know you did your best."

"Oh, God, I'm sorry to be such a girl."

"I wish all my men were such girls," Percy said with a catch in his voice.

She detached herself from his embrace and wiped her eyes with her sleeve. "Take no notice."

He turned away and blew his nose into a big handkerchief. "Tea or whisky?" he said.

"Tea, I think." She looked around. The room was full of shabby furniture, hastily in-stalled in 1940 and never replaced: a cheap desk, a worn rug, mismatched chairs. She sank into a sagging armchair. "I'll fall asleep if I have booze."

She watched Percy as he made tea. He could be tough as well as compassionate. Much decorated in the First World War, he had become a rabble-rousing labor orga-nizer in the twenties, and was a veteran of the 1936 Battle of Cable Street, when Cock-neys attacked Fascists who were trying to

march through a Jewish neighborhood in
London's East End. He would ask searching
questions about her plan, but he would be
open-minded.

He handed her a mug of tea with milk and
sugar. "There's a meeting later this morning," he said. "I have to get a briefing note
to the boss by nine ack emma. Hence the
hurry."

She sipped the sweet tea and felt a pleasant jolt of energy. She told him what had
happened in the square at Sainte-Cécile. He
sat at the desk and made notes with a sharp
pencil. "I should have called it off," she finished. "Based on Antoinette's misgivings
about the intelligence, I should have postponed the raid and sent you a radio message saying we were outnumbered."

Percy shook his head sadly. "This is no
time for postponements. The invasion can't
be more than a few days away. If you had
consulted us, I doubt it would have made
any difference. What could we do? We
couldn't send you more men. I think we
would have ordered you to go ahead regardless. It had to be tried. The telephone exchange is too important."

"Well, that's some consolation." Flick was

glad she did not have to believe Albert had died because she had made a tactical error. But that would not bring him back.

"And Michel is all right?" Percy said.

"Mortified, but recovering." When SOE had recruited Flick, she had not told them her husband was in the Resistance. If they had known, they might have steered her toward different work. But she had not really known it herself, though she had guessed. In May 1940 she had been in England, visiting her mother, and Michel had been in the army, like most able-bodied young Frenchmen, so the fall of France had left them stranded in different countries. By the time she returned as a secret agent, and learned for certain what role her husband was playing, too much training had been invested in her, and she was already too useful to SOE, for her to be fired on account of hypothetical emotional distractions.

"Everyone hates a bullet in the backside," Percy mused. "People think you must have been running away." He stood up. "Well, you'd better go home and get some sleep."

"Not yet," Flick said. "First I want to know what we're going to do next."

"I'm going to write this report—"

"No, I mean about the telephone exchange. If it's so important, we *have* to knock it out."

He sat down again and looked at her shrewdly. "What have you got in mind?"

She took Antoinette's pass out of her bag and threw it on his desk. "Here's a better way to get inside. That's used by the cleaners who go in every night at seven o'clock."

Percy picked up the pass and scrutinized it. "Clever girl," he said with something like admiration in his voice. "Go on."

"I want to go back."

A look of pain passed briefly over Percy's face, and Flick knew he was dreading her risking her life again. But he said nothing.

"This time I'll take a full team with me," she went on. "Each of them will have a pass like that. We'll substitute for the cleaners in order to get into the château."

"I take it the cleaners are women?"

"Yes. I'd need an all-female team."

He nodded. "Not many people around here will object to that—you girls have proved yourselves. But where would you find the women? Virtually all our trained people are over there already."

"Get approval for my plan, and I'll find the

women. I'll take SOE rejects, people who failed the training course, anybody. We must have a file of people who have dropped out for one reason or another."

"Yes—because they were physically unfit, or couldn't keep their mouths shut, or enjoyed violence too much, or lost their nerve in parachute training and refused to jump out of the plane."

"It doesn't matter if they're second-raters," Flick argued earnestly. "I can deal with that." At the back of her mind, a voice said *Can you, really?* But she ignored it. "If the invasion fails, we've lost Europe. We won't try again for years. This is the turning point, we have to throw everything at the enemy."

"You couldn't use French women who are already there, Resistance fighters?"

Flick had already considered and rejected that idea. "If I had a few weeks, I might put together a team from women in half a dozen different Resistance circuits, but it would take too long to find them and get them to Reims."

"It might still be possible."

"And then we have to have a forged pass with a photo for each woman. That's hard to arrange over there. Here, we can do it in a day or two."

"It's not that easy." Percy held Antoinette's pass up to the light of a naked bulb hanging from the ceiling. "But you're right, our people do work miracles in that department." He put it down. "All right. It has to be SOE rejects, then."

Flick felt a surge of triumph. He was going for it.

Percy went on, "But assuming you can find enough French-speaking girls, will it work? What about the German guards? Don't they know the cleaners?"

"It's probably not the same women every night—they must have days off. And men never notice who cleans up after them."

"I'm not sure. Soldiers are generally sex-hungry youngsters who pay great attention to all the women with whom they come into contact. I imagine the men in this château flirt with the younger ones, at least."

"I watched these women entering the château last night, and I didn't see any signs of flirting."

"Still, you can't be sure the men won't notice the appearance of a completely strange crew."

"I can't be certain, but I'm confident enough to take the chance."

"All right, what about the French people inside? The telephone operators are local women, aren't they?"

"Some are local, but most are brought in from Reims by bus."

"Not every French person likes the Resistance, we both know that. There are some who approve of the Nazis' ideas. God knows, there were plenty of fools in Britain who thought Hitler offered the kind of strong modernizing government we all needed—although you don't hear much from those people nowadays."

Flick shook her head. Percy had not been to occupied France. "The French have had four years of Nazi rule, remember. Everyone over there is hoping desperately for the invasion. The switchboard girls will keep mum."

"Even though the RAF bombed them?"

Flick shrugged. "There may be a few hostile ones, but the majority will keep them under control."

"You hope."

"Once again, I think it's a chance worth taking."

"You still don't know how heavily guarded that basement entrance is."

"That didn't stop us trying yesterday."

"Yesterday you had fifteen Resistance fighters, some of them seasoned. Next time, you'll have a handful of dropouts and rejects."

Flick played her trump card. "Listen, all kinds of things could go wrong, but so what? The operation is low-cost, and we're risking the lives of people who aren't contributing to the war effort anyway. What have we got to lose?"

"I was coming to that. Look, I like this plan. I'm going to put it up to the boss. But I think he will reject it, for a reason we haven't yet discussed."

"What?"

"No one but you could lead this team. But the trip you've just returned from should be your last. You know too much. You've been going in and out for two years. You've had contact with most of the Resistance circuits in northern France. We can't send you back. If you were captured, you could give them all away."

"I know," Flick said grimly. "That's why I carry a suicide pill."

CHAPTER 8

General Sir Bernard Montgomery, commander of the 21st Army Group that was about to invade France, had set up improvised headquarters in west London, at a school whose pupils had been evacuated to safer accommodation in the countryside. By coincidence, it was the school Monty himself had attended as a boy. Meetings were held in the model room, and everyone sat on the schoolboys' hard wooden benches—generals and politicians and, on one famous occasion, the King himself.

The Brits thought this was cute. Paul Chancellor from Boston, Massachusetts, thought it was bullshit. What would it have cost them to bring in a few chairs? He liked the British, by and large, but not when they were showing off how eccentric they were.

Paul was on Monty's personal staff. A lot of people thought this was because his father was a general, but that was an unfair assumption. Paul was comfortable with senior officers, partly because of his father, partly because before the war the U.S. Army had been the biggest customer for his business, which was making educational gramophone records, language courses mainly. He liked the military virtues of obedience, punctuality, and precision, but he could think for himself, too, and Monty had come to rely on him more and more.

His area of responsibility was intelligence. He was an organizer. He made sure the reports Monty needed were on his desk when he wanted them, chased those that came late, set up meetings with key people, and made supplementary inquiries on the boss's behalf.

He did have experience of clandestine work. He had been with the Office of Strategic Services, the American secret agency, and had served under cover in France and French-speaking North Africa. (As a child he had lived in Paris, where Pa was military attaché at the U.S. Embassy.) Paul had been wounded six months ago in a shoot-out with the Gestapo in Marseilles. One bullet had taken off most of his left ear but harmed nothing other than his looks. The other smashed his right kneecap, which would never be the same again, and that was the real reason he had a desk job.

The work was easy, by comparison with living on the run in occupied territory, but never dull. They were planning Operation Overlord, the invasion that would end the war. Paul was one of a few hundred people in the world who knew the date, although many more could guess. In fact, there were three possible dates, based on the tides, the currents, the moon, and the hours of daylight. The invasion needed a late-rising moon, so that the army's initial movements would be shrouded in darkness, but there would be moonlight later, when the first paratroopers jumped from their planes and gliders. A low tide at dawn was necessary to expose the obstacles Rommel had scattered on the beaches. And another low tide before nightfall was needed for the landing of follow-up forces. These requirements left only a narrow window: the fleet could sail next Monday, June 5, or on the following Tuesday or Wednesday. The final decision would be made at the last minute, depending on the weather, by the Allied Supreme Commander, General Eisenhower.

Three years ago, Paul would have been desperately scheming for a place in the invasion force. He would have been itching for action and embarrassed at being a stay-at-home. Now he was older and wiser. For one thing, he had paid his dues: in high school he had captained the side that won the Massachusetts championship, but he would never again kick a ball with his right foot. More importantly, he knew that his organizational talents could do more to win the war than his ability to shoot straight.

He was thrilled to be part of the team that was planning the greatest invasion of all time. With the thrill came anxiety, of course. Battles never went according to plan (although it was a weakness of Monty's to pretend that his did). Paul knew that any error he made—a slip of the pen, a detail overlooked, a piece of intelligence not double-checked—could kill Allied troops. Despite the huge size of the invasion force, the battle could still go either way, and the smallest of mistakes could tip the balance.

Today at ten a.m. Paul had scheduled fifteen minutes on the French Resistance. It was Monty's idea. He was nothing if not a detail man. The way to win battles, he believed, was to refrain from fighting until all preparations were in place.

At five to ten, Simon Fortescue came into the model room. He was one of the senior men at MI6, the secret intelligence department. A tall man in a pin-striped suit, he had a smoothly authoritative manner, but Paul doubted if he knew much about clandestine work in the real world. He was followed by John Graves, a nervous-looking civil servant from the Ministry of Economic Warfare, the government department that oversaw SOE. Graves wore the Whitehall uniform of black jacket and striped gray pants. Paul frowned. He had not invited Graves. "Mr. Graves!" he said sharply. "I didn't know you had been asked to join us."

"I'll explain in a second," Graves said, and he sat down on a schoolboy bench, looking flustered, and opened his briefcase.

Paul was irritated. Monty hated surprises. But Paul could not throw Graves out of the room.

A moment later, Monty walked in. He was a small man with a pointed nose and receding hair. His face was deeply lined either side of his close-clipped moustache. He was fifty-six, but looked older. Paul liked him. Monty was so meticulous that some people became impatient with him and called him an old woman. Paul believed that Monty's fussiness saved men's lives.

With Monty was an American Paul did not know. Monty introduced him as General Pickford. "Where's the chap from SOE?" Monty snapped, looking at Paul.

Graves answered. "I'm afraid he was summoned by the Prime Minister, and sends his profound apologies. I hope I'll be able to help . . ."

"I doubt it," Monty said crisply.

Paul groaned inwardly. It was a snafu, and he would be blamed. But there was something else going on here. The Brits were playing some game he did not know about. He watched them carefully, looking for clues.

Simon Fortescue said smoothly, "I'm sure I can fill in the gaps."

Monty looked angry. He had promised General Pickford a briefing, and the key person was absent. But he did not waste time on recriminations. "In the coming battle," he

said without further ado, "the most dangerous moments will be the first." It was unusual
for him to speak of dangerous moments,
Paul thought. His way was to talk as if everything would go like clockwork. "We will
be hanging by our fingertips from a cliff edge
for a day." Or two days, Paul said to himself,
or a week, or more. "This will be the enemy's
best opportunity. He has only to stamp on
our fingers with the heel of his jackboot."

So easy, Paul thought. Overlord was the
largest military operation in human history:
thousands of boats, hundreds of thousands
of men, millions of dollars, tens of millions
of bullets. The future of the world depended
on the outcome. Yet this vast force could
be repelled so easily, if things went wrong
in the first few hours.

"Anything we can do to slow the enemy's
response will be of crucial importance,"
Monty finished, and he looked at Graves.

"Well, F Section of SOE has more than a
hundred agents in France—in fact, virtually
all our people are over there," Graves began. "And under them, of course, are thousands of French Resistance fighters. Over
the last few weeks we have dropped them

many hundreds of tons of guns, ammunition, and explosives."

It was a bureaucrat's answer, Paul thought; it said everything and nothing. Graves would have gone on, but Monty interrupted with the key question: "How effective will they be?"

The civil servant hesitated, and Fortescue jumped in. "My expectations are modest," he said. "The performance of SOE is nothing if not uneven."

There was a subtext here, Paul knew. The old-time professional spies at MI6 hated the newcomers of SOE with their swashbuckling style. When the Resistance struck at German installations they stirred up Gestapo investigations which then sometimes caught MI6's people. Paul took SOE's side: striking at the enemy was the whole point of war.

Was that the game here? A bureaucratic spat between MI6 and SOE?

"Any *particular* reason for your pessimism?" Monty asked Fortescue.

"Take last night's fiasco," Fortescue replied promptly. "A Resistance group under an SOE commander attacked a telephone exchange near Reims."

General Pickford spoke for the first time. "I thought it was our policy not to attack telephone exchanges—we're going to need them ourselves if the invasion is success-ful."

"You're quite right," Monty said. "But Sainte-Cécile has been made an exception. It's an access node for the new cable route to Germany. Most of the telephone and telex traffic between the High Command in Berlin and German forces in France passes through that building. Knocking it out wouldn't do us much harm—we won't be calling Germany—but would wreak havoc with the enemy's communications."

Pickford said, "They'll switch to wireless communication."

"Exactly," said Monty. "Then we'll be able to read their signals."

Fortescue put in, "Thanks to our code-breakers at Bletchley."

Paul knew, though not many other people did, that British intelligence had cracked the codes used by the Germans and therefore could read much of the enemy's radio traffic. MI6 was proud of this, although in truth they deserved little credit: the work had been done not by intelligence staff but by an irregular group of mathematicians and cross-word-puzzle enthusiasts, many of whom would have been arrested if they had entered an MI6 office in normal times. Sir Stewart Menzies, the foxhunting head of MI6, hated intellectuals, communists, and homosexuals, but Alan Turing, the mathematical genius who led the codebreakers, was all three.

However, Pickford was right: if the Germans could not use the phone lines, they would have to use radio, and then the Allies would know what they were saying. Destroying the telephone exchange at Sainte-Cécile would give the Allies a crucial advantage.

But the mission had gone wrong. "Who was in charge?" Monty asked.

Graves said, "I haven't seen a full report—"

"I can tell you," Fortescue interjected. "Major Clairet." He paused. "A girl."

Paul had heard of Felicity Clairet. She was something of a legend among the small group who knew the secret of the Allies' clandestine war. She had survived under cover in France longer than anyone. Her code name was Leopardess, and people said she moved around the streets of occupied France with the silent footsteps of a dangerous cat. They also said she was a pretty girl with a heart of stone. She had killed more than once.

"And what happened?" Monty said.

"Poor planning, an inexperienced commander, and a lack of discipline among the men all played their part," Fortescue replied. "The building was not heavily guarded, but the Germans there are trained troops, and they simply wiped out the Resistance force."

Monty looked angry. Pickford said, "Looks like we shouldn't rely too heavily on the French Resistance to disrupt Rommel's supply lines."

Fortescue nodded. "Bombing is the more reliable means to that end."

"I'm not sure that's quite fair," Graves protested feebly. "Bomber Command has its successes and failures, too. And SOE is a good deal cheaper."

"We're not here to be fair to people, for God's sake," Monty growled. "We just want to win the war." He stood up. "I think we've heard enough," he said to General Pickford.

Graves said, "But what shall we do about

the telephone exchange? SOE has come up with a new plan—"

"Good God," Fortescue interrupted. "We don't want another balls-up, do we?"

"Bomb it," said Monty.

"We've tried that," Graves said. "They hit the building, but the damage was not sufficient to put the telephone exchange out of action for longer than a few hours."

"Then bomb it again," said Monty, and he walked out.

Graves threw a look of petulant fury at the man from MI6. "Really, Fortescue," he said. "I mean to say . . . *really.*"

Fortescue did not respond.

They all left the room. In the hallway outside, two people were waiting: a man of about fifty in a tweed jacket, and a short blonde woman wearing a worn blue cardigan over a faded cotton dress. Standing in front of a display of sporting trophies, they looked almost like a head teacher chatting to a schoolgirl, except that the girl wore a bright yellow scarf tied with a touch of style that looked, to Paul, distinctly French. Fortescue hurried past them, but Graves stopped. "They turned you down," he said. "They're going to bomb it again."

Paul guessed that the woman was the Leopardess, and he looked at her with interest. She was small and slim, with curly blonde hair cut short, and—Paul noticed—rather lovely green eyes. He would not have called her pretty: her face was too grown-up for that. The initial schoolgirl impression was fleeting. There was an aggressive look to her straight nose and chisel-shaped chin. And there was something sexy about her, something that made Paul think about the slight body under the shabby dress.

She reacted with indignation to Graves's statement. "There's no point in bombing the place from the air, the basement is reinforced. For God's sake, why did they make that decision?"

"Perhaps you should ask this gentleman," Graves said, turning to Paul. "Major Chancellor, meet Major Clairet and Colonel Thwaite."

Paul was annoyed at being put in the position of defending someone else's decision. Caught off guard, he replied with undiplomatic frankness. "I don't see that there's much to explain," he said brusquely. "You screwed up and you're not being given a second chance."

The woman glared up at him—she was a foot shorter than he—and spoke angrily. "Screwed up?" she said. "What the hell do you mean by that?"

Paul felt himself flush. "Maybe General Montgomery was misinformed, but wasn't this the first time you had commanded an action of this kind, Major?"

"Is *that* what you've been told? That it was my lack of experience?"

She was beautiful, he saw now. Anger made her eyes wide and her cheeks pink. But she was being very rude, so he decided to give it to her with both barrels. "That and poor planning—"

"There was nothing wrong with the damn plan!"

"—and the fact that trained troops were defending the place against an undisciplined force."

"You arrogant pig!"

Paul took an involuntary step back. He had never been spoken to this way by a woman. She may be five feet nothing, he thought, but I bet she scares the damn Nazis. Looking at her furious face, he realized that she was most angry with herself. "You think it's your fault," he said. "No one gets this mad about other people's mistakes."

It was her turn to be taken aback. Her mouth dropped open, and she was speechless.

Colonel Thwaite spoke for the first time. "Calm down, Flick, for God's sake," he said. Turning to Paul, he went on, "Let me guess—this account was given to you by Simon Fortescue of MI6, was it not?"

"That's correct," Paul said stiffly.

"Did he mention that the attack plan was based on intelligence supplied by his organization?"

"I don't believe he did."

"I thought not," said Thwaite. "Thank you, Major, I don't need to trouble you any further."

Paul did not feel the conversation was really over, but he had been dismissed by a senior officer, and he had no choice but to walk away.

He had obviously got caught in the crossfire of a turf war between MI6 and SOE. He felt most angry with Fortescue, who had used the meeting to score points. Had Monty made the right decision in choosing to bomb the telephone exchange rather than let SOE have another go at it? Paul was not sure.

As he turned into his own office he glanced back. Major Clairet was still arguing with Colonel Thwaite, her voice low but her face animated, expressing outrage with large gestures. She stood like a man, hand on hip, leaning forward, making her point with a belligerent forefinger, but all the same there was something enchanting about her. Paul wondered what it would be like to hold her in his arms and run his hands over her lithe body. Although she's tough, he thought, she's all woman.

But was she right? Was bombing futile?

He decided to ask some more questions.

CHAPTER 9

The vast, sooty bulk of the cathedral loomed over the center of Reims like a divine reproach. Dieter Franck's sky-blue Hispano-Suiza pulled up at midday outside the Hotel Frankfort, taken over by the German occupiers. Dieter got out and glanced up at the stubby twin towers of the great church. The original medieval design had featured elegant pointed spires, which had never been built for lack of money. So mundane obstacles frustrated the holiest of aspirations.

Dieter told Lieutenant Hesse to drive to the château at Sainte-Cécile and make sure the Gestapo were ready to cooperate. He did not want to risk being repulsed a second time by Major Weber. Hesse drove off, and

Dieter went up to the suite where he had left Stéphanie last night.

She got up from her chair as he walked in. He drank in the welcome sight. Her red hair fell on bare shoulders, and she wore a chestnut silk negligee and high-heeled slippers. He kissed her hungrily and ran his hands over her slim body, grateful for the gift of her beauty.

"How nice that you're so pleased to see me," she said with a smile. They spoke French together, as always.

Dieter inhaled the scent of her. "Well, you smell better than Hans Hesse, especially when he's been up all night."

She brushed his hair back with a soft hand. "You always make fun. But you wouldn't have protected Hans with your own body."

"True." He sighed and let her go. "Christ, I'm tired."

"Come to bed."

He shook his head. "I have to interrogate the prisoners. Hesse's coming back for me in an hour." He slumped on the couch.

"I'll get you something to eat." She pressed the bell, and a minute later an elderly French waiter tapped at the door.

Stéphanie knew Dieter well enough to order for him. She asked for a plate of ham with warm rolls and potato salad. "Some wine?" she asked him.

"No—it'll send me to sleep."

"A pot of coffee, then," she told the waiter. When the man had gone, she sat on the couch beside Dieter and took his hand. "Did everything go according to plan?"

"Yes. Rommel was quite complimentary to me." He frowned anxiously. "I just hope I can live up to the promises I made him."

"I'm sure you will." She did not ask for details. She knew he would tell her as much as he wanted to and no more.

He looked fondly at her, wondering whether to say what was on his mind. It might spoil the pleasant atmosphere—but it needed to be said. He sighed again. "If the invasion is successful, and the Allies win back France, it will be the end for you and me. You know that."

She winced, as if at a sudden pain, and let go of his hand. "Do I?"

He knew that her husband had been killed early in the war, and they had had no children. "Do you have any family at all?" he asked her.

"My parents died years ago. I have a sister in Montreal."

"Maybe we should be thinking about how to send you over there."

She shook her head. "No."

"Why?"

She would not meet his eye. "I just wish the war would be over," she muttered.

"No, you don't."

She showed a rare flash of irritation. "Of course I do."

"How uncharacteristically conventional of you," he said with a hint of scorn.

"You can't possibly think war is a good thing!"

"You and I would not be together, were it not for the war."

"But what about all the suffering?"

"I'm an existentialist. War enables people to be what they really are: the sadists become torturers, the psychopaths make brave front-line troops, the bullies and the victims alike have scope to play their roles to the hilt, and the whores are always busy."

She looked angry. "That tells me pretty clearly what part I play."

He stroked her soft cheek and touched

her lips with the tip of his finger. "You're a courtesan—and very good at it."

She moved her head away. "You don't mean any of this. You're improvising on a tune, the way you do when you sit at the piano."

He smiled and nodded: he could play a little jazz, much to his father's dismay. The analogy was apt. He was trying out ideas, rather than expressing a firm conviction. "Perhaps you're right."

Her anger evaporated, and she looked sad. "Did you mean the part about us separating, if the Germans leave France?"

He put his arm around her shoulders and pulled her to him. She relaxed and laid her head on his chest. He kissed the top of her head and stroked her hair. "It's not going to happen," he said.

"Are you certain?"

"I guarantee it."

It was the second time today he had made a promise he might not be able to keep.

The waiter returned with his lunch, and the spell was broken. Dieter was almost too tired to be hungry, but he ate a few mouthfuls and drank all the coffee. Afterwards he washed and shaved, and then he felt better. As he was buttoning a clean uniform shirt, Lieutenant Hesse tapped at the door. Dieter kissed Stéphanie and went out.

The car was diverted around a blocked street: there had been another bombing raid overnight, and a whole row of houses near the railway station had been destroyed. They got out of town and headed for Sainte-Cécile.

Dieter had told Rommel that the interrogation of the prisoners *might* enable him to cripple the Resistance before the invasion— but Rommel, like any military commander, took a maybe for a promise and would now expect results. Unfortunately, there was nothing guaranteed about an interrogation. Clever prisoners told lies that were impossible to check. Some found ingenious ways to kill themselves before the torture became unbearable. If security was really tight in their particular Resistance circuit, each would know only the minimum about the others, and have little information of value. Worst of all, they might have been fed false information by the perfidious Allies, so that when they finally broke under torture, what they said was part of a deception plan.

Dieter began to put himself in the mood. He needed to be completely hard-hearted and calculating. He must not allow himself to be touched by the physical and mental suffering he was about to inflict on human beings. All that mattered was whether it worked. He closed his eyes and felt a profound calm settle over him, a familiar bone-deep chill that he sometimes thought must be like the cold of death itself.

The car pulled into the grounds of the château. Workmen were repairing the smashed glass in the windows and filling the holes made by grenades. In the ornate hall, the telephonists murmured into their microphones in a perpetual undertone. Dieter marched through the perfectly proportioned rooms of the east wing, with Hans Hesse in tow. They went down the stairs to the fortified basement. The sentry at the door saluted and made no attempt to detain Dieter, who was in uniform. He found the door marked Interrogation Center and went in.

In the outer room, Willi Weber sat at the table. Dieter barked, "Heil Hitler!" and saluted, forcing Weber to stand. Then Dieter pulled out a chair, sat down, and said, "Please be seated, Major."

Weber was furious at being invited to sit in his own headquarters, but he had no choice.

Dieter said, "How many prisoners do we have?"

"Three."

Dieter was disappointed. "So few?"

"We killed eight of the enemy in the skirmish. Two more died of their wounds overnight."

Dieter grunted with dismay. He had ordered that the wounded be kept alive. But there was no point now in questioning Weber about their treatment.

Weber went on, "I believe two escaped—"

"Yes," Dieter said. "The woman in the square, and the man she carried away."

"Exactly. So, from a total of fifteen attackers, we have three prisoners."

"Where are they?"

Weber looked shifty. "Two are in the cells."

Dieter narrowed his eyes. "And the third?"

Weber inclined his head toward the inner room. "The third is under interrogation at this moment."

Dieter got up, apprehensive, and opened

the door. The hunched figure of Sergeant Becker stood just inside the room, holding in his hand a wooden club like a large policeman's truncheon. He was sweating and breathing hard, as if he had been taking vigorous exercise. He was staring at a prisoner who was tied to a post.

Dieter looked at the prisoner, and his fears were confirmed. Despite his self-imposed calm, he grimaced with revulsion. The prisoner was the young woman, Geneviève, who had carried a Sten gun under her coat. She was naked, tied to the pillar by a rope that passed under her arms and supported her slumped weight. Her face was so swollen that she could not have opened her eyes. Blood from her mouth covered her chin and most of her chest. Her body was discolored with angry bruises. One arm hung at an odd angle, apparently dislocated at the shoulder. Her pubic hair was matted with blood.

Dieter said to Becker, "What has she told you?"

Becker looked embarrassed. "Nothing."

Dieter nodded, suppressing his rage. It was as he had expected.

He went close to the woman. "Geneviève, listen to me," he said in French.

She showed no sign of having heard.

"Would you like to rest now?" he tried.

There was no response.

He turned around. Weber was standing in the doorway, looking defiant. Dieter, coldly furious, said, "You were expressly told that I would conduct the interrogation."

"We were ordered to give you access," Weber replied with smug pedantry. "We were not prohibited from questioning the prisoners ourselves."

"And are you satisfied with the results you have achieved?"

Weber did not answer.

Dieter said, "What about the other two?"

"We have not yet begun their interrogation."

"Thank God for that." Dieter was nonetheless dismayed. He had expected half a dozen subjects, not two. "Take me to them."

Weber nodded at Becker, who put down his club and led the way out of the room. In the bright lights of the corridor, Dieter could see the bloodstains on Becker's uniform. The sergeant stopped at a door with a judas peephole. Dieter slid back the panel and looked inside.

It was a bare room with a dirt floor. The only item of furniture was a bucket in the corner. Two men sat on the ground, not talking, staring into space. Dieter studied them carefully. He had seen both yesterday. The older one was Gaston, who had set the charges. He had a large piece of sticking-plaster covering a scalp wound that looked superficial. The other was very young, about seventeen, and Dieter recalled that his name was Bertrand. He had no visible injuries, but Dieter, recalling the skirmish, thought he might have been stunned by the explosion of a hand grenade.

Dieter watched them for a while, taking time to think. He had to do this right. He could not afford to waste another captive: these two were the only assets left. The kid would be scared, he foresaw, but might withstand a lot of pain. The other was too old for serious torture—he might die before he cracked—but he would be soft-hearted. Dieter began to see a strategy for interrogating them.

He closed the judas and returned to the interview room. Becker followed, reminding him again of a stupid but dangerous dog. Dieter said, "Sergeant Becker, untie the woman and put her in the cell with the other two."

Weber protested, "A woman in a man's cell?"

Dieter stared at him incredulously. "Do you think she will feel the indignity?"

Becker went into the torture chamber and reemerged carrying the broken body of Geneviève. Dieter said, "Make sure the old man gets a good look at her, then bring him here."

Becker went out.

Dieter decided he would prefer to get rid of Weber. However, he knew that if he gave a direct order, Weber would resist. So he said, "I think you should remain here to witness the interrogation. You could learn a lot from my techniques."

As Dieter had expected, Weber did the opposite. "I don't think so," he said. "Becker can keep me informed." Dieter faked an indignant expression, and Weber went out.

Dieter caught the eye of Lieutenant Hesse, who had quietly taken a seat in the corner. Hesse understood how Dieter had manipulated Weber and was looking admiringly at Dieter. Dieter shrugged. "Sometimes it's too easy," he said.

Becker returned with Gaston. The older man was pale. No doubt he had been badly shocked by the sight of Geneviève. Dieter said in German, "Please have a seat. Do you like to smoke?"

Gaston looked blank.

That established that he did not understand German, which was worth knowing.

Dieter motioned him to a seat and offered him cigarettes and matches. Gaston took a cigarette and lit it with shaking hands.

Some prisoners broke at this stage, before torture, just from fear of what would happen. Dieter hoped that might be the case today. He had shown Gaston the alternatives: on one hand, the dreadful sight of Geneviève; on the other, cigarettes and kindness.

Now he spoke in French, using a friendly tone. "I'm going to ask you some questions."

"I don't know anything," Gaston said.

"Oh, I think you do," Dieter said. "You're in your sixties, and you've probably lived in or around Reims all your life." Gaston did not deny this. Dieter went on: "I realize that the members of a Resistance cell use code names and give one another the minimum of personal information, as a security precaution." Gaston involuntarily gave a slight nod of agreement. "But you've known most of these people for decades. A man may call himself Elephant or Priest or Aubergine when the Resistance meet, but you know his face, and you recognize him as Jean-Pierre the postman, who lives in the rue du Parc and surreptitiously visits the widow Martineau on Tuesdays when his wife thinks he is playing bowls."

Gaston looked away, unwilling to meet Dieter's eye, confirming that Dieter was right.

Dieter went on, "I want you to understand that you are in control of everything that happens here. Pain, or the relief of pain; the sentence of death, or reprieve; all depend on your choices." He saw with satisfaction that Gaston looked even more terrified. "You will answer my questions," he went on. "Everyone does, in the end. The only imponderable is how soon."

This was the moment when a man might break down, but Gaston did not. "I can't tell you anything," he said in a near-whisper. He was scared, but he still had some courage left, and he was not going to give up without a fight.

Dieter shrugged. It was to be the hard way, then. He spoke to Becker in German. "Go back to the cell. Make the boy strip naked. Bring him here and tie him to the pillar in the next room."

"Very good, Major," Becker said eagerly.

Dieter turned back to Gaston. "You're going to tell me the names and code names of all the men and women who were with you yesterday, and any others in your Resistance circuit." Gaston shook his head, but Dieter ignored that. "I want to know the address of every member, and of every house used by members of the circuit."

Gaston drew hard on his cigarette and stared at the glowing end.

In fact, these were not the most important questions. Dieter's main aim was to get information that would lead him to other Resistance circuits. But he did not want Gaston to know that.

A moment later, Becker returned with Bertrand. Gaston stared open-mouthed as the naked boy was marched through the interview room into the chamber beyond.

Dieter stood up. He said to Hesse, "Keep an eye on this old man." Then he followed Becker into the torture chamber.

He was careful to leave the door a little ajar so that Gaston could hear everything.

Becker tied Bertrand to the pillar. Before Dieter could intervene, Becker punched Bertrand in the stomach. It was a powerful blow from a strong man, and it made a sickening thud. The young man groaned and writhed in agony.

"No, no, no," Dieter said. As he had expected, Becker's approach was completely unscientific. A strong young man could withstand being punched almost indefinitely. "First, you blindfold him." He produced a large cotton bandanna from his pocket and tied it over Bertrand's eyes. "This way, every blow comes as a dreadful shock, and every moment between blows is an agony of anticipation."

Becker picked up his wooden club. Dieter nodded, and Becker swung the club, hitting the side of the victim's head with a loud crack of solid wood on skin and bone. Bertrand cried out in pain and fear.

"No, no," Dieter said again. "Never hit the head. You may dislocate the jaw, preventing the subject from speaking. Worse, you may damage the brain, then nothing he says will be of any value." He took the wooden club from Becker and replaced it in the umbrella stand. From the selection of weapons there he chose a steel crowbar and handed it to Becker.

"Now, remember, the object is to inflict unbearable agony without endangering the subject's life or his ability to tell us what we need to know. Avoid vital organs. Concentrate on the bony parts: ankles, shins, knee-caps, fingers, elbows, shoulders, ribs."

A crafty look came over Becker's face. He walked around the pillar then, taking careful aim, struck hard at Bertrand's elbow with the steel bar. The boy gave a scream of real agony, a sound Dieter recognized.

Becker looked pleased. God forgive me, Dieter thought, for teaching this brute how to inflict pain more efficiently.

On Dieter's orders, Becker struck at Bertrand's bony shoulder, then his hand, then his ankle. Dieter made Becker pause between blows, allowing just enough time for the pain to ease slightly and for the subject to begin to dread the next stroke.

Bertrand began to appeal for mercy. "No

more, please," he implored, hysterical with pain and fear. Becker raised the crowbar, but Dieter stopped him. He wanted the begging to go on. "Please don't hit me again," Bertrand cried. "Please, please."

Dieter said to Becker, "It is often a good idea to break a leg early in the interview. The pain is quite excruciating, especially when the broken bone is struck again." He selected a sledgehammer from the umbrella stand. "Just below the knee," he said, handing it to Becker. "As hard as you can."

Becker took careful aim and swung mightily. The crack as the shin broke was loud enough to hear. Bertrand screamed and fainted. Becker picked up a bucket of water that stood in a corner and threw the water in Bertrand's face. The young man came to and screamed again.

Eventually, the screams subsided to heartrending groans. "What do you want?" Bertrand implored. "Please, tell me what you want from me!" Dieter did not ask him any questions. Instead, he handed the steel crowbar to Becker and pointed to the broken leg where a jagged white edge of bone stuck through the flesh. Becker struck the leg at that point. Bertrand screamed and passed out again.

Dieter thought that might be enough.

He went into the next room. Gaston sat where Dieter had left him, but he was a different man. He was bent over in his chair, face in his hands, crying with great sobs, moaning and praying to God. Dieter knelt in front of him and prized his hands away from his wet face. Gaston looked at him through tears. Dieter said softly, "Only you can make it stop."

"Please, stop it, please," Gaston moaned.

"Will you answer my questions?"

There was a pause. Bertrand screamed again. "Yes!" Gaston yelled. "Yes, yes, I'll tell you everything, if you just stop!"

Dieter raised his voice. "Sergeant Becker!"

"Yes, Major?"

"No more for now."

"Yes, Major." Becker sounded disappointed.

Dieter reverted to French. "Now, Gaston, let's begin with the leader of the circuit. Name and code name. Who is he?"

Gaston hesitated. Dieter looked toward the open door of the torture chamber. Gaston quickly said, "Michel Clairet. Code name Monet."

It was the breakthrough. The first name was the hardest. The rest would follow effortlessly. Concealing his satisfaction, Dieter gave Gaston a cigarette and held a match. "Where does he live?"

"In Reims." Gaston blew out smoke and his shaking began to subside. He gave an address near the cathedral.

Dieter nodded to Lieutenant Hesse, who took out a notebook and began to record Gaston's responses. Patiently, Dieter took Gaston through each member of the attack team. In a few cases Gaston knew only the code names, and there were two men he claimed never to have seen before Sunday. Dieter believed him. There had been two getaway drivers waiting a short distance away, Gaston said: a young woman called Gilberte and a man codenamed Maréchal. There were others in the group, which was known as the Bollinger circuit.

Dieter asked about relationships between Resistance members. Were there any love affairs? Were any of them homosexual? Was anyone sleeping with someone else's wife? Although the torture had stopped, Bertrand continued to groan and sometimes scream with the agony of his wounds, and now Gaston said, "Is he going to be looked after?"

Dieter shrugged.

"Please, get a doctor for him."

"Very well . . . when we have finished our talk."

Gaston told Dieter that Michel and Gilberte were lovers, even though Michel was married to Flick, the blonde girl in the square.

So far, Gaston had been talking about a circuit that was mostly destroyed, so his information had been mainly of academic interest. Now Dieter moved on to more important questions. "When Allied agents come to this district, how do they make contact?"

No one was supposed to know how that was handled, Gaston said. There was a cutout. However, he knew part of the story. The agents were met by a woman codenamed Bourgeoise. Gaston did not know where she met them, but she took them to her home, then she passed them on to Michel.

No one had ever met Bourgeoise, not even Michel.

Dieter was disappointed that Gaston knew so little about the woman. But that was the idea of a cut-out.

"Do you know where she lives?"

Gaston nodded. "One of the agents gave it away. She has a house in the rue du Bois. Number eleven."

Dieter tried not to look jubilant. This was a key fact. The enemy would probably send more agents in an attempt to rebuild the Bollinger circuit. Dieter might be able to catch them at the safe house.

"And when they leave?"

They were picked up by plane in a field codenamed Champ de Pierre, actually a pasture near the village of Chatelle, Gaston revealed. There was an alternative landing field, codenamed Champ d'Or, but he did not know where it was.

Dieter asked Gaston about liaison with London. Who had ordered the attack on the telephone exchange? Gaston explained that Flick—Major Clairet—was the circuit's commanding officer, and she had brought orders from London. Dieter was intrigued. A woman in command. But he had seen her courage under fire. She would make a good leader.

In the next room, Bertrand began to pray aloud for death to come. "Please," Gaston said. "A doctor."

"Just tell me about Major Clairet," Dieter said. "Then I'll get someone to give Bertrand an injection."

"She is a very important person," Gaston said, eager now to give Dieter information that would satisfy him. "They say she has survived longer than anyone else under cover. She has been all over northern France."

Dieter was spellbound. "She has contact with different circuits?"

"So I believe."

That was unusual—and it meant she could be a fountain of information about the French Resistance. Dieter said, "She got away yesterday after the skirmish. Where do you think she went?"

"Back to London, I'm sure," Gaston said. "To report on the raid."

Dieter cursed silently. He wanted her in France, where he could catch her and interrogate her. If he got his hands on her, he could destroy half the French Resistance—as he had promised Rommel. But she was out of reach.

He stood up. "That's all for now," he said. "Hans, get a doctor for the prisoners. I don't want any of them to die today—they may have more to tell us. Then type up your notes and bring them to me in the morning."

"Very good, Major."

"Make a copy for Major Weber—but don't give it to him until I say so."

"Understood."

"I'll drive myself back to the hotel." Dieter went out.

The headache began as he stepped into the open air.

Rubbing his forehead with his hand, he made his way to the car and drove out of the village, heading for Reims. The afternoon sun seemed to reflect off the road surface straight into his eyes. These migraines often struck him after an interrogation. In an hour he would be blind and helpless. He had to get back to the hotel before the attack reached its peak. Reluctant to brake, he sounded his horn constantly. Vineyard workers making their slow way home scattered out of his path. Horses reared and a cart was driven into the ditch. His eyes watered with the pain, and he felt nauseous.

He reached the town without crashing the

car. He managed to steer into the center. Outside the Hotel Frankfort, he did not so much park the car as abandon it. Staggering inside, he made his way to the suite.

Stéphanie knew immediately what had happened. While he stripped off his uniform tunic and shirt, she got the field medical kit out of her suitcase and filled a syringe with the morphine mixture. Dieter fell on the bed, and she plunged the needle into his arm. Almost immediately, the pain eased. Stéphanie lay down beside him, stroking his face with gentle fingertips.

A few moments later, Dieter was unconscious.

CHAPTER 10

Flick's home was a bedsitter in a big old house in Bayswater. Her room was in the attic: if a bomb came through the roof it would land on her bed. She spent little time there, not for fear of bombs but because real life went on elsewhere—in France, at SOE headquarters, or at one of SOE's training centers around the country. There was little of her in the room: a photo of Michel playing a guitar, a shelf of Flaubert and Molière in French, a watercolor of Nice she had painted at the age of fifteen. The small chest had three drawers of clothing and one of guns and ammunition.

Feeling weary and depressed, she undressed and lay down on the bed, looking through a copy of *Parade* magazine. Berlin had been bombed by a force of 1,500 planes last Wednesday, she read. It was hard to imagine. She tried to picture what it must have been like for the ordinary Germans living there, and all she could think of was a medieval painting of Hell, with naked people being burned alive in a hail of fire. She turned the page and read a silly story about second-rate "V-cigarettes" being passed off as Woodbines.

Her mind kept returning to yesterday's failure. She reran the battle in her mind, imagining a dozen decisions she might have made differently, leading to victory instead of defeat. As well as losing the battle, she feared she might be losing her husband, and she wondered if there was a link. Inadequate as a leader, inadequate as a wife, perhaps there was some flaw deep in her character.

Now that her alternative plan had been rejected, there was no prospect of redeeming herself. All those brave people had died for nothing.

Eventually she drifted into an uneasy sleep. She was awakened by someone banging on the door and calling, "Flick! Telephone!" The voice belonged to one of the girls in the flat below.

The clock on Flick's bookshelf said six. "Who is it?" she called.

"He just said the office."

"I'm coming." She pulled on a dressing gown. Unsure whether it was six in the morning or evening, she glanced out of her little window. The sun was setting over the elegant terraces of Ladbroke Grove. She ran downstairs to the phone in the hall.

Percy Thwaite's voice said, "Sorry to wake you."

"That's all right." She was always glad to hear Percy's voice on the other end of the phone. She had become very fond of him, even though he constantly sent her into danger. Running agents was a heartbreaking job, and some senior officers anaesthetized themselves by adopting a hard-hearted attitude toward the death or capture of their people, but Percy never did that. He felt every loss as a bereavement. Consequently, Flick knew he would never take an unnecessary risk with her. She trusted him.

"Can you come to Orchard Court?"

She wondered if the authorities had reconsidered her new plan for taking out the telephone exchange, and her heart leaped with hope. "Has Monty changed his mind?"

"I'm afraid not. But I need you to brief someone."

She bit her lip, suppressing her disappointment. "I'll be there in a few minutes."

She dressed quickly and took the Underground to Baker Street. Percy was waiting for her in the flat in Portman Square. "I've found a radio operator. No experience, but he's done the training. I'm sending him to Reims tomorrow."

Flick glanced reflexively at the window, to check the weather, as agents always did when a flight was mentioned. Percy's curtains were drawn, for security, but anyway she knew the weather was fine. "Reims? Why?"

"We've heard nothing from Michel today. I need to know how much of the Bollinger circuit is left."

Flick nodded. Pierre, the radio operator, had been in the attack squad. Presumably he was captured or dead. Michel might have been able to locate Pierre's radio transceiver, but he had not been trained to operate it, and he certainly did not know the codes. "But what's the point?"

"We've sent them tons of explosives and ammunition in the last few months. I want them to light some fires. The telephone exchange is the most important target, but it's not the only one. Even if there's no one left but Michel and a couple of others, they can blow up railway lines, cut telephone wires, and shoot sentries—it all helps. But I can't direct them if I have no communication."

Flick shrugged. To her, the château was the only target that mattered. Everything else was chicken feed. But what the hell. "I'll brief him, of course."

Percy gave her a hard look. He hesitated, then said, "How was Michel—apart from his bullet wound?"

"Fine." Flick was silent for a moment. Percy stared at her. She could not deceive him, he knew her too well. At last she sighed and said, "There's a girl."

"I was afraid of that."

"I don't know whether there's anything left of my marriage," she said bitterly.

"I'm sorry."

"It would help if I could tell myself that I'd made a sacrifice for a purpose, struck a magnificent blow for our side, made the invasion more likely to succeed."

"You've done more than most, over the last two years."

"But there's no second prize in a war, is there?"

"No."

She stood up. She was grateful for Percy's fond sympathy, but it was making her maudlin. "I'd better brief the new radio man."

"Code name Helicopter. He's waiting in the study. Not the sharpest knife in the box, I'm afraid, but a brave lad."

This seemed sloppy to Flick. "If he's not too bright, why send him? He might endanger others."

"As you said earlier—this is our big chance. If the invasion fails, we've lost Europe. We've got to throw everything we have at the enemy now, because we won't get another chance."

Flick nodded grimly. He had turned her own argument against her. But he was right. The only difference was that the lives being endangered, in this case, included Michel's. "Okay," she said. "I'd better get on with it."

"He's eager to see you."

She frowned. "Eager? Why?"

Percy gave a wry smile. "Go and find out for yourself."

Flick left the drawing room of the apartment, where Percy had his desk, and went along the corridor. His secretary was typing in the kitchen, and she directed Flick to another room.

Flick paused outside the door. This is how it is, she told herself: you pick yourself up and carry on working, hoping you will eventually forget.

She entered the study, a small room with a square table and a few mismatched chairs. Helicopter was a fair-skinned boy of about twenty-two, wearing a tweed suit in a checked pattern of mustard, orange, and green. You could tell he was English from a distance of a mile. Fortunately, before he got on the plane he would be kitted out in clothing that would look inconspicuous in a French town. SOE employed French tailors and dressmakers who sewed continental-style clothes for agents (then spent hours making the clothes look worn and shabby so that they would not attract attention by their newness). There was nothing they could do about Helicopter's pink complexion and red-blond hair, except hope that the

Gestapo would think he must have some German blood.

Flick introduced herself, and he said, "Yes, we've met before, actually."

"I'm sorry, I don't remember."

"You were at Oxford with my brother, Charles."

"Charlie Standish—of course!" Flick remembered another fair boy in tweeds, taller and slimmer than Helicopter, but probably no cleverer—he had not taken a degree. Charlie spoke fluent French, she recalled—something they had had in common.

"You came to our house in Gloucestershire once, actually."

Flick recalled a weekend in a country house in the thirties, and a family with an amiable English father and a chic French mother. Charlie had had a kid brother, Brian, an awkward adolescent in knee shorts, very excited about his new camera. She had talked to him a bit, and he had developed a little crush on her. "So how is Charlie? I haven't seen him since we graduated."

"He's dead, actually." Brian looked suddenly grief-stricken. "Died in forty-one. Killed in the b-b-bloody desert, actually."

Flick was afraid he would cry. She took

his hand in both of hers and said, "Brian, I'm so terribly sorry."

"Jolly nice of you." He swallowed hard. With an effort he brightened. "I've seen you since then, just once. You gave a lecture to my SOE training group. I didn't get a chance to speak to you afterwards."

"I hope my talk was useful."

"You spoke about traitors within the Resistance and what to do about them. 'It's quite simple,' you said. 'You put the barrel of your pistol to the back of the bastard's head and pull the trigger twice.' Scared us all to death, actually."

He was looking at her with something like hero-worship in his eyes, and she began to see what Percy had been hinting at. It looked as if Brian still had a crush on her. She moved away from him, sat at the other side of the table, and said, "Well, we'd better begin. You know you're going to make contact with a Resistance circuit that has been largely wiped out."

"Yes, I'm to find out how much of it is left and what it is still capable of doing, if anything."

"It's likely that some members were captured during the skirmish yesterday and are under Gestapo interrogation as we speak. So you'll have to be especially careful. Your contact in Reims is a woman codenamed Bourgeoise. Every day at eleven in the morning she goes to the crypt of the cathedral to pray. She's generally the only person there but, in case there are others, she'll be wearing odd shoes, one black and one brown."

"Easy enough to remember."

"You say to her, 'Pray for me.' She replies, 'I pray for peace.' That's the code."

He repeated the words.

"She'll take you to her house, then put you in touch with the head of the Bollinger circuit, whose code name is Monet." She was talking about her husband, but Brian did not need to know that. "Don't mention the address or real name of Bourgeoise to other members of the circuit when you meet them, please: for security reasons, it's better they don't know." Flick herself had recruited Bourgeoise and set up the cut-out. Even Michel had not met the woman.

"I understand."

"Is there anything you want to ask me?"

"I'm sure there are a hundred things, but I can't think of any."

She stood up and came around the table to shake his hand. "Well, good luck."

He kept hold of her hand. "I never forgot that weekend you came to our house," he said. "I expect I was a frightful bore, but you were very kind to me."

She smiled and said lightly, "You were a nice kid."

"I fell in love with you, actually."

She wanted to jerk her hand out of his and walk away, but he might die tomorrow, and she could not bring herself to be so cruel. "I'm flattered," she said, trying to maintain an amiably bantering tone.

It was no good: he was in earnest. "I was wondering . . . would you . . . just for luck, give me a kiss?"

She hesitated. Oh, hell, she thought. She stood on tiptoe and kissed him lightly on the lips. She let the kiss linger for a second, then broke away. He looked transfixed by joy. She patted his cheek softly with her hand. "Stay alive, Brian," she said. Then she went out.

She returned to Percy's room. He had a pile of books and a scatter of photographs on his desk. "All done?" he said.

She nodded. "But he's not perfect secret agent material, Percy."

Percy shrugged. "He's brave, he speaks French like a Parisian, and he can shoot straight."

"Two years ago you would have sent him back to the army."

"True. Now I'm going to send him off to Sandy." At a large country house in the village of Sandy, near the Tempsford airstrip, Brian would be dressed in French-style clothes and given the forged papers he needed to pass through Gestapo checkpoints and buy food. Percy got up and went to the door. "While I'm seeing him off, have a look at that rogues' gallery, will you?" He pointed to the photos on the desk. "Those are all the pictures MI6 has of German officers. If the man you saw in the square at Sainte-Cécile should happen to be among them, I'd be interested to know his name." He went out.

Flick picked up one of the books. It was a graduation yearbook from a military academy, showing postage stamp-sized photos of a couple of hundred fresh-faced young men. There were a dozen or more similar books, and several hundred loose photos.

She did not want to spend all night looking at mug shots, but perhaps she could narrow it down. The man in the square had seemed about forty. He would have graduated at the age of twenty-two, roughly, so the year must have been about 1926. None of the books was that old.

She turned her attention to the loose photographs. As she flicked through, she recalled all she could of the man. He was quite tall and well dressed, but that would not show in a photo. He had thick dark hair, she thought, and although he was clean-shaven, he looked as if he could grow a heavy beard. She remembered dark eyes, clearly marked eyebrows, a straight nose, a square chin . . . quite the matinee idol, in fact.

The loose photos had been taken in all sorts of different situations. Some were news pictures, showing officers shaking hands with Hitler, inspecting troops, or looking at tanks and airplanes. A few seemed to have been snapped by spies. These were the most candid shots, taken in crowds, from cars, or through windows, showing the officers shopping, talking to children, hailing a taxi, lighting a pipe.

She scanned the photos as fast as she

could, tossing them to one side. She hesitated over each dark-haired man. None was as handsome as the one she recalled from the square. She passed over a photo of a man in police uniform, then went back to it. The uniform had at first put her off, but on careful study she thought this was him.

She turned the photograph over. Pasted to the back was a typewritten sheet. She read:

FRANCK, Dieter Wolfgang, sometimes "Frankie"; born Cologne 3 June 1904; educ. Humboldt University of Berlin & Koln Police Academy; mar. 1930 Waltraud Loewe, 1 son 1 dtr; Superintendent, Criminal Investigation Department, Cologne police, to 1940; Major, Intelligence Section, Afrika Korps, to ?

A star of Rommel's intelligence staff, this officer is said to be a skilled interrogator and a ruthless torturer.

Flick shuddered to think she had been so near to such a dangerous man. An experienced police detective who had turned his skills to military intelligence was a frightening enemy. The fact that he had a family in Cologne did not prevent his having a mistress in France, it seemed.

Percy returned, and she handed him the picture. "This is the man."

"Dieter Franck!" said Percy. "We know of him. How interesting. From what you overheard of his conversation in the square, Rommel seems to have given him some kind of counter-Resistance job." He made a note on his pad. "I'd better let MI6 know, as they loaned us their photos."

There was a tap at the door, and Percy's secretary looked in. "There's someone to see you, Colonel Thwaite." The girl looked coquettish. The fatherly Percy never inspired that sort of behavior in secretaries, so Flick guessed the visitor must be an attractive man. "An American," the girl added. That might explain it, Flick thought. Americans were the height of glamour, to secretaries at least.

"How did he find this place?" Percy said. Orchard Court was supposed to be a secret address.

"He went to number sixty-four Baker Street, and they sent him here."

"They shouldn't do that. He must be very persuasive. Who is he?"

"Major Chancellor."

Percy looked at Flick. She did not know anyone called Chancellor. Then she remembered the arrogant major who had been so rude to her this morning at Monty's headquarters. "Oh, God, him," she said in disgust. "What does he want?"

"Send him in," said Percy.

Paul Chancellor came in. He walked with a limp that Flick had not noticed this morning. It probably got worse as the day wore on. He had a pleasant American face, with a big nose and a jutting chin. Any chance he might have had of being handsome was spoiled by his left ear, or what remained of it, which was the lower one-third, mostly lobe. Flick assumed he had been wounded in action.

Chancellor saluted and said, "Good evening, Colonel. Good evening, Major."

Percy said, "We don't do a lot of saluting at SOE, Chancellor. Please sit down. What brings you here?"

Chancellor took a chair and removed his uniform cap. "I'm glad I caught you both," he said. "I've spent most of the day thinking about this morning's conversation." He gave a self-effacing grin. "Part of the time, I have to confess, I was composing wittily crushing remarks I could have made if only I had thought of them in time."

Flick could not help smiling. She had done the same.

Chancellor went on. "You hinted, Colonel Thwaite, that MI6 might not have told the whole truth about the attack on the telephone exchange, and that played on my mind. The fact that Major Clairet here was so rude to me did not necessarily mean she was lying about the facts."

Flick had been halfway to forgiving him, but now she bridled. "Rude? Me?"

Percy said, "Shut up, Flick."

She closed her mouth.

"So I sent for your report, Colonel. Of course the request came from Monty's office, not me personally, so it was brought to our headquarters by a FANY motorcyclist in double-quick time."

He was a no-nonsense type who knew how to pull the levers of the military machine, Flick thought. He might be an arrogant pig, but he would make a useful ally.

"When I read it, I realized the main reason for defeat was wrong intelligence."

"Supplied by MI6!" Flick said indignantly.

"Yes, I noticed that," Chancellor said with mild sarcasm. "Obviously, MI6 was covering up its own incompetence. I'm not a career soldier myself, but my father is, so I'm familiar with the tricks of military bureaucrats."

"Oh," said Percy thoughtfully. "Are you the son of General Chancellor?"

"Yes."

"Go on."

"MI6 would never have gotten away with it if your boss had been at the meeting this morning to tell SOE's side of the story. It seemed too much of a coincidence that he had been called away at the last minute."

Percy looked dubious. "He was summoned by the Prime Minister. I don't see how MI6 could have arranged that."

"The meeting was not attended by Churchill. A Downing Street aide took the chair. And it *had* been arranged at the instigation of MI6."

"Well, I'm damned," Flick said angrily. "They're such snakes!"

Percy said, "I wish they were as clever

about gathering intelligence as they are about deceiving their colleagues."

Chancellor said, "I also looked in detail at your plan, Major Clairet, for taking the château by stealth, with a team disguised as cleaners. It's risky, of course, but it could work."

Did that mean it would be reconsidered? Flick hardly dared to ask.

Percy gave Chancellor a level look. "So what are you going to do about all this?"

"By chance, I had dinner with my father tonight. I told him the whole story and asked him what a general's aide should do in these circumstances. We were at the Savoy."

"What did he say?" Flick asked impatiently. She did not care which restaurant they had gone to.

"That I should go to Monty and tell him we had made a mistake." He grimaced. "Not easy with any general. They never like to revisit decisions. But sometimes it has to be done."

"And will you?" Flick said hopefully.

"I already have."

Percy said in surprise, "You don't waste time, do you!"

Flick held her breath. It hardly seemed

possible, after a day of despair, that she might be given the second chance she longed for.

Chancellor said, "Monty was remarkably good about it, in the end."

Flick could not contain her agitation. "For God's sake, what did he say about my plan?"

"He's authorized it."

"Thank God!" She jumped up, unable to sit still. "Another chance!"

Percy said, "Splendid!"

Chancellor held up a warning hand. "Two more things. The first one you may not like. He's put me in charge of the operation."

"You!" Flick said.

"Why?" said Percy.

"You don't cross-examine the general when he gives an order. I'm sorry you seem dismayed. Monty has faith in me, even if you don't."

Percy shrugged.

Flick said, "What's the other stipulation?"

"There's a time constraint. I can't tell you when the invasion will be, and in fact the date has not been finally decided. But I can tell you that we have to accomplish our mission very quickly. If you haven't achieved the objective by midnight next Monday, it will probably be too late."

"Next Monday!" said Flick.

"Yes," said Paul Chancellor. "We have exactly one week."

THE THIRD DAY

Tuesday, May 30, 1944

CHAPTER 11

Flick left London at dawn, driving a Vincent Comet motorcycle with a powerful 500cc engine. The roads were deserted. Gas was severely rationed, and drivers could be jailed for making "unnecessary" journeys. She drove very fast. It was dangerous but exciting. The thrill was worth the risk.

She felt the same about the mission, scared but eager. She had stayed up late last night with Percy and Paul, drinking tea and planning. There must be six women in the team, they had decided, as it was the unvarying number of cleaners on a shift. One had to be an explosives expert; another, a telephone engineer, to decide exactly where the charges should be placed to ensure the exchange was crippled. She wanted one good marksman and two tough soldiers. With herself, that would make six.

She had one day to find them. The team would need a minimum of two days' training—they had to learn to parachute, if nothing else. That would take up Wednesday and Thursday. They would be dropped near Reims on Friday night, and enter the château on Saturday evening or Sunday. That left one spare day as a margin for error.

She crossed the river at London Bridge. Her motorbike roared through the bomb-ravaged wharves and tenements of Bermondsey and Rotherhithe, then she took the Old Kent Road, traditional route of pilgrims, toward Canterbury. As she left the suburbs behind, she opened the throttle and gave the bike its head. For a while she let the wind blow the worries out of her hair.

It was not yet six o'clock when she reached Somersholme, the country house of the barons of Colefield. The baron himself, William, was in Italy, fighting his way toward Rome with the Eighth Army, Flick knew. His sister, the Honorable Diana Colefield, was the only member of the family living here now. The vast house, with its dozens of bedrooms for houseguests and their servants, was being used as a convalescent home for wounded soldiers.

Flick slowed the bike to walking speed and drove up the avenue of hundred-year-old lime trees, gazing at the great pile of pink granite ahead, with its bays, balconies, gables, and roofs, acres of windows and scores of chimneys. She parked on the gravel forecourt next to an ambulance and a scatter of jeeps.

In the hall, nurses bustled about with cups of tea. The soldiers might be here to convalesce, but they still had to be wakened at daybreak. Flick asked for Mrs. Riley, the housekeeper, and was directed to the basement. She found her staring worriedly at the furnace in the company of two men in overalls.

"Hello, Ma," said Flick.

Her mother hugged her hard. She was even shorter than her daughter and just as thin, but like Flick she was stronger than she looked. The hug squeezed the breath out of Flick. Gasping and laughing, she extricated herself. "Ma, you'll crush me!"

"I never know if you're alive until I see you," her mother said. In her voice there was still a trace of the Irish accent: she had left Cork with her parents forty-five years ago.

"What's the matter with the furnace?"

"It was never designed to produce so much hot water. These nurses are mad for cleanliness, they force the poor soldiers to bathe every day. Come to my kitchen and I'll make you some breakfast."

Flick was in a hurry, but she told herself she had time for her mother. Anyway, she had to eat. She followed Ma up the stairs and into the servants' quarters.

Flick had grown up in this house. She had played in the servants' hall, run wild in the woods, attended the village school a mile away, and returned here from boarding school and university for the vacations. She had been extraordinarily privileged. Most women in her mother's position were forced to give up their jobs when they had a child. Ma had been allowed to stay, partly because the old baron had been somewhat unconventional, but mainly because she was such a good housekeeper that he had dreaded losing her. Flick's father had been butler, but he had died when she was six years old. Every February, Flick and her Ma had accompanied the family to their villa in

Nice, which was where Flick had learned French.

The old baron, father of William and Diana, had been fond of Flick and had encouraged her to study, even paying her school fees. He had been very proud when she had won a scholarship to Oxford University. When he died, soon after the start of the war, Flick had been as heartbroken as if he had been her real father.

The family now occupied only a small corner of the house. The old butler's pantry had become the kitchen. Flick's mother put the kettle on. "Just a piece of toast will be fine, Ma," said Flick.

Her mother ignored her and started frying bacon. "Well, I can see you're all right," she said. "How is that handsome husband?"

"Michel's alive," Flick said. She sat at the kitchen table. The smell of bacon made her mouth water.

"Alive, is he? But not well, evidently. Wounded?"

"He got a bullet in his bum. It won't kill him."

"You've seen him, then."

Flick laughed. "Ma, stop it! I'm not supposed to say."

"Of course not. Is he keeping his hands off other women? If *that's* not a military secret."

Flick never ceased to be startled by the accuracy of her mother's intuition. It was quite eerie. "I hope he is."

"Hmm. Anyone in particular, that you hope he's keeping his hands off?"

Flick did not answer the question directly. "Have you noticed, Ma, that men sometimes don't seem to realize when a girl is really stupid?"

Ma made a disgusted noise. "So that's the way of it. She's pretty, I suppose."

"Mmm."

"Young?"

"Nineteen."

"Have you had it out with him?"

"Yes. He promised to stop."

"He might keep his promise—if you're not away too long."

"I'm hopeful."

Ma looked crestfallen. "So you're going back."

"I can't say."

"Have you not done enough?"

"We haven't won the war yet, so no, I suppose I haven't."

Ma put a plate of bacon and eggs in front of Flick. It probably represented a week's rations. But Flick suppressed the protest that came to her lips. Better to accept the gift gracefully. Besides, she was suddenly ravenous. "Thanks, Ma," she said. "You spoil me."

Her mother smiled, satisfied, and Flick tucked in hungrily. As she ate, she reflected wryly that Ma had effortlessly got out of her everything she wanted to know, despite Flick's attempts to avoid answering questions. "You should work for military intelligence," she said through a mouthful of fried egg. "They could use you as an interrogator. You've made me tell you everything."

"I'm your mother, I've a right to know."

It didn't much matter. Ma would not repeat any of it.

She sipped a cup of tea as she watched Flick eat. "You've got to win the war all on your own, of course," she said with fond sarcasm. "You were that way from a child— independent to a fault."

"I don't know why. I was always looked after. When you were busy there were half a dozen housemaids doting on me."

"I think I encouraged you to be self-sufficient because you didn't have a father. Whenever you wanted me to do something for you, like fix a bicycle chain, or sew on a button, I used to say, 'Try it yourself, and if you can't manage I'll help you.' Nine times out of ten I heard no more about it."

Flick finished the bacon and wiped her plate with a slice of bread. "A lot of the time, Mark used to help me." Mark was Flick's brother, a year older.

Her mother's face froze. "Is that right," she said.

Flick suppressed a sigh. Ma had quarreled with Mark two years ago. He worked in the theater as a stage manager, and lived with an actor called Steve. Ma had long known that Mark was "not the marrying kind," as she put it. But in a burst of excessive honesty Mark had been foolish enough to tell Ma that he loved Steve, and they were like husband and wife. She had been mortally offended and had not spoken to her son since.

Flick said, "Mark loves you, Ma."

"Does he, now."

"I wish you'd see him."

"No doubt." Ma picked up Flick's empty plate and washed it in the sink.

Flick shook her head in exasperation. "You're a bit stubborn, Ma."

"I daresay that's where you get it from, then."

Flick had to smile. She had often been accused of stubbornness. "Mulish" was Percy's word. She made an effort to be conciliatory. "Well, I suppose you can't help the way you feel. Anyway, I'm not going to argue with you, especially after such a wonderful breakfast." All the same, it was her ambition to get the two of them to make up.

But not today. She stood up.

Ma smiled. "It's lovely to see you. I worry about you."

"I've got another reason for coming. I need to talk to Diana."

"Whatever for?"

"Can't say."

"I hope you're not thinking of taking her to France with you."

"Ma, hush! Who said anything about going to France?"

"I suppose it's because she's so handy with a gun."

"I can't say."

"She'll get you killed! She doesn't know what discipline is, why should she? She wasn't brought up that way. Not her fault, of course. But you'd be a fool to rely on her."

"Yes, I know," Flick said impatiently. She had made a decision and she was not going to review it with Ma.

"She's had several war jobs, and been sacked from every one."

"I know." But Diana was a crack shot, and Flick did not have time to be fussy. She had to take what she could get. Her main worry was that Diana might refuse. No one could be forced to do undercover work. It was strictly for volunteers. "Where is Diana now, do you know?"

"I believe she's in the woods," Ma said. "She went out early, after rabbits."

"Of course." Diana loved all the blood sports: foxhunting, deerstalking, hare coursing, grouse shooting, even fishing. If there was nothing else to do, she would shoot rabbits.

"Just follow the sound of gunfire."

Flick kissed her mother's cheek. "Thanks for breakfast." She went to the door.

"And don't get on the wrong side of her gun," Ma called after her.

Flick left by the staff door, crossed the

kitchen garden, and entered the woods at the rear of the house. The trees were bright with new leaves, and the nettles grew waist-high. Flick tramped through the undergrowth in her heavy motorcycle boots and leather trousers. The best way to attract Diana, she thought, would be by issuing a challenge.

When she had gone a quarter of a mile into the woods, she heard the report of a shotgun. She stopped, listened, and shouted, "Diana!" There was no reply.

She walked toward the sound, calling out every minute or so. Eventually she heard, "Over here, you noisy idiot, whoever you are!"

"Coming, just put down the gun."

She came upon Diana in a clearing, sitting on the ground with her back against an oak tree, smoking a cigarette. A shotgun lay across her knees, broken open for reloading, and there were half a dozen dead rabbits beside her. "Oh, it's you!" she said. "You scared all the game away."

"They'll come back tomorrow." Flick studied her childhood companion. Diana was pretty in a boyish way, with dark hair cut short and freckles across her nose. She wore a shooting jacket and corduroy trousers. "How are you, Diana?"

"Bored. Frustrated. Depressed. Otherwise fine."

Flick sat on the grass beside her. This might be easier than she had thought. "What's the matter?"

"I'm rotting away in the English countryside while my brother's conquering Italy."

"How is William?"

"He's all right, he's part of the war effort, but no one will give me a proper job."

"I might be able to help you there."

"You're in the FANYs." Diana drew on her cigarette and blew out smoke. "Darling, I can't be a *chauffeuse.*"

Flick nodded. Diana was too grand to do the menial war work that most women were offered. "Well, I'm here to propose something more interesting."

"What?"

"You might not like it. It's very difficult, and dangerous."

Diana looked skeptical. "What does it involve, driving in the blackout?"

"I can't tell you much about it, because it's secret."

"Flick, darling, don't tell me you're involved in cloak-and-dagger stuff."

"I didn't get promoted to major by driving generals to meetings."

Diana looked hard at her. "Do you mean this?"

"Absolutely."

"Good Lord." Against her will, Diana was impressed.

Flick had to get her positive agreement to volunteer. "So—are you willing to do something very dangerous? I mean it, you really are quite likely to get killed."

Diana looked excited rather than discouraged. "Of course I'm willing. William's risking his life, why shouldn't I?"

"You mean it?"

"I'm very serious."

Flick concealed her relief. She had recruited her first team member.

Diana was so keen that Flick decided to press her advantage. "There's a condition, and you may find it worse than the danger."

"What?"

"You're two years older than I, and all our lives you've been my social superior. You're the baron's daughter, and I'm the housekeeper's brat. Nothing wrong with that, and

I'm not complaining. Ma would say that's how it should be."

"Yes, dear, so what's your point?"

"I'm in charge of the operation. You'll have to defer to me."

Diana shrugged. "That's fine."

"It will be a problem," Flick insisted. "You'll find it strange. But I'll be hard on you until you get used to it. This is a warning."

"Yes, sir!"

"We don't bother too much about the formalities in my department, so you won't need to call me sir, or ma'am. But we do enforce military discipline, especially once an operation has begun. If you forget that, my anger will be the least of your worries. Disobeying orders can get you killed in my line of work."

"Darling, how dramatic! But of course I understand."

Flick was not at all sure Diana did understand, but she had done her best. She took a scratch pad from her blouse and wrote down an address in Hampshire. "Pack a case for three days. This is where you need to go. You get the train from Waterloo to Brockenhurst."

Diana looked at the address. "Why, this is Lord Montagu's estate."

"Most of it is occupied by my department now."

"What *is* your department?"

"The Inter Services Research Bureau," Flick said, using the usual cover name.

"I trust it's more exciting than it sounds."

"You can bet on that."

"When do I start?"

"You need to get there today." Flick got to her feet. "Your training starts at dawn tomorrow."

"I'll come back to the house with you and start packing." Diana stood up. "Tell me something?"

"If I can."

Diana fiddled with her shotgun, seeming embarrassed. When she looked at Flick, her face showed an expression of frankness for the first time. "Why me?" she said. "You must know I've been turned down by everyone."

Flick nodded. "I'll be blunt." She looked at the bloodstained rabbit corpses on the ground, then lifted her gaze to Diana's pretty face. "You're a killer," she said. "And that's what I need."

CHAPTER 12

Dieter slept until ten. He woke with a headache from the morphine, but otherwise he felt good: excited, optimistic, confident. Yesterday's bloody interrogation had given him a hot lead. The woman codenamed Bourgeoise, with her house in the rue du Bois, could be his way into the heart of the French Resistance.

Or it might go nowhere.

He drank a liter of water and took three aspirins to get rid of the morphine hangover, then he picked up the phone.

First he called Lieutenant Hesse, who was staying in a less grand room at the same hotel. "Good morning, Hans, did you sleep well?"

"Yes, thank you, Major. Sir, I went to the

town hall to check out the address in the rue du Bois."

"Good lad," Dieter said. "What did you find out?"

"The house is owned and occupied by one person, a Mademoiselle Jeanne Lemas."

"But there may be other people staying there."

"I also drove past, just to have a look, and the place seemed quiet."

"Be ready to leave, with my car, in an hour."

"Very good."

"And, Hans—well done for using your initiative."

"Thank you, sir."

Dieter hung up. He wondered what Mademoiselle Lemas was like. Gaston said no one in the Bollinger circuit had ever met her, and Dieter believed him: the house was a security cut-out. Incoming agents knew nothing more than where to contact the woman: if caught, they could not reveal any information about the Resistance. At least, that was the theory. There was no such thing as perfect security.

Presumably Mademoiselle Lemas was

unmarried. She could be a young woman who had inherited the house from her parents, a middle-aged spinster looking for a husband, or an old maid. It might help to take a woman with him, he decided.

He returned to the bedroom. Stéphanie had brushed her abundant red hair and was sitting up in bed, with her breasts showing over the top of the sheet. She really knew how to look tempting. But he resisted the impulse to get back into bed. "Would you do something for me?" he said.

"I would do anything for you."

"Anything?" He sat on the bed and touched her bare shoulder. "Would you watch me with another woman?"

"Of course," she said. "I would lick her nipples while you made love to her."

"You would, I know." He laughed with pleasure. He had had mistresses before, but none like her. "It's not that, though. I want you to come with me while I arrest a woman in the Resistance."

Her face showed no emotion. "Very well," she said calmly.

He was tempted to press her for a reaction, to ask her how she felt about this, and was she sure she was happy about it, but he decided to take her consent at face value. "Thank you," he said, and he returned to the living room.

Mademoiselle Lemas might be alone but, on the other hand, the house could be crawling with Allied agents, all armed to the teeth. He needed some backup. He consulted his notebook and gave the hotel operator Rommel's number in La Roche-Guyon.

When the Germans had first occupied the country, the French telephone system had been swamped. Since then, the Germans had improved the equipment, adding thousands of kilometers of cable and installing automatic exchanges. The system was still overloaded, but it was better than it had been.

He asked for Rommel's aide Major Goedel. A moment later he heard the familiar cold, precise voice: "Goedel."

"This is Dieter Franck," he said. "How are you, Walter?"

"Busy," Goedel said crisply. "What is it?"

"I'm making rapid progress here. I don't want to give details, because I'm speaking on a hotel phone, but I'm about to arrest at least one spy, perhaps several. I thought the Field Marshal might like to know that."

"I shall tell him."

"But I could use some assistance. I'm doing all this with one lieutenant. I'm so desperate, I'm using my French girlfriend to help me."

"That seems unwise."

"Oh, she's trustworthy. But she won't be much use against trained terrorists. Can you get me half a dozen good men?"

"Use the Gestapo—that's what they're for."

"They're unreliable. You know they're cooperating with us only reluctantly. I need people I can rely on."

"It's out of the question," Goedel said.

"Look, Walter, you know how important Rommel feels this is—he's given me the job of making sure the Resistance can't hamper our mobility."

"Yes. But the Field Marshal expects you to do it without depriving him of combat troops."

"I'm not sure I can."

"For God's sake, man!" Goedel raised his voice. "We're trying to defend the entire Atlantic coastline with a handful of soldiers, and you're surrounded by able-bodied men who have nothing better to do than track down scared old Jews hiding in barns. Get on with the job and don't pester me!" There was a click as the phone was hung up.

Dieter was startled. It was uncharacteristic for Goedel to blow his top. No doubt they were all tense about the threat of invasion. But the upshot was clear. Dieter had to do this on his own.

With a sigh, he jiggled the rest and placed a call to the château at Sainte-Cécile.

He reached Willi Weber. "I'm going to raid a Resistance house," he said. "I may need some of your heavyweights. Will you send four men and a car to the Hotel Frankfort? Or do I need to speak to Rommel again?"

The threat was unnecessary. Weber was keen to have his men along on the operation. That way, the Gestapo could claim the credit for any success. He promised a car in half an hour.

Dieter was worried about working with the Gestapo. He could not control them. But he had no choice.

While shaving, he turned on the radio, which was tuned to a German station. He learned that the first-ever tank battle in the Pacific theater had developed yesterday on the island of Biak. The occupying Japanese had driven the invading American 162d Infantry back to their beachhead. Push them into the sea, Dieter thought.

He dressed in a dark gray worsted suit, a fine cotton shirt with pale gray stripes, and a black tie with small white dots. The dots were woven into the fabric rather than printed on it, a detail that gave him pleasure. He thought for a moment, then removed the jacket and strapped on a shoulder holster. He took his Walther P38 automatic pistol from the bureau and slid it into the holster, then put his jacket back on.

He sat down with a cup of coffee and watched Stéphanie dressing. The French made the most beautiful underwear in the world, he thought as she stepped into silk cami-knickers the color of clotted cream. He loved to see her pull on her stockings, smoothing the silk over her thighs. "Why did the old masters not paint this moment?" he said.

"Because Renaissance women didn't have sheer silk stockings," said Stéphanie.

When she was ready, they left.

Hans Hesse was waiting outside with Dieter's Hispano-Suiza. The young man gazed at Stéphanie with awestruck admiration. To him, she was infinitely desirable and at the same time untouchable. He made Dieter think of a poor woman staring into Cartier's shop window.

Behind Dieter's car was a black Citroën Traction Avant containing four Gestapo men in plain clothes. Major Weber had decided to come himself, Dieter saw: he sat in the front passenger seat of the Citroën, wearing a green tweed suit that made him look like a farmer on his way to church. "Follow me," Dieter told him. "When we get there, please stay in your car until I call you."

Weber said, "Where the hell did you get a car like that?"

"It was a bribe from a Jew," Dieter said. "I helped him escape to America."

Weber grunted in disbelief, but in fact the story was true.

Bravado was the best attitude to take with men such as Weber. If Dieter had tried to keep Stéphanie hidden away, Weber would immediately have suspected that she was Jewish and might have started an investigation. But because Dieter flaunted her, the thought never crossed Weber's mind.

Hans took the wheel, and they headed for the rue du Bois.

Reims was a substantial country town with a population of more than 100,000, but there were few motor vehicles on the streets. Cars were used only by those on official business: the police, doctors, firemen, and, of course, the Germans. The citizens went about by bicycle or on foot. Petrol was available for deliveries of food and other essential supplies, but many goods were transported by horse-drawn cart. Champagne was the main industry here. Dieter loved champagne in all its forms: the nutty older vintages, the fresh, light, nonvintage cuvées, the refined blanc de blancs, the demi-sec dessert varieties, even the playful pink beloved of Paris courtesans.

The rue du Bois was a pleasant tree-lined street on the outskirts of town. Hans pulled up outside a tall house at the end of a row, with a little courtyard to one side. This was the home of Mademoiselle Lemas. Would Dieter be able to break her spirit? Women were more difficult than men. They cried and screamed, but held out longer. He had sometimes failed with a woman, though never with a man. If this one defeated him, his investigation was dead.

"Come if I wave to you," he said to Stéphanie as he got out of the car. Weber's Citroën drew up behind, but the Gestapo men stayed in the car, as instructed.

Dieter glanced into the courtyard beside the house. There was a garage. Beyond that, he saw a small garden with clipped hedges, rectangular flower beds, and a raked gravel path. The owner had a tidy mind.

Beside the front door was an old-fashioned red-and-yellow rope. He pulled it and heard from inside the metallic ring of a mechanical bell.

The woman who opened the door was about sixty. She had white hair tied up at the back with a tortoiseshell clasp. She wore a blue dress with a pattern of small white flowers. Over it she had a crisp white apron. "Good morning, monsieur," she said politely.

Dieter smiled. She was an irreproachably genteel provincial lady. Already he had thought of a way to torture her. His spirits lifted with hope.

He said, "Good morning . . . Mademoiselle Lemas?"

She took in his suit, noticed the car at the curb, and perhaps heard the trace of a German accent, and fear came into her eyes. There was a tremor in her voice as she said, "How may I help you?"

"Are you alone, Mademoiselle?" He watched her face carefully.

"Yes," she said. "Quite alone."

She was telling the truth. He was sure. A woman such as this could not lie without betraying herself with her eyes.

He turned and beckoned Stéphanie. "My colleague will join us." He was not going to need Weber's men. "I have some questions to ask you."

"Questions? About what?"

"May I come in?"

"Very well."

The front parlor was furnished with dark wood, highly polished. There was a piano under a dust cover and an engraving of Reims cathedral on the wall. The mantelpiece bore a selection of ornaments: a spun-glass swan, a china flower girl, a transparent globe containing a model of the palace at Versailles, and three wooden camels.

Dieter sat on a plush-upholstered couch. Stéphanie sat beside him, and Mademoiselle Lemas took an upright chair opposite. She was plump, Dieter observed. Not many French people were plump after four years of occupation. Food was her vice.

On a low table was a cigarette box and a heavy lighter. Dieter flipped the lid and saw that the box was full. "Please feel free to smoke," he said.

She looked mildly offended: women of her generation did not use tobacco. "I don't smoke."

"Then who are these for?"

She touched her chin, a sign of dishonesty. "Visitors."

"And what kind of visitors do you get?"

"Friends . . . neighbors . . ." She looked uncomfortable.

"And British spies."

"That is absurd."

Dieter gave her his most charming smile. "You are obviously a respectable lady who has become mixed up in criminal activities from misguided motives," he said in a tone of friendly candor. "I'm not going to toy with you, and I hope you will not be so foolish as to lie to me."

"I shall tell you nothing," she said.

Dieter feigned disappointment, but he was pleased to be making such rapid progress. She had already abandoned the pretense that she did not know what he was talking about. That was as good as a confession. "I'm going to ask you some questions," he said. "If you don't answer them, I shall ask you again at Gestapo headquarters."

She gave him a defiant look.

He said, "Where do you meet the British agents?"

She said nothing.

"How do they recognize you?"

Her eyes met his in a steady gaze. She was no longer flustered, but resigned. A brave woman, he thought. She would be a challenge.

"What is the password?"

She did not answer.

"Who do you pass the agents on to? How do you contact the Resistance? Who is in charge of it?"

Silence.

Dieter stood up. "Come with me, please."

"Very well," she said staunchly. "Perhaps you will permit me to put on my hat."

"Of course." He nodded to Stéphanie. "Go with Mademoiselle, please. Make sure she does not use the telephone or write anything down." He did not want her to leave any kind of message.

He waited in the hall. When they returned, Mademoiselle Lemas had taken off her apron and wore a light coat and a cloche hat that had gone out of fashion long before the outbreak of war. She carried a sturdy tan leather handbag. As the three of them were heading for the front door, Mademoiselle Lemas said, "Oh! I forgot my key."

"You don't need it," Dieter said.

"The door locks itself," she said. "I need a key to get back in."

Dieter looked her in the eye. "Don't you understand?" he said. "You've been sheltering British terrorists in your house, you have been caught, and you are in the hands of the Gestapo." He shook his head in an expression of sorrow that was not entirely fake. "Whatever happens, Mademoiselle, you're never coming home again."

She realized the full horror of what was happening to her. Her face turned white, and she staggered. She steadied herself by grabbing the edge of a kidney-shaped table.

A Chinese vase containing a spray of dried grasses wobbled dangerously but did not fall. Then Mademoiselle Lemas recovered her poise. She straightened up and let go of the table. She gave him that defiant look again, then walked out of her house with her head held high.

Dieter asked Stéphanie to take the front passenger seat, while he sat in the back of the car with the prisoner. As Hans drove them to Sainte-Cécile, Dieter made polite conversation. "Were you born in Reims, Mademoiselle?"

"Yes. My father was choirmaster at the cathedral."

A religious background. This was good news for the plan that was forming in Dieter's mind. "Is he retired?"

"He died five years ago, after a long illness."

"And your mother?"

"Died when I was quite young."

"So, I imagine you nursed your father through his illness?"

"For twenty years."

"Ah." That explained why she was single. She had spent her life caring for an invalid father. "And he left you the house."

She nodded.

"Small reward, some might think, for a life of dedicated service," Dieter said sympathetically.

She gave him a haughty look. "One does not do such things for reward."

"Indeed not." He did not mind the implied rebuke. It would help his plan if she could convince herself that she was somehow Dieter's superior, morally and socially. "Do you have brothers and sisters?"

"None."

Dieter saw the picture vividly. The agents she sheltered, all young men and women, must have been like her children. She had fed them, done their laundry, talked to them, and probably kept an eye on the relationships between the sexes, making sure there was no immorality, at least not under her roof.

And now she would die for it.

But first, he hoped, she would tell him everything.

The Gestapo Citroën followed Dieter's car to Sainte-Cécile. When they had parked in the grounds of the château, Dieter spoke to Weber. "I'm going to take her upstairs and put her in an office," he said.

"Why? There are cells in the basement."

"You'll see."

Dieter led the prisoner up the stairs to the Gestapo offices. Dieter looked into all the rooms and picked the busiest, a combination typing pool and post room. It was occupied by young men and women in smart shirts and ties. Leaving Mademoiselle Lemas in the corridor, he closed the door and clapped his hands for attention. In a quiet voice he said, "I'm going to bring a French woman in here. She is a prisoner, but I want you all to be friendly and polite to her, is that understood? Treat her as a guest. It's important that she feels respected."

He brought her in, sat her at a table and, with a murmured apology, handcuffed her ankle to the table leg. He left Stéphanie with her and took Hesse outside. "Go to the canteen and ask them to prepare lunch on a tray. Soup, a main course, a little wine, a bottle of mineral water, and plenty of coffee. Bring cutlery, glasses, a napkin. Make it look nice."

The lieutenant grinned admiringly. He had no idea what his boss was up to, but he felt sure it would be something clever.

A few minutes later he returned with a

tray. Dieter took it from him and carried it into the office. He set it in front of Mademoiselle Lemas. "Please," he said. "It's lunchtime."

"I couldn't eat anything, thank you."

"Perhaps just a little soup." He poured wine into her glass.

She added water to the wine and sipped it, then tried a mouthful of soup.

"How is it?"

"Very good," she admitted.

"French food is so refined. We Germans cannot imitate it." Dieter talked nonsense to her, trying to relax her, and she drank most of the soup. He poured her a glass of water.

Major Weber came in and stared incredulously at the tray in front of the prisoner. Speaking German, he said, "Are we now rewarding people for harboring terrorists?"

Dieter said, "Mademoiselle is a lady. We must treat her correctly."

"God in heaven," Weber said, and he turned on his heel.

She refused the main course but drank all the coffee. Dieter was pleased. Everything was going according to plan. When she had finished, he asked her all the questions again. "Where do you meet the Allied agents? How do they recognize you? What is the password?" She looked worried, but she still refused to answer.

He looked sadly at her. "I am very sorry that you refuse to cooperate with me, after I have treated you kindly."

She looked somewhat bewildered. "I appreciate your kindness, but I cannot tell you anything."

Stéphanie, sitting beside Dieter, also looked puzzled. He guessed that she was thinking: *Did you really imagine that a nice meal would be sufficient to make this woman talk?*

"Very well," he said. He stood up as if to go.

"And now, Monsieur," said Mademoiselle Lemas. She looked embarrassed. "I must ask to . . . ah . . . visit the ladies' powder room."

In a harsh voice, Dieter said, "You want to go to the toilet?"

She reddened. "In a word, yes."

"I'm sorry, Mademoiselle," Dieter said. "That will not be possible."

CHAPTER 13

The last thing Monty had said to Paul Chancellor, late on Monday night, had been, "If you only do one thing in this war, make sure that telephone exchange is destroyed."

Paul had woken this morning with those words echoing in his mind. It was a simple instruction. If he could fulfill it, he would have helped win the war. If he failed, men would die—and he might spend the rest of his life reflecting that he had helped *lose* the war.

He went to Baker Street early, but Percy Thwaite was already there, sitting in his office, puffing his pipe and staring at six boxes of files. He seemed a typical military duffer, with his check jacket and toothbrush moustache. He looked at Paul with mild hostility. "I don't know why Monty's put you in charge of this operation," he said. "I don't mind that you're only a major, and I'm a colonel—that's all stuff and nonsense. But you've never run a clandestine operation, whereas I've been doing it for three years. Does it make sense to you?"

"Yes," Paul said briskly. "When you want to make absolutely sure that a job gets done, you give it to someone you trust. Monty trusts me."

"But not me."

"He doesn't know you."

"I see," Percy said grumpily.

Paul needed Percy's cooperation, so he decided to mollify him. Looking around the office, he saw a framed photograph of a young man in lieutenant's uniform and an older woman in a big hat. The boy could have been Percy thirty years ago. "Your son?" Paul guessed.

Percy softened immediately. "David's out in Cairo," he said. "We had some bad moments during the desert war, especially after Rommel reached Tobruk, but now, of course, he's well out of the line of fire, and I must say I'm glad."

The woman was dark-haired and dark-eyed, with a strong face, handsome rather than pretty. "And Mrs. Thwaite?"

"Rosa Mann. She became famous as a suffragette, in the twenties, and she's always used her maiden name."

"Suffragette?"

"Campaigner for votes for women."

Percy liked formidable women, Paul concluded; that was why he was fond of Flick. "You know, you're right about my shortcomings," he said candidly. "I have been at the sharp end of clandestine operations, but this will be my first time as an organizer. So I'll be very grateful for your help."

Percy nodded. "I begin to see why you have a reputation for getting things done," he said with a hint of a smile. "But if you'll hear a word of advice . . ."

"Please."

"Be guided by Flick. No one else has spent as much time under cover and survived. Her knowledge and experience are matchless. I may be in charge of her in theory, but what I do is give her the support she needs. I would never try to tell her what to do."

Paul hesitated. He had been given command by Monty, and he was not about to hand it over on anyone's advice. "I'll bear that in mind," he said.

Percy seemed satisfied. He gestured to the files. "Shall we get started?"

"What are these?"

"Records of people who were considered by us as possible agents, then rejected for some reason."

Paul took off his jacket and rolled back his cuffs.

They spent the morning going through the files together. Some of the candidates had not even been interviewed; others had been rejected after they had been seen; and many had failed some part of the SOE training course—baffled by codes, hopeless with guns, or frightened to the point of hysteria when asked to jump out of a plane with a parachute. They were mostly in their early twenties, and they had only one other thing in common: they all spoke a foreign language with native fluency.

There were a lot of files, but few suitable candidates. By the time Percy and Paul had eliminated all the men, and the women whose language was something other than French, they were left with only three names.

Paul was disheartened. They had run into a major obstacle when they had hardly begun. "Four is the minimum number we need, even assuming that Flick recruits the woman she has gone to see this morning."

"Diana Colefield."

"And none of these is either an explosives expert or a telephone engineer!"

Percy was more optimistic. "They weren't when SOE interviewed them, but they might be now. Women have learned to do all sorts of things."

"Well, let's find out."

It took a while to track the three down. A further disappointment was that one was dead. The other two were in London. Ruby Romain, unfortunately, was in His Majesty's Prison for Women at Holloway, three miles north of Baker Street, awaiting trial for murder. And Maude Valentine, whose file said simply "psychologically unsuitable," was a driver with the FANYs.

"Down to two!" Paul said despondently.

"It's not the numbers but the quality that bothers me," Percy said.

"We knew from the start we'd be looking at rejects."

Percy's tone became angry. "But we can't risk Flick's life with people like these!"

Percy was desperate to protect Flick, Paul realized. The older man had been willing to hand over control of the operation but was not able to give up his role as Flick's guardian angel.

Their argument was interrupted by a phone call. It was Simon Fortescue, the pin-striped spook from MI6 who had blamed SOE for the failure at Sainte-Cécile. "What can I do for you?" Paul said guardedly. Fortescue was not a man to trust.

"I think I may be able to do something for you," Fortescue said. "I know you're going ahead with Major Clairet's plan."

"Who told you?" Paul asked suspiciously. It was supposed to be a secret.

"Let's not go into that. I naturally wish you success with your mission, even though I was against it, and I'd like to help."

Paul was angry that the mission was being talked about, but there was no point in pursuing that. "Do you know a female telephone engineer who speaks perfect French?" he asked.

"Not quite. But there's someone you should see. Her name is Lady Denise Bowyer. Terribly nice girl, her father was the Marquess of Inverlocky."

Paul was not interested in her pedigree. "How did she learn French?"

"Brought up by her French stepmother, Lord Inverlocky's second wife. She's ever so keen to do her bit."

Paul was suspicious of Fortescue, but he was desperate for suitable recruits. "Where do I find her?"

"She's with the RAF at Hendon." The word "Hendon" meant nothing to Paul, but Fortescue explained. "It's an airfield in the north London suburbs."

"Thank you."

"Let me know how she gets on." Fortescue hung up.

Paul explained the call to Percy, who said, "Fortescue wants a spy in our camp."

"We can't afford to turn her down for that reason."

"Quite."

They saw Maude Valentine first. Percy arranged for them to meet her at the Fenchurch Hotel, around the corner from SOE headquarters. Strangers were never brought to number sixty-four, he explained. "If we reject her, she may guess that she's been considered for secret work, but she won't know the name of the organization that interviewed her nor where its office is, so even if she blabs she can't do much harm."

"Very good."

"What's your mother's maiden name?"

Paul was mildly startled and had to think for a moment. "Thomas. She was Edith Thomas."

"So, you'll be Major Thomas and I'll be Colonel Cox. No point in giving our real names."

Percy was not such a duffer, Paul reflected.

He met Maude in the hotel lobby. She piqued his interest right away. She was a pretty girl with a flirtatious manner. Her uniform blouse was tight across the chest, and she wore her cap at a jaunty angle. Paul spoke to her in French. "My colleague is waiting in a private room."

She gave him an arch look and replied in the same language. "I don't usually go to hotel rooms with strange men," she said pertly. "But in your case, Major, I'll make an exception."

He blushed. "It's a meeting room, with a table and so on, not a bedroom."

"Oh, well, that's all right, then," she said, mocking him.

He decided to change the subject. He had

noticed that she spoke with a south of France accent, so he said, "Where are you from?"

"I was born in Marseilles."

"And what do you do in the FANYs?"

"I drive Monty."

"Do you?" Paul was not supposed to give any information about himself, but he could not help saying, "I worked for Monty for a while, but I don't recall seeing you."

"Oh, it's not always Monty. I drive all the top generals."

"Ah. Well, come this way, please."

He took her to the room and poured her a cup of tea. Maude was enjoying the attention, Paul realized. While Percy asked questions, he studied the girl. She was petite, though not as tiny as Flick, and she was cute: she had a rosebud mouth accentuated with red lipstick, and there was a beauty spot—which might even have been fake—on one cheek. Her dark hair was wavy.

"My family came to London when I was ten years old," she said. "My papa is a chef."

"And where does he work?"

"He's the head pastry cook at Claridge's Hotel."

"Very impressive."

Maude's file was on the table, and Percy

discreetly moved it an inch closer to Paul. Paul's eye was caught by the slight movement, and his eye fell on a note made when Maude was first interviewed. *Father: Armand Valentin, 39, kitchen porter at Claridge's,* he read.

When they had finished, they asked her to wait outside. "She lives in a fantasy world," Percy said as soon as she was outside the door. "She's promoted her father to chef, and changed her name to Valentine."

Paul nodded agreement. "In the lobby, she told me she was Monty's driver—which I know she's not."

"No doubt that was why she was rejected before."

Paul thought Percy was getting ready to reject Maude. "But now we can't afford to be so particular," he said.

Percy looked at him in surprise. "She'd be a menace on an undercover operation!"

Paul made a helpless gesture. "We don't have any choice."

"This is mad!"

Percy was half in love with Flick, Paul decided, but, being older and married, he expressed his love in a paternal, protective way. Paul liked him better for that, but realized at the same time that he would have to fight Percy's caution if he was going to get this job done. "Listen," he said. "We shouldn't eliminate Maude. Flick can make up her own mind when she meets her."

"I suppose you're right," Percy said reluctantly. "And the ability to invent stories can be useful under interrogation."

"All right. Let's get her on board." Paul called her back in. "I'd like you to be part of a team I'm setting up," he told her. "How would you feel about taking on something dangerous?"

"Would we be going to Paris?" Maude said eagerly.

It was an odd response. Paul hesitated, then said, "Why do you ask?"

"I'd love to go to Paris. I've never been. They say it's the most beautiful city in the world."

"Wherever you go, you won't have time for sightseeing," Percy said, letting his irritation show.

Maude did not seem to notice. "Shame," she said. "I'd still like to go, though."

"How do you feel about the danger?" Paul persisted.

"That's all right," Maude said airily. "I'm not scared."

Well, you should be, Paul thought, but he kept his mouth shut.

They drove north from Baker Street and passed through a working-class neighborhood that had suffered heavily from the bombing. In every street at least one house was a blackened shell or a pile of rubble.

Paul was to meet Flick outside the prison and they would interview Ruby Romain together. Percy would go on to Hendon to see Lady Denise Bowyer.

Percy, at the wheel, confidently wound his way through the grimy streets. Paul said, "You know London well."

"I was born in this neighborhood," Percy replied.

Paul was intrigued. He knew it was unusual for a boy from a poor family to rise as high as colonel in the British army. "What did your father do for a living?"

"Sold coal off the back of a horse-drawn cart."

"He had his own business?"

"No, he worked for a coal merchant."

"Did you go to school around here?"

Percy smiled. He knew he was being probed, but he did not seem to mind. "The local vicar helped me get a scholarship to a good school. That was where I lost my London accent."

"Intentionally?"

"Not willingly. I'll tell you something. Before the war, when I was involved in politics, people would sometimes say to me, 'How can you be a socialist, with an accent like that?' I explained that I was flogged in school for dropping my aitches. That silenced one or two smug bastards."

Percy stopped the car on a tree-lined street. Paul looked out and saw a fantasy castle, with battlements and turrets and a high tower. "This is a jail?"

Percy made a gesture of helplessness. "Victorian architecture."

Flick was waiting at the entrance. She wore her FANY uniform: a four-pocket tunic, a divided skirt, and a little cap with a turned-up brim. The leather belt that was tightly cinched around her small waist emphasized her diminutive figure, and her fair curls spilled out from under the cap. For a moment she took Paul's breath away. "She's such a pretty girl," he said.

"She's married," Percy remarked crisply.

I'm being warned off, Paul thought with amusement. "To whom?"

Percy hesitated, then said, "You need to know this, I think. Michel is in the French Resistance. He's the leader of the Bollinger circuit."

"Ah. Thanks." Paul got out of the car and Percy drove on.

He wondered if Flick would be angry that he and Percy had turned up so few prospects from the files. He had met her only twice, and on both occasions she had yelled at him. However, she seemed cheerful, and when he told her about Maude, she said, "So we have three team members, including me. That means we're halfway there, and it's only two pip emma."

Paul nodded. That was one way of looking at it. He was worried, but there was nothing to be gained by saying so.

The entrance to Holloway was a medieval lodge with arrowslit windows. "Why didn't they go the whole way and build a portcullis and a drawbridge?" said Paul. They passed through the lodge into a courtyard, where a few women in dark dresses were cultivating vegetables. Every patch of waste ground in London was planted with vegetables.

The prison loomed up in front of them. The entrance was guarded by stone monsters, massive winged griffins holding keys and shackles in their claws. The main gatehouse was flanked by four-story buildings, each story represented by a long row of narrow, pointed windows. "What a place!" said Paul.

"This is where the suffragettes went on hunger strike," Flick told him. "Percy's wife was force-fed in here."

"My God."

They went in. The air smelled of strong bleach, as if the authorities hoped that disinfectant would kill the bacteria of crime. Paul and Flick were shown to the office of Miss Lindleigh, a barrel-shaped assistant governor with a hard, fat face. "I don't know why you wish to see Romain," she said. With a note of resentment she added, "Apparently I'm not to be told."

A scornful look came over Flick's face, and Paul could see that she was about to say something derisory, so he hastily intervened. "I apologize for the secrecy," he said with his most charming smile. "We're just following orders."

"I suppose we all have to do that," said Miss Lindleigh, somewhat mollified. "Anyway, I must warn you that Romain is a violent prisoner."

"I understand she's a killer."

"Yes. She should be hanged, but the courts are too soft nowadays."

"They sure are," said Paul, although he did not really think so.

"She was in here originally for drunkenness, then she killed another prisoner in a fight in the exercise yard, so now she's awaiting trial for murder."

"A tough customer," Flick said with interest.

"Yes, Major. She may seem reasonable at first, but don't be fooled. She's easily riled and loses her temper faster than you can say knife."

"And deadly when she does," Paul said.

"You've got the picture."

"We're short of time," Flick said impatiently. "I'd like to see her now."

Paul added hastily, "If that's convenient to you, Miss Lindleigh."

"Very well." The assistant governor led

them out. The hard floors and bare walls made the place echo like a cathedral, and there was a constant background accompaniment of distant shouts, slamming doors, and the clang of boots on iron catwalks. They went via narrow corridors and steep stairs to an interview room.

Ruby Romain was already there. She had nut-brown skin, straight dark hair, and fierce black eyes. However, she was not the traditional gypsy beauty: her nose was hooked and her chin curved up, giving her the look of a gnome.

Miss Lindleigh left them with a warder in the next room watching through a glazed door. Flick, Paul, and the prisoner sat around a cheap table with a dirty ashtray on it. Paul had brought a pack of Lucky Strikes. He put them on the table and said in French, "Help yourself." Ruby took two, putting one in her mouth and the other behind her ear.

Paul asked a few routine questions to break the ice. She replied clearly and politely but with a strong accent. "My parents are traveling folk," she said. "When I was a girl, we went around France with a funfair. My father had a rifle range and my mother sold hot pancakes with chocolate sauce."

"How did you come to England?"

"When I was fourteen, I fell in love with an English sailor I met in Calais. His name was Freddy. We got married—I lied about my age, of course—and came to London. He was killed two years ago, his ship was sunk by a U-boat in the Atlantic." She shivered. "A cold grave. Poor Freddy."

Flick was not interested in the family history. "Tell us why you're in here," she said.

"I got myself a little brazier and sold pancakes in the street. But the police kept harassing me. One night, I'd had some cognac—a weakness of mine, I admit—and anyway, I got into a dispute." She switched to cockney-accented English. "The copper told me to fuck off out of it, and I gave him a mouthful of abuse. He shoved me and I knocked him down."

Paul looked at her with a touch of amusement. She was no more than average height, and wiry, but she had big hands and muscular legs. He could imagine her flattening a London policeman.

Flick asked, "What happened next?"

"His two mates came around the corner, and I was a bit slow to leave, on account of the brandy, so they gave me a kicking and took me down the nick." Seeing Paul's frown of incomprehension, she added: "The police station, that is. Anyway, the first copper was ashamed to do me for assault, didn't want to admit he'd been floored by a girl, so I got fourteen days for drunk and disorderly."

"And then you got into another fight."

She gave Flick an appraising look. "I don't know if I can explain to someone of your sort what it's like in here. Half the girls are mad, and they've all got weapons. You can file the edge of a spoon to make a blade, or sharpen the end of a bit of wire for a stiletto, or twist threads together for a garotte. And the warders never intervene in a fight between convicts. They like to watch us tear each other apart. That's why so many of the inmates have scars."

Paul was shocked. He had never had contact with people in jail. The picture painted by Ruby was horrifying. Perhaps she was exaggerating, but she seemed quietly sincere. She did not appear to care whether she was believed or not but recited the facts in the dry, unhurried manner of someone who is not greatly interested but has nothing better to do.

Flick said, "What happened with the woman you killed?"

"She stole something of mine."

"What?"

"A cake of soap."

My God, thought Paul. She killed her for a piece of soap.

Flick said, "What did you do?"

"I took it back."

"And then?"

"She went for me. She had a chair leg that she'd made into a club with a bit of plumber's lead fixed to the business end. She hit me over the head with it. I thought she was going to kill me. But I had a knife. I'd found a long, pointed sliver of glass, like a shard from a broken window pane, and I wrapped the broad end in a length of worn-out bicycle tire for a handle. I stuck it in her throat. So she didn't get to hit me a second time."

Flick suppressed a shudder and said, "It sounds like self-defense."

"No. You've got to prove you couldn't possibly have run away. And I'd premeditated the murder by making a knife out of a piece of glass."

Paul stood up. "Wait here with the guard

for a moment, please," he said to Ruby. "We'll just step outside."

Ruby smiled at him, and for the first time she looked, not quite pretty but pleasant. "You're so polite," she said appreciatively.

In the corridor, Paul said, "What a dreadful story!"

"Remember, everyone in here says they're innocent," Flick said guardedly.

"All the same, I think she might be more sinned against than sinning."

"I doubt it. I think she's a killer."

"So we reject her."

"On the contrary," said Flick. "She's exactly what I want."

They went back into the room. Flick said to Ruby, "If you could get out of here, would you be willing to do dangerous war work?"

She responded with another question. "Would we be going to France?"

Flick raised her eyebrows. "What leads you to ask that?"

"You spoke French to me at the start. I assume you were checking if I speak the language."

"Well, I can't tell you much about the job."

"I bet it involves sabotage behind enemy lines."

Paul was startled: Ruby was very quick on the uptake.

Seeing his surprise, Ruby went on, "Look, at first I thought you might want me to do a bit of translation for you, but there's nothing dangerous about that. So we must be going to France. And what would the British Army do there except blow up bridges and railway lines?"

Paul said nothing, but he was impressed by her powers of deduction.

Ruby frowned. "What I can't figure out is why it's an all-woman team."

Flick's eyes widened. "What makes you think that?"

"If you could use men, why would you be talking to me? You must be desperate. It can't be that easy to get a murderess out of jail, even for vital war work. So what's special about me? I'm tough, but there must be hundreds of tough men who speak perfect French and would be gung-ho for a bit of cloak-and-dagger stuff. The only reason for picking me rather than one of them is that I'm female. Perhaps women are less likely to be questioned by the Gestapo . . . is that it?"

"I can't say," Flick said.

"Well, if you want me, I'll do it. Can I have another one of those cigarettes?"

"Sure," said Paul.

Flick said, "You do understand that the job is dangerous."

"Yeah," said Ruby, lighting a Lucky Strike. "But not as dangerous as being in this fucking prison."

They returned to the assistant governor's office after leaving Ruby. "I need your help, Miss Lindleigh," Paul said, once again flattering her. "Tell me what you would need in order to be able to release Ruby Romain."

"Release her! But she's a murderer! Why would she be released?"

"I'm afraid I can't tell you. But I can assure you that if you knew where she was going, you wouldn't think she'd had a lucky escape—quite the contrary."

"I see," she said, not entirely mollified.

"I must have her out of here tonight," Paul went on. "But I don't want to put you in any kind of awkward position. That's why I need to know exactly what authorization you require." What he really wanted was to make sure she would have no excuse to be obstructive.

"I can't release her under any circumstances," said Miss Lindleigh. "She has been remanded here by a magistrate's court, so only the court can free her."

Paul was patient. "And what do you think that would require?"

"She would have to be taken, in police custody, before a magistrate. The public prosecutor, or his representative, would have to tell the magistrate that all charges against Romain had been dropped. Then the magistrate would be obliged to say she was free to go."

Paul frowned, looking ahead for snags. "She would have to sign her army joining-up papers before seeing the magistrate, so that she would be under military discipline as soon as the court released her . . . otherwise she might just walk away."

Miss Lindleigh was still incredulous. "Why would they drop the charges?"

"This prosecutor is a government official?"

"Yes."

"Then it won't be a problem." Paul stood up. "I will be back here later this evening, with a magistrate, someone from the prosecutor's department, and an army driver to take Ruby to . . . her next port of call. Can you foresee any snags?"

Miss Lindleigh shook her head. "I follow orders, Major, just as you do."

"Good."

They took their leave. When they got outside, Paul stopped and looked back. "I've never been to a prison before," he said. "I don't know what I expected, but it wasn't something out of a fairy tale."

He was making an inconsequential remark about the building, but Flick looked sour. "Several women have been hanged here," she said. "Not much of a fairy tale."

He wondered why she was grumpy. "I guess you identify with the prisoners," he said. Suddenly he realized why. "It's because you might end up in a jail in France."

She looked taken aback. "I think you're right," she said. "I didn't know why I hated that place so much, but that's it."

She might be hanged, too, he realized, but he kept that thought to himself.

They walked away, heading for the nearest Tube station. Flick was thoughtful. "You're very perceptive," she said. "You understood how to keep Miss Lindleigh on our side. I would have made an enemy of her."

"No point in that."

"Exactly. And you turned Ruby from a tigress into a pussycat."

"I wouldn't want a woman like that to dislike me."

Flick laughed. "Then you told me something that I hadn't figured out about myself."

Paul was pleased that he had impressed her, but he was already looking ahead to the next problem. "By midnight, we should have half a team at the training center in Hampshire."

"We call it the Finishing School," Flick said. "Yes: Diana Colefield, Maude Valentine, and Ruby Romain."

Paul nodded grimly. "An undisciplined aristocrat, a pretty flirt who can't tell fantasy from reality, and a murdering gypsy with a short temper." When he thought of the possibility that Flick could be hanged by the Gestapo, he felt as worried as Percy about the caliber of the recruits.

"Beggars can't be choosers," Flick said cheerfully. Her sour mood had vanished.

"But we still don't have an explosives expert or a telephone engineer."

Flick glanced at her wrist. "It's still only four pip emma. And maybe the RAF has taught Denise Bowyer how to blow up a telephone exchange."

Paul grinned. Flick's optimism was irresistible.

They reached the station and caught a train. They could not talk about the mission because there were other passengers within earshot. Paul said, "I learned a little about Percy this morning. We drove through the neighborhood where he was brought up."

"He's adopted the manners and even the accent of the British upper class, but don't be fooled. Under that old tweed jacket beats the heart of a real street brawler."

"He told me he was flogged at school for speaking with a low-class accent."

"He was a scholarship boy. They generally have a hard time in swanky British schools. I know, I was a scholarship girl."

"Did you have to change your accent?"

"No. I grew up in an earl's household. I always spoke like this."

Paul guessed that was why Flick and Percy got on so well: they were both lower-class people who had climbed the social ladder. Unlike Americans, the British thought there was nothing wrong with class prejudice. Yet they were shocked at Southerners who told them Negroes were inferior. "I think Percy's very fond of you," Paul said.

"I love him like a father."

The sentiment seemed genuine, Paul thought, but she was also firmly setting him straight about her relationship with Percy.

Flick had arranged to meet Percy back at Orchard Court. When they arrived, there was a car outside the building. Paul recognized the driver, one of Monty's entourage. "Sir, there's someone in the car waiting for you," the man said.

The back door opened and out stepped Paul's younger sister, Caroline. He grinned with delight. "Well, I'll be damned!" he said. She stepped into his arms and he hugged her. "What are you doing in London?"

"I can't say, but I have a couple of hours off, and I persuaded Monty's office to lend me a car to come and see you. Want to buy me a drink?"

"I don't have a minute to spare," he said. "Not even for you. But you can drive me to Whitehall. I have to find a man called a public prosecutor."

"Then I'll take you there, and we'll catch up in the car."

"Of course," he said. "Let's go!"

CHAPTER 14

Flick turned at the building door and saw a pretty girl wearing the uniform of an American lieutenant step out of the car and throw her arms around Paul. She noted the delighted smile on his face and the force of his hug. This was obviously his wife, girlfriend, or fiancée, probably making an unexpected visit to London. She must be with the U. S. forces in Britain, preparing for the invasion. Paul jumped into her car.

Flick went into Orchard Court, feeling a little sad. Paul had a girl, they were nuts about one another, and they had been granted a surprise meeting. Flick wished Michel could show up just like that, out of the blue. But he was lying wounded on a couch in Reims with a shameless nineteen-year-old beauty nursing him.

Percy was already back from Hendon. She found him making tea. "How was your RAF girl?" she asked.

"Lady Denise Bowyer—she's on her way to the Finishing School," he said.

"Wonderful! Now we have four!"

"But I'm worried. She's a braggart. She boasted about the work she's doing in the Air Force, told me all sorts of details she should have kept quiet about. You'll have to see what you think of her in training."

"I don't suppose she knows anything about telephone exchanges."

"Not a thing. Nor explosives. Tea?"

"Please."

He handed her a cup and sat behind the cheap old desk. "Where's Paul?"

"Gone to find the public prosecutor. He's hoping to get Ruby Romain out of jail this evening."

Percy gave her a quizzical glance. "Do you like him?"

"More than I did initially."

"Me too."

Flick smiled. "He charmed the socks off the old battleax running the prison."

"How was Ruby Romain?"

"Terrifying. She slit the throat of another inmate in a quarrel over a bar of soap."

"Jesus." Percy shook his head in incredulity. "What the hell kind of a team are we putting together, Flick?"

"Dangerous. Which is what it's supposed to be. That's not the problem. Besides, the way things are going, we may have the luxury of eliminating the least satisfactory one or two during training. My worry is that we don't have the experts we need. There's no point taking a team of tough girls into France, then destroying the wrong cables."

Percy drained his teacup and began to fill his pipe. "I know a woman explosives expert who speaks French."

Flick was surprised. "But this is great! Why didn't you say so before?"

"When I first thought of her, I dismissed her out of hand. She's not at all suitable. But I hadn't realized how desperate we'd be."

"How is she unsuitable?"

"She's about forty. SOE rarely uses anyone so old, especially on a parachute mission." He struck a match.

Age was not going to be an obstacle at this stage, Flick thought. Excited, she said, "Will she volunteer?"

"I should think there's a good chance, especially if I ask her."

"You're friends."

He nodded.

"How did she become an explosives expert?"

Percy looked embarrassed. Still holding the burning match, he said, "She's a safebreaker. I met her years ago, when I was doing political work in the East End." The match burned down, and he struck another.

"Percy, I had no idea your past was so raffish. Where is she now?"

Percy looked at his watch. "It's six o'clock. At this time of the evening, she'll be in the private bar of the Mucky Duck."

"A pub."

"Yes."

"Then get that damn pipe alight and let's go there now."

In the car, Flick said, "How do you know she's a safebreaker?"

Percy shrugged. "Everyone knows."

"Everyone? Even the police?"

"Yes. In the East End, police and villains grow up together, go to the same schools, live in the same streets. They all know one another."

"But if they know who the criminals are, why don't they put them in jail? I suppose they can't prove anything."

"This is the way it works," Percy said. "When they need a conviction, they arrest someone who is in that line of business. If it's a burglary, they arrest a burglar. It doesn't matter whether he was responsible for that particular crime, because they can always manufacture a case: suborn witnesses, counterfeit confessions, manufacture forensic evidence. Of course, they sometimes make mistakes, and jail innocent people, and they often use the system to pay off personal grudges, and so on; but nothing in life is perfect, is it?"

"So you're saying the whole rigmarole of courts and juries is a farce?"

"A highly successful, long-running farce that provides lucrative employment for otherwise useless citizens who act the parts of detectives, solicitors, barristers, and judges."

"Has your friend the safebreaker been to jail?"

"No. You can escape prosecution if you're willing to pay hefty bribes, *and* you're careful to cultivate warm friendships with detectives. Let's say you live in the same street as Detective-Inspector Callahan's dear old mum. You drop in once a week, ask her if she needs any shopping done, look at photos of her grandchildren . . . makes it hard for D.I. Callahan to put you in jail."

Flick thought of the story Ruby had told a few hours ago. For some people, life in London was almost as bad as being under the Gestapo. Could things really be so different from what she had imagined? "I can't tell if you're serious," she said to Percy. "I don't know what to believe."

"Oh, I'm serious," he said with a smile. "But I don't expect you to believe me."

They were in Stepney, not far from the docks. The bomb damage here was the worst Flick had seen. Whole streets were flattened. Percy turned into a narrow cul-de-sac and parked outside a pub.

"Mucky Duck" was a humorous sobriquet: the pub was called The White Swan. The private bar was not private, but was so called to distinguish it from the public bar, where there was sawdust on the floor and the beer was a penny a pint cheaper. Flick found herself thinking about explaining these idiosyncrasies to Paul. He would be amused.

Geraldine Knight sat on a stool at the end of the bar, looking as if she might own the place. She had vivid blonde hair and heavy makeup, expertly applied. Her plump figure had the apparent firmness that could only have come from a corset. The cigarette burning in the ashtray bore a ring of bright lipstick around the end. It was hard to imagine anyone who looked less like a secret agent, Flick thought despondently.

"Percy Thwaite, as I live and breathe!" the woman said. She sounded like a Cockney who had been to elocution lessons. "What are you doing slumming around here, you bloody old communist?" She was obviously delighted to see him.

"Hello, Jelly, meet my friend Flick," Percy said.

"Pleased to know you, I'm sure," she said, shaking Flick's hand.

"Jelly?" Flick inquired.

"No one knows where I got that nickname."

"Oh," said Flick. "Jelly Knight, gelignite."

Jelly ignored that. "I'll have a gin-and-It, Percy, while you're buying."

Flick spoke to her in French. "Do you live in this part of London?"

"Since I was ten," she replied, speaking French with a North American accent. "I was born in Quebec."

That was not so good, Flick thought. Germans might not notice the accent, but the French certainly would. Jelly would have to pose as a Canadian-born French citizen. It was a perfectly plausible history, but just unusual enough to attract curiosity. Damn. "But you consider yourself British."

"English, not British," said Jelly with arch indignation. She switched back to the English language. "I'm Church of England, I vote Conservative, and I dislike foreigners, heathens, and republicans." With a glance at Percy, she added, "Present company excepted, of course."

Percy said, "You ought to live in Yorkshire, on a hill farm, someplace where they haven't seen a foreigner since the Vikings came. I don't know how you can bear to live in London, surrounded by Russian Bolsheviks, German Jews, Irish Catholics, and nonconformist Welshmen building little chapels all over the place like moles disfiguring the lawn."

"London's not what it was, Perce."

"Not what it was when you were a foreigner?"

This was obviously a familiar old argument. Flick interrupted it impatiently. "I'm very glad to hear that you're so patriotic, Jelly."

"And why would you be interested in such a thing, may I ask?"

"Because there's something you could do for your country."

Percy put in, "I told Flick about your . . . expertise, Jelly."

She looked at her vermilion fingernails. "Discretion, Percy, please. Discretion is the better part of valor, it says in the Bible."

Flick said, "I expect you know that there have been some fascinating recent developments in the field. Plastic explosives, I mean."

"I try to keep up to date," Jelly said with airy modesty. Her expression changed, and she looked shrewdly at Flick. "This is something to do with the war, isn't it?"

"Yes."

"Count me in. I'll do anything for England."

"You'll be away for a few days."

"No problem."

"You might not come back."

"What the hell does that mean?"

"It will be very dangerous," Flick said quietly.

Jelly looked dismayed. "Oh." She swallowed. "Well, that makes no difference," she said unconvincingly.

"Are you sure?"

Jelly looked thoughtful, as if she were calculating. "You want me to blow something up."

Flick nodded silently.

"It's not overseas, is it?"

"Could be."

Jelly paled beneath her makeup. "Oh, my gordon. You want me to go to France, don't you?"

Flick said nothing.

"Behind enemy lines! God's truth, I'm too bloody old for that sort of thing. I'm . . ." She hesitated. "I'm thirty-seven."

She was about five years older than that, Flick thought, but she said, "Well, we're almost the same age, I'm nearly thirty. We're not too old for a bit of adventure, are we?"

"Speak for yourself, dear."

Flick's heart sank. Jelly was not going to agree.

The whole scheme had been misconceived, she decided. It was never going to be possible to find women who could do these jobs and speak perfect French. The plan had been doomed from the start. She turned away from Jelly. She felt like crying.

Percy said, "Jelly, we're asking you to do a job that's really crucial for the war effort."

"Pull the other leg, Perce, it's got bells on," she said, but her mockery was half-hearted, and she looked solemn.

He shook his head. "No exaggeration. It could make a difference to whether we win or lose."

She stared at him, saying nothing. Conflict twisted her face into a grimace of indecision.

Percy said, "And you're the only person in the country who can do it."

"Get off," she said skeptically.

"You're a female safebreaker who speaks French—how many others do you think there are? I'll tell you: none."

"You mean this, don't you."

"I was never more serious in my life."

"Bloody hell, Perce." Jelly fell silent. She did not speak for a long moment. Flick held her breath. At last Jelly said, "All right, you bastard, I'll do it."

Flick was so pleased she kissed her.

Percy said, "God bless you, Jelly."

Jelly said, "When do we start?"

"Now," said Percy. "If you'll finish up that gin, I'll take you home to pack a case, then I'll drive you to the training center."

"What, tonight?"

"I told you it was important."

She swallowed the remains of her drink. "All right, I'm ready."

She slid her ample bottom off the bar stool, and Flick thought: I wonder how she'll manage with a parachute.

They left the pub. Percy said to Flick, "You'll be all right going back on the Tube?"

"Of course."

"Then we'll see you tomorrow at the Finishing School."

"I'll be there," said Flick, and they parted company.

She headed for the nearest station, feeling jubilant. It was a mild summer evening, and the East End was alive: a group of dirty-faced boys played cricket with a stick and a bald tennis ball; a tired man in soiled work clothes headed home for a late tea; a uniformed soldier, on leave with a packet of cigarettes and a few shillings in his pocket, strode along the pavement with a jaunty air, as if all the world's pleasures were his for the taking; three pretty girls in sleeveless dresses and straw hats giggled at the soldier. The fate of all these people would be decided in the next few days, Flick thought somberly.

On the train to Bayswater, her spirits fell again. She still did not have the most crucial member of the team. Without a telephone engineer, Jelly might place the explosives in the wrong location. They would still do damage but, if the damage could be repaired in a day or two, the enormous effort and risk of life would have been wasted.

When she returned to her bedsitting room, she found her brother Mark waiting there. She hugged and kissed him. "What a nice surprise!" she said.

"I've got a night off, so I thought I'd take you for a drink," he said.

"Where's Steve?"

"Giving his Iago to the troops in Lyme Regis. We both work for ENSA most of the time, now." ENSA was the Entertainments National Service Association, which organized shows for the armed forces. "Where shall we go?"

Flick was tired, and her first inclination was to turn him down. Then she remembered that she was going to France on Friday, and this could be the last time she ever saw her brother. "How about the West End," she said.

"We'll go to a nightclub."

"Perfect!"

They left the house and walked arm-in-arm along the street. Flick said, "I saw Ma this morning."

"How is she?"

"All right, but she hasn't softened her attitude to you and Steve, I'm sorry to say."

"I didn't expect it. How did you happen to see her?"

"I went down to Somersholme. It would take too long to explain why."

"Something hush-hush, I suppose."

She smiled acknowledgment, then sighed as she remembered her problem. "I don't suppose you happen to know a female telephone engineer who speaks French, do you?"

He stopped. "Well," he said, "sort of."

CHAPTER 15

Mademoiselle Lemas was in agony. She sat rigid on the hard upright chair behind the little table, her face frozen into a mask of self-control. She did not dare to move. She still wore her cloche hat and clutched her sturdy leather handbag on her lap. Her fat little hands squeezed the handle of the bag rhythmically. Her fingers bore no rings; in fact she wore only one piece of jewelry, a small silver cross on a chain.

Around her, late-working clerks and secretaries in their well-pressed uniforms carried on typing and filing. Following Dieter's instructions, they smiled politely when they caught her eye, and every now and again one of the girls would speak a word to her, offering her water or coffee.

Dieter sat watching her, with Lieutenant

Hesse on one side of him and Stéphanie on the other. Hans Hesse was the best type of sturdy, unflappable working-class German. He looked on stoically: he had seen many tortures. Stéphanie was more excitable, but she was exercising self-control. She looked unhappy, but said nothing: her aim in life was to please Dieter.

Mademoiselle Lemas's pain was not just physical, Dieter knew. Even worse than her bursting bladder was the terror of soiling herself in a room full of polite, well-dressed people going about their normal business. For a respectable elderly lady, that was the worst of nightmares. He admired her fortitude and wondered if she would break, and tell him everything, or hold out.

A young corporal clicked his heels beside Dieter and said, "Pardon me, Major, I have been sent to ask you to step into Major Weber's office."

Dieter considered sending a reply saying *If you want to talk to me, come and see me,* but he decided there was nothing to be gained by being combative before it was strictly necessary. Weber might even become a little more cooperative if he was allowed to score a few points. "Very well." He turned to Hesse. "Hans, you know what to ask her if she breaks."

"Yes, Major."

"In case she doesn't . . . Stéphanie, would you go to the Café des Sports and get me a bottle of beer and a glass, please?"

"Of course." She seemed grateful for a reason to leave the room.

Dieter followed the corporal to Willi Weber's office. It was a grand room at the front of the château, with three tall windows overlooking the square. Dieter gazed out at the sun setting over the town. The slanting light picked out the curved arches and buttresses of the medieval church. He saw Stéphanie crossing the square in her high heels, walking like a racehorse, dainty and powerful at the same time.

Soldiers were at work in the square, erecting three stout wooden pillars in a neat row. Dieter frowned. "A firing squad?"

"For the three terrorists who survived Sunday's skirmish," Weber answered. "I understand you have finished interrogating them."

Dieter nodded. "They have told me all they know."

"They will be shot in public as a warning

to others who may think of joining the Resistance."

"Good idea," Dieter said. "However, though Gaston is fit, both Bertrand and Geneviève are seriously injured—I'll be surprised if they can walk."

"Then they will be carried to their fate. But I did not summon you to discuss them. My superiors in Paris have been asking me what further progress has been made."

"And what did you tell them, Willi?"

"That after forty-eight hours of investigation you have arrested one old woman who may or may not have sheltered Allied agents in her house, and who has so far told us nothing."

"And what would you *wish* to tell them?"

Weber banged his desk theatrically. "That we have broken the back of the French Resistance!"

"That may take longer than forty-eight hours."

"Why don't you torture this old cow?"

"I am torturing her."

"By refusing to let her go to the toilet! What kind of torture is that?"

"In this case, the most effective one, I believe."

"You think you know best. You always were arrogant. But this is the new Germany, Major. You are no longer assumed to have superior judgment just because you are the son of a professor."

"Don't be ridiculous."

"Do you really think you would have become the youngest-ever head of the Cologne criminal intelligence department if your father had not been an important man in the university?"

"I had to pass the same exams as everyone else."

"How strange that other people, just as capable as you, never seemed to do quite so well."

Was that the fantasy Weber told himself? "For God's sake, Willi, you can't believe the entire Cologne police force conspired to give me better marks than you because my father was professor of music—it's risible!"

"Such things were commonplace in the old days."

Dieter sighed. Weber was half right. Patronage and nepotism had existed in Germany. But that was not why Willi had failed to win promotion. The truth was that he was stupid. He would never get on anywhere except in an organization where fanaticism was more important than ability.

Dieter had had enough of this stupid talk. "Don't worry about Mademoiselle Lemas," he said. "She'll talk soon." He went to the door. "And we will break the back of the French Resistance, too. Just wait a little longer."

He returned to the main office. Mademoiselle Lemas was now making low moaning noises. Weber had made Dieter impatient, and he decided to speed up the process. When Stéphanie returned, he put the glass on the table, opened the bottle, and poured the beer slowly in front of the prisoner. Tears of pain squeezed from her eyes and rolled down her plump cheeks. Dieter took a long drink of beer and put the glass down. "Your agony is almost over, Mademoiselle," he said. "Relief is at hand. In a few moments you will answer my questions, then you will find ease."

She closed her eyes.

"Where do you meet the British agents?" He paused. "How do you recognize one another?" She said nothing. "What is the password?"

He waited a moment, then said, "Have

the answers ready, in the forefront of your mind, and make sure they are clear, so that when the time comes, you can tell me quickly, without hesitation or explanations; then you can seek rapid release from your pain."

He took the key to the handcuffs from his pocket. "Hans, hold her wrist firmly." He bent down and unlocked the cuffs that fastened her ankle to the table leg. He took her by the arm. "Come with us, Stéphanie," he said. "We're going to the ladies' toilet."

They left the room, Stéphanie leading the way, Dieter and Hans holding the prisoner, who hobbled along with difficulty, bent at the waist, biting her lip. They went to the end of the corridor and stopped at a door marked *Damen.* Mademoiselle Lemas groaned loudly when she saw it.

Dieter said to Stéphanie, "Open the door."

She did so. It was a clean, white-tiled room, with a wash basin, a towel on a rail, and a row of cubicles. "Now," said Dieter. "The pain is about to end."

"Please," she whispered. "Let me go."

"Where do you meet the British agents?"

Mademoiselle Lemas began to cry.

Dieter said gently, "Where do you meet these people?"

"In the cathedral," she sobbed. "In the crypt. Please let me go!"

Dieter breathed a long sigh of satisfaction. She had broken. "When do you meet them?"

"Three o'clock any afternoon, I go every day."

"And how do you recognize one another?"

"I wear odd shoes, black and brown, now can I go?"

"One more question. What is the password?"

" 'Pray for me.' "

She tried to move forward, but Dieter held her tightly, and Hans did the same. "Pray for me," Dieter repeated. "Is that what you say, or what the agent says?"

"The agent, oh, I beg you!"

"And your reply?"

" 'I pray for peace,' that's my reply."

"Thank you," Dieter said, and released her.

She rushed inside.

Dieter nodded at Stéphanie, who followed her in and closed the door.

He could not conceal his satisfaction. "There, Hans, we make progress."

Hans, too, was pleased. "The cathedral crypt, three p.m. any day, black and brown shoes, 'Pray for me,' and the response 'I pray for peace.' Very good!"

"When they come out, put the prisoner in a cell and turn her over to the Gestapo. They'll arrange for her to disappear into a camp somewhere."

Hans nodded. "It seems harsh, sir. Her being an elderly lady, I mean."

"It does—until you think of the German soldiers and French civilians killed by the terrorists she sheltered. Then it seems hardly punishment enough."

"That does throw a different light on it, yes, sir."

"You see how one thing leads to another," Dieter said reflectively. "Gaston gives us a house, the house gives us Mademoiselle Lemas, she gives us the crypt, and the crypt will give us . . . who knows?" He began to think about the best way to exploit the new information.

The challenge was to capture agents without letting London know. If the thing was handled right, the Allies would send more people along the same route, wasting vast resources. It had been done in Holland: more than fifty expensively trained sabo-teurs had parachuted straight into the arms of the Germans.

Ideally, the next agent sent by London would go to the crypt of the cathedral and find Mademoiselle Lemas waiting there. She would take the agent home, and he would send a wireless message to London saying all was well. Then, when he was out of the house, Dieter could get hold of his code books. After that, Dieter could arrest the agent but continue to send messages to London in his name—and read the replies. In effect, he would be running a Resistance circuit that was entirely fictional. It was a thrilling prospect.

Willi Weber walked by. "Well, Major, has the prisoner talked?"

"She has."

"Not a moment too soon. Did she say anything useful?"

"You may tell your superiors that she has revealed the location of her rendezvous and the passwords used. We can pick up any further agents as they arrive."

Weber looked interested despite his hostility. "And where is the rendezvous?"

Dieter hesitated. He would have preferred not to tell Weber anything. But it was difficult to refuse without giving offense, and he needed the man's help. He had to tell him. "The cathedral crypt, afternoons at three."

"I shall inform Paris." Weber walked on.

Dieter resumed thinking about his next step. The house in the rue du Bois was a cut-out. No one in the Bollinger circuit had met Mademoiselle Lemas. Agents coming in from London did not know what she looked like—hence the need for recognition signals and passwords. If he could get someone to impersonate her . . . but who?

Stéphanie came out of the ladies' toilet with Mademoiselle Lemas.

She could do it.

She was much younger than Mademoiselle Lemas, and looked completely different, but the agents would not know that. She was obviously French. All she had to do was take care of the agent for a day or so.

He took Stéphanie's arm. "Hans will deal with the prisoner now. Come, let me buy you a glass of champagne."

He walked her out of the château. In the

square, the soldiers had done their work, and the three stakes threw long shadows in the evening light. A handful of local people stood silent and watchful outside the church door.

Dieter and Stéphanie went into the café. Dieter ordered a bottle of champagne. "Thank you for helping me today," he said. "I appreciate it."

"I love you," she said. "And you love me, I know, even though you never say it."

"But how do you feel about what we did today? You're French, and you have that grandmother whose race we mustn't speak of, and as far as I know you're not a Fascist."

She shook her head violently. "I no longer believe in nationality, or race, or politics," she said passionately. "When I was arrested by the Gestapo, no French people helped me. No Jews helped me. No socialists or liberals or communists either. And I was so cold in that prison." Her face changed. Her lips lost the sexy half-smile she wore most of the time, and the glint of teasing invitation went from her eyes. She was looking at another scene in another time. She crossed her arms and shivered, although it was a warm summer evening. "Not just cold on the outside, not just the skin. I felt cold in my heart and my bowels and my bones. I felt I would never be warm again, I would just go cold to my grave." She was silent for a long moment, her face drawn and pale, and Dieter felt at that instant that war was a terrible thing. Then she said, "I'll never forget the fire in your apartment. A coal fire. I had forgotten what it was like to feel that blazing warmth. It made me human again." She came out of her trance. "You saved me. You gave me food and wine. You bought me clothes." She smiled her old smile, the one that said *You can, if you dare.* "And you loved me, in front of that coal fire."

He held her hand. "It wasn't difficult."

"You keep me safe, in a world where almost no one is safe. So now I believe only in you."

"If you really mean that . . ."

"Of course."

"There's something else you could do for me."

"Anything."

"I want you to impersonate Mademoiselle Lemas."

She raised one perfectly plucked eyebrow.

"Pretend to be her. Go to the cathedral

crypt every afternoon at three o'clock, wearing one black shoe and one brown. When someone approaches you and says, 'Pray for me,' reply, 'I pray for peace.' Take the person to the house in the rue du Bois. Then call me."

"It sounds simple."

The champagne arrived, and he poured two glasses. He decided to level with her. "It should be simple. But there is a slight risk. If the agent has met Mademoiselle Lemas before, he will know you're an impostor. Then you could be in danger. Will you take that chance?"

"Is it important to you?"

"It's important for the war."

"I don't care about the war."

"It's important to me, too."

"Then I'll do it."

He raised his glass. "Thank you," he said.

They clinked glasses and drank.

Outside, in the square, there was a volley of gunfire. Dieter looked through the window. He saw three bodies tied to the wooden pillars, slumped in death; a row of soldiers lowering their rifles; and a crowd of citizens looking on, silent and still.

CHAPTER 16

Wartime austerity had made little real difference to Soho, the red-light district in the heart of London's West End. The same groups of young men staggered through the streets, drunk on beer, though most of them were in uniform. The same painted girls in tight dresses strolled along the pavements, eyeing potential customers. The illuminated signs outside clubs and bars were switched off, because of the blackout, but all the establishments were open.

Mark and Flick arrived at the Criss-Cross Club at ten o'clock in the evening. The manager, a young man wearing a dinner jacket with a red bow tie, greeted Mark like a friend. Flick's spirits were high. Mark knew a female telephone engineer. Flick was about to meet her, and she felt optimistic.

Mark had not said much about her, except that her name was Greta, like the film star. When Flick tried to question him, he just said, "You have to see her for yourself."

As Mark paid the entrance fee and exchanged commonplaces with the manager, Flick saw an alteration come over him. He grew more extrovert, his voice took on a lilt, and his gestures became theatrical. Flick wondered if her brother had another persona that he put on after dark.

They went down a flight of stairs to a basement. The place was dimly lit and smoky. Flick could see a five-piece band on a low stage, a small dance floor, a scatter of tables, and a number of booths around the dark perimeter of the room. She had wondered if it would be a men-only club, the kind of place that catered to chaps like Mark who were "not the marrying kind." Although the patrons were mostly male, there was a good sprinkling of girls, some of them very glamorously dressed.

A waiter said, "Hello, Markie," and put a hand on Mark's shoulder, but gave Flick a hostile glare.

"Robbie, meet my sister," Mark said. "Her

name's Felicity, but we've always called her Flick."

The waiter's attitude changed, and he gave Flick a friendly smile. "Very nice to meet you." He showed them to a table.

Flick guessed that Robbie had suspected she might be a girlfriend, and had resented her for persuading Mark to change sides, as it were. Then he had warmed to her when he learned she was Mark's sister.

Mark smiled up at Robbie and said, "How's Kit?"

"Oh, all right, I suppose," Robbie said with the hint of a flounce.

"You've had a row, haven't you?"

Mark was being charming. He was almost flirting. This was a side of him Flick had never seen. In fact, she thought, it might be the real Mark. The other persona, his discreet daytime self, was probably the pretense.

"When have we not had a row?" Robbie said.

"He doesn't appreciate you," Mark said with exaggerated melancholy, touching Robbie's hand.

"You're right, bless you. Something to drink?"

Flick ordered scotch and Mark asked for a martini.

Flick did not know much about men such as these. She had been introduced to Mark's friend, Steve, and had visited the flat they shared, but had never met any of their friends. Although she was madly curious about their world, it seemed prurient to ask questions.

She didn't even know what they called themselves. All the words she knew were more or less unpleasant: queer, homo, fairy, nancy-boy. "Mark," she said. "What do *you* call men who, you know, prefer men?"

He grinned. "Musical, darling," he said, waving his hand in a feminine gesture.

I must remember that, Flick thought. Now I can say to Mark, "Is he musical?" She had learned the first word of their secret code.

A tall blonde in a red cocktail dress came swishing onto the stage to a burst of applause. "This is Greta," said Mark. "She's a telephone engineer by day."

Greta began to sing "Nobody Knows You When You're Down and Out." She had a powerful, bluesy voice, but Flick noticed immediately that she had a German accent. Shouting into Mark's ear over the sound of the band, she said, "I thought you said she was French."

"She *speaks* French," he corrected. "But she's German."

Flick was bitterly disappointed. This was no good. Greta would have just as much of a German accent when she spoke French.

The audience loved Greta, clapping each number enthusiastically, cheering and whistling when she accompanied the music with bump-and-grind movements. But Flick could not relax and enjoy the show. She was too worried. She still did not have her telephone engineer, and she had wasted the latter half of the evening coming here on a wild-goose chase.

But what was she going to do? She wondered how long it would take her to pick up the rudiments of telephone engineering herself. She had no difficulty with technical things. She had built a radio at school. Anyway, she needed to know only enough to destroy the equipment effectively. Could she do a two-day course, maybe with some people from the General Post Office?

The trouble was, nobody could be quite sure what kind of equipment the saboteurs would find when they entered the château.

It could be French or German or a mixture, possibly even including imported American machinery—the U.S.A. was far ahead of France in phone technology. There were many kinds of equipment, and the château served several different functions. It had a manual exchange, an automatic exchange, a tandem exchange for connecting other exchanges to one another, and an amplification station for the all-important new trunk route to Germany. But only an experienced engineer could be confident of recognizing whatever he saw when he walked in.

There were engineers in France, of course, and she might find a woman—if she had time. It was not a promising idea, but she thought it through. SOE could send a message to every Resistance circuit. If there was a woman who could fit the bill, it would take her a day or two to get to Reims, which was all right. But the plan was so uncertain. Was there a woman telephone engineer in the French Resistance? If not, Flick would waste two days to learn that the mission was doomed.

No, she needed something more sure. She thought again about Greta. She could not pass for French. The Gestapo might not notice her accent, since they spoke French the same way, but the French police would. Did she have to pretend to be French? There were plenty of German women in France: officers' wives, young women in the armed services, drivers and typists and wireless operators. Flick began to feel excited again. Why not? Greta could pose as an army secretary. No, that could cause problems—an officer might start giving her orders. It would be safer for her to pose as a civilian. She could be the young wife of an officer, living with her husband in Paris—no, Vichy, it was farther away. There would have to be a story about why Greta was traveling with a group of French women. Perhaps one of the team could pose as her French maid.

What about when they entered the château? Flick was pretty sure there were no German women working as cleaners in France. How could Greta evade suspicion? Once again, Germans probably would not notice her accent, but French people would. Could she avoid speaking to any French people? Pretend she had laryngitis?

She might be able to get away with it for a few minutes, Flick thought.

It was not exactly watertight, but it was better than any other option.

Greta finished her act with a hilariously suggestive blues called "Kitchen Man," full of double-entendres. The audience loved the line: "When I eat his doughnuts, all I leave is the hole." She left the stage to gales of applause. Mark got up, saying, "We can talk to her in her dressing room."

Flick followed him through a door beside the stage, down a smelly concrete corridor, into a dingy area crammed with cardboard boxes of beer and gin. It was like the cellar of a run-down pub. They came to a door that had a pink paper cutout star fixed to it with thumbtacks. Mark knocked and opened it without waiting for a reply.

The tiny room had a dressing table, a mirror surrounded by bright makeup lights, a stool, and a movie poster showing Greta Garbo in *Two-Faced Woman.* An elaborate blonde wig rested on a stand shaped like a head. The red dress Greta had worn on stage hung from a hook on the wall. Sitting on the stool in front of the mirror, Flick saw, to her utter astonishment, was a young man with a hairy chest.

She gasped.

It was Greta, no question. The face was heavily made up, with vivid lipstick and false eyelashes, plucked eyebrows, and a layer of makeup hiding the shadow of a dark beard. The hair was cut brutally short, no doubt to accommodate the wig. The false bosom was presumably fixed inside the dress, but Greta still wore a half-slip, stockings, and red high-heeled shoes.

Flick rounded on Mark. "You didn't tell me!" she accused.

He laughed delightedly. "Flick, meet Gerhard," he said. "He loves it when people don't realize."

Flick saw that Gerhard was looking pleased. Of course he would be happy that she had taken him for a real woman. It was a tribute to his art. She did not need to worry that she had insulted him.

But he was a man. And she needed a woman telephone engineer.

Flick was painfully disappointed. Greta would have been the last piece in the jigsaw, the woman who made the team complete. Now the mission was in doubt again.

She was angry with Mark. "This was so mean of you!" she said. "I thought you'd solved my problem, but you were just playing a joke."

"It's not a joke," Mark said indignantly. "If you need a woman, take Greta."

"I couldn't," Flick said. It was a ridiculous idea.

Or was it? Greta had convinced *her*. She could probably do the same to the Gestapo. If they arrested her and stripped her they would learn the truth, but if they got to that stage it was generally all over anyway.

She thought of the hierarchy at SOE, and Simon Fortescue at MI6. "The top brass would never agree to it."

"Don't tell them," Mark suggested.

"Not tell them!" Flick was at first shocked, then intrigued by that idea. If Greta was to fool the Gestapo, she ought also to be able to deceive everyone at SOE.

"Why not?" said Mark.

"Why not?" Flick repeated.

Gerhard said, "Mark, sweetie, what is all this about?" His German accent was stronger in speech than in song.

"I don't really know," Mark told him. "My sister is involved in something hush-hush."

"I'll explain," Flick said. "But first, tell me

about yourself. How did you come to London?"

"Well, sweetheart, where shall I begin?" Gerhard lit a cigarette. "I'm from Hamburg. Twelve years ago, when I was a boy of sixteen, and an apprentice telephone engineer, it was a wonderful town, bars and nightclubs full of sailors making the most of their shore leave. I had the best time. And when I was eighteen I met the love of my life. His name was Manfred."

Tears came to Gerhard's eyes, and Mark held his hand.

Gerhard sniffed, in a very unladylike fashion, and carried on. "I've always adored women's clothes, lacy underwear and high heels, hats and handbags. I love the swish of a full skirt. But I did it so crudely in those days. I really didn't even know how to put on eyeliner. Manfred taught me everything. He wasn't a cross-dresser himself, you know." A fond look came over Gerhard's face. "He was *extremely* masculine, in fact. He worked in the docks, as a stevedore. But he loved me in drag, and he taught me how to do it right."

"Why did you leave?"

"They took Manfred away. The bloody

fucking Nazis, sweetheart. We had five years together, but one night they came for him, and I never saw him again. He's probably dead, I think prison would kill him, but I don't know anything for sure." Tears dissolved his mascara and ran down his powdered cheeks in black streaks. "He could still be alive in one of their bloody fucking camps, you know."

His grief was infectious, and Flick found herself fighting back tears. What got into people that made them persecute one another? she asked herself. What made the Nazis torment harmless eccentrics like Gerhard?

"So I came to London," Gerhard said. "My father was English. He was a sailor from Liverpool who got off his ship in Hamburg and fell in love with a pretty German girl and married her. He died when I was two, so I never really knew him, but he gave me my surname, which is O'Reilly, and I always had dual nationality. It still cost me all my savings to get a passport, in 1939. As things turned out, I was just in time. Happily, there's always work for a telephone engineer in any city. So here I am, the toast of London, the deviant diva."

JACKDAWS   271

"It's a sad story," Flick said. "I'm very sorry."

"Thank you, sweetheart. But the world is full of sad stories these days, isn't it? Why are you interested in mine?"

"I need a female telephone engineer."

"What on earth for?"

"I can't tell you much. As Mark said, it's hush-hush. One thing I can say is that the job is very dangerous. You might get killed."

"How absolutely chilling! But you can imagine that I'm not very good at rough stuff. They said I was psychologically un-suited to service in the army, and quite bloody rightly. Half the squaddies would have wanted to beat me up and the other half would have been sneaking into bed with me at night."

"I've got all the tough soldiers I need. What I want from you is your expertise."

"Would it mean a chance to hurt those bloody fucking Nazis?"

"Absolutely. If we succeed, it will do a very great deal of damage indeed to the Hitler regime."

"Then, sweetheart, I'm your girl."

Flick smiled. My God, she thought; I've done it.

THE FOURTH DAY

Wednesday, May 31, 1944

CHAPTER 17

In the middle of the night, the roads of southern England were thronged with traffic. Great convoys of army trucks rumbled along every highway, roaring through the darkened towns, heading for the coast. Bemused villagers stood at their bedroom windows, staring in incredulity at the endless stream of traffic that was stealing their sleep.

"My God," said Greta. "There really is going to be an invasion."

She and Flick had left London shortly after midnight in a borrowed car, a big white Lincoln Continental that Flick loved to drive. Greta wore one of her less eye-popping outfits, a simple black dress with a brunette wig. She would not be Gerhard again until the mission was over.

Flick hoped Greta was as expert as Mark had claimed. She worked for the General Post Office as an engineer, so presumably she knew what she was talking about. But Flick had not been able to test her. Now, as they crawled along behind a tank transporter, Flick explained the mission, anxiously hoping the conversation would not reveal gaps in Greta's knowledge. "The château contains a new automatic exchange put in by the Germans to handle all the extra telephone and teleprinter traffic between Berlin and the occupying forces."

At first Greta was skeptical about the plan. "But, sweetheart, even if we succeed, what's to stop the Germans just rerouting calls around the network?"

"Volume of traffic. The system is overloaded. The army command center called 'Zeppelin' outside Berlin handles one hundred twenty thousand long-distance calls and twenty thousand telex messages a day. There will be more when we invade France. But much of the French system still consists of manual exchanges. Now imagine that the main automatic exchange is out of service and all those calls have to be made the old-fashioned way, by hello girls, taking ten times as long. Ninety percent of them will never get through."

"The military could prohibit civilian calls."

"That won't make much difference. Civilian traffic is only a tiny fraction anyway."

"All right." Greta was thoughtful. "Well, we could destroy the common equipment racks."

"What do they do?"

"Provide the tones and ringing voltages and so on for automatic calls. And the register translators, they transform the dialed area code into a routing instruction."

"Would that make the whole exchange unworkable?"

"No. And the damage could be repaired. You need to knock out the manual exchange, the automatic exchange, the long-distance amplifiers, the telex exchange, and the telex amplifiers—which are probably all in different rooms."

"Remember, we can't carry a great quantity of explosives with us—only what six women could hide in their everyday bags."

"That's a problem."

Michel had been through all this with Arnaud, a member of the Bollinger circuit who worked for the French PTT—*Postes,*

Télégraphes, Téléphones—but Flick had not queried the details, and Arnaud was dead, killed in the raid. "There must be some equipment common to all the systems."

"Yes, there is—the MDF."

"What's that?"

"The Main Distribution Frame. Two sets of terminals on large racks. All the cables from outside come to one side of the frame; all the cables from the exchange come to the other; and they're connected by jumper links."

"Where would that be?"

"In a room next to the cable chamber. Ideally, you'd want a fire hot enough to melt the copper in the cables."

"How long would it take to reconnect the cables?"

"A couple of days."

"Are you sure? When the cables in my street were severed by a bomb, one old Post Office engineer had us reconnected in a few hours."

"Street repairs are simple, just a matter of connecting broken ends together, red to red and blue to blue. But an MDF has hundreds of cross-connections. Two days is conservative, and that assumes the repair-men have the record cards."

"Record cards?"

"They show how the cables are con-nected. They're normally kept in a cabinet in the MDF room. If we burn them, too, it will take weeks of trial and error to figure out the connections."

Flick now recalled Michel saying the Re-sistance had someone in the PTT who was ready to destroy the duplicate records kept at headquarters. "This is sounding good. Now, listen. In the morning, when I explain our mission to the others, I'm going to tell them something completely different, a cover story."

"Why?"

"So that our mission won't be jeopardized if one of us is captured and interrogated."

"Oh." Greta found this a sobering thought. "How dreadful."

"You're the only one who knows the true story, so keep it to yourself for now."

"Don't worry. Us queers are used to keep-ing secrets."

Flick was startled by her choice of words, but made no comment.

The Finishing School was located on the

grounds of one of England's grandest stately homes. Beaulieu, pronounced Bewly, was a sprawling estate in the New Forest near the south coast. The main residence, Palace House, was the home of Lord Montagu. Hidden away in the surrounding woods were numerous large country houses in extensive grounds of their own. Most of these had been vacated early in the war: younger owners had gone on active service, and older ones generally had the means to flee to safer locations. Twelve of the houses had been requisitioned by SOE and were used for training agents in security, wireless operation, map reading, and dirtier skills such as burglary, sabotage, forgery, and silent killing.

They reached the place at three o'clock in the morning. Flick drove down a rough track and crossed a cattle grid before pulling up in front of a large house. Coming here always felt like entering a fantasy world, one where deception and violence were talked of as commonplace. The house had an appropriate air of unreality. Although it had about twenty bedrooms, it was built in the style of a cottage—an architectural affectation that had been popular in the years before the First World War. It looked quaint in the moonlight, with its chimneys and dormer windows, hipped roofs and tile-hung bays. It was like an illustration in a children's novel, a big rambling house where you could play hide-and-seek all day.

The place was silent. The rest of the team was here, Flick knew, but they would be asleep. She was familiar with the house and found two vacant rooms on the attic floor. She and Greta went gratefully to bed. Flick lay awake for a while, wondering how she would ever weld this bunch of misfits into a fighting unit, but she soon fell asleep.

She got up again at six. From her window she could see the estuary of the Solent. The water looked like mercury in the gray morning light. She boiled a kettle for shaving and took it to Greta's room. Then she roused the others.

Percy and Paul were first to arrive in the big kitchen at the back of the house, Percy demanding tea and Paul coffee. Flick told them to make it themselves. She had not joined SOE to wait on men.

"I make tea for you sometimes," Percy said indignantly.

"You do it with an air of noblesse oblige,"

she replied. "Like a duke holding a door for a housemaid."

Paul laughed. "You guys," he said. "You crack me up."

An army cook arrived at half past six, and before long they were sitting around the big table eating fried eggs and thick rashers of bacon. Food was not rationed for secret agents: they needed to build up their reserves. Once they went into action, they might have to go for days without proper nourishment.

The girls came down one by one. Flick was startled by her first sight of Maude Valentine: neither Percy nor Paul had said how pretty she was. She appeared immaculately dressed and scented, her rosebud mouth accentuated by bright lipstick, looking as if she were off to lunch at the Savoy. She sat next to Paul and said with a suggestive air, "Sleep well, Major?"

Flick was relieved to see the dark pirate face of Ruby Romain. She would not have been surprised to learn that Ruby had run off in the night, never to be seen again. Of course, Ruby could then be rearrested for the murder. She had not been pardoned: rather, the charges had been dropped. They could always be picked up again. That ought to keep Ruby from disappearing, but she was as tough as a boot, and she might have decided to take the chance.

Jelly Knight looked her age, this early in the morning. She sat beside Percy and gave him a fond smile. "I suppose you slept like a top," she said.

"Clear conscience," he replied.

She laughed. "You haven't got a bloody conscience."

The cook offered her a plate of bacon and eggs, but she made a face. "No, thank you, dear," she said. "I've got to watch my figure." Her breakfast was a cup of tea and several cigarettes.

When Greta came through the door, Flick held her breath.

She wore a pretty cotton dress with a small false bosom. A pink cardigan softened her shoulder line and a chiffon scarf concealed her masculine throat. She wore the short dark wig. Her face was heavily powdered, but she had used only a little lipstick and eye makeup. By contrast with her sassy on-stage personality, today she was playing the part of a rather plain young woman who was perhaps a little embarrassed about being so tall. Flick introduced her and watched the reactions of the other women. This was the first test of Greta's impersonation.

They all smiled pleasantly, showing no sign that they saw anything wrong, and Flick breathed easier.

Along with Maude, the other woman Flick had not met before was Lady Denise Bowyer. Percy had interviewed her at Hendon and had recruited her despite signs that she was indiscreet. She turned out to be a plain girl with a lot of dark hair and a defiant air. Although she was the daughter of a marquess, she lacked the easy self-confidence typical of upper-class girls. Flick felt a little sorry for her, but Denise was too charmless to be likable.

This is my team, Flick thought: one flirt, one murderess, one safebreaker, one female impersonator, and one awkward aristocrat. There was someone missing, she realized: the other aristocrat. Diana had not appeared. And it was now half past seven.

Flick said to Percy, "You did tell Diana that reveille was at six?"

"I told everyone."

"And I banged on her door at a quarter

past." Flick stood up. "I'd better check on her. Bedroom Ten, right?"

She went upstairs and knocked at Diana's door. There was no response, so she went in. The room looked as if a bomb had hit it—a suitcase open on the rumpled bed, pillows on the floor, knickers on the dressing table—but Flick knew this was normal. Diana had always been surrounded by people whose job it was to tidy up after her. Flick's mother had been one of those people. No, Diana had simply gone off somewhere. She was going to have to realize that her time was no longer her own, Flick thought with irritation.

"She's disappeared," she told the others. "We'll start without her." She stood at the head of the table. "We have two days' training in front of us. Then, on Friday night, we parachute into France. We're an all-female team because it is much easier for women to move around occupied France—the Gestapo are less suspicious. Our mission is to blow up a railway tunnel near the village of Marles, not far from Reims, on the main railway line between Frankfurt and Paris."

Flick glanced at Greta, who knew the

story was false. She sat quietly buttering toast and did not meet Flick's eye.

"The agent's course is normally three months," Flick went on. "But this tunnel has to be destroyed by Monday night. In two days, we hope to give you some basic security rules, teach you how to parachute, do some weapons training, and show you how to kill people without making a noise."

Maude looked pale despite her makeup. "Kill people?" she said. "Surely you don't expect girls to do that?"

Jelly gave a grunt of disgust. "There is a bloody war on, you know."

Diana came in from the garden with bits of vegetation clinging to her corduroy trousers. "I've been for a tramp in the woods," she said enthusiastically. "Marvelous. And look what the greenhouseman gave me." She took a handful of ripe tomatoes from her pocket and rolled them onto the kitchen table.

Flick said, "Sit down, Diana, you're late for the briefing."

"I'm sorry, darling, have I missed your lovely talk?"

"You're in the military now," Flick said with exasperation. "When you're told to be in the kitchen by seven, it's not a suggestion."

"You're not going to get all headmistressy with me, are you?"

"Sit down and shut up."

"Frightfully sorry, darling."

Flick raised her voice. "Diana, when I say shut up, you don't say 'Frightfully sorry' to me, and you don't call me darling, ever. Just shut up."

Diana sat down in silence, but she looked mutinous. Oh, hell, Flick thought, I didn't handle that very well.

The kitchen door opened with a bang and a small, muscular man of about forty came in. He had sergeant's chevrons on his uniform shirt. "Good morning, girls!" he said heartily.

Flick said, "This is Sergeant Bill Griffiths, one of the instructors." She did not like Bill. An army PT instructor, he showed an unpleasant relish in physical combat and never seemed sorry enough when he hurt someone. She had noticed that he was worse with women. "We're just about ready for you, Sergeant, so why don't you begin?" She moved aside and leaned against the wall.

"Your wish is my command," he said unnecessarily. He took her place at the head of the table. "Landing with a parachute," he began, "is like jumping off a wall fourteen feet high. The ceiling of this kitchen is a bit less than that, so it's like leaping into the garden from upstairs."

Flick heard Jelly say quietly, "Oh, my gordon."

"You cannot come down on your feet and stay upright," Bill continued. "If you try to land in a standing position, you will break your legs. The only safe way is to fall. So the first thing we're going to teach you is how to fall. If anyone wishes to keep their clothing clean, please go into the boot room just there and put on overalls. If you will assemble outside in three minutes, we will begin."

While the women were changing, Paul took his leave. "We need a parachute training flight tomorrow, and they're going to tell me there are no planes available," he said to Flick. "I'm going to London to kick ass. I'll be back tonight." Flick wondered if he was going to see his girl as well.

In the garden were an old pine table, an ugly mahogany wardrobe from the Victorian era, and a stepladder fourteen feet high.

Jelly was dismayed. "You're not going to make us jump off the top of that bloody wardrobe, are you?" she said to Flick.

"Not before we show you how," she said. "You'll be surprised how easy it is."

Jelly looked at Percy. "You bugger," she said. "What have you let me in for?"

When they were all ready, Bill said, "First we're going to learn to fall from zero height. There are three ways: forwards, backwards, and sideways."

He demonstrated each method, dropping to the ground effortlessly and springing up again with a gymnast's agility. "You must keep your legs together." He looked arch and added, "As all young ladies should." No one laughed. "Do not throw out your arms to break your fall, but keep them at your sides. Do not worry about hurting yourself. If you break an arm it will hurt a hell of a lot worse."

As Flick expected, the younger girls had no difficulty: Diana, Maude, Ruby, and Denise were all able to fall like athletes as soon as they were shown how. Ruby, having done it once from the standing position, lost patience with the exercise. She climbed to the top of the stepladder. "Not yet!" Bill shouted at her, but he was too late. She jumped off the top and landed perfectly. Then she walked off, sat under a tree, and lit a cigarette. I think she's going to give me trouble, Flick thought.

Flick was more worried about Jelly. She was a key member of the team, the only one who knew about explosives. But she had lost her girlish suppleness some years ago. Parachuting was going to be difficult for her. However, she was game. Falling from the standing position, she hit the ground with a grunt and cursed as she got up, but she was ready to try again.

To Flick's surprise, the worst student was Greta. "I can't do this," she said to Flick. "I told you I'm no good at rough stuff."

It was the first time Greta had spoken more than a couple of words, and Jelly frowned and muttered, "Funny accent."

"Let me help you," Bill said to Greta. "Stand still. Just relax." He took her by the shoulders. Then, with a sudden strong motion, he threw her to the ground. She landed heavily and gave a gasp of pain. She struggled to her feet and, to Flick's dismay, she began to cry. "For God's sake," Bill said disgustedly. "What kind of people are they sending us?"

Flick glared at him. She did not want to lose her telephone engineer through Bill's brutishness. "Just go easy," she snapped at him.

He was unrepentant. "The Gestapo are a lot worse than me!"

Flick would have to mend the damage herself. She took Greta by the hand. "We'll do a little special training on our own." They went around the house to another part of the garden.

"I'm sorry," Greta said. "I just hate that little man."

"I know. Now, let's do this together. Kneel down." They knelt facing one another and held hands. "Just do what I do." Flick leaned slowly sideways. Greta mirrored her action. Together, they fell to the ground, still holding hands. "There," Flick said. "That was all right, wasn't it?"

Greta smiled. "Why can't he be like you?"

Flick shrugged. "Men," she said with a grin. "Now, are you ready to try falling from a standing position? We'll do it the same way, holding hands."

She took Greta through all the exercises Bill was doing with the others. Greta quickly gained confidence. They returned to the group. The others were jumping off the table. Greta joined in and landed perfectly, and they gave her a round of applause.

They progressed to jumping from the top of the wardrobe, then finally the stepladder. When Jelly jumped off the ladder, rolled perfectly, and stood upright, Flick hugged her. "I'm proud of you," she said. "Well done."

Bill looked disgusted. He turned to Percy. "What the hell kind of army is it when you get a hug for doing what you're bloody well told?"

"Get used to it, Bill," said Percy.

CHAPTER 18

At the tall house in the rue du Bois, Dieter carried Stéphanie's suitcase up the stairs and into Mademoiselle Lemas's bedroom. He looked at the tightly made single bed, the old-fashioned walnut chest of drawers, and the prayer stool with the rosary on its lectern. "It's not going to be easy to pretend this is your house," he said anxiously, putting the case on the bed.

"I'll say I've inherited it from a maiden aunt, and I've been too lazy to fix it up to my taste," she said.

"Clever. All the same, you'll need to mess it up a little."

She opened the case, took out a black negligee, and draped it carelessly over the prayer stool.

"Better already," Dieter said. "What will you do if the phone rings?"

Stéphanie thought for a minute. When she spoke, her voice was lower, and her high-class Paris accent had been replaced by the tones of provincial gentility. "Hello, yes, this is Mademoiselle Lemas, who is calling, please?"

"Very good," said Dieter. The impersonation might not fool a close friend or relative, but a casual caller would notice nothing wrong, especially with the distortion of a telephone line.

They explored the house. There were four more bedrooms, each ready to receive a guest, the beds made up, a clean towel on each washstand. In the kitchen, where there should have been a selection of small saucepans and a one-cup coffee pot, they found large casserole dishes and a sack of rice that would have fed Mademoiselle Lemas for a year. The wine in the cellar was cheap *vin ordinaire,* but there was half a case of good scotch whisky. The garage at the side of the house contained a little pre-war Simca Cinq, the French version of the Fiat the Italians called the Topolino. It was in good condition with a tank full of petrol.

He cranked the starting handle, and the engine turned over immediately. There was no way the authorities would have allowed Mademoiselle Lemas to buy scarce petrol and spare parts for a car to take her shopping. The vehicle must have been fueled and maintained by the Resistance. He wondered what cover story she had used to explain her ability to drive around. Perhaps she pretended to be a midwife. "The old cow was well organized," Dieter remarked.

Stéphanie made lunch. They had shopped on the way. There was no meat or fish in the shops, but they had bought some mushrooms and a lettuce, and a loaf of *pain noir,* the bread the French bakers made with the poor flour and bran, which was all they could get. Stéphanie prepared a salad, and used the mushrooms to make a risotto, and they found some cheese in the larder to finish off. With crumbs on the dining room table and dirty pans in the kitchen sink, the house began to look more lived in.

"The war must have been the best thing that ever happened to her," Dieter said as they drank coffee.

"How can you say that? She's on her way to a prison camp."

"Think of the life she led before. A woman alone, no husband, no family, her parents dead. Then into her life come all these young people, brave boys and girls on dare-devil missions. They probably tell her all about their loves and their fears. She hides them in her house, gives them whisky and cigarettes, and sends them on their way, wishing them luck. It was probably the most exciting time of her life. I bet she's never been so happy."

"Perhaps she would have preferred a peaceful life, shopping for hats with a woman friend, arranging the flowers for the cathedral, going to Paris once a year for a concert."

"Nobody really prefers a peaceful life." Dieter glanced out of the dining room window. "Damn!" A young woman was coming up the path, pushing a bicycle with a large basket over its front wheel. "Who the hell is this?"

Stéphanie stared at the approaching visitor. "What shall I do?"

Dieter did not answer for a moment. The intruder was a plain, fit-looking girl in muddy trousers and a work shirt with big sweat patches under the armpits. She did not ring the doorbell but pushed her bicycle into the courtyard. He was dismayed. Was his charade to be exposed so soon? "She's coming to the back door. She must be a friend or relation. You'll just have to improvise. Go and meet her, I'll stay here and listen."

They heard the kitchen door open and close, and the girl called out in French, "Good morning, it's me."

Stéphanie went into the kitchen. Dieter stood by the dining room door. He could hear everything clearly. The girl's startled voice said, "Who are you?"

"I'm Stéphanie, the niece of Mademoiselle Lemas."

The visitor did not bother to conceal her suspicion. "I didn't know she had a niece."

"She didn't tell me about you, either." Dieter heard the note of amiable amusement in Stéphanie's voice, and realized she was being charming. "Would you like to sit down? What's in that basket?"

"Some provisions. I'm Marie. I live in the country. I'm able to get extra food and I bring some for . . . for Mademoiselle."

"Ah," said Stéphanie. "For her . . . guests." There was a rustling sound, and Dieter guessed Stéphanie was looking through the paper-wrapped food in the basket. "This is wonderful! Eggs . . . pork . . . strawberries . . ."

This explained how Mademoiselle Lemas managed to remain plump, Dieter thought.

"You know, then," said Marie.

"I know about Auntie's secret life, yes." Hearing her say "Auntie," Dieter realized that neither he nor Stéphanie had ever asked Mademoiselle Lemas's first name. The pretense would be over if Marie found out that Stéphanie did not even know the name of her "aunt."

"Where is she?"

"She went to Aix. Do you remember Charles Menton, who used to be dean at the cathedral?"

"No, I don't."

"Perhaps you're too young. He was the best friend of Auntie's father, until he retired and went to live in Provence." Stéphanie was improvising brilliantly, Dieter thought with admiration. She had cool nerves and she was imaginative. "He has suffered a heart attack, and she has gone to nurse him. She asked me to take care of any guests while she's away."

"When will she come back?"

"Charles is not expected to live long. On the other hand, the war may be over soon."

"She didn't tell anyone about this Charles."

"She told me."

It looked as if Stéphanie might get away with it, Dieter thought. If she could keep this up a little longer, Marie would go away convinced. She would report what had happened, to someone or other, but Stéphanie's story was plausible, and exactly the kind of thing that happened in Resistance movements. It was not like the army: someone like Mademoiselle Lemas could easily make a unilateral decision to leave her post and put someone else in charge. It drove Resistance leaders mad, but there was nothing they could do: all their troops were volunteers.

He began to feel hopeful.

"Where are you from?" said Marie.

"I live in Paris."

"Does your aunt Valérie have any other nieces hidden away?"

So, Dieter thought, Mademoiselle Lemas's name is Valérie.

"I don't think so—none that I know."

"You're a liar."

Marie's tone had changed. Something had gone wrong. Dieter sighed and drew the automatic pistol from beneath his jacket.

Stéphanie said, "What on earth are you talking about?"

"You're lying. You don't even know her name. It's not Valérie, it's Jeanne."

Dieter thumbed the safety lever on the left of the slide up to the fire position.

Stéphanie carried on gamely. "I always call her Auntie. You're being very rude."

Marie said scornfully, "I knew from the start. Jeanne would never trust someone like you, with your high heels and perfume."

Dieter stepped into the kitchen. "What a shame, Marie," he said. "If you had been more trusting, or less clever, you might have got away. As it is, you're under arrest."

Marie looked at Stéphanie and said, "You're a Gestapo whore."

It was a wounding gibe, and Stéphanie blushed.

Dieter was so infuriated that he almost pistol-whipped Marie. "You'll regret that remark when you're in the hands of the Gestapo," he said coldly. "There's a man called Sergeant Becker who is going to question you. When you're screaming and bleeding and begging for mercy, remember that careless insult."

Marie looked poised to flee. Dieter almost hoped she would. Then he could shoot her and the problem would be solved. But she did not run. After a long moment, her shoulders slumped and she began to cry.

Her tears did not move him. "Lie facedown on the floor with your hands behind your back."

She obeyed.

He put away the gun. "I think I saw a rope in the cellar," he said to Stéphanie.

"I'll get it."

She returned with a length of washing line. Dieter tied Marie's hands and feet. "I'll have to take her to Sainte-Cécile," he said. "We can't have her here in case a British agent comes in today." He looked at his watch. It was two o'clock. He had time to take her to the château and be back by three. "You'll have to go to the crypt on your own," he told Stéphanie. "Use the little car in the garage. I'll be in the cathedral, though you may not see me." He kissed her. Almost like a husband going to the office, he thought with grim amusement. He picked Marie up and slung her over his shoulder.

"I'll have to hurry," he said, and went to the back door.

He stepped outside, then turned back. "Hide the bicycle."

"Don't worry," Stéphanie replied.

He carried the bound girl through the courtyard and into the street. He opened the trunk of his car and put her inside. Had it not been for the "whore" comment, he would have put her on the backseat.

He slammed the lid and looked around. He saw no one, but there were always watchers in a street such as this, peering through their shutters. They would have seen Mademoiselle Lemas being taken away yesterday and would have remarked the big sky-blue car. As soon as he drove away, they would be talking about the man who had put a girl into the trunk of his car. In normal times, they would have called the police, but no one in occupied territory would talk to the police unless they had to, especially where the Gestapo might be involved.

The key question for Dieter was: Would the Resistance hear of the arrest of Mademoiselle Lemas? Reims was a city, not a village. People were arrested every day: thieves, murderers, smugglers, black marketeers, communists, Jews. There was a good chance that no report of the events in the rue du Bois would reach the ears of Michel Clairet.

But there was no guarantee.

Dieter got into the car and headed for Sainte-Cécile.

CHAPTER 19

The team had got through the morning's instruction reasonably well, to Flick's relief. Everyone had learned the falling technique, which was the hardest part of parachuting. The map-reading session had been less successful. Ruby had never been to school and could barely read: a map was like a page of Chinese to her. Maude was baffled by directions such as north-northeast, and fluttered her eyelids prettily at the instructor. Denise, despite her expensive education, proved completely incapable of under-standing coordinates. If the group got split up in France, Flick thought worriedly, she would not be able to rely on them finding their own way.

In the afternoon they moved on to the rough stuff. The weapons instructor was

Captain Jim Cardwell, a character quite different from Bill Griffiths. Jim was an easy-going man with a craggy face and a thick black moustache. He grinned amiably when the girls discovered how difficult it was to hit a tree at six paces with a .45 caliber Colt automatic pistol.

Ruby was comfortable with an automatic in her hand and could shoot accurately: Flick suspected she had used handguns before. Ruby was even more comfortable when Jim put his arms around her to show her how to hold the Lee-Enfield "Canadian" rifle. He murmured something in her ear, and she smiled up at him with a wicked gleam in her black eyes. She had been in a women's prison for three months, Flick reflected: no doubt she was enjoying being touched by a man.

Jelly, too, handled the firearms with relaxed familiarity. But Diana was the star of the session. Using the rifle, she hit the center of the target with every shot, emptying the magazine of both its five-round clips in a steady burst of deadly fire. "Very good!" Jim said in surprise. "You can have my job."

Diana looked triumphantly at Flick. "There

are *some* things you're not best at," she said.

What the heck did I do to deserve that? Flick asked herself. Was Diana thinking of their schooldays, when Flick had always done so much better? Did that childhood rivalry still rankle?

Greta was the only failure. Once again, she was more feminine than the real women. She put her hands over her ears, jumped nervously at every bang, and closed her eyes in terror as she pulled the trigger. Jim worked with her patiently, giving her earplugs to muffle the noise, holding her hand to teach her how to squeeze the trigger gently, but it was no good: she was too skittish ever to be a good shot. "I'm just not cut out for this kind of thing!" she said in despair.

Jelly said, "Then what the hell are you doing here?"

Flick interposed quickly. "Greta's an engineer. She's going to tell you where to place the charges."

"Why do we need a German engineer?"

"I'm English," Greta said. "My father was born in Liverpool."

Jelly snorted skeptically. "If that's a Liverpool accent, I'm the Duchess of Devonshire."

"Save your aggression for the next session," Flick said. "We're about to do hand-to-hand combat." This bickering bothered her. She needed them to trust one another.

They returned to the garden of the house, where Bill Griffiths was waiting. He had changed into shorts and tennis shoes, and was doing push-ups on the grass with his shirt off. When he stood up, Flick got the feeling he wanted them to admire his physique.

Bill liked to teach self-defense by giving the student a weapon and saying, "Attack me." Then he would demonstrate how an unarmed man could repel an attacker. It was a dramatic and memorable lesson. Bill was sometimes unnecessarily violent but, Flick always thought, the agents might as well get used to that.

Today he had a selection of weapons laid out on the old pine table: a wicked-looking knife that he claimed was SS equipment, a Walther P38 automatic pistol of the kind Flick had seen German officers carrying, a French policeman's truncheon, a length of black-and-yellow electrical cord that he called a garotte, and a beer bottle with the neck snapped to leave a rough circle of sharp glass.

He put his shirt back on for the training session. "How to escape from a man who is pointing a gun at you," he began. He picked up the Walther, thumbed the safety catch up to the firing position, and handed the gun to Maude. She pointed it at him. "Sooner or later, your captor is going to want you to go somewhere." He turned and put his hands in the air. "Chances are, he'll follow close behind you, poking the gun in your back." He walked around in a wide circle, with Maude behind. "Now, Maude, I want you to pull the trigger the moment you think I'm trying to escape." He quickened his pace slightly, forcing Maude to step out a little faster to keep up with him, and as she did so he moved sideways and back. He caught her right wrist under his arm and hit her hand with a sharp, downward-chopping motion. She cried out and dropped the gun.

"This is where you can make a bad mistake," he said as Maude rubbed her wrist. "Do *not* run away at this point. Otherwise your Kraut copper will just pick up his gun and shoot you in the back. What you have to do is . . ." He picked up the Luger, pointed it at Maude, and pulled the trigger. There was a bang. Maude screamed, and so did Greta. "This gun is loaded with blanks, of course," Bill said.

Sometimes Flick wished Bill would not be quite so dramatic in his demonstrations.

"We'll practice all these techniques on one another in a few minutes," he went on. He picked up the electrical cord and turned to Greta. "Put that around my neck. When I give the word, pull it as tight as you can." He handed her the cord. "Your Gestapo man, or your traitorous collaborationist French gendarme, could kill you with the cord, but he can't hold your weight with it. All right, Greta, strangle me." Greta hesitated, then pulled the cord tight. It dug into Bill's muscular neck. He kicked out forward with both feet and fell to the ground, landing on his back. Greta lost her grip on the cord.

"Unfortunately," Bill said, "this leaves you lying on the ground with your enemy standing over you, which is an unfavorable situation." He got up. "We'll do it again. But this time, before I drop to the ground, I'm going to take hold of my captor by one wrist."

They resumed the position, and Greta pulled the cord tight. Bill grabbed her wrist, fell to the ground, pulling her forward and down. As she fell on top of him, he bent one leg and kneed her viciously in the stomach.

She rolled off him and curled up, gasping for breath and retching. Flick said, "For Christ's sake, Bill, that's a bit rough!"

He looked pleased. "The Gestapo are a lot worse than me," he said.

She went to Greta and helped her up. "I'm sorry," she said.

"He's a bloody fucking Nazi," Greta gasped.

Flick helped Greta into the house and sat her down in the kitchen. The cook, who was peeling potatoes for lunch, offered her a cup of tea, and Greta accepted gratefully.

When Flick returned to the garden, Bill had picked his next victim, Ruby, and handed her the policeman's truncheon. There was a cunning look on Ruby's face, and Flick thought: If I were Bill I'd be careful with her.

Flick had seen Bill demonstrate this technique before. When Ruby raised her right hand to hit him with the truncheon, Bill was going to grab her arm, turn, and throw her over his shoulder. She would land flat on her back with a painful thump.

"Right, gypsy girl," Bill said. "Hit me with the truncheon, as hard as you like."

Ruby lifted her arm, and Bill moved toward her, but the action did not follow the usual pattern. When Bill reached for Ruby's arm, it was not there. The truncheon fell to the ground. Ruby moved close to Bill and brought her knee up hard into his groin. He gave a sharp cry of pain. She grabbed his shirt front, pulled him toward her sharply, and butted his nose. Then, with her sturdy black laced shoe, she kicked his shin, and he fell to the ground, blood pouring from his nose.

"You bitch, you weren't supposed to do that!" he yelled.

"The Gestapo are a lot worse than me," said Ruby.

CHAPTER 20

It was a minute before three when Dieter parked outside the Hotel Frankfort. He hurried across the cobbled square to the cathedral under the stony gaze of the carved angels in the buttresses. It was almost too much to hope that an Allied agent would show up at the rendezvous the first day. On the other hand, if the invasion really were imminent, the Allies would be throwing in every last asset.

He saw Mademoiselle Lemas's Simca Cinq parked to one side of the square, which meant that Stéphanie was already here. He was relieved to have arrived in time. If anything should go wrong, he would not want her to have to deal with it alone.

He passed through the great west door into the cool gloom of the interior. He looked for Hans Hesse and saw him sitting in the back row of pews. They nodded briefly to one another but did not speak.

Right away Dieter felt like a violator. The business he was engaged upon should not take place in this atmosphere. He was not very devout—less so than the average German, he thought—but he was certainly no unbeliever. He felt uncomfortable catching spies in a place that had been a holy sanctuary for hundreds of years.

He shook off the feeling as superstitious.

He crossed to the north side of the building and walked up the long north aisle, his footsteps ringing on the stone floor. When he reached the transept, he saw the gate, railing, and steps leading down to the crypt, which was below the high altar. Stéphanie was down there, he assumed, wearing one black shoe and one brown. From here he could see in both directions: back the way he had come the length of the north aisle, and forward around the curved ambulatory at the other end of the building. He knelt down and folded his hands in prayer.

He said, "O Lord, forgive me for the suffering I inflict on my prisoners. You know I'm trying my best to do my duty. And forgive me for my sin with Stéphanie. I know it's wrong, but You made her so lovely that I can't resist the temptation. Watch over my dear Waltraud, and help her to care for Rudi and little Mausi, and protect them from the bombs of the RAF. And be with Field Marshal Rommel when the invasion comes, and give him the power to push the Allied invaders back into the sea. It's a short prayer to have so much in it, but You know that I have a lot to do right now. Amen."

He looked around. There was no service going on, but a handful of people were scattered around the pews in the side chapels, praying or just sitting quietly in the sacred stillness. A few tourists walked around the aisles, talking in hushed voices about the medieval architecture, bending their necks to peer up into the vastness of the vaulting.

If an Allied agent showed up today, Dieter planned simply to watch and make sure nothing went wrong. Ideally he would not have to do anything. Stéphanie would talk to the agent, exchange passwords, and take him home to the rue du Bois.

After that, his plans were vaguer. Somehow, the agent would lead him to others. At some point, there would be a breakthrough:

an unwise person would be found to have a written list of names and addresses; a wireless set and a code book would fall into Dieter's hands; or he would capture someone like Flick Clairet, who would, under torture, betray half the French Resistance.

He checked his watch. It was five past three. Probably no one would come today. He looked up. To his horror, he saw Willi Weber.

What the hell was he doing here?

Weber was in plain clothes, wearing his green tweed suit. With him was a younger Gestapo man in a check jacket. They were coming from the east end of the church, walking around the ambulatory toward Dieter, though they had not seen him. They drew level with the crypt door and stopped.

Dieter cursed under his breath. This could ruin everything. He almost hoped that no British agent would come today.

Looking along the north aisle, he saw a young man carrying a small suitcase. Dieter narrowed his eyes: most of the people in the church were older. The man was wearing a shabby blue suit of French cut, but he looked like a Viking, with red hair, blue eyes, and pale pink skin. It was a very English combination, but could also be German. At first glance, the young man might be an officer in mufti, seeing the sights or even intending to pray.

However, his behavior gave him away. He walked purposefully along the aisle, neither looking at the pillars like a tourist nor taking a seat like a worshiper. Dieter's heart beat faster. An agent on the first day! And the bag he carried was almost certainly a suitcase radio. That meant he had a code book, too. This was more than Dieter had dared to hope for.

But Weber was here to mess everything up.

The agent passed Dieter and slowed his walk, obviously looking for the crypt.

Weber saw the man, gave him a hard look, then turned and pretended to study the fluting on a column.

Maybe it was going to be all right, Dieter thought. Weber had done a stupid thing in coming here, but perhaps he was just planning to observe. Surely he was not such an imbecile as to interfere? He could ruin a unique opportunity.

The agent found the crypt gate and disappeared down the stone steps.

Weber looked across the north transept and gave a nod. Following his gaze, Dieter saw two more Gestapo men lurking beneath the organ loft. That was a bad sign. Weber did not need four men just to observe. Dieter wondered if he had time to speak to Weber, get him to call his men off. But Weber would argue, and there would be a row, and then—

As it turned out, there was no time. Almost immediately, Stéphanie came up from the crypt with the agent right behind her.

When she reached the top of the steps she saw Weber. A look of shock came over her face. She was disoriented by his unexpected presence, as if she had walked on stage and found herself in the wrong play. She stumbled, and the young agent caught her elbow and steadied her. She recovered her composure with characteristic speed and gave him a grateful smile. Well done, my girl, Dieter thought.

Then Weber stepped forward.

"No!" Dieter said involuntarily. No one heard him.

Weber took the agent by the arm and said something. Dieter's heart sank as he realized Weber was making an arrest. Stéphanie backed away from the little tableau, looking bewildered.

Dieter got up and walked quickly toward the group. He could only think that Weber had decided to grab the glory by capturing an agent. It was insane but possible.

Before Dieter got close, the agent shook off Weber's hand and bolted.

Weber's young companion in the check jacket reacted fast. He took two big strides after the agent, flung himself forward in a flying tackle, and threw his arms around the agent's knees. The agent stumbled, but he was moving strongly, and the Gestapo man could not hold him. The agent recovered his balance, straightened up, and ran on, still clutching his suitcase.

The sudden running steps, and the grunts made by both men, sounded loud in the hushed cathedral, and everyone looked. The agent ran toward Dieter. Dieter saw what was going to happen and groaned. The second pair of Gestapo men stepped out of the north transept. The agent saw them and seemed to guess what they were, for he swerved left, but he was too late. One of the men stuck out a foot and tripped him. He fell headlong, his chunky body hitting the stone floor with a thwack. The suitcase went flying. Both Gestapo men jumped on him. Weber came running up, looking pleased.

"Shit," Dieter said aloud, forgetting where he was. The mad fools were ruining everything.

Maybe he could still save the situation.

He reached into his jacket, drew his Walther P38, thumbed the safety catch, and pointed it at the Gestapo men who were holding the agent down. Speaking French, he yelled at the top of his voice, "Get off him now, or I shoot!"

Weber said, "Major, I—"

Dieter fired into the air. The report of the pistol crashed around the cathedral vaults, drowning Weber's giveaway words. "Silence!" Dieter shouted in German. Weber looked scared and shut up.

Dieter poked the nose of the pistol hard into the face of one of the Gestapo men. Reverting to French, he screamed, "Off! Off! Get off him!"

With terrified faces the two men stood up and backed away.

Dieter looked at Stéphanie. Calling her by Mademoiselle Lemas's name, he shouted, "Jeanne! Go! Get away!" Stéphanie began to run. She circled widely around the Gestapo men and dashed for the west door.

The agent was scrambling to his feet. "Go with her! Go with her!" Dieter shouted at him, pointing. The man grabbed his suitcase and ran, vaulting over the backs of the wooden choir stalls and haring down the middle of the nave.

Weber and his three associates looked bemused. "Lie facedown!" Dieter ordered them. As they obeyed, he backed away, still threatening them with the gun. Then he turned and ran after Stéphanie and the agent.

As the other two fled through the doorway, Dieter stopped and spoke to Hans, who stood near the back of the church, looking stolid. "Talk to those damn fools," Dieter said breathlessly. "Explain what we're doing and make sure they don't follow us." He holstered the pistol and ran outside.

The engine of the Simca was turning over. Dieter pushed the agent into the cramped backseat and got into the front passenger seat. Stéphanie stamped on the pedal and the little car shot out of the square like a champagne cork.

As they raced along the street, Dieter

turned and looked through the back window. "No one following," he said. "Slow down. We don't want to get stopped by a gendarme."

The agent said in French, "I'm Helicopter. What the hell happened in there?"

Dieter realized that "Helicopter" must be a code name. He recalled that Gaston had told him Mademoiselle Lemas's code name. "This is Bourgeoise," he said, indicating Stéphanie. "And I'm Charenton," he improvised, thinking for some reason of the prison where the Marquis de Sade had been incarcerated. "Bourgeoise has become suspicious, in the last few days, that the cathedral rendezvous might be watched, so she asked me to come with her. I'm not part of the Bollinger circuit—Bourgeoise is a cutout."

"Yes, I understand that."

"Anyway, we now know the Gestapo had set a trap, and it's just fortunate that she had asked me to be there as backup for her."

"You were brilliant!" Helicopter said enthusiastically. "God, I was so scared, I thought I'd blown it on my first day."

You have, Dieter thought silently.

It seemed to Dieter that he might have saved the situation. Helicopter now firmly believed that Dieter was a member of the Resistance. Helicopter's French sounded perfect, but obviously he was not quite good enough to identify Dieter's slight accent. Was there anything else that might cause him to be suspicious, perhaps later when he thought things over? Dieter had stood up and said "No!" right at the start of the rumpus, but a plain "No" did not mean much, and anyway he did not think anyone had heard him. Willi Weber had shouted "Major" in German at Dieter, and Dieter had fired his weapon to drown out any further indiscretion. Had Helicopter heard that one word, did he know what it meant, and would he remember it later and puzzle over it? No, Dieter decided. If Helicopter had understood the word, he would have assumed Weber was addressing one of the other Gestapo men: they were all in plain clothes so could be any rank.

Helicopter would now trust Dieter in all things, being convinced Dieter had snatched him from the clutches of the Gestapo.

Others might not be quite so easy to fool.

The existence of a new Resistance member codenamed Charenton and recruited by Mademoiselle Lemas would have to be plausibly explained, both to London and to the leader of the Bollinger circuit, Michel Clairet. Both might ask questions and run checks. Dieter would just have to deal with them in due course. It was not possible to anticipate everything.

He allowed himself a moment of triumph. He was one step closer to his goal of crippling the Resistance in northern France. He had pulled it off despite the stupidity of the Gestapo. And it had been exhilarating.

The challenge now was to make maximum use of Helicopter's trust. The agent must continue to operate, believing himself unsuspected. That way he could lead Dieter to more agents, perhaps dozens more. But it was a subtle trick to pull off.

They arrived at the rue du Bois and Stéphanie drove into Mademoiselle Lemas's garage. They entered the house by the back door and sat in the kitchen. Stéphanie got a bottle of scotch from the cellar and poured them all a drink.

Dieter was desperately anxious to confirm that Helicopter had a radio. He said,

"You'd better send a message to London right away."

"I'm supposed to broadcast at eight p.m. and receive at eleven."

Dieter made a mental note. "But you need to tell them as soon as possible that the cathedral rendezvous is compromised. We don't want them to send any more men there. And there could be someone else on his way tonight."

"Oh, my God, yes," the young man said. "I'll use the emergency frequency."

"You can set up your wireless right here in the kitchen."

Helicopter lifted the heavy case onto the table and opened it.

Dieter hid a sigh of profound satisfaction. There it was.

The interior of the case was divided into four: two side compartments and, in the middle, one front and one back. Dieter could see immediately that the rear middle compartment contained the transmitter, with the Morse key in the lower right-hand corner, and the front middle was the receiver, with a socket for headphone connections. The right-side compartment was the power supply. The function of the left-side compartment became clear when the agent lifted the lid to reveal a selection of accessories and spare parts: a power lead, adaptors, aerial wire, connection cables, a headset, spare tubes, fuses, and a screwdriver.

It was a neat, compact set, Dieter thought admiringly; the kind of thing the Germans would have made, not at all what he would expect from the untidy British.

He already knew Helicopter's times for transmission and reception. Now he had to learn the frequencies used and—most important—the code.

Helicopter plugged a lead into the power socket. Dieter said, "I thought it was battery-operated."

"Battery or mains power. I believe the Gestapo's favorite trick, when they're trying to locate the source of an illicit radio transmission, is to switch off the town's electricity block by block until the broadcast is cut off."

Dieter nodded.

"Well, with this set, if you lose the house current, you just have to reverse this plug, and it switches to battery operation."

"Very good." Dieter would pass that on to the Gestapo, in case they did not already know.

Helicopter plugged the power lead into an electrical outlet, then took the aerial wire and asked Stéphanie to drape it over a tall cupboard. Dieter looked in the kitchen drawers and found a pencil and a scratch pad that Mademoiselle Lemas had probably used to make shopping lists. "You can use this to encode your message," he said helpfully.

"First I'd better figure out what to say." Helicopter scratched his head then began to write in English:

ARRIVED OK STOP CRYPT RENDEZ-VOUS UNSAFE STOP NABBED BY GESTAPO BUT GOT AWAY OVER

"I suppose that's it for now," he said.

Dieter said, "We should give them a new rendezvous for future incomers. Say the Café de la Gare next to the railway station."

Helicopter wrote it down.

He took from the case a silk handkerchief printed with a complex table showing letters in pairs. He also took out a pad of a dozen or so sheets of paper printed with five-letter nonsense words. Dieter recognized the makings of a one-time-pad encryption system. It was unbreakable—unless you had the pad.

Over the words of his message, Helicopter wrote the five-letter groups from the pad; then he used the letters he had written to select transpositions from the silk handkerchief. Over the first five letters of AR-RIVED he had written the first group from his one-time pad, which was BGKRU. The first letter, B, told him which column to use from the grid on the silk handkerchief. At the top of column B were the letters Ae. That told him to replace the A of ARRIVED with the letter e.

The code could not be broken in the usual way, because the next A would be represented not by e but by some other letter. In fact, any letter could stand for any other letter, and the only way to decrypt the message was by using the pad with the five-letter groups. Even if the codebreakers could get hold of a coded message and its plain-language original, they could not use them to read another message, because the next message would be encoded with a different sheet from the pad—which was why it was called a "one-time" pad. Each sheet was used once, then burned.

When he had encrypted his message, Helicopter flicked the on/off switch and turned a knob marked in English "Crystal Selector." Looking carefully, Dieter saw that the dial bore three faint markings in yellow wax crayon. Helicopter had mistrusted his memory and had marked his broadcast positions. The crystal he was using would be reserved for emergencies. Of the other two, one would be for transmission and the other for reception.

Finally he tuned in, and Dieter saw that the frequency dial was also marked with yellow crayon.

Before sending his message, he checked in with the receiving station by sending:

HLCP DXDX QTC1 QRK? K

Dieter frowned, figuring. The first group had to be the call sign "Helicopter." The next one, "DXDX," was a mystery. The number one at the end of "QTC1" suggested that this group meant something like: "I have one message to send you." The question mark at the end of "QRK?" made him think this asked if he was being received loud and clear. "K" meant "Over," he knew. That left the mysterious "DXDX."

He tried a guess. "Don't forget your security tag," he said.

"I haven't," Helicopter said.

That must be "DXDX," Dieter concluded.

Helicopter turned to "receive" and they all heard the Morse reply:

HLCP QRK QRV K

Once again, the first group was Helicopter's call sign. The second group, "QRK," had appeared in the original message. Without the question mark, it presumably meant "I am receiving you loud and clear." He was not sure about "QRV," but he guessed it must mean "Go ahead."

As Helicopter tapped out his message in Morse, Dieter watched, feeling elated. This was the spycatcher's dream: he had an agent in his hands and the agent did not know he had been captured.

When the message was sent, Helicopter shut down the radio quickly. Because the Gestapo used radio direction-finding equipment to track down spies, it was dangerous to operate a set for more than a few minutes.

In England, the message had to be transcribed, decoded, and passed to Helicopter's controller, who might have to consult with others before replying; all of which could take several hours, so Helicopter would wait until the appointed hour for a response.

Now Dieter had to separate him from the wireless set and, more importantly, from his coding materials. "I presume you want to contact the Bollinger circuit now," he said.

"Yes. London needs to know how much of it is left."

"We'll put you in touch with Monet, that's the code name of the leader." He looked at his wristwatch and suffered a moment of sheer panic: it was a standard-issue German Army officer's watch, and if Helicopter recognized it the game would be up. Trying to keep the tremor out of his voice, Dieter said, "We've got time, I'll drive you to his house."

"Is it far?" Helicopter said eagerly.

"Center of town."

Monet, whose real name was Michel Clairet, would not be at home. He was no longer using the house; Dieter had checked. The neighbors claimed to have no idea where he was. Dieter was not surprised. Monet had guessed that his name and address would be given away by one of his comrades under interrogation, and he had gone into hiding.

Helicopter began to close up the radio. Dieter said, "Does that battery need recharging from time to time?"

"Yes—in fact they tell us to plug it in at every opportunity, so that it's always fully charged."

"So why don't you leave it where it is for now? We can come back for it later, by which time it will be charged. If anyone should come in the meantime, Bourgeoise can hide it away in a few seconds."

"Good idea."

"Then let's go." Dieter led the way to the garage and backed the Simca Cinq out. Then he said, "Wait here a minute, I have to tell Bourgeoise something."

He went back into the house. Stéphanie was in the kitchen, staring at the suitcase radio on the kitchen table. Dieter took the one-time-pad and the silk handkerchief from the accessories compartment. "How long will it take you to copy these?" he said.

She made a face. "All those gibberish letters? At least an hour."

"Do it as fast as you can, but don't make any mistakes. I'll keep him out for an hour and a half."

He returned to the car and drove Helicopter into the city center.

Michel Clairet's home was a small, elegant town house near the cathedral. Dieter waited in the car while Helicopter went to the door. After a few minutes, the agent came back and said, "No answer."

"You can try again in the morning," Dieter said. "Meanwhile, I know a bar used by the Resistance." He knew no such thing. "Let's go there and see if I recognize anyone."

He parked near the station and picked a bar at random. The two of them sat drinking watery beer for an hour, then returned to the rue du Bois.

When they entered the kitchen, Stéphanie gave Dieter a slight nod. He took it to mean she had succeeded in copying everything. "Now," Dieter said to Helicopter, "you'd probably like a bath, having spent a night in the open. And you certainly should

shave. I'll show you your room, and Bourgeoise will run your bath."

"How kind you are."

Dieter put him in an attic room, the one
farthest from the bathroom. As soon as he
heard the man splashing in the bath, he
went into the room and searched his
clothes. Helicopter had a change of underwear and socks, all bearing the labels of
French shops. In his jacket pockets were
French cigarettes and matches, a handkerchief with a French label, and a wallet. In
the wallet was a lot of cash—half a million
francs, enough to buy a luxury car, if there
had been any new cars for sale. The identity
papers seemed impeccable, though they
had to be forgeries.

There was also a photograph.

Dieter stared at it in surprise. It showed
Flick Clairet. There was no mistake. It was
the woman he had seen in the square at
Sainte-Cécile. Finding it was a wonderful
piece of luck for Dieter—and a disaster for
her.

She was wearing a swimsuit that revealed
muscular legs and suntanned arms. Beneath the costume she had neat breasts, a
small waist, and delightfully rounded hips.

There was a glimmer of moisture, either water or perspiration, at her throat, and she was looking into the camera with a faint smile. Behind her and slightly out of focus, two young men in bathing trunks seemed about to dive into a river. The picture had obviously been taken at an innocent swimming party. But her seminakedness, the wetness at her throat, and the slight smile combined to make a picture that seemed sexually charged. Had it not been for the boys in the background, she might have been about to take the swimsuit off and reveal her body to the person behind the camera. That was how a woman smiled at her man when she wanted him to make love to her, Dieter thought. He could see why a young fellow would treasure the photo.

Agents were not supposed to carry photos with them into enemy territory—for very good reasons. Helicopter's passion for Flick Clairet might destroy her, and much of the French Resistance too.

Dieter slipped the photo into his pocket and left the room. All in all, he thought, he had done a very good day's work.

CHAPTER 21

Paul Chancellor spent the day fighting the military bureaucracy—persuading, threatening, pleading, cajoling, and as a last resort using the name of Monty—and, in the end, he got a plane for the team's parachute training tomorrow.

When he caught the train back to Hampshire, he found he was eager to see Flick again. He liked her a lot. She was smart, tough, and a pleasure to look at. He wished to hell she was single.

On the train he read the war news in the paper. The long lull on the eastern front had been broken, yesterday, by a surprisingly powerful German attack in Rumania. The continuing resilience of the Germans was formidable. They were in retreat everywhere, but they kept fighting back.

The train was delayed, and he missed six o'clock dinner at the Finishing School. After dinner there was always another lecture, then at nine the students were free to relax for an hour or so before bed. Paul found most of the team gathered in the drawing room of the house, which had a bookcase, a cupboard full of games, a wireless set, and a half-size billiards table. He sat on the sofa beside Flick and said quietly, "How did it go today?"

"Better than we had a right to expect," she said. "But everything is so compressed. I don't know how much they're going to remember when they're in the field."

"I guess anything is better than nothing."

Percy Thwaite and Jelly were playing poker for pennies. Jelly was a real character, Paul thought. How could a professional safebreaker consider herself a respectable English lady? "How was Jelly?" he asked Flick.

"Not bad. She has more difficulty than the others with the physical training but, my goodness, she just grit her teeth and got on with it, and in the end she did everything the youngsters did." Flick paused and frowned.

Paul said, "What?"

"Her hostility to Greta is a problem."

"It's not surprising that an Englishwoman should hate Germans."

"It's illogical, though—Greta has suffered more from the Nazis than Jelly has."

"Jelly doesn't know that."

"She knows that Greta's prepared to fight against the Nazis."

"People aren't logical about these things."

"Too bloody right."

Greta herself was talking to Denise. Or rather, Paul thought, Denise was talking and Greta was listening. "My stepbrother, Lord Foules, pilots fighter-bombers," he heard her say in her half-swallowed aristocratic accent. "He's been training to fly support missions for the invasion troops."

Paul frowned. "Did you hear that?" he asked Flick.

"Yes. Either she's making it up, or she's being dangerously indiscreet."

He studied Denise. She was a rawboned girl who always looked as if she had just been insulted. He did not think she was fantasizing. "She doesn't seem the imaginative type," he said.

"I agree. I think she's giving away real secrets."

"I'd better arrange a little test tomorrow."

"Okay."

Paul wanted to get Flick to himself so that they could talk more freely. "Let's take a stroll around the garden," he said.

They stepped outside. The air was warm and there was an hour of daylight left. The house had a large garden with several acres of lawn dotted with trees. Maude and Diana were sitting on a bench under a copper beech. Maude had flirted with Paul at first, but he had given her no encouragement, and she seemed to have given up. Now she was listening avidly to something Diana was saying, looking into Diana's face with an attitude almost of adoration. "I wonder what Diana's saying?" Paul said. "She's got Maude fascinated."

"Maude likes to hear about the places she's been," Flick said. "The fashion shows, the balls, the ocean liners."

Paul recalled that Maude had surprised him by asking whether the mission would take them to Paris. "Maybe she wanted to go to America with me," he said.

"I noticed her making a play for you," Flick said. "She's pretty."

"Not my type, though."

"Why not?"

"Candidly? She's not smart enough."

"Good," Flick said. "I'm glad."

He raised an eyebrow at her. "Why?"

"I would have thought less of you otherwise."

He thought this was a little condescending. "I'm glad to have your approval," he said.

"Don't be ironic," she reprimanded him. "I was paying you a compliment."

He grinned. He could not help liking her, even when she was being high-handed. "Then I'll quit while I'm ahead," he said.

They passed close to the two women, and heard Diana say, "So the contessa said, 'Keep your painted claws off my husband,' then poured a glass of champagne over Jennifer's head, whereupon Jennifer pulled the contessa's hair—and it came off in her hand, because it was a wig!"

Maude laughed. "I wish I'd been there!"

Paul said to Flick, "They all seem to be making friends."

"I'm pleased. I need them to work as a team."

The garden merged gradually with the forest, and they found themselves walking through woodland. It was only half light under the canopy of leaves. "Why is it called the New Forest?" Paul said. "It looks old."

"Do you still expect English names to be logical?"

He laughed. "I guess I don't."

They walked in silence for a while. Paul felt quite romantic. He wanted to kiss her, but she was wearing a wedding ring.

"When I was four years old, I met the King," Flick said.

"The present king?"

"No, his father, George V. He came to Somersholme. I was kept out of his way, of course, but he wandered into the kitchen garden on Sunday morning and saw me. He said, 'Good morning, little girl, are you ready for church?' He was a small man, but he had a booming voice."

"What did you say?"

"I said, 'Who are you?' He replied, 'I'm the King.' And then, according to family legend, I said, 'You can't be, you're not big enough.' Fortunately, he laughed."

"Even as a child, you had no respect for authority."

"So it seems."

Paul heard a low moan. Frowning, he looked toward the sound and saw Ruby Romain with Jim Cardwell, the firearms instructor. Ruby had her back to a tree and Jim was embracing her. They were kissing passionately. Ruby moaned again.

They were not just embracing, Paul realized, and he felt both embarrassed and aroused. Jim's hands were busy inside Ruby's blouse. Her skirt was up around her waist. Paul could see all of one brown leg and a thick patch of dark hair at her groin. The other leg was raised and bent at the knee, and Ruby's foot rested high on Jim's hip. The movement they were making together was unmistakable.

Paul looked at Flick. She had seen the same thing. She stared for a moment, her expression showing shock and something else. Then she turned quickly away. Paul followed suit, and they went back the way they had come, walking as quietly as they could.

When they were out of earshot, he said, "I'm terribly sorry about that."

"Not your fault," she said.

"Still, I'm sorry I led you that way."

"I really don't mind. I've never seen anyone . . . doing that. It was rather sweet."

"Sweet?" It was not the word he would have chosen. "You know, you're kind of unpredictable."

"Have you only just noticed?"

"Don't be ironic, I was paying you a compliment," he said, repeating her own words.

She laughed. "Then I'll quit while I'm ahead."

They emerged from the woods. Daylight was fading fast, and the blackout curtains were drawn in the house. Maude and Diana had gone from their seat under the copper beech. "Let's sit here for a minute," Paul said. He was in no hurry to go inside.

Flick complied without speaking.

He sat sideways, looking at her. She bore his scrutiny without comment, but she was thoughtful. He took her hand and stroked her fingers. She looked at him, her face unreadable, but she did not pull away her hand. He said, "I know I shouldn't, but I really want to kiss you." She made no reply but continued to look at him with that enigmatic expression, half amused and half sad. He took silence for assent, and kissed her.

Her mouth was soft and moist. He closed his eyes, concentrating on the sensation. To his surprise, her lips parted, and he felt the tip of her tongue. He opened his mouth.

He put his arms around her and pulled her to him, but she slipped out of his embrace and stood up. "Enough," she said. She turned away and walked toward the house.

He watched her go in the fading light. Her small, neat body suddenly seemed the most desirable thing in the world.

When she had disappeared inside, he followed. In the drawing room, Diana sat alone, smoking a cigarette, looking thoughtful. On impulse, Paul sat close to her and said, "You've known Flick since you were kids."

Diana smiled with surprising warmth. "She's adorable, isn't she?"

Paul did not want to give away too much of what was in his heart. "I like her a lot, and I wish I knew more about her."

"She always yearned for adventure," Diana said. "She loved those long trips we made to France every February. We would spend a night in Paris, then take the Blue Train all the way to Nice. One winter, my father decided to go to Morocco. I think it was the best time of Flick's life. She learned a few words of Arabic and talked to the merchants in the souks. We used to read the memoirs of those doughty Victorian lady explorers who traveled the Middle East dressed as men."

"She got on well with your father?"

"Better than I did."

"What's her husband like?"

"All Flick's men are slightly exotic. At Oxford, her best friend was a Nepalese boy, Rajendra, which caused great consternation in the senior common room at St. Hilda's, I can tell you, although I'm not sure she ever, you know, misbehaved with him. A boy called Charlie Standish was desperately in love with her, but he was just too boring for her. She fell for Michel because he's charming and foreign and clever, which is what she likes."

"Exotic," Paul repeated.

Diana laughed. "Don't worry, you'll do. You're American, you've only got one and a half ears, and you're as smart as a whip. You're in with a chance, at least."

Paul stood up. The conversation was taking an uncomfortably intimate turn. "I'll take that as a compliment," he said with a smile. "Goodnight."

On his way upstairs, he passed Flick's room. There was a light under the door.

He put on his pyjamas and got into bed, but he lay awake. He was too excited and happy to sleep. He relived the kiss again and again. He wished he and Flick could be like Ruby and Jim, and give in to their desires shamelessly. Why not? he thought. Why the hell not?

The house fell quiet.

A few minutes after midnight, Paul got up. He went along the corridor to Flick's room. He tapped gently on the door and stepped inside.

"Hello," she said quietly.

"It's me."

"I know."

She lay on her back in the single bed, her head propped up on two pillows. The curtains were drawn back, and moonlight came in at the small window. He could see, quite clearly, the straight line of her nose and the chisel chin that he had once thought not to be pretty. Now they seemed angelic.

He knelt by the bed.

"The answer is no," she said.

He took her hand and kissed her palm. "Please," he said.

"No."

He leaned over her to kiss her, but she turned her head away.

"Just a kiss?" he said.

"If I kiss you, I'll be lost."

That pleased him. It told him she was feeling the same way he did. He kissed her hair, then her forehead and her cheek, but she kept her face averted. He kissed her shoulder through the cotton of her night-dress, then brushed his lips over her breast. "You want to," he said.

"Out," she commanded.

"Don't say that."

She turned to him. He bent his face to kiss her, but she put a finger on his lips as if to hush him. "Go," she said. "I mean it."

He looked at her lovely face in the moon-light. Her expression was set with determi-nation. Although he hardly knew her, he understood that her will could not be over-ridden. Reluctantly, he stood up.

He gave it one more try. "Look, let's—"

"No more talk. Go."

He turned away and left the room.

THE FIFTH DAY
Thursday, June 1, 1944

CHAPTER 22

Dieter slept a few hours at the Hotel Frankfort and got up at two a.m. He was alone: Stéphanie was at the house in the rue du Bois with the British agent Helicopter. Some time this morning, Helicopter would go in search of the head of the Bollinger circuit, and Dieter had to follow him. He knew Helicopter would start at Michel Clairet's house, so he had decided to put a surveillance team there by first light.

He drove to Sainte-Cécile in the early hours, winding through the moonlit vineyards in his big car, and parked in front of the château. He went first to the photo lab in the basement. There was no one in the darkroom, but his prints were there, pegged on a line to dry like laundry. He had asked for two copies of Helicopter's picture of Flick

Clairet. He took them off the line and studied one, remembering the way she had run through gunfire to rescue her husband. He tried to see some of that steely nerve in the carefree expression of the pretty girl in the swimsuit, but there was no sign of it. No doubt it had come with war.

He pocketed the negative and picked up the original photo, which would have to be returned surreptitiously to Helicopter. He found an envelope and a sheet of plain paper, thought for a moment, and wrote:

My darling,
While Helicopter is shaving, please put this in his inside jacket pocket, so that it will look as if it slipped out of his wallet. Thank you.
D.

He put the note and the picture in the envelope, sealed it, and wrote: "Mlle. Lemas" on the front. He would drop it off later.

He passed the cells and looked through a judas at Marie, the girl who had surprised him yesterday by showing up at the house in the rue du Bois with food for Mademoiselle Lemas's "guests." She lay on a bloodstained sheet, staring at the wall with a wide-eyed gaze of horror, emitting a constant low moan like a piece of machinery that was broken but not switched off.

Dieter had interrogated Marie last night. She had had no useful information. She had claimed she knew no one in the Resistance, only Mademoiselle Lemas. Dieter had been inclined to believe her, but he had let Sergeant Becker torture her just in case. However, she had not changed her story, and he now felt confident that her disappearance would not alert the Resistance to the impostor in the rue du Bois.

He suffered a moment of depression as he stared at the wrecked body. He remembered her coming up the path yesterday with her bicycle, a picture of vigorous health. She had been a happy girl, albeit foolish. She had made a simple mistake, and now her life was coming to a ghastly end. She deserved her fate, of course; she had helped terrorists. All the same, it was horrible to contemplate.

He put her out of his mind and went up the stairs. On the ground floor, the night shift telephonists were at their switchboards. Above that, on what had once been a floor of impossibly grand bedrooms, were the Gestapo offices.

Dieter had not seen Weber since the fiasco in the cathedral and assumed the man was licking his wounds somewhere. However, he had spoken to Weber's deputy and asked for four Gestapo men to be here in plain clothes at three a.m. ready for a day's surveillance. Dieter had also ordered Lieutenant Hesse to be here. Now he pulled aside a blackout blind and looked out. Moonlight illuminated the parking lot, and he could see Hans walking across the yard, but there was no sign of anyone else.

He went to Weber's office and was surprised to find him there alone, behind his desk, pretending to work on some papers by the light of a green-shaded lamp. "Where are the men I asked for?" Dieter said.

Weber stood up. "You pulled a gun on me yesterday," he said. "What the devil do you mean by threatening an officer?"

Dieter had not expected this. Weber was being aggressive about an incident in which he had made a fool of himself. Was it possible that he did not understand what a dreadful mistake he had made? "It was your own damn fault, you idiot," Dieter said in exasperation. "I didn't want that man arrested."

"You can be court-martialed for what you did."

Dieter was about to ridicule the idea, then he stopped himself. It was true, he realized. He had simply done what was necessary to rescue the situation; but it was not impossible, in the bureaucratic Third Reich, for an officer to be arraigned for using his initiative. His heart sank, and he had to feign confidence. "Go ahead, report me, I think I can justify myself in front of a tribunal."

"You actually fired your gun!"

Dieter could not resist saying, "I suppose that's something you haven't often witnessed, in your military career."

Weber flushed. He had never seen action. "Guns should be used against the enemy, not fellow officers."

"I fired into the air. I'm sorry if I frightened you. You were in the process of ruining a first-class counterintelligence coup. Don't you think a military court would take that into account? What orders were *you* following? You were the one who showed lack of discipline."

"I arrested a British terrorist spy."

"And what's the point of that? He's just one. They have plenty more. But, left to go free, he will lead us to others—perhaps many others. Your insubordination would have destroyed that chance. Fortunately for you, I saved you from a ghastly error."

Weber looked sly. "Certain people in authority would find it highly suspicious that you're so keen to free an Allied agent."

Dieter sighed. "Don't be stupid. I'm not some wretched Jewish shopkeeper, to be frightened by the threat of malicious gossip. You can't pretend I'm a traitor, no one will believe you. Now, where are my men?"

"The spy must be arrested immediately."

"No, he mustn't, and if you try I'll shoot you. Where are the men?"

"I refuse to assign much-needed men to such an irresponsible task."

"You *refuse?*"

"Yes."

Dieter stared at him. He had not thought Weber brave enough or foolish enough to do this. "What do you imagine will happen to you when the Field Marshal hears about this?"

Weber looked scared but defiant. "I am

not in the army," he said. "This is the Gestapo."

Unfortunately, he was right, Dieter
thought despondently. It was all very well
for Walter Goedel to order Dieter to use Gestapo personnel instead of taking much-
needed fighting troops from the coast, but
the Gestapo were not obliged to take orders
from Dieter. The name of Rommel had frightened Weber for a while, but the effect had
worn off.

And now Dieter was left with no staff but
Lieutenant Hesse. Could he and Hans manage the shadowing of Helicopter without assistance? It would be difficult, but there was
no alternative.

He tried one more threat. "Are you sure
you're willing to bear the consequences of
this refusal, Willi? You're going to get into
the most dreadful trouble."

"On the contrary, I think it is you who are
in trouble."

Dieter shook his head in despair. There
was no more to be said. He had already
spent too much time arguing with this idiot.
He went out.

He met Hans in the hall and explained the
situation. They went to the back of the

château, where the engineering section was housed in the former servants' quarters. Last night Hans had arranged to borrow a PTT van and a moped, the kind of motorized bicycle whose small engine was started by pedaling.

Dieter wondered whether Weber might have found out about the vehicles and ordered the engineers not to lend them. He hoped not: dawn was due in half an hour, and he did not have time for more arguments. But there was no trouble. Dieter and Hans put on overalls and drove away, with the moped in the back of the van.

They went to Reims and drove along the rue du Bois. They parked around the corner and Hans walked back, in the faint light of dawn, and put the envelope containing the photo of Flick into the letter box. Helicopter's bedroom was at the back, so there was no serious risk that he might see Hans, and recognize him later.

The sun was rising when they arrived outside Michel Clairet's house in the center of town. Hans parked a hundred meters down the road and opened a PTT manhole. He pretended to be working while watching the house. It was a busy street with numerous parked vehicles, so the van was not conspicuous.

Dieter stayed in the van, keeping out of sight, brooding over the row with Weber. The man was stupid, but he had a point. Dieter was taking a dangerous risk. Helicopter could give him the slip and disappear. Then Dieter would have lost the thread. The safe and easy course would be to torture Helicopter. But though letting him go was risky, it promised rich rewards. If things went right, Helicopter could be solid gold. When Dieter thought of the triumph that hung just beyond his grasp, he lusted for it with a passion that made his pulse race.

On the other hand, if things went wrong, Weber would make the most of it. He would tell everyone how he had opposed Dieter's risky plan. But Dieter would not allow himself to worry about such bureaucratic point-scoring. Men such as Weber, who played those games, were the most contemptible people on earth.

The town came slowly to life. First to appear were the women walking to the bakery opposite Michel's house. The shop was closed, but they stood patiently outside, waiting and talking. Bread was rationed, but

Dieter guessed it sometimes ran out anyway, so dutiful housewives shopped early to make sure they got their share. When eventually the doors opened, they all tried to get in at once—unlike German housewives, who would have formed an orderly queue, Dieter thought with a feeling of superiority. When he saw them come out with their loaves, he wished he had eaten some breakfast.

After that, the working men appeared in their boots and berets, each carrying a bag or cheap fiber case containing his lunch. The children were just beginning to set out for school when Helicopter appeared, pedaling the bicycle that had belonged to Marie. Dieter sat upright. In the bicycle's basket was a rectangular object covered with a rag: the suitcase radio, Dieter guessed.

Hans put his head up out of the manhole and watched.

Helicopter went to Michel's door and knocked. There was no reply, of course. He stood on the step for a while, then looked in at the windows, then walked up and down the street looking for a back entrance. There was none, Dieter knew.

Dieter had suggested to Helicopter what

to do next. "Go to the bar along the street, Chez Régis. Order coffee and rolls, and wait." Dieter's hope was that the Resistance might be watching Michel's house, alert for an emissary from London. He did not expect full-time surveillance, but perhaps a sympathetic neighbor might have agreed to keep an eye on the place. Helicopter's evident guilelessness would reassure such a watcher. Anyone could tell, just by the way he walked around, that he was not a Gestapo man or an agent of the Milice, the French security police. Dieter felt sure that somehow the Resistance would be alerted, and before too long someone would show up and speak to Helicopter—and *that* person might lead Dieter to the heart of the Resistance.

A minute later Helicopter did as Dieter had suggested. He wheeled his bicycle along the street to the bar and sat at a pavement table, apparently enjoying the sunshine. He got a cup of coffee. It had to be ersatz, made with roasted grain, but he drank it with apparent relish.

After twenty minutes or so he got another coffee and a newspaper from inside. He began to read the paper thoroughly. He had a patient air, as if he was prepared to wait all day. That was good.

The morning wore on. Dieter began to wonder whether this was going to work. Maybe the Bollinger circuit had been so decimated by the slaughter at Sainte-Cécile that it was no longer operational, and there was no one left to perform even the most essential tasks. It would be a profound disappointment if Helicopter did not lead him to other terrorists. And it would please Weber no end.

The time approached when Helicopter would have to order lunch to justify continuing to use the table. A waiter came out and spoke to him, then brought him a pastis. That, too, would be ersatz, made with a synthetic substitute for aniseed, but all the same Dieter licked his lips: he would have liked a drink.

Another customer sat down at the table next to Helicopter's. There were five tables, and it would have been natural to take one farther away. Dieter's hopes rose. The newcomer was a long-limbed man in his thirties. He wore a blue chambray shirt and navy canvas trousers, but to Dieter's intuition he did not have the air of a working man. He was something else, perhaps an artist who affected a proletarian look. He sat back in his chair and crossed his legs, resting his right ankle on his left knee, and the pose struck Dieter as familiar. Had he seen this man before?

The waiter came out and the customer ordered something. For a minute or so nothing happened. Was the man covertly studying Helicopter? Or just waiting for his drink? The waiter brought a glass of pale beer on a tray. The man took a long pull and wiped his mouth with a satisfied air. Dieter began to think gloomily that he was just a man with a thirst. But at the same time he felt he had seen that mouth-wiping gesture before.

Then the newcomer spoke to Helicopter.

Dieter tensed. Could this be what he had been waiting for?

They exchanged a few casual words. Even at this distance, Dieter sensed that the newcomer had an engaging personality: Helicopter was smiling and talking with enthusiasm. After a few moments, Helicopter pointed to Michel's house, and Dieter guessed he was asking where the owner might be found. The other man gave a typical French shrug, and Dieter could imagine him saying, "Me, I don't know." But Helicopter seemed to persist.

The newcomer drained his beer glass, and Dieter had a flash of recollection. He suddenly knew exactly who this man was, and the realization so startled him that he jumped in his seat. He had seen the man in the square at Sainte-Cécile, at another café table, sitting with Flick Clairet, just before the skirmish—for this was her husband, Michel himself.

"Yes!" Dieter said, and he thumped the dashboard with his fist in satisfaction. His strategy had been proved right—Helicopter had led him to the heart of the local Resistance.

But he had not been expecting this degree of success. He had thought a messenger might come, and the messenger might take Helicopter—and Dieter—to Michel. Now Dieter had a dilemma. Michel was a very big prize. Should Dieter arrest him right away? Or follow him, in the hope of catching even bigger fish?

Hans replaced the manhole cover and got into the van. "Contact, sir?"

"Yes."

"What next?"

Dieter did not know what to do next—arrest Michel, or follow him?

Michel stood up, and Helicopter did the same.

Dieter decided to follow them.

"What shall I do?" Hans said anxiously.

"Get out the bike, quick."

Hans opened the back doors of the van and took out the moped.

The two men put money on the café tables and moved away. Dieter saw that Michel walked with a limp, and recalled that he had taken a bullet during the skirmish.

He said to Hans, "You follow them, I'll follow you." He started the engine of the van.

Hans climbed on the moped and started pedaling, which fired the engine. He drove slowly along the street, keeping a hundred meters behind his quarry. Dieter followed Hans.

Michel and Helicopter turned a corner. Following a minute later, Dieter saw that they had stopped to look in a shop window. It was a pharmacy. They were not shopping for medicines, of course: this was a precaution against surveillance. As Dieter drove by, they turned and headed back the way they had come. They would be watching for a vehicle that made a U-turn, so Dieter could not pursue them. However, he saw Hans pull behind a truck and turn back, remaining on the far side of the street but keeping the two men in sight.

Dieter went around the block and caught up with them again. Michel and Helicopter were approaching the railway station, with Hans still following.

Dieter asked himself whether they knew they were being followed. The trick at the pharmacy might indicate that they were suspicious. He did not think they had noticed the PTT van, for he had been out of their sight most of the time, but they could have spotted the moped. Most likely, Dieter thought, the reversal of direction was a precaution taken routinely by Michel, who was presumably an experienced undercover operator.

The two men crossed the gardens in front of the station. There were no flowers in the beds, but a few trees were blossoming in defiance of the war. The station was a solidly classical building with pilasters and pediments, heavyweight and overdecorated, no doubt like the nineteenth-century businessmen who had built it.

What would Dieter do if Michel and Helicopter caught a train? It was too risky for Dieter to get on the same train. Helicopter would certainly recognize him, and it was even possible that Michel might remember him from the square at Sainte-Cécile. No, Hans would have to board the train, and Dieter would follow by road.

They entered the station through one of three classical arches. Hans left his moped and followed them inside. Dieter pulled up and did the same. If the two men went to the booking office, he would tell Hans to stand behind them in the queue and buy a ticket to the same destination.

They were not at the ticket window. Dieter entered the station just in time to see Hans go down a flight of steps to the tunnel beneath the lines that connected the platforms. Perhaps Michel had bought tickets in advance, Dieter thought. That was not a problem. Hans would just get on the train without a ticket.

On either side of the tunnel, steps led up to the platforms. Dieter followed Hans past all the platform entrances. Sensing danger, he quickened his pace as he mounted the stairs to the station's rear entrance. He

caught up with Hans and they emerged together into the rue de Courcelles.

Several of the buildings had been
bombed recently, but cars were parked on
those stretches of the road that were clear
of rubble. Dieter scanned the street, fear
leaping in his chest. A hundred meters away,
Michel and Helicopter were jumping into a
black car. Dieter and Hans would never
catch them. Dieter put his hand on his gun,
but the range was too great for a pistol. The
car pulled away. It was a black Renault
Monaquatre, one of the commonest cars in
France. Dieter could not read its license
plate. It tore off along the street and turned
a corner.

Dieter cursed. It was a simple ploy but
infallible. By entering the tunnel, they had
forced their pursuers to abandon their vehicles; then they had a car waiting at the other
side, enabling them to escape. They might
not even have detected their shadows: like
the change of direction outside the pharmacy, the tunnel trick had probably been a
routine precaution.

Dieter sank into gloom. He had gambled
and lost. Weber would be overjoyed.

"What do we do now?" said Hans.

"Go back to Sainte-Cécile."

They returned to the van, put the moped in the back, and drove to headquarters.

Dieter had just one ray of hope. He knew Helicopter's times for radio contact, and the frequencies assigned to him. That information might yet be used to recapture him. The Gestapo had a sophisticated system, developed and refined throughout the war, for detecting illicit broadcasts and following them to their source. Many Allied agents had been captured that way. As British training improved, so the wireless operators had adopted better security precautions, always broadcasting from a different location, never staying on air longer than fifteen minutes; but careless ones could still be caught.

Would the British suspect that Helicopter had been found out? Helicopter would by now be giving Michel a full account of his adventures. Michel would question him closely about the arrest in the cathedral and subsequent escape. He would be particularly interested in the newcomer codenamed Charenton. However, he would have no reason to suspect that Mademoiselle Lemas was not who she claimed to be. Michel had never met her, so he would not be alerted even if Helicopter happened to mention that she was an attractive young redhead rather than a middle-aged spinster. And Helicopter had no idea that his one-time pad and his silk handkerchief had been meticulously copied out by Stéphanie, or that his frequencies had been noted—from the yellow wax crayon marks on the dials—by Dieter.

Perhaps, Dieter began to think, all was not yet lost.

When they got back to the château, Dieter ran into Weber in the hallway. Weber looked hard at him and said, "Have you lost him?"

Jackals can smell blood, Dieter thought. "Yes," he admitted. It was beneath his dignity to lie to Weber.

"Ha!" Weber was triumphant. "You should leave such work to the experts."

"Very well, then I shall," Dieter said. Weber looked surprised. Dieter went on, "He's due to broadcast to England at eight o'clock tonight. Here's your chance to prove your expertise. Show how good you are. Track him down."

CHAPTER 23

The Fisherman's Rest was a big pub that stood on the estuary shore like a fort, with chimneys for gun turrets and smoked-glass windows instead of observation slits. A fading sign in its front garden warned customers to stay off the beach, which had been mined back in 1940 in anticipation of a German invasion.

Since SOE had moved into the neighborhood, the pub had been busy every night; its lights blazing behind the blackout curtains, its piano loud, its bars crowded and spilling over into the garden on warm summer evenings. The singing was raucous, the drinking was heavy, and the canoodling was kept only just within the bounds of decency. An atmosphere of abandon prevailed, for everyone knew that some of the youngsters who were laughing uproariously at the bar tonight would embark tomorrow on missions from which they might never return.

Flick and Paul took their team to the pub at the end of their two-day training course. The girls dressed up for the outing. Maude was prettier than ever in a pink summer frock. Ruby would never be pretty, but she looked sultry in a black cocktail dress she had borrowed from somewhere. Lady Denise had on an oyster-colored silk dress that looked as if it had cost a fortune, though it did nothing for her bony figure. Greta wore one of her stage outfits, a cocktail dress and red shoes. Even Diana was wearing a smart skirt instead of her usual country corduroys and, to Flick's astonishment, had put on a smear of lipstick.

The team had been given the code name Jackdaws. They were going to parachute in near Reims, and Flick remembered the legend of the Jackdaw of Reims, the bird that stole the bishop's ring. "The monks couldn't figure out who had taken it, so the bishop cursed the unknown thief," she explained to Paul as they both sipped scotch, hers with water and his on the rocks. "Next thing they knew, the jackdaw appeared all bedraggled, and they realized he was suffering from the effects of the curse, and must be the culprit. I learned the whole thing at school:

> *The day was gone*
> *The night came on*
> *The monks and the friars, they*
> *   searched till dawn*
> *When the sacristan saw*
> *On crumpled claw*
> *Come limping a poor little lame*
> *   jackdaw*
> *No longer gay*
> *As on yesterday*
> *His feathers all seemed to be turned*
> *   the wrong way*
> *His pinions drooped, he could hardly*
> *   stand*
> *His head was as bald as the palm of*
> *   your hand*
> *His eye so dim*
> *So wasted each limb*
> *That, heedless of grammar, they all*
> *   cried: "That's him!"*

"Sure enough, they found the ring in his nest."

Paul nodded, smiling. Flick knew he

would have nodded and smiled in exactly the same way if she had been speaking Icelandic. He did not care what she said, he just wanted to watch her. She did not have vast experience, but she could tell when a man was in love, and Paul was in love with her.

She had got through the day on autopilot. Last night's kisses had shocked and thrilled her. She told herself that she did not want to have an illicit affair, she wanted to win back the love of her faithless husband. But Paul's passion had upended her priorities. She asked herself angrily why she should stand in line for Michel's affections when a man such as Paul was ready to throw himself at her feet. She had very nearly let him into her bed—in fact, she wished he had been less of a gentleman, for if he had ignored her refusal, and climbed between the sheets, she might have given in.

At other moments she was ashamed that she had even kissed him. It was frightfully common: all over England, girls were forgetting about husbands and boyfriends on the front line and falling in love with visiting American servicemen. Was she as bad as those empty-headed shop assistants who went to bed with their Yanks just because they talked like movie stars?

Worst of all, her feelings for Paul threatened to distract her from the job. She held in her hands the lives of six people, plus a crucial element in the invasion plan, and she really did not need to be thinking about whether his eyes were hazel or green. He was no matinée idol anyway, with his big chin and his shot-off ear, although there was a certain charm to his face—

"What are you thinking?" he said.

She realized she must have been staring at him. "Wondering whether we can pull this off," she lied.

"We can, with a little luck."

"I've been lucky so far."

Maude sat herself next to Paul. "Speaking of luck," she said, batting her eyelashes, "can I have one of your cigarettes?"

"Help yourself." He pushed the Lucky Strike pack along the table.

She put a cigarette between her lips and he lit it. Flick glanced across to the bar and caught an irritated look from Diana. Maude and Diana had become great friends, and Diana had never been good at sharing. So why was Maude flirting with Paul? To annoy

Diana, perhaps. It was a good thing Paul was not coming to France, Flick thought: he could not help being a disruptive influence in a group of young women.

She looked around the room. Jelly and Percy were playing a gambling game called Spoof, which involved guessing how many coins the other player held in a closed fist. Percy was buying round after round of drinks. This was deliberate. Flick needed to know what the Jackdaws were like under the influence of booze. If any of them became rowdy, indiscreet, or aggressive, she would have to take precautions once they were in the field. She was most worried about Denise, who even now was sitting in a corner talking animatedly to a man in captain's uniform.

Ruby was drinking steadily, too, but Flick trusted her. She was a curious mixture: she could barely read or write, and had been hopeless in classes on map reading and encryption, but nevertheless she was the brightest and most intuitive of the group. Ruby gave Greta a hard look now and again, and she may have guessed that Greta was a man, but to her credit she had said nothing.

Ruby was sitting at the bar with Jim Cardwell, the firearms instructor, talking to the barmaid but at the same time discreetly stroking the inside of Jim's thigh with a small brown hand. They were having a whirlwind romance. They kept disappearing. During the morning coffee break, the half-hour rest period after lunch, the afternoon tea time, or at any opportunity, they would sneak off for a few minutes. Jim looked as if he had jumped out of a plane and had not yet opened his parachute. His face wore a permanent expression of bemused delight. Ruby was no beauty, with her hooked nose and turned-up chin, but she was obviously a sex bomb, and Jim was reeling from the explosion. Flick almost felt jealous. Not that Jim was her type—all the men she had ever fallen for were intellectuals, or at least very bright—but she envied Ruby's lustful happiness.

Greta was leaning on the piano with some pink cocktail in her hand, talking to three men who looked to be local residents rather than Finishing School types. It seemed they had got over the shock of her German accent—no doubt she had told the story of her Liverpudlian father—and now she held them enthralled with tales about Hamburg nightclubs. Flick could see they had no suspicions about Greta's gender: they were treating her like an exotic but attractive woman, buying her drinks and lighting her cigarettes and laughing in a pleased way when she touched them.

As Flick watched, one of the men sat at the piano, played some chords, and looked up at Greta expectantly. The bar went quiet, and Greta launched into "Kitchen Man":

How that boy can open clams
No one else can touch my hams

The audience quickly realized that every line was a sexual innuendo, and the laughter was uproarious. When Greta finished, she kissed the pianist on the lips, and he looked thrilled.

Maude left Paul and returned to Diana at the bar. The captain who had been talking to Denise now came over and said to Paul, "She told me everything, sir."

Flick nodded, disappointed but not surprised.

Paul asked him, "What did she say?"

"That she's going in tomorrow night to

blow up a railway tunnel at Marles, near Reims."

It was the cover story, but Denise thought it was the truth, and she had revealed it to a stranger. Flick was furious.

"Thank you," Paul said.

"I'm sorry." The captain shrugged.

Flick said, "Better to find out now than later."

"Do you want to tell her, sir, or shall I deal with it?"

"I'll talk to her first," Paul replied. "Just wait outside for her, if you wouldn't mind."

"Yes, sir."

The captain left the pub, and Paul beckoned Denise.

"He left suddenly," Denise said. "Rather bad behavior, I thought." She obviously felt slighted. "He's an explosives instructor."

"No, he's not," Paul said. "He's a policeman."

"What do you mean?" Denise was mystified. "He's wearing a captain's uniform and he told me—"

"He told you lies," Paul said. "His job is to catch people who blab to strangers. And he caught you."

Denise's jaw dropped, then she recovered her composure and became indignant. "So it was a trick? You tried to trap me?"

"I succeeded, unfortunately," Paul said. "You told him everything."

Realizing she was found out, Denise tried to make light of it. "What's my punishment? A hundred lines and no playtime?"

Flick wanted to slap her face. Denise's boasting could have endangered the lives of the whole team.

Paul said coldly, "There's no punishment, as such."

"Oh. Thank you so much."

"But you're off the team. You won't be coming with us. You'll be leaving tonight, with the captain."

"I shall feel rather foolish going back to my old job at Hendon."

Paul shook his head. "He's not taking you to Hendon."

"Why not?"

"You know too much. You can't be allowed to walk around free."

Denise began to look worried. "What are you going to do to me?"

"You'll be posted to some place where you can't do any damage. I believe it's usually an isolated base in Scotland, where their main function is to file regimental accounts."

"That's as bad as prison!"

Paul reflected for a moment, then nodded. "Almost."

"For how long?" Denise said in dismay.

"Who knows? Until the war is over, probably."

"You absolute rotter," Denise said furiously. "I wish I'd never met you."

"You may leave now," said Paul. "And be grateful I caught you. Otherwise it might have been the Gestapo."

Denise stalked out.

Paul said, "I hope that wasn't unnecessarily cruel."

Flick did not think so. The silly cow deserved a lot worse. However, she wanted to make a good impression on Paul, so she said, "No point in crushing her. Some people just aren't suited to this work. It's not her fault."

Paul smiled. "You're a rotten liar," he said. "You think I was too easy on her, don't you?"

"I think crucifixion would be too easy on her," Flick said angrily, but Paul laughed, and his humor softened her wrath until she had to smile. "I can't pull the wool over your eyes, can I?"

"I hope not." He became serious again. "It's fortunate that we had one team member more than we really needed. We could afford to lose Denise."

"But now we're down to the bare minimum." Flick stood up wearily. "We'd better get the rest to bed. This will be their last decent night's sleep for a while."

Paul looked around the room. "I don't see Diana and Maude."

"They must have stepped out for a breath of air. I'll find them if you'll round up the rest." Paul nodded agreement, and Flick went outside.

There was no sign of the two girls. She paused for a moment to look at the evening light glowing on the calm water of the estuary. Then she walked around the side of the pub to the parking lot. A tan-colored army Austin was pulling away, and Flick glimpsed Denise in the back, crying.

There was no sign of Diana or Maude. Frowning, puzzled, Flick crossed the tarmac and went to the back of the pub. She came to a yard with old barrels and stacked crates. Across the yard was a small outbuilding with a wooden door that stood open. She went in.

At first she could see nothing in the gloom, but she knew she was not alone, for she could hear breathing. Instinct told her to remain silent and still. Her eyes adjusted to the dim light. She was in a tool shed, with neat rows of wrenches and shovels on hooks, and a big lawn mower in the middle of the floor. Diana and Maude were in a far corner.

Maude was leaning against the wall and Diana was kissing her. Flick's jaw dropped. Diana's blouse was undone, revealing a large, severely practical brassiere. Maude's pink gingham skirt was rucked up around her waist. As the picture became clearer, she saw that Diana's hand was thrust down the front of Maude's panties.

Flick stood there for a moment, frozen with shock. Maude saw her and met her eye. "Have you had a good look?" she said saucily. "Or do you want to take a photo?"

Diana jumped, snatching her hand away and stepping back from Maude. She turned around, and a look of horror came over her face. "Oh, my *God,*" she said. She pulled the front of her blouse together with one hand and covered her mouth with the other in a gesture of shame.

Flick stammered: "I-I-I just came to say we're leaving." Then she turned around and stumbled out.

CHAPTER 24

Wireless operators were not quite invisible. They lived in a spirit world where their ghostly shapes could be dimly seen. Peering into the gloom, searching for them, were the men of the Gestapo's radio detection team, housed in a cavernous, darkened hall in Paris. Dieter had visited the place. Three hundred round oscilloscope screens flickered with a greenish light. Radio broadcasts appeared as vertical lines on the monitors, the position of the line showing the frequency of the transmission, the height indicating the strength of the signal. The screens were tended, day and night, by silent, watchful operators, who made him think of angels observing the sins of humankind.

The operators knew the regular stations, either German-controlled or foreign-based, and were able to spot a rogue instantly. As soon as this happened, the operator would pick up a telephone at his desk and call three tracking stations: two in southern Germany, at Augsburg and Nuremberg, and one in Brittany, at Brest. He would give them the frequency of the rogue broadcast. The tracking stations were equipped with goniometers, apparatus for measuring angles, and each could say within seconds which direction the broadcast was coming from. They would send this information back to Paris, where the operator would draw three lines on a huge wall map. The lines intersected where the suspect radio was located. The operator then telephoned the Gestapo office nearest to the location. The local Gestapo had cars waiting in readiness, equipped with their own detection apparatus.

Dieter was now sitting in such a car, a long black Citroën parked on the outskirts of Reims. With him were three Gestapo men experienced in wireless detection. Tonight the help of the Paris center was not required: Dieter already knew the frequency Helicopter would use, and he assumed Helicopter would broadcast from somewhere in the city (because it was too difficult for a wireless operator to lose himself in the countryside). The car's receiver was tuned to Helicopter's frequency. It measured the strength, as well as the direction, of the broadcast, and Dieter would know he was getting nearer to the transmitter when the needle rose on the dial.

In addition, the Gestapo man sitting next to Dieter wore a receiver and an aerial concealed beneath his raincoat. On his wrist was a meter like a watch that showed the strength of the signal. When the search narrowed down to a particular street, city block, or building, the walker would take over.

The Gestapo man in the front seat held on his lap a sledgehammer, for breaking doors down.

Dieter had been hunting once. He did not much like country pursuits, preferring the more refined pleasures of city life, but he was a good shot. Now he was reminded of that, as he waited for Helicopter to begin sending his coded report home to England. This was like lying in the hide in the early dawn, tense with anticipation, impatient for the deer to start moving, savoring the thrill of anticipation.

The Resistance were not deer but foxes, Dieter thought, skulking in their holes, coming out to cause carnage in the chicken house, then going to earth again. He was mortified to have lost Helicopter. He was so keen to recapture the man that he hardly minded having to rely on the help of Willi Weber. He just wanted to kill the fox.

It was a fine summer evening. The car was parked at the northern end of the city. Reims was a small town, and Dieter reckoned a car could drive from one side to the other in less than ten minutes.

He checked his watch: one minute past eight. Helicopter was late coming on air. Perhaps he would not broadcast tonight . . . but that was unlikely. Today Helicopter had met up with Michel. As soon as possible, he would want to report his success to his superiors, and tell them just how much was left of the Bollinger circuit.

Michel had phoned the house in the rue du Bois two hours ago. Dieter had been there. It was a tense moment. Stéphanie had answered, in her imitation of Mademoiselle Lemas's voice. Michel had given his code name, and asked whether "Bourgeoise" remembered him—a question that reassured Stéphanie, because it indicated that Michel did not know Mademoiselle Lemas very well and therefore would not realize this was an impersonator.

He had asked her about her new recruit, codenamed Charenton. "He's my cousin," Stéphanie had said gruffly. "I've known him since we were children, I would trust him with my life." Michel had told her she had no right to recruit people without at least discussing it with him, but he had appeared to believe her story, and Dieter had kissed Stéphanie and told her she was a good enough actor to join the Comédie Française.

All the same, Helicopter would know that the Gestapo would be listening and trying to find him. That was a risk he had to run: if he sent no messages home he was of no use. He would stay on air only for the minimum length of time. If he had a lot of information to send, he would break it into two or more messages and send them from different locations. Dieter's only hope was that he would be tempted to stay on the air just a little too long.

The minutes ticked by. There was silence in the car. The men smoked nervously. Then, at five past eight, the receiver beeped.

By prearrangement, the driver set off immediately, driving south.

The signal grew stronger, but slowly, making Dieter worry that they were not heading directly for the source.

Sure enough, as they passed the cathedral in the center of town, the needle fell back.

In the passenger seat, a Gestapo man talked into a short-wave radio. He was consulting with someone in a radio-detection truck a mile away. After a moment he said, "Northwest quarter."

The driver immediately turned west, and the signal began to strengthen.

"Got you," Dieter breathed.

But five minutes had elapsed.

The car raced west, and the signal strengthened, as Helicopter continued to tap on the Morse key of his suitcase radio in his hiding place—a bathroom, an attic, a warehouse—somewhere in the northwest of the city. Back at the château of Sainte-Cécile, a German radio operator had tuned to the same frequency and was taking down the coded message. It was also being registered on a wire recorder. Later, Dieter would decrypt it, using the one-time pad copied by Stéphanie. But the message was not as important as the messenger.

They entered a neighborhood of large old houses, mostly decrepit and subdivided into small apartments and bedsitting rooms for students and nurses. The signal grew louder, then suddenly began to fade. "Overshoot, overshoot!" said the Gestapo man in the front passenger seat. The driver reversed the car, then braked.

Ten minutes had passed.

Dieter and the three Gestapo men sprang out. The one with the portable detection unit under his raincoat walked rapidly along the pavement, consulting his wrist dial constantly, and the others followed. He went a hundred meters, then suddenly turned back. He stopped and pointed to a house. "That one," he said. "But the transmission has ended."

Dieter noticed that there were no curtains in the windows. The Resistance liked to use derelict houses for their transmissions.

The Gestapo man carrying the sledgehammer broke the door down with two blows. They all rushed in.

The floors were bare and the place had

a musty smell. Dieter threw open a door and looked into an empty room.

Dieter opened the door of the back room. He crossed the vacant room in three strides and looked into an abandoned kitchen.

He ran up the stairs. On the next floor was a window overlooking a long back garden. Dieter glanced out—and saw Helicopter and Michel running across the grass. Michel was limping, Helicopter was carrying his little suitcase. Dieter swore. They must have escaped through a back door as the Gestapo were breaking down the front. Dieter turned and yelled, "Back garden!" The Gestapo men ran and he followed.

As he reached the garden, he saw Michel and Helicopter scrambling over the back fence into the grounds of another house. He joined in the chase, but the fugitives had a long lead. With the three Gestapo men, he climbed the fence and ran through the second garden.

They reached the next street just in time to see a black Renault Monaquatre disappearing around the corner.

"Hell," Dieter said. For the second time in a day, Helicopter had slipped through his grasp.

CHAPTER 25

When they got back to the house, Flick made cocoa for the team. It was not regular practice for officers to make cocoa for their troops, but in Flick's opinion that only showed how little the army knew about leadership.

Paul stood in the kitchen watching her as she waited for the kettle to boil. She felt his eyes on her like a caress. She knew what he was going to say, and she had prepared her reply. It would have been easy to fall in love with Paul, but she was not going to betray the husband who was risking his life fighting the Nazis in occupied France.

However, his question surprised her. "What will you do after the war?"

"I'm looking forward to being bored," she said.

He laughed. "You've had enough excitement."

"Too much." She thought for a moment. "I still want to be a teacher. I'd like to share my love of French culture with young people. Educate them about French literature and painting, and also about less highbrow things like cooking and fashion."

"So you'll become a don?"

"Finish my doctorate, get a job at a university, be condescended to by narrow-minded old male professors. Maybe write a guide book to France, or even a cookbook."

"Sounds tame, after this."

"It's important, though. The more young people know about foreigners, the less likely they are to be as stupid as we were, and go to war with their neighbors."

"I wonder if that's right."

"What about you? What's your plan for after the war?"

"Oh, mine is real simple. I want to marry you and take you to Paris for a honeymoon. Then we'll settle down and have children."

She stared at him. "Were you thinking of asking my consent?" she said indignantly.

He was quite solemn. "I haven't thought of anything else for days."

"I already have a husband."

"But you don't love him."

"You have no right to say that!"

"I know, but I can't help it."

"Why did I used to think you were a smooth talker?"

"Usually I am. That kettle's boiling."

She took the kettle off the hob and poured boiling water over the cocoa mixture in a big stoneware jug. "Put some mugs on a tray," she told Paul. "A little housework might cure you of dreams of domesticity."

He complied. "You can't put me off by being bossy," he said. "I kind of like it."

She added milk and sugar to the cocoa and poured it into the mugs he had laid out. "In that case, carry that tray into the living room."

"Right away, boss."

When they entered the living room they found Jelly and Greta having a row, standing face to face in the middle of the room while the others looked on, half amused and half horrified.

Jelly was saying, "You weren't using it!"

"I was resting my feet on it," Greta replied.

"There aren't enough chairs." Jelly was

holding a small stuffed pouffe, and Flick guessed she had snatched it away from Greta rudely.

Flick said, "Ladies, please!"

They ignored her. Greta said, "You only had to ask, sweetheart."

"I don't have to ask permission from foreigners in my own country."

"I'm not a foreigner, you fat bitch."

"Oh!" Jelly was so stung by the insult that she reached out and pulled Greta's hair. Greta's brunette wig came off in her hand.

With her head of close-cropped dark hair exposed, Greta suddenly looked unmistakably like a man. Percy and Paul were in on the secret, and Ruby had guessed, but Maude and Diana were shocked rigid. Diana said, "Good God!" and Maude gave a little scream of fright.

Jelly was the first to recover her wits. "A pervert!" she said triumphantly. "Oh, my gordon, it's a foreign pervert!"

Greta was in tears. "You bloody fucking Nazi," she sobbed.

"I bet she's a spy!" Jelly said.

Flick said, "Shut up, Jelly. She's not a spy. I knew she was a man."

"You knew!"

"So did Paul. So did Percy."

Jelly looked at Percy, who nodded solemnly.

Greta turned to leave, but Flick caught her arm. "Don't go," she said. "Please. Sit down."

Greta sat down. "Jelly, give me the damn wig."

Jelly handed it to Flick.

Flick stood in front of Greta and put the wig back on. Ruby, quickly understanding what Flick was trying to do, lifted the mirror from over the mantelpiece and held it in front of Greta, who studied her reflection while she adjusted the wig and blotted her tears with a handkerchief.

"Now listen to me, all of you," said Flick. "Greta is an engineer, and we can't accomplish our mission without an engineer. We have a much better chance of survival in occupied territory as an all-woman team. The upshot is, we need Greta and we need her to be a woman. So get used to it."

Jelly gave a contemptuous grunt.

"There's something else I ought to explain," Flick said. She looked hard at Jelly. "You may have noticed that Denise is no longer with us. A little test was set for her tonight, and she failed it. She's off the team. Unfortunately, she's learned some secrets in the last two days, and she can't be allowed to return to her old posting. So she's gone to a remote base in Scotland, where she'll stay, probably for the rest of the war, with no leave."

Jelly said, "You can't do that!"

"Of course I can, you idiot," Flick said impatiently. "There's a war on, remember? And what I've done to Denise, I'll do to anyone who has to be fired from this team."

"I never even joined the army!" Jelly protested.

"Yes, you did. You were commissioned as an officer, yesterday, after tea. You all were. And you're getting officer's pay, although you haven't seen any yet. That means you're under military discipline. And you all know too much."

"So we're prisoners?" Diana said.

"You're in the army," Flick said. "It's much the same thing. So drink your cocoa and go to bed."

They drifted off one by one until only Diana was left. Flick had been expecting this. Seeing the two women in a sexual clinch had been a real shock. She recalled that at school some of the girls had developed crushes on one another, sending loving notes, holding hands, and sometimes even kissing; but as far as she knew it had not gone any further. At some point she and Diana had practiced French kissing on one another, so that they would know what to do when they got boyfriends, and now Flick guessed those kisses had meant more to Diana than they had to her. But she had never known a grown woman who desired other women. Theoretically, she was aware that they existed, the female equivalents of her brother Mark and of Greta, but she had never really imagined them . . . well, feeling each other up in a garden shed.

Did it matter? Not in everyday life. Mark and his kind were happy, or at least they were when people left them alone. But would Diana's relationship with Maude affect the mission? Not necessarily. Flick herself worked with her husband in the Resistance, after all. This was not quite the same, admittedly. A passionate new romance might prove a distraction.

Flick could try to keep the two lovers separate—but that might make Diana even more insubordinate. And the affair could just as easily be an inspiration. Flick had been trying desperately to get the women to work together as a team, and this might help. She had decided to leave well enough alone. But Diana wanted to talk.

"It's not what it seems, really it isn't," Diana said without preamble. "Christ, you've got to believe me. It was just a stupid thing, a joke—"

"Would you like more cocoa?" Flick said. "I think there's some left in the jug."

Diana stared at her, nonplussed. After a moment she said, "How can you talk about cocoa?"

"I just want you to calm down and realize that the world is not going to come to an end simply because you kissed Maude. You kissed me, once—remember?"

"I knew you'd bring that up. But that was just kid stuff. With Maude, it wasn't just a kiss." Diana sat down. Her proud face crumpled and she began to cry. "You know it was more than that, you could see, oh, God, the things I did. What on earth did you think?"

Flick chose her words carefully. "I thought the two of you looked very sweet."

"Sweet?" Diana was incredulous. "You weren't disgusted?"

"Certainly not. Maude is a pretty girl, and you appear to have fallen in love with her."

"That's exactly what happened."

"So stop being ashamed."

"How can I not be ashamed? I'm queer!"

"I wouldn't look at it that way if I were you. You ought to be discreet, to avoid offending narrow-minded people such as Jelly, but there's no need for shame."

"Will I always be like this?"

Flick considered. The answer was probably yes, but she did not want to be brutal. "Look," she said, "I think some people, like Maude, just love to be loved, and they can be made happy by a man or a woman." In truth, Maude was shallow, selfish, and tarty, but Flick suppressed that thought firmly. "Others are more inflexible," she went on. "You should keep an open mind."

"I suppose that's the end of the mission for me and Maude."

"It most certainly is not."

"You'll still take us?"

"I still need you. And I don't see why this should make any difference."

Diana took out a handkerchief and blew her nose. Flick got up and went to the window, giving her time to recover her composure. After a minute, Diana spoke in a calmer voice. "You're frightfully kind," she said with a touch of her old hauteur.

"Go to bed," Flick said.

Diana got up obediently.

"And if I were you . . ."

"What?"

"I'd go to bed with Maude."

Diana looked shocked.

Flick shrugged. "It may be your last chance," she said.

"Thank you," Diana whispered. She stepped toward Flick and spread her arms, as if to hug her; then she stopped. "You may not want me to kiss you," she said.

"Don't be silly," Flick said, and embraced her.

"Goodnight," said Diana. She left the room.

Flick turned and looked out at the garden. The moon was three-quarters full. In a few days' time it would be full, and the Allies would invade France. A wind was disturbing the new leaves in the forest: the weather was going to change. She hoped there would not be a storm in the English Channel. The entire invasion plan could be ruined by the capricious British climate. She guessed a lot of people were praying for good weather.

She ought to get some sleep. She left the room and climbed the stairs. She thought of what she had said to Diana: *I'd go to bed with Maude. It may be your last chance.* She hesitated outside Paul's door. It was different for Diana—she was single. Flick was married.

But it might be her last chance.

She knocked at the door and stepped inside.

CHAPTER 26

Sunk in gloom, Dieter returned to the château at Sainte-Cécile in the Citroën with the radio detection team. He went to the wireless listening room in the bombproofed basement. Willi Weber was there, looking angry. The one consolation from tonight's fiasco, Dieter thought, was that Weber was not able to crow that he had succeeded where Dieter had failed. But Dieter could have put up with all the triumphalism Weber could muster in return for having Helicopter in the torture chamber.

"You have the message he sent?" Dieter asked.

Weber handed him a carbon copy of the typed message. "It has already been sent to the cryptanalysis office in Berlin."

Dieter looked at the meaningless strings

of letters. "They won't be able to decode it. He's using a one-time pad." He folded the sheet and slipped it into his pocket.

"What can you do with it?" Weber said.

"I have a copy of his code book," Dieter said. It was a petty victory, but he felt better.

Weber swallowed. "The message may tell us where he is."

"Yes. He's scheduled to receive a reply at eleven p.m." He looked at his watch. It was a few minutes before eleven. "Let's record that, and I will decrypt the two together."

Weber left. Dieter waited in the windowless room. On the dot of eleven, a receiver tuned to Helicopter's listening frequency began to chatter with the long-and-short beeps of Morse. An operator wrote the letters down while at the same time a wire recorder ran. When the chattering stopped, the operator pulled a typewriter toward him and typed out what he had on his notepad. He gave Dieter a carbon copy.

The two messages could be everything or nothing, Dieter thought as he got behind the wheel of his own car. The moon was bright as he followed the twisting road through the vineyards to Reims and parked in the rue du Bois. It was good weather for an invasion.

Stéphanie was waiting for him in the kitchen of Mademoiselle Lemas's house. He put the coded messages on the table and took out the copies Stéphanie had made of the pad and the silk handkerchief. He rubbed his eyes and began to decode the first message, the one Helicopter had sent, writing the decrypt on the scratch pad Mademoiselle Lemas had used to make her shopping lists.

Stéphanie brewed a pot of coffee. She looked over his shoulder for a while, asked a couple of questions, then took the second message and began to decode it herself.

Dieter's decrypt gave a concise account of the incident at the cathedral, naming Dieter as Charenton and saying he had been recruited by Bourgeoise (Mademoiselle Lemas) because she was worried about the security of the rendezvous. It said Monet (Michel) had taken the unusual step of phoning Bourgeoise to confirm that Charenton was trustworthy, and he was satisfied.

It listed the code names of those members of the Bollinger circuit who had not fallen in the battle last Sunday and were still active. There were only four.

It was useful, but it did not tell him where to find the spies.

He drank a cup of coffee while he waited for Stéphanie to finish. She handed him a sheet of paper covered with her flamboyant handwriting.

When he read it, he could hardly believe his luck. It said:

PREPARE RECEIVE GROUP OF SIX
NUMBER PARACHUTISTS
CODENAMED JACKDAWS LEADER
LEOPARDESS ARRIVING ELEVEN
PIP EMMA FRIDAY SECOND JUNE
CHAMP DE PIERRE.

"My God," he whispered.

Champ de Pierre was a code name, but Dieter knew what it meant, for Gaston had told him during the very first interrogation. It was a drop zone in a pasture outside Chatelle, a small village five miles from Reims. Dieter now knew exactly where Helicopter and Michel would be tomorrow night, and could pick them up.

He could also capture six more Allied agents as they parachuted to earth.

And one of them was "Leopardess": Flick Clairet, the woman who knew more than anyone else about the French Resistance, the woman who, under torture, would give him the information he needed to break the back of the Resistance—just in time to stop them aiding the invasion force.

"Jesus Christ Almighty," Dieter said. "What a break."

THE SIXTH DAY

Friday, June 2, 1944

CHAPTER 27

Paul and Flick were talking.

They lay side by side on his bed. The lights were off, but the moon shone through the window. He was naked, as he had been when she entered the room. He always slept naked. He wore pyjamas only to walk along the corridor to the bathroom.

He had been asleep when she came in, but he had wakened fast and leaped out of bed, his unconscious mind assuming that a clandestine visit in the night must mean the Gestapo. He had had his hands around her throat before he realized who it was.

He was astonished, thrilled, and grateful. He had closed the door, then kissed her, standing there, for a long time. He was unprepared, and it felt like a dream. He was afraid he might wake up.

She had caressed him, feeling his shoulders and his back and his chest. Her hands were soft but her touch was firm, exploring. "You have a lot of hair," she had whispered.

"Like an ape."

"But not as handsome," she teased.

He looked at her lips, delighting in the way they moved when she spoke, thinking that in a moment he would touch them with his own, and it would be lovely. He smiled. "Let's lie down."

They lay on the bed, facing one another, but she did not take off any clothes, not even her shoes. He found it strangely exciting to be naked with a woman who was fully dressed. He enjoyed it so much that he was in no hurry to move to the next base. He wanted this moment to last forever.

"Tell me something," she said in a lazy, sensual voice.

"What?"

"Anything. I feel I don't know you."

What was this? He had never had a girl behave like this. She came to his room in the night, she lay on his bed but kept her clothes on, then she questioned him. "Is that why you came?" he said lightly, watching her face. "To interrogate me?"

She laughed softly. "Don't worry, I want to make love to you, but not in a hurry. Tell me about your first lover."

He stroked her cheek with light fingertips, tracing the curve of her jaw. He did not know what she wanted, where she was going. She had thrown him off balance. "Can we touch while we talk?"

"Yes."

He kissed her lips. "And kiss, too?"

"Yes."

"Then I think we should talk for just a little while, maybe a year or two."

"What was her name?"

Flick was not as confident as she pretended to be, he decided. In fact she was nervous, and that was the reason for the questions. If it made her comfortable, he would answer. "Her name was Linda. We were terribly young—I'm embarrassed at how young we were. The first time I kissed her, she was twelve, and I was fourteen, can you imagine?"

"Of course I can." She giggled, and for an instant she was a girl again. "I used to kiss boys when I was twelve."

"We always had to pretend we were going out with a bunch of friends, and usually we started the evening that way, but pretty soon we would peel off from the crowd and go to a movie or something. We did that for a couple of years before we had real sex."

"Where was this, in America?"

"Paris. My father was military attaché at the embassy. Linda's parents owned a hotel that catered specially for American visitors. We used to run with a whole crowd of expatriate kids."

"Where did you make love?"

"In the hotel. We had it easy. There were always empty rooms."

"What was it like the first time? Did you use any, you know, precautions?"

"She stole one of her father's rubbers."

Flick's fingertips traced a course down his belly. He closed his eyes. She said, "Who put it on?"

"She did. It was very exciting. I nearly came right then. And if you're not careful . . ."

She moved her hand to his hip. "I'd like to have known you when you were sixteen."

He opened his eyes. He no longer wanted to make this moment last forever. In fact, he found he was in a great hurry to move on. "Would you . . ." His mouth was dry, and he swallowed. "Would you like to take off some clothes?"

"Yes. But speaking of precautions . . ."

"In my billfold. On the bedside table."

"Good." She sat upright and unlaced her shoes, throwing them on the floor. She stood up and unbuttoned her blouse. She was tense, he could see, so he said, "Take your time, we have all night."

It was a couple of years since Paul had watched a woman undress. He had been living on a diet of pin-ups, and they always wore elaborate confections of silk and lace, corsets and garter belts and transparent negligees. Flick was wearing a loose cotton chemise, not a brassiere, and he guessed that the small, neat breasts he could see tantalizingly outlined beneath it did not need support. She dropped her skirt. Her panties were plain white cotton with frills around the legs. Her body was tiny but muscular. She looked like a schoolgirl getting changed for hockey practice, but he found that more exciting than a pin-up.

She lay down again. "Is that better?" she said.

He stroked her hip, feeling the warm skin, then the soft cotton, then skin again. She was not yet ready, he could tell. He forced himself to be patient and let her set the pace. "You haven't told me about your first time," he said.

To his surprise, she blushed. "It wasn't as nice as yours."

"In what way?"

"It was a horrible place, a dusty storeroom."

He felt indignant. What kind of idiot could take a girl as special as Flick and submit her to a furtive quickie in a cupboard? "How old were you?"

"Twenty-two."

He had expected her to say seventeen. "Jeepers. At that age you deserve a comfortable bed."

"That wasn't it, though."

She was relaxing again, Paul could tell. He encouraged her to talk some more. "So what was wrong?"

"Probably that I didn't really want to do it. I was talked into it."

"Didn't you love the guy?"

"Yes, I did. But I wasn't ready."

"What was his name?"

"I don't want to tell you."

Paul guessed it was her husband, Michel,

and decided not to question her any more. He kissed her and said, "May I touch your breasts?"

"You can touch anything you like."

No one had ever said that to him. He found her openness startling and exciting. He began to explore her body. In his experience, most women closed their eyes at this point, but she kept hers open, studying his face with a mixture of desire and curiosity that inflamed him more. It was as if by watching him she was exploring him, instead of the other way around. His hands discovered the pert shape of her breasts, and his fingertips got to know her shy nipples, learning what they liked. He took off her panties. She had curly hair the color of honey, lots of it, and under the hair, on the left side, a birthmark like a splash of tea. He bent his head and kissed her there, his lips feeling the crisp brush of her hair, his tongue tasting her moisture.

He sensed her yielding to pleasure. Her nervousness vanished. Her arms and legs spread out in a star shape, slack, abandoned, but her hips strained toward him eagerly. He explored the folds of her sex with slow delight. Her movements became more urgent.

She pushed his head away. Her face was flushed and she was breathing hard. She reached across to the bedside table, opened his billfold, and found the rubbers, three of them in a small paper packet. She ripped the pack with fumbling fingers, took one out, and put it on him. Then she straddled him as he lay on his back. She bent to kiss him, and said into his ear, "Oh, boy, you feel so good inside me." Then she sat upright and began to move.

"Take off your chemise," he said.

She pulled it over her head.

He watched her above him, her lovely face drawn into an expression of fierce concentration, her pretty breasts moving delightfully. He felt like the luckiest man in the world. He wanted this to go on forever: no dawn, no tomorrow, no plane, no parachute, no war.

In all of life, he thought, there was nothing better than love.

When it was over, Flick's first thought was: What will I say to Michel?

She did not feel unhappy. She was full of love and desire for Paul. In a short time she had come to feel more intimate with him than she ever had with Michel. She wanted to make love to him every day for the rest of her life. That was the trouble. Her marriage was over. And she would have to tell Michel as soon as she saw him. She could not pretend, even for a few minutes, to feel the same about him.

Michel was the only man she had been intimate with before Paul. She would have told Paul that, but she felt disloyal talking about Michel. It seemed more of a betrayal than simple adultery. One day she would tell Paul he was only her second lover, and she might say he was her best, but she would never talk to him about how sex was with Michel.

However, it was not just sex that was different with Paul, it was herself. She had never asked Michel, the way she had questioned Paul, about his early sexual experiences. She had never said to him *You can touch anything you like.* She had never put a rubber on him, or climbed on top of him to make love, or told him he felt good inside her.

When she had lain down on the bed beside Paul, another personality had seemed to come out of her, just as a transformation had come over Mark when he walked into the Criss-Cross Club. She suddenly felt she could say anything she liked, do anything that took her fancy, be herself without worrying what would be thought of her.

It had never been like that with Michel. Beginning as his student, wanting to impress him, she had never really got on an even footing with him. She had continued to seek his approval, something he had never done with her. In bed, she tried to please him, not herself.

After a while, Paul said, "What are you thinking?"

"About my marriage," she said.

"What about it?"

She wondered how much to confess. He had said, earlier in the evening, that he wanted to marry her, but that was before she came to his bedroom. Men never married girls who slept with them first, according to female folklore. It was not always true, Flick knew from her own experience with Michel. But all the same she decided to tell Paul half the truth. "That it's over."

"A drastic decision."

She raised herself on her elbow and looked at him. "Does that bother you?"

"On the contrary. I hope it means we might see each other again."

"Do you mean that?"

He put his arms around her. "I'm scared to tell you how much I mean it."

"Scared?"

"Of frightening you off. I said a foolish thing earlier."

"About marrying me and having children?"

"I meant it, but I said it in an arrogant way."

"That's okay," she said. "When people are perfectly polite, it usually means they don't really care. A little awkwardness is more sincere."

"I guess you're right. I never thought of that."

She stroked his face. She could see the bristles of his beard, and she realized the dawn light was strengthening. She forced herself not to look at her watch: she did not want to keep checking how much time they had left.

She ran her hand over his face, mapping

his features with her fingertips: the bushy eyebrows, the deep eye sockets, the big nose, the shot-off ear, the sensual lips, the lantern jaw. "Do you have hot water?" she said suddenly.

"Yes, it's a swanky room. There's a basin in the corner."

She got up.

He said, "What are you doing?"

"Stay there." She padded across the floor in her bare feet, feeling his eyes on her naked body, wishing she were not quite so broad across the hips. On a shelf over the sink was a mug containing toothpaste and a wooden toothbrush that she recognized as French. Next to the glass were a safety razor, a brush, and a bowl of shaving soap. She ran the hot tap, dipped the shaving brush in it, and worked up a lather in his soap bowl.

"Come on," he said. "What is this?"

"I'm going to shave you."

"Why?"

"You'll see."

She covered his face with lather, then got his safety razor and filled the tooth mug with hot water. She straddled him the way she had when they made love and shaved his face with careful, tender strokes.

"How did you learn to do this?" he asked.

"Don't speak," she said. "I watched my mother do it for my father, many times. Dad was a drunk, and toward the end he couldn't hold the razor steady, so Ma had to shave him every day. Lift your chin."

He did so obediently, and she shaved the sensitive skin of his throat. When she had finished she soaked a flannel in hot water and wiped his face with it, then patted him dry with a clean towel. "I should put on some face cream, but I bet you're too masculine to use it."

"It never occurred to me that I should."

"Never mind."

"What next?"

"Do you remember what you were doing to me just before I reached for your wallet?"

"Yes."

"Did you wonder why I didn't let you go on longer?"

"I thought you were impatient for . . . intercourse."

"No, your bristles were scratching my thighs, right where the skin is most tender."

"Oh, I'm sorry."

"Well, you can make it up to me."

He frowned. "How?"

She groaned with mock frustration. "Come on, Einstein. Now that your bristles have gone . . ."

"Oh—I see! Is that why you shaved me? Yes, of course it is. You want me to . . ."

She lay on her back, smiling, and parted her legs. "Is this enough of a hint?"

He laughed. "I guess it is," he said, and he bent over her.

She closed her eyes.

CHAPTER 28

The old ballroom was in the bombed west wing of the château at Sainte-Cécile. The room was only partly damaged: one end was a pile of debris, square stones and carved pediments and chunks of painted wall in a dusty heap, but the other remained intact. The effect was picturesque, Dieter thought, with the morning sun shining through a great hole in the ceiling onto a row of broken pillars, like a Victorian painting of classical ruins.

Dieter had decided to hold his briefing in the ballroom. The alternative was to meet in Weber's office, and Dieter did not want to give the men the impression that Willi was in charge. There was a small dais, presumably intended for the orchestra, on which he had placed a blackboard. The men had

brought chairs from other parts of the building and had placed them in front of the dais
in four neat rows of five—very German,
Dieter thought with a secret smile; French
men would have scattered the chairs any
which way. Weber, who had assembled the
team, sat on the dais facing the men, to em-
phasize that he was one of the commanders, not subordinate to Dieter.

The presence of two commanders, equal
in rank and hostile to one another, was the
greatest threat to the operation, Dieter
thought.

On the blackboard he had chalked a neat
map of the village of Chatelle. It consisted
of three large houses—presumably farms or
wineries—plus six cottages and a bakery.
The buildings were clustered around a
crossroads, with vineyards to the north,
west, and south, and to the east a large cow
pasture, a kilometer long, bordered by a
broad pond. Dieter guessed that the field
was used for grazing because the ground
was too wet for grapes.

"The parachutists will aim to land in the
pasture," Dieter said. "It must be a regular
landing-and-takeoff field: it's level, plenty
big enough for a Lysander, and long enough

even for a Hudson. The pond next to it would be a useful landmark, visible from the air. There is a cowshed at the southern end of the field where the reception committee probably take shelter while they are waiting for the plane."

He paused. "The most important thing for everyone here to remember is that *we want these parachutists to land.* We must avoid any action that might betray our presence to the reception committee or the pilot. We have to be silent and invisible. If the plane turns around and returns home with the agents on board, we will have lost a golden opportunity. One of the parachutists is a woman who can give us information on most of the Resistance circuits in northern France—if only we can get our hands on her."

Weber spoke, mainly to remind them that he was here. "Allow me to underline what Major Franck has said. Take no risks! Do nothing ostentatious! Stick to the plan!"

"Thank you, Major," Dieter said. "Lieutenant Hesse has divided you into two-man teams, designated A through L. Each building on the map is marked with a team letter. We will arrive at the village at twenty hundred hours. Very swiftly, we will enter every building. All the residents will be brought to the largest of the three big houses, known as La Maison Grandin, and held there until it is all over."

One of the men raised a hand. Weber barked, "Schuller! You may speak."

"Sir, what if the Resistance people call at a house? They will find it empty and they may become suspicious."

Dieter nodded. "Good question. But I don't think they will. My guess is the reception committee are strangers here. They don't usually have agents parachute in near where sympathizers live—it's an unnecessary security risk. I'm betting they arrive after dark and go straight to the cowshed without bothering the villagers."

Weber spoke again. "This would be normal Resistance procedure," he said with the air of a doctor giving a diagnosis.

"The Maison Grandin will be our headquarters," Dieter continued. "Major Weber will be in command there." This was his scheme for keeping Weber away from the real action. "The prisoners will be locked away in some convenient place, ideally a cellar. They must be kept quiet, so that we can hear the vehicle in which the reception committee arrive, and later the plane."

Weber said, "Any prisoner who persistently makes noise may be shot."

Dieter continued, "As soon as the villagers have been incarcerated, teams A, B, C, and D will take up concealed positions on the roads leading into the village. If any vehicles or personnel enter the village, you will report by short-wave radio, but you will do nothing more. At this point, you will not prevent people entering the village, and you will not do anything that might betray your presence." Looking around the room, Dieter wondered pessimistically whether the Gestapo men had brains enough to follow these orders.

"The enemy needs transport for six parachutists plus the reception committee, so they will arrive in a truck or bus, or possibly several cars. I believe they will enter the pasture by this gate—the ground is quite dry at this time of year, so there is no danger of cars becoming bogged down—and park between the gate and the cowshed, just here." He pointed to the spot on the map.

"Teams E, F, G, and H will be in this cluster of trees beside the pond, each equipped with a large battery searchlight. Teams I and J will remain at La Maison Grandin to guard the prisoners and maintain the command post with Major Weber." Dieter did not want Weber at the scene of the arrest. "Teams K and L will be with me, behind this hedge near the cowshed." Hans had found out which of the men were the best shots and assigned them to work with Dieter.

"I will be in radio contact with all teams and will be in command in the pasture. When we hear the plane—we do nothing! When we see the parachutists—we do nothing! We will watch the parachutists land and wait for the reception committee to round them up and assemble them near where the vehicles are parked." Dieter raised his voice, mainly for the benefit of Weber. *"Not until this process has been completed will we arrest anyone!"* The men would not jump the gun unless a skittish officer told them to.

"When we are ready, I will give the signal. From this moment on, until the order to stand down is given, teams A, B, C, and D will arrest anyone attempting to enter or leave the village. Teams E, F, G, and H, will switch on their searchlights and turn them on the enemy. Teams K and L will approach them with me and arrest them. No one is to fire on the enemy—is that clear?"

Schuller, obviously the thinker among the group, raised his hand again. "What if they fire on us?"

"Do not return their fire. These people are useless to us dead! Lie flat and keep the lights trained on them. Only teams E and F are permitted to use their weapons, and they have orders to shoot to wound. We want to interrogate these parachutists, not kill them."

The phone in the room rang, and Hans Hesse picked it up. "It's for you," he said to Dieter. "Rommel's headquarters."

The timing was lucky, Dieter thought as he took the phone. He had called Walter Goedel at La Roche-Guyon earlier and had left a message asking Goedel to call back. Now he said, "Walter, my friend, how is the Field Marshal?"

"Fine, what do you want?" said Goedel, abrupt as ever.

"I thought the Field Marshal might like to know that we expect to carry off a small coup tonight—the arrest of a group of saboteurs as they arrive." Dieter hesitated to give details over the phone, but this was a German military line, and the risk that the Resistance might be listening was very small. And it was crucial to get Goedel's support for the operation. "My information is that one of them could tell us a great deal about several Resistance circuits."

"Excellent," said Goedel. "As it happens, I am calling you from Paris. How long would it take me to drive to Reims—two hours?"

"Three."

"Then I will join you on the raid."

Dieter was delighted. "By all means," he said, "if that is what the Field Marshal would like. Meet us at the château of Sainte-Cécile not later than nineteen hundred." He looked at Weber, who had gone slightly pale.

"Very good." Goedel hung up.

Dieter handed the phone back to Hesse. "Field Marshal Rommel's personal aide, Major Goedel, will be joining us tonight," he said triumphantly. "Yet another reason for us to make sure that everything is done with impeccable efficiency." He smiled around the room, bringing his gaze to rest finally on Weber. "Aren't we fortunate?"

CHAPTER 29

All morning the Jackdaws drove north in a small bus. It was a slow journey through leafy woods and fields of green wheat, zigzagging from one sleepy market town to the next, circling London to the west. The countryside seemed oblivious of the war or indeed of the twentieth century, and Flick hoped it would long remain so. As they wound their way through medieval Winchester, she thought of Reims, another cathedral city, with uniformed Nazis strutting on the streets and the Gestapo everywhere in their black cars, and she gave a short prayer of thanks that they had stopped at the English Channel. She sat next to Paul and watched the countryside for a while, then—having been awake all night making love—she fell into a blissful sleep with her head on his shoulder.

At two in the afternoon they reached the village of Sandy in Bedfordshire. The bus went down a winding country road, turned onto an unpaved lane through a wood, and arrived at a large mansion called Tempsford House. Flick had been here before: it was the assembly point for the nearby Tempsford Airfield. The mood of tranquillity left her. Despite the eighteenth-century elegance of the place, to her it symbolized the unbearable tension of the hours immediately before a flight into enemy territory.

They were too late for lunch, but they got tea and sandwiches in the dining room. Flick drank her tea but felt too anxious to eat. However, the others tucked in heartily. Afterwards they were shown to their rooms.

A little later the women met in the library. The room looked more like the wardrobe of a film studio. There were racks of coats and dresses, boxes of hats and shoes, cardboard cartons labeled *Culottes, Chaussettes,* and *Mouchoirs,* and a trestle table in the middle of the room with several sewing machines.

In charge of the operation was Madame

Guillemin, a slim woman of about fifty in a shirtwaist dress with a chic little matching jacket. She had spectacles on the end of her nose and a measuring tape around her neck, and she spoke to them in perfect French with a Parisian accent. "As you know, French clothes are distinctively different from British clothes. I won't say they are more stylish, but, you know, they are . . . more stylish." She gave a French shrug, and the girls laughed.

It was not just a question of style, Flick thought somberly: French jackets were normally about ten inches longer than British, and there were numerous differences of detail, any of which could be the fatal clue that betrayed an agent. So all the clothes here had been bought in France, exchanged with refugees for new British clothes, or faithfully copied from French originals, then worn for a while so that they would not look new.

"Now it is summer so we have cotton dresses, light wool suits, and showerproof coats." She waved a hand at two young women sitting at sewing machines. "My assistants will make alterations if the clothes don't fit quite perfectly."

Flick said, "We need clothes that are fairly

expensive, but well worn. I want us to look like respectable women in case we're questioned by the Gestapo." When they needed to pose as cleaners, they could quickly downgrade their appearance by taking off their hats, gloves, and belts.

Madame Guillemin began with Ruby. She looked hard at her for a minute, then picked from the rack a navy dress and a tan raincoat. "Try those. It's a man's coat, but in France today no one can afford to be particular." She pointed across the room. "You can change behind that screen if you wish, and for the very shy there is a little anteroom behind the desk. We think the owner of the house used to lock himself in there to read dirty books." They laughed again, all but Flick, who had heard Madame Guillemin's jokes before.

The seamstress looked hard at Greta, then moved on, saying, "I'll come back to you." She picked outfits for Jelly, Diana, and Maude, and they all went behind the screen. Then she turned to Flick and said in a low voice, "Is this a joke?"

"Why do you say that?"

She turned to Greta. "You're a man."

Flick gave a grunt of frustration and

turned away. The seamstress had seen through Greta's disguise in seconds. It was a bad omen. Madame added, "You might fool a lot of people, but not me. I can tell."

Greta said, "How?"

Madame Guillemin shrugged. "The proportions are all wrong—your shoulders are too broad, your hips too narrow, your legs too muscular, your hands too big—it's obvious to an expert."

Flick said irritably, "She has to be a woman, for this mission, so please dress her as best you can."

"Of course—but for God's sake, try not to let her be seen by a dressmaker."

"No problem. The Gestapo don't employ many of those." Flick's confidence was faked. She did not want Madame Guillemin to know how worried she was.

The seamstress looked again at Greta. "I'll give you a contrasting skirt and blouse, to reduce your height, and a three-quarter-length coat." She selected clothes and handed them to Greta.

Greta looked at them with disapproval. Her taste ran to more glamorous outfits. However, she did not complain. "I'm going to be shy and lock myself in the anteroom," she said.

Finally Madame gave Flick an apple-green dress with a matching coat. "The color shows off your eyes," she said. "As long as you're not ostentatious, why shouldn't you look pretty? It may help you charm your way out of trouble."

The dress was loose and looked like a tent on Flick, but she put on a leather belt to give it a waist. "You are so chic, just like a French girl," said Madame Guillemin. Flick did not tell her that the main purpose of the belt was to hold a gun.

They all put on their new clothes and paraded around the room, preening and giggling. Madame Guillemin had chosen well, and they liked what they had been given, but some of the garments needed adjusting. "While we are making alterations you can choose some accessories," Madame said.

They rapidly lost their inhibitions, and clowned around in their underwear, trying on hats and shoes, scarves and bags. They had momentarily forgotten the dangers ahead, Flick thought, and were taking simple pleasure in their new outfits.

Greta came out of the anteroom looking

surprisingly glamorous. Flick studied her with interest. She had turned up the collar of the plain white blouse so that it looked stylish and wore the shapeless coat draped over her shoulders cloak-style. Madame Guillemin raised an eyebrow but made no comment.

Flick's dress had to be shortened. While that was being done she studied the coat. Working undercover had given her a sharp eye for detail, and she anxiously checked the stitching, the lining, the buttons, and the pockets to make sure they were in the normal French style. She found no fault. The label in the collar said "Galeries Lafayette."

Flick showed Madame Guillemin her lapel knife. It was only three inches long, with a thin blade, but it was wickedly sharp. It had a small handle and no hilt. It came in a slim leather sheath pierced with holes for thread. "I want you to sew this to the coat under the lapel," Flick said.

Madame Guillemin nodded. "I can do this."

She gave them each a little pile of underwear, two of everything, all with the labels of French shops. With unerring accuracy she had picked not just the right size but the preferred style of each woman: corsets for Jelly, pretty lacy slips for Maude, navy knickers and boned brassieres for Diana, simple chemises and panties for Ruby and Flick. "The handkerchiefs bear the laundry marks of different *blanchisseries* in Reims," said Madame Guillemin with a touch of pride.

Finally she produced an assortment of bags: a canvas duffel, a gladstone bag, a rucksack, and a selection of cheap fiber suitcases in different colors and sizes. Each woman got one. Inside she found a toothbrush, toothpaste, face powder, shoe polish, cigarettes and matches—all French brands. Even though they were going in only for a short time, Flick had insisted on the full kit for each of them.

"Remember," Flick said, "you may not take with you *anything* that you have not been given this afternoon. Your life depends on that."

The giggling stopped as they remembered the danger they would face in a few hours.

Flick said, "All right, everybody, please go back to your rooms and change into your

French outfits, including underwear. Then we'll meet downstairs for dinner."

In the main drawing room of the house a bar had been set up. When Flick walked in, it was occupied by a dozen or so men, some in RAF uniform, all of them—Flick knew from previous visits—destined to make clandestine flights over France. A blackboard bore the names or code names of those who would leave tonight, together with the times they needed to depart from the house. Flick read:

Aristotle—19:50
Capt. Jenkins & Lieut. Ramsey—20:05
All Jackdaws—20:30
Colgate & Bunter—21.00
Mr. Blister, Paradox, Saxophone—
22:05

She looked at her watch. It was six-thirty. Two hours to go.

She sat at the bar and looked around, wondering which of them would come back and which would die in the field. Some were terribly young, smoking and telling jokes, looking as if they had no cares. The older ones looked hardened, and savored their whisky and gin in the grim knowledge it might be their last. She thought about their parents, their wives or girlfriends, their babies and children. Tonight's work would leave some of them with a grief that would never entirely go away.

Her somber reflections were interrupted by a sight that astonished her. Simon Fortescue, the slippery bureaucrat from MI6, walked into the bar in a pinstriped suit—accompanied by Denise Bowyer.

Flick's jaw dropped.

"Felicity, I'm so glad I caught you," said Simon. Without waiting for an invitation he pulled up a stool for Denise. "Gin and tonic, please, barman. What would you like, Lady Denise?"

"A martini, very dry."

"And for you, Felicity?"

Flick did not answer the question. "She's supposed to be in Scotland!" she said.

"Look, there seems to have been some misunderstanding. Denise has told me all about this policeman fellow—"

"No misunderstanding," Flick said abruptly. "Denise failed the course. That's all there is to it."

Denise made a disgusted sound.

Fortescue said, "I really don't see how a perfectly intelligent girl from a good family could fail—"

"She's a blabbermouth."

"What?"

"She can't keep her damn mouth shut. She's not trustworthy. She shouldn't be walking around free!"

Denise said, "You insolent cat."

Fortescue controlled his temper with an effort and lowered his voice. "Look, her brother is the Marquess of Inverlocky, who's *very* close to the Prime Minister. Inverlocky himself asked me to make sure Denise got a chance to do her bit. So, you see, it would be dreadfully tactless to turn her down."

Flick raised her voice. "Let me get this straight." One or two of the men nearby looked up. "As a favor to your upper-class friend, you're asking me to take someone untrustworthy on a dangerous mission behind enemy lines. Is that it?"

As she was speaking, Percy and Paul walked in. Percy glared at Fortescue with undisguised malevolence. Paul said, "Did I hear right?"

Fortescue said, "I've brought Denise with me because it would be, frankly, an embarrassment to the government if she were left behind—"

"And a danger to me if she were to come!" Flick interrupted. "You're wasting your breath. She's off the team."

"Look, I don't want to have to pull rank—"

"What rank?" said Flick.

"I resigned from the Guards as a colonel—"

"Retired!"

"—and I'm the civil service equivalent of a brigadier."

"Don't be ridiculous," Flick said. "You're not even in the army."

"I'm *ordering* you to take Denise with you."

"Then I'll have to consider my response," said Flick.

"That's better. I'm sure you won't regret it."

"All right, here is my response. Fuck off."

Fortescue went red. He had probably never been told to fuck off by a girl. He was uncharacteristically speechless.

"Well!" said Denise. "We've certainly found out what type of person we're dealing with."

Paul said, "You're dealing with me." He

turned to Fortescue. "I'm in command of this operation, and I won't have Denise on the team at any price. If you want to argue, call Monty."

"Well said, my boy," Percy added.

Fortescue found his voice at last. He wagged a finger at Flick. "The time will come, Mrs. Clairet, when you will regret saying that to me." He got off his stool. "I'm sorry about this, Lady Denise, but I think we've done all we can here."

They left.

"Stupid prat," Percy muttered.

"Let's have dinner," said Flick.

The others were already in the dining room, waiting. As the Jackdaws began their last meal in England, Percy gave each of them an expensive gift: silver cigarette cases for the smokers, gold powder compacts for the others. "They have French hallmarks, so you can take them with you," he said. The women were pleased, but he brought their mood back down with his next remark. "They have a purpose, too. They are items that can easily be pawned for emergency funds if you get into real trouble."

The food was plentiful, a banquet by wartime standards, and the Jackdaws tucked in with relish. Flick did not feel very hungry, but she forced herself to eat a big steak, knowing it was more meat than she would get in a week in France.

When they finished supper, it was time to go to the airfield. They returned to their rooms to pick up their French bags, then boarded the bus. It took them along another country lane and across a railway line, then approached what looked like a cluster of farm buildings at the edge of a large, flat field. A sign said Gibraltar Farm, but Flick knew that this was RAF Tempsford, and the barns were heavily disguised Nissen huts.

They went into what looked like a cowshed and found a uniformed RAF officer standing guard over steel racks of equipment. Before they were given their gear, each of them was searched. A box of British matches was found in Maude's suitcase; Diana had in her pocket a half-completed crossword torn from the *Daily Mirror,* which she swore she had intended to leave on the plane; and Jelly, the inveterate gambler, had a pack of playing cards with *"Made in Birmingham"* printed on every one.

Paul distributed their identity cards, ration cards, and clothing coupons. Each woman was given a hundred thousand French francs, mostly in grubby thousand-franc notes. It was the equivalent of five hundred pounds, enough to buy two Ford cars.

They also got weapons, .45 caliber Colt automatic pistols and sharp double-bladed Commando knives. Flick declined both. She took her personal gun, a Browning nine-millimeter automatic. Around her waist she wore the leather belt, into which she could push the pistol or, at a pinch, the submachine gun. She also took her lapel knife instead of the Commando knife. The Commando knife was longer and deadlier, but more cumbersome. The great advantage of the lapel knife was that when the agent was asked to produce papers, she could innocently reach toward an inside pocket, then at the last moment pull the knife.

In addition there was a Lee-Enfield rifle for Diana and a Sten Mark II submachine gun with silencer for Flick.

The plastic explosive Jelly would need was distributed evenly among the six women so that even if one or two bags were lost there would still be enough to do the job.

Maude said, "It might blow me up!"

Jelly explained that it was extraordinarily

safe. "I knew a bloke who thought it was chocolate and ate some," she said. "Mind you," she added, "it didn't half give him the runs."

They were offered the usual round Mills grenades with the conventional turtleshell finish, but Flick insisted on general-purpose grenades in square cans, because they could also be used as explosive charges.

Each woman got a fountain pen with a hollow cap containing a suicide pill.

There was a compulsory visit to the bathroom before putting on the flying suit. It had a pistol pocket so that the agent could defend herself immediately on landing, if necessary. With the suit, they donned helmet and goggles and finally shrugged into the parachute harness.

Paul asked Flick to step outside for a moment. He had held back the all-important special passes that would enable the women to enter the château as cleaners. If a Jackdaw were to be captured by the Gestapo, this pass would betray the true purpose of the mission. For safety, he gave all the passes to Flick, to be distributed at the last minute.

Then he kissed her. She kissed him back

with desperate passion, clutching his body to hers, shamelessly thrusting her tongue into his mouth until she had to gasp for breath.

"Don't get killed," he said into her ear.

They were interrupted by a discreet cough. Flick smelled Percy's pipe. She broke the clinch.

Percy said to Paul, "The pilot is waiting for a word with you."

Paul nodded and moved away.

"Make sure he understands that Flick is the officer in command," Percy called after him.

"Sure," Paul replied.

Percy looked grim, and Flick had a bad feeling. "What's wrong?" she said.

He took a sheet of paper from his jacket pocket and handed it to her. "A motorcycle courier from London brought this from SOE headquarters just before we left the house. It came in from Brian Standish last night." He sucked anxiously on his pipe and blew out clouds of smoke.

Flick looked at the sheet of paper in the evening sunlight. It was a decrypt. Its contents hit her like a punch in the stomach.

She looked up, dismayed. "Brian has been in the hands of the Gestapo!"

"Only for a few seconds."

"So this claims."

"Any reason to think otherwise?"

"Ah, *fuck* it," she said loudly. A passing airman looked up sharply, surprised to hear a woman's voice utter such words. Flick crumpled the paper and threw it on the ground.

Percy bent down, picked it up, and smoothed out the creases. "Let's try to stay calm and think clearly."

Flick took a deep breath. "We have a rule," she said insistently. "Any agent who is captured by the enemy, *whatever the circumstances,* must immediately be returned to London for debriefing."

"Then you'll have no wireless operator."

"I can manage without one. And what about this Charenton?"

"I suppose it's natural that Mademoiselle Lemas might have recruited someone to help her."

"All recruits are supposed to be vetted by London."

"You know that rule has never been followed."

"At a minimum they should be approved by the local commander."

"Well, he has been now—Michel is satisfied that Charenton is trustworthy. And Charenton saved Brian from the Gestapo. That whole scene in the cathedral can't have been deliberately staged, can it?"

"Perhaps it never took place at all, and this message comes straight from Gestapo headquarters."

"But it has all the right security codes. Anyway, they wouldn't invent a story about his being captured and then released. They'd know that would arouse our suspicions. They would just say he had arrived safely."

"You're right, but still I don't like it."

"No, nor do I," he said, surprising her. "But I don't know what to do."

She sighed. "We have to take the risk. There's no time for precautions. If we don't disable the telephone exchange in the next three days it will be too late. We have to go anyway."

Percy nodded. Flick saw that there were tears in his eyes. He put his pipe in his mouth and took it out again. "Good girl," he said, his voice reduced to a whisper. "Good girl."

THE SEVENTH DAY

Saturday, June 3, 1944

CHAPTER 30

SOE had no planes of its own. It had to borrow them from the RAF, which was like pulling teeth. In 1941, the air force had reluctantly handed over two Lysanders, too slow and heavy for their intended role in battlefield support but ideal for clandestine landings in enemy territory. Later, under pressure from Churchill, two squadrons of obsolete bombers were assigned to SOE, although the head of Bomber Command, Arthur Harris, never stopped scheming to get them back. By the spring of 1944, when dozens of agents were flown into France in preparation for the invasion, SOE had the use of thirty-six aircraft.

The plane the Jackdaws boarded was an American-made twin-engined Hudson light bomber, manufactured in 1939 and since made obsolete by the four-engined Lancaster heavy bomber. A Hudson came with two machine guns in the nose, and the RAF added a rear turret with two more. At the back of the passenger cabin was a slide like a water chute, down which the parachutists would glide into space. There were no seats inside, and the six women and their dispatcher lay down on the metal floor. They were cold and uncomfortable and scared, but Jelly got a fit of the giggles, which cheered them all up.

They shared the cabin with a dozen metal containers, each as tall as a man and equipped with a parachute harness, all containing—Flick presumed—guns and ammunition to enable some other Resistance circuit to run interference behind German lines during the invasion. After dropping the Jackdaws at Chatelle, the Hudson would fly on to another destination before turning around and heading back to Tempsford.

Takeoff had been delayed by a faulty altimeter, which had to be replaced, so it was one o'clock in the morning when they left the English coastline behind. Over the Channel, the pilot dropped the plane to a few hundred feet above the sea, trying to hide below the level of enemy radar, and Flick silently hoped they would not be shot at by ships of the Royal Navy, but he soon climbed again to eight thousand feet to cross the fortified French coastline. He stayed high to traverse the "Atlantic Wall," the heavily defended coastal strip, then descended again to three hundred feet, to make navigation less difficult.

The navigator was constantly busy with his maps, calculating the plane's position by dead reckoning and trying to confirm it by landmarks. The moon was waxing, and only three days from full, so large towns were easily visible, despite the blackout. However, they generally had antiaircraft batteries, so had to be avoided, as did army camps and military sites, for the same reason. Rivers and lakes were the most useful terrain features, especially when the moon was reflected off the water. Forests showed as dark patches, and the unexpected absence of one was a sure sign that the flight had gone astray. The gleam of railway lines, the glow of a steam engine's fire, and the headlights of the occasional blackout-breaking car were all helpful.

All the way, Flick brooded over the news

about Brian Standish and the newcomer Charenton. The story was probably true. The Gestapo had learned about the cathedral crypt rendezvous from one of the prisoners they had taken last Sunday at the château, and they had set a trap, which Brian had walked into, but he had escaped, with help from Mademoiselle Lemas's new recruit. It was all perfectly possible. However, Flick hated plausible explanations. She felt safe only when events followed standard procedure and no explanations were required.

As they approached the Champagne region, another navigation aid came into play. It was a recent invention known as Eureka/Rebecca. A radio beacon broadcast a call sign from a secret location somewhere in Reims. The crew of the Hudson did not know exactly where it was, but Flick did, for Michel had placed it in the tower of the cathedral. This was the Eureka half. On the plane was Rebecca, a radio receiver, shoehorned into the cabin next to the navigator. They were about fifty miles north of Reims when the navigator picked up the signal from the Eureka in the cathedral.

The intention of the inventors was that the

Eureka should be in the landing field with the reception committee, but this was impracticable. The equipment weighed more than a hundred pounds, it was too bulky to be transported discreetly, and it could not be explained away to even the most gullible Gestapo officer at a checkpoint. Michel and other Resistance leaders were willing to place a Eureka in a permanent position, but refused to carry them around.

So the navigator had to revert to traditional methods to find Chatelle. However, he was lucky in having Flick beside him, someone who had landed there on several occasions and could recognize the place from the air. In the event, they passed about a mile to the east of the village, but Flick spotted the pond and redirected the pilot.

They circled around and flew over the cow pasture at three hundred feet. Flick could see the flare path, four weak, flickering lights in an L shape, with the light at the toe of the L flashing the prearranged code. The pilot climbed toward six hundred feet, the ideal altitude for a parachute drop: any higher, and the wind could blow the parachutists away from the dropping zone; much lower, and the chute might not have time to open fully before the agent hit the ground.

"Ready when you are," said the pilot.

"I'm not ready," Flick said.

"What's the matter?"

"Something's wrong." Flick's instincts were sounding alarm bells. It was not just her worries about Brian Standish and Charenton. There was something else. She pointed west, to the village. "Look, no lights."

"That surprises you? There's a blackout. And it's after three o'clock in the morning."

Flick shook her head. "This is the countryside, they're careless about the blackout. And there's always someone up: a mother with a new baby, an insomniac, a student cramming for finals. I've never seen it completely dark."

"If you really feel there's something wrong, we should get out of here fast," the pilot said nervously.

Something else was bothering her. She tried to scratch her head and found her helmet in the way. The thought evaded her.

What should she do? She could hardly abort the mission just because the villagers of Chatelle were obeying the blackout rules for once.

The plane overflew the field and banked to turn. The pilot said anxiously, "Remember, each time we overfly increases the risk. Everyone in that village can hear our engines, and one of them might call the police."

"Exactly!" she said. "We must have awakened the entire place. Yet no one has switched on a light!"

"I don't know, country folk can be very incurious. They like to keep themselves to themselves, as they always say."

"Nonsense. They're as nosy as anyone. This is peculiar."

The pilot looked more and more worried, but he continued circling.

Suddenly it came to her. "The baker should have lit his oven. You can normally see the glow from the air."

"Could he be closed today?"

"What day is it? Saturday. A baker might close on a Monday or a Tuesday but never on a Saturday. What's happened? This is like a ghost town!"

"Then let's get out of here."

It was as if someone had rounded up the

villagers, including the baker, and locked them in a barn—which was probably what the Gestapo would have done if they were lying in wait for her.

She could not abort the mission. It was too important. But every instinct told her not to parachute into Chatelle. "A risk is a risk," she said.

The pilot was losing patience. "So what do you want to do?"

Suddenly she remembered the containers of supplies in the passenger cabin. "What's your next destination?"

"I'm not supposed to tell you."

"Not usually, no. But now I really need to know."

"It's a field north of Chartres."

That meant the Vestryman circuit. "I know them," Flick said with mounting excitement. This could be the solution. "You could drop us with the containers. There will be a reception committee waiting, they can take care of us. We could be in Paris this afternoon, Reims by tomorrow morning."

He reached for the joystick. "Is that what you want to do?"

"Is it possible?"

"I can drop you there, no problem. The

tactical decision is yours. You're in command of the mission—that was made very clear to me."

Flick considered, worrying. Her suspicions might be unfounded, in which case she would need to get a message to Michel via Brian's radio, saying that although her landing had been aborted, she was still on her way. But in case Brian's radio was in Gestapo hands, she would have to give the minimum of information. However, that was feasible. She could write a brief radio signal for the pilot to take back to Percy: Brian would have it in a couple of hours.

She would also have to change the arrangements for picking up the Jackdaws after the mission. At present, a Hudson was scheduled to land at Chatelle at two a.m. on Sunday, and if the Jackdaws were not there, to return the following night at the same time. If Chatelle had been betrayed to the Gestapo and could no longer be used, she would have to divert the Hudson to another landing field at Laroque, to the west of Reims, codenamed Champ d'Or. The mission would take an extra day, because they would have to travel from Chartres to Reims, so the pickup flight would have to come down at two a.m. on Monday, with a fall-back on Tuesday at the same hour.

She weighed consequences. Diverting to Chartres meant the loss of a day. But landing at Chatelle could mean the entire mission failed and all the Jackdaws ended up in Gestapo torture chambers. It was no contest. "Go to Chartres," she said to the pilot.

"Roger, wilco."

As the aircraft banked and turned, Flick went back to the cabin. The Jackdaws all looked expectantly at her. "There's been a change of plan," she said.

CHAPTER 31

Dieter lay beneath a hedge and watched, bewildered, while the British plane circled over the cow pasture.

Why the delay? The pilot had made two passes over the landing site. The flare path, such as it was, was in place. Had the reception leader flashed the wrong code? Had the Gestapo men done something to arouse suspicion? It was maddening. Felicity Clairet was a few yards away from him. If he fired his pistol at the plane, a lucky shot might hit her.

Then the plane banked, turned, and roared away to the south.

Dieter was mortified. Flick Clairet had evaded him—in front of Walter Goedel, Willi Weber, and twenty Gestapo men.

For a moment, he buried his face in his hands.

What had gone wrong? There could be a dozen reasons. As the drone of the plane's engines receded, Dieter could hear shouts of indignation in French. The Resistance seemed as perplexed as he was. His best guess was that Flick, an experienced team leader, had smelled a rat and aborted the jump.

Walter Goedel, lying in the dirt beside him, said, "What are you going to do now?"

Dieter considered briefly. There were four Resistance people here: Michel the leader, still limping from his bullet wound; Helicopter, the British radio operator; a Frenchman Dieter did not recognize, and a young woman. What should he do with them? His strategy of letting Helicopter run free had been a good one in theory, but it had now led to two humiliating reverses, and he did not have the nerve to continue it. He had to get something out of tonight's fiasco. He was going to have to revert to traditional methods of interrogation and hope to salvage the operation—and his reputation.

He brought the mouthpiece of the short-wave radio to his lips. "All units, this is Major Franck," he said softly. "Action, I repeat, action." Then he got to his feet and drew his automatic pistol.

The searchlights concealed in the trees blazed into life. The four terrorists in the middle of the field were mercilessly lit up, looking suddenly bewildered and vulnerable. Dieter called out in French, "You are surrounded! Raise your hands!"

Beside him, Goedel drew his Luger. The four Gestapo men with Dieter aimed their rifles at the legs of the Resistance people. There was a moment of uncertainty: Would the Resistance open fire? If they did, they would be mowed down. With luck, they might be only wounded. But Dieter had not had much luck tonight. And if these four were killed, he would be left empty-handed.

They hesitated.

Dieter stepped forward, moving into the light, and the four riflemen moved with him. "Twenty guns are aimed at you," he shouted. "Do not draw your weapons."

One of them started to run.

Dieter swore. He saw a flash of red hair in the lights: it was Helicopter, stupid boy, heading across the field like a charging bull. "Shoot him," Dieter said quietly. All four riflemen took careful aim and fired. The shots crashed out in the silent meadow. Helicopter ran another two paces, then fell to the ground.

Dieter looked at the other three, waiting. Slowly, they raised their hands in the air.

Dieter spoke into the short-wave radio. "All teams in the pasture, move in and secure the prisoners." He put away his pistol.

He walked over to where Helicopter lay. The body was still. The Gestapo riflemen had shot at his legs, but it was hard to hit a moving target in the dark, and one of them had aimed too high, putting a bullet through his neck, severing his spinal cord, or his jugular vein, or both. Dieter knelt beside him and felt for a pulse, but there was none. "You weren't the cleverest agent I've ever met, but you were a brave boy," he said quietly. "God rest your soul." He closed the eyes.

He looked over the other three as they were disarmed and fettered. Michel would resist interrogation well: Dieter had seen him in action, and he had courage. His weakness was probably vanity. He was handsome, and a womanizer. The way to torture him would be in front of a mirror: break his nose, knock out his teeth, scar his cheeks, make him understand that with every minute that he continued to resist, he was getting irreversibly uglier.

The other man had the air of a professional, perhaps a lawyer. A Gestapo man searched him and showed Dieter a pass that permitted Dr. Claude Bouler to be out after curfew. Dieter assumed it was a forgery, but when they searched the Resistance cars they found a genuine doctor's bag, full of instruments and drugs. Under arrest he looked pale but composed: he, too, would be a difficult subject.

The girl was the most promising. She was about nineteen, and pretty, with long dark hair and big eyes, but she had a vacant look. Her papers showed that she was Gilberte Duval. Dieter knew from his interrogation of Gaston that Gilberte was the lover of Michel and the rival of Flick. Handled correctly, she might prove easy to turn.

The German vehicles were brought from the barn at La Maison Grandin. The prisoners went in a truck with the Gestapo men. Dieter gave orders that they should be kept in separate cells and prevented from communicating with one another.

He and Goedel were driven back to

Sainte-Cécile in Weber's Mercedes. "What a damned farce," Weber said scornfully. "A complete waste of time and manpower."

"Not quite," said Dieter. "We have taken four subversive agents out of circulation—which is, after all, what the Gestapo is supposed to do—and, even better, three of them are still alive for interrogation."

Goedel said, "What do you hope to get from them?"

"The dead man, Helicopter, was a wireless operator," Dieter explained. "I have a copy of his code book. Unfortunately, he did not have his set with him. If we can find the set, we can impersonate Helicopter."

"Surely you can use any radio transmitter, so long as you know the frequency assigned to him?"

Dieter shook his head. "Every transmitter sounds different to the experienced ear. And these little suitcase radios are particularly distinctive. All nonessential circuits are omitted, to minimize the size, and the result is poor tone quality. If we had one exactly like his, captured from another agent, it might be similar enough to take the risk."

"We may have one somewhere."

"If we do, it will be in Berlin. It's easier to find Helicopter's."

"How will you do that?"

"The girl will tell me where it is."

For the rest of the journey, Dieter brooded over his interrogation strategy. He could torture the girl in front of the men, but they might resist that. More promising would be to torture the men in front of the girl. But there might be an easier way.

A plan was forming in his mind when they passed the public library in the center of Reims. He had noticed the building before. It was a little jewel, an art deco design in tan stone, standing in a small garden. "Would you mind stopping the car for a moment, please, Major Weber?" he said.

Weber muttered an order to his driver.

"Do you have any tools in the trunk?"

"I have no idea," said Weber. "What is this about?"

The driver said, "Of course, Major, we have the regulation tool kit."

"Is there a good-sized hammer?"

"Yes." The driver jumped out.

"This won't take a moment," Dieter said. He got out of the car.

The driver handed him a long-handled

hammer with a chunky steel head. Dieter walked past a bust of Andrew Carnegie up to the library. The place was closed and dark, of course. The glass doors were protected by an elaborate wrought-iron grille. He walked around to the side of the building and found a basement entrance with a plain wood door marked Archives Municipales.

Dieter swung at the door with the hammer, hitting the lock. It broke after four blows. He went inside, turning on the lights. He ran up a narrow staircase to the main floor and crossed the lobby to the fiction section. There he located the letter F for Flaubert and picked out a copy of the book he was looking for, *Madame Bovary*. It was not particularly lucky: that was the one book that must be available in every library in the country.

He turned to chapter nine and located the passage he was thinking about. He had remembered it accurately. It would serve his purpose very well.

He returned to the car. Goedel was looking amused. Weber said incredulously, "You needed something to read?"

"Sometimes I find it difficult to get to sleep," Dieter replied.

Goedel laughed. He took the book from Dieter and read its title. "A classic of world literature," he said. "All the same, I imagine that's the first time someone broke down the library door to borrow it."

They drove on to Sainte-Cécile. By the time they reached the château, Dieter's plan was fully formed.

He ordered Lieutenant Hesse to prepare Michel by stripping him naked and tying him to a chair in the torture chamber. "Show him the instrument used for pulling out fingernails," he said. "Leave it on the table in front of him." While that was being done, he got a pen, a bottle of ink, and a pad of letter paper from the offices on the upper floor. Walter Goedel ensconced himself in a corner of the torture chamber to watch.

Dieter studied Michel for a few moments. The Resistance leader was a tall man, with attractive wrinkles around his eyes. He had a kind of bad-boy look that women liked. Now he was scared but determined. He was thinking grimly about how to hold out as long as possible against torture, Dieter guessed.

Dieter put the pen, ink, and paper on the table next to the fingernail pliers, to show that they were alternatives. "Untie his hands," he said.

Hesse complied. Michel's face showed enormous relief combined with a fear that this might not be real.

Dieter explained to Walter Goedel, "Before questioning the prisoners, I will take samples of their handwriting."

"Their handwriting?"

Dieter nodded, watching Michel, who seemed to have understood the brief exchange in German. He looked hopeful.

Dieter took *Madame Bovary* from his pocket, opened it, and put it down on the table. "Copy out chapter nine," he said to Michel in French.

Michel hesitated. It seemed a harmless request. He suspected a trick, Dieter could tell, but he could not see what it was. Dieter waited. The Resistance were told to do everything they could to put off the moment when torture began. Michel was bound to see this as a means of postponement. It was unlikely to be harmless, but it had to be better than having his fingernails pulled out. "Very well," he said after a long pause. He began writing.

Dieter watched him. His handwriting was

large and flamboyant. Two pages of the printed book took up six sheets of the letter paper. When Michel turned the page, Dieter stopped him. He told Hans to return Michel to his cell and bring Gilberte.

Goedel looked over what Michel had written, and shook his head bemusedly. "I can't figure out what you're up to," he said. He handed the sheets back and returned to his chair.

Dieter tore one of the pages very carefully to leave only certain words.

Gilberte came in looking terrified but defiant. She said, "I won't tell you anything. I will never betray my friends. Besides, I don't know anything. All I do is drive cars."

Dieter told her to sit down and offered her coffee. "The real thing," he said as he handed her a cup. French people could get only ersatz coffee.

She sipped it and thanked him.

Dieter studied her. She was quite beautiful, with long dark hair and dark eyes, although there was something bovine about her expression. "You're a lovely woman, Gilberte," he said. "I don't believe you are a murderer at heart."

"No, I'm not!" she said gratefully.

"A woman does things for love, doesn't she?"

She looked at him with surprise. "You understand."

"I know all about you. You are in love with Michel."

She bowed her head without replying.

"A married man, of course. This is regrettable. But you love him. And that's why you help the Resistance. Out of love, not hate."

She nodded.

"Am I right?" he said. "You must answer."

She whispered, "Yes."

"But you have been misguided, my dear."

"I know I've done wrong—"

"You misunderstand me. You've been misguided, not just in breaking the law but in loving Michel."

She looked at him in puzzlement. "I know he's married, but—"

"I'm afraid he doesn't really love you."

"But he does!"

"No. He loves his wife. Felicity Clairet, known as Flick. An Englishwoman—not chic, not very beautiful, some years older than you—but he loves her."

Tears came to her eyes, and she said, "I don't believe you."

"He writes to her, you know. I imagine he gets the couriers to take his messages back to England. He sends her love letters, saying how much he misses her. They're rather poetic, in an old-fashioned way. I've read some."

"It's not possible."

"He was carrying one when we arrested all of you. He tried to destroy it, just now, but we managed to save a few scraps." Dieter took from his pocket the sheet he had torn and handed it to her. "Isn't that his handwriting?"

"Yes."

"And is it a love letter . . . or what?"

Gilberte read it slowly, moving her lips:

I think of you constantly. The memory of you drives me to despair. Ah! Forgive me! I will leave you! Farewell! I will go far away, so far that you will never hear of me again; and yet—today—I know not what force impelled me toward you. For one doesn't struggle against heaven; one cannot resist the smile of angels; one is carried away by that which is beautiful, charming, adorable.

She threw down the paper with a sob.

"I'm sorry to be the one to tell you," Dieter said gently. He took the white linen handkerchief from the breast pocket of his suit and handed it to her. She buried her face in it.

It was time to turn the conversation imperceptibly toward interrogation. "I suppose Michel has been living with you since Flick left."

"Longer than that," she said indignantly. "For six months, every night except when *she* was in town."

"In your house?"

"I have an apartment. Very small. But it was enough for two . . . two people who loved each other." She continued to cry.

Dieter strove to maintain a light conversational tone as he obliquely approached the topic he was really interested in. "Wasn't it difficult to have Helicopter living with you as well, in a small place?"

"He's not living there. He only came today."

"But you must have wondered where he was going to stay."

"No. Michel found him a place, an empty

room over the old bookshop in the rue Molière."

Walter Goedel suddenly shifted in his chair: he had realized where this was heading. Dieter carefully ignored him, and casually asked Gilberte, "Didn't he leave his stuff at your place when you went to Chatelle to meet the plane?"

"No, he took it to the room."

Dieter asked the key question. "Including his little suitcase?"

"Yes."

"Ah." Dieter had what he wanted. Helicopter's radio set was in a room over the bookshop in the rue Molière. "I've finished with this stupid cow," he said to Hans in German. "Turn her over to Becker."

Dieter's own car, the blue Hispano-Suiza, was parked in front of the château. With Walter Goedel beside him and Hans Hesse in the backseat, he drove fast through the villages to Reims and quickly found the bookshop in the rue Molière.

They broke down the door and climbed a bare wooden staircase to the room over the shop. It was unfurnished but for a palliasse covered with a rough blanket. On the floor beside the rough bed stood a bottle of whisky, a bag containing toiletries, and the small suitcase.

Dieter opened it to show Goedel the radio. "With this," Dieter said triumphantly, "I can become Helicopter."

On the way back to Sainte-Cécile, they discussed what message to send. "First, Helicopter would want to know why the parachutists did not drop," Dieter said. "So he will ask, 'What happened?' Do you agree?"

"And he would be angry," Goedel said.

"So he will say, 'What the blazes happened?' perhaps."

Goedel shook his head. "I studied in England before the war. That phrase, 'What the blazes,' is too polite. It's a coy euphemism for 'What the hell.' A young man in the military would never use it."

"Maybe he should say, 'What the fuck?' instead."

"Too coarse," Goedel objected. "He knows the message may be decoded by a female."

"Your English is better than mine, you choose."

"I think he would say, 'What the devil happened?' It expresses his anger, and it's a masculine curse that would not offend most women."

"Okay. Then he wants to know what he should do next, so he will ask for further orders. What would he say?"

"Probably, 'Send instructions.' English people dislike the word 'order,' they think it's not refined."

"All right. And we'll ask for a quick response, because Helicopter would be impatient, and so are we."

They reached the château and went to the wireless listening room in the basement. A middle-aged operator called Joachim plugged the set in and tuned it to Helicopter's emergency frequency while Dieter scribbled the agreed message:

WHAT THE DEVIL HAPPENED? SEND
INSTRUCTIONS. REPLY
IMMEDIATELY.

Dieter forced himself to control his impatience and carefully show Joachim how to encode the message, including the security tags.

Goedel said, "Won't they know it's not Helicopter at the machine? Can't they recognize the individual 'fist' of the sender, like handwriting?"

"Yes," Joachim said. "But I've listened to this chap sending a couple of times, and I can imitate him. It's a bit like mimicking someone's accent, talking like a Frankfurt man, say."

Goedel was skeptical. "You can do a perfect impersonation after hearing him twice?"

"Not perfect, no. But agents are often under pressure when they broadcast, in some hiding place and worried about us catching up with them, so small variations will be put down to strain." He began to tap out the letters.

Dieter reckoned they had a wait of at least an hour. At the British listening station, the message had to be decrypted, then passed to Helicopter's controller, who was surely in bed. The controller might get the message by phone and compose a reply on the spot, but even then the reply had to be encrypted and transmitted, then decrypted by Joachim.

Dieter and Goedel went to the kitchen on the ground floor, where they found a mess corporal starting work on breakfast, and got him to give them sausages and coffee.

Goedel was impatient to get back to Rommel's headquarters, but he wanted to stay and see how this turned out.

It was daylight when a young woman in SS uniform came to tell them that the reply had come in and Joachim had almost finished typing it.

They hurried downstairs. Weber was already there, with his usual knack of showing up where the action was. Joachim handed the typed message to him and carbon copies to Dieter and Goedel.

Dieter read:

JACKDAWS ABORTED DROP BUT HAVE LANDED ELSEWHERE AWAIT CONTACT FROM LEOPARDESS

Weber said grumpily, "This does not tell us much."

Goedel agreed. "What a disappointment."

"You're both wrong!" Dieter said jubilantly. "Leopardess is in France—and I have a picture of her!" He pulled the photos of Flick Clairet from his pocket with a flourish and handed one to Weber. "Get a printer out of bed and have a thousand copies made. I want to see that picture all over Reims within the next twelve hours. Hans, get my car filled up with petrol."

"Where are you going?" said Goedel.

"To Paris, with the other photograph, to do the same thing there. I've got her now!"

CHAPTER 32

The parachute drop went smoothly. The containers were pushed out first so that there was no possibility of one landing on the head of a parachutist; then the Jackdaws took turns to sitting on the top of the slide and, when tapped on the shoulder by the dispatcher, slithering down the chute and out into space.

Flick went last. As she fell, the Hudson turned north and disappeared into the night. She wished the crew luck. It was almost dawn: because of the night's delays, they would have to fly the last part of their journey in dangerous daylight.

Flick landed perfectly, with her knees bent and her arms tucked into her sides as she fell to the ground. She lay still for a moment. French soil, she thought with a shiver of fear; enemy territory. Now she was a criminal, a terrorist, a spy. If she was caught, she would be executed.

She put the thought out of her mind and stood up. A few yards away, a donkey stared at her in the moonlight, then bent its head to graze. She could see three containers nearby. Farther away, scattered across the field, were half a dozen Resistance people, working in pairs, picking up the bulky containers and carrying them away.

She struggled out of her parachute harness, helmet, and flying suit. While she was doing so, a young man ran up to her and said in breathless French, "We weren't expecting any personnel, just supplies!"

"A change of plan," she said. "Don't worry about it. Is Anton with you?" Anton was the code name of the leader of the Vestryman circuit.

"Yes."

"Tell him Leopardess is here."

"Ah—you are Leopardess?" He was impressed.

"Yes."

"I'm Chevalier. I'm so pleased to meet you."

She glanced up at the sky. It was turning

from black to gray. "Find Anton as quickly as you can, please, Chevalier. Tell him we have six people who need transport. There's no time to spare."

"Very good." He hurried away.

She folded her parachute into a neat bundle, then set out to find the other Jackdaws. Greta had landed in a tree, and had bruised herself crashing through the upper branches, but had come to rest without serious injury, and had been able to slip out of her harness and climb down to the ground. The others had all come down safely on the grass. "I'm very proud of myself," said Jelly, "but I wouldn't do it again for a million pounds."

Flick noted that the Resistance people were carrying the containers to the southern end of the field, and she took the Jackdaws in that direction. There she found a builder's van, a horse and cart, and an old Lincoln limousine with the hood removed and some kind of steam motor powering it. She was not surprised: gas was available only for essential business, and French people tried all kinds of ingenious ways to run their cars.

The Resistance men had loaded the cart with containers and were now hiding them under empty vegetable boxes. More containers were going into the back of the builder's van. Directing the operation was Anton, a thin man of forty in a greasy cap and a short blue workman's jacket, with a yellow French cigarette stuck to his lip. He stared in astonishment. "Six women?" he said. "Is this a sewing circle?"

Jokes about women were best ignored, Flick had found. She spoke solemnly to him. "This is the most important operation I've ever run, and I need your help."

"Of course."

"We have to catch a train to Paris."

"I can get you to Chartres." He glanced at the sky, calculating the time until daylight, then pointed across the field to a farmhouse, dimly visible. "You can hide in a barn for now. When we have disposed of these containers, we'll come back for you."

"Not good enough," Flick said firmly. "We have to get going."

"The first train to Paris leaves at ten. I can get you there by then."

"Nonsense. No one knows when the trains will run." It was true. The combination of Allied bombing, Resistance sabotage, and deliberate mistakes by anti-Nazi railway workers had wrecked all schedules, and the only thing to do was go to the station and wait until a train came. But it was best to get there early. "Put the containers in the barn and take us now."

"Impossible," he said. "I have to stash the supplies before daylight."

The men stopped work to listen to the argument.

Flick sighed. The guns and ammunition in the containers were the most important thing in the world to Anton. They were the source of his power and prestige. She said, "This is more important, believe me."

"I'm sorry—"

"Anton, listen to me. If you don't do this for me, I promise you, you will never again receive a single container from England. You know I can do this, don't you?"

There was a pause. Anton did not want to back down in front of his men. However, if the supply of arms dried up, the men would go elsewhere. This was the only leverage British officers had over the French Resistance.

But it worked. He glared at her. Slowly, he removed the stub of the cigarette from his mouth, pinched out the end, and threw it away. "Very well," he said. "Get in the van."

The women helped unload the containers, then clambered in. The floor was filthy with cement dust, mud, and oil, but they found some scraps of sacking and used them to keep the worst of the dirt off their clothes as they sat on the floor. Anton closed the door on them.

Chevalier got into the driving seat. "So, ladies," he said in English. "Off we go!"

Flick replied coldly in French. "No jokes, please, and no English."

He drove off.

Having flown five hundred miles on the metal floor of a bomber, the Jackdaws now drove twenty miles in the back of a builder's van. Surprisingly it was Jelly—the oldest, the fattest, and the least fit of the six—who was most stoical, joking about the discomfort and laughing at herself when the van took a sharp bend and she rolled over helplessly.

But when the sun came up, and the van entered the small city of Chartres, their mood became somber again. Maude said, "I can't believe I'm doing this," and Diana squeezed her hand.

Flick was planning ahead. "From now on, we split up into pairs," she said. The teams had been decided back at the Finishing School. Flick had put Diana with Maude, for otherwise Diana would make a fuss. Flick paired herself with Ruby, because she wanted to be able to discuss problems with someone, and Ruby was the cleverest Jackdaw. Unfortunately, that left Greta with Jelly.

"I still don't see why I have to go with the foreigner," Jelly said.

"This isn't a tea party," Flick said, irritated. "You don't get to sit by your best friend. It's a military operation and you do what you're told."

Jelly shut up.

"We'll have to modify our cover stories, to explain the train trip," Flick went on. "Any ideas?"

Greta said, "I'm the wife of Major Remmer, a German officer working in Paris, traveling with my French maid. I was to be visiting the cathedral at Reims. Now, I suppose, I could be returning from a visit to the cathedral at Chartres."

"Good enough. Diana?"

"Maude and I are secretaries working for the electric company in Reims. We've been to Chartres because . . . Maude has lost contact with her fiancé and we thought he might be here. But he isn't."

Flick nodded, satisfied. There were thousands of French women searching for missing relatives, especially young men, who might have been injured by bombing, arrested by the Gestapo, sent to labor camps in Germany, or recruited by the Resistance.

She said, "And I'm the widow of a stockbroker who was killed in 1940. I went to Chartres to fetch my orphaned cousin and bring her to live with me in Reims."

One of the great advantages women had as secret agents was that they could move around the country without attracting suspicion. By contrast, a man found outside the area where he worked would automatically be assumed to be in the Resistance, especially if he was young.

Flick spoke to the driver, Chevalier. "Look for a quiet spot to let us out." The sight of six respectably dressed women getting out of the back of a builder's van would be somewhat remarkable, even in occupied France, where people used any means of transport they could get. "We can find the station on our own."

A couple of minutes later he stopped the van and reversed into a turn, then jumped out and opened the back door. The Jackdaws got out and found themselves in a narrow cobbled alley with high houses on either side. Through a gap between roofs she glimpsed part of the cathedral.

Flick reminded them of the plan. "Go to the station, buy one-way tickets to Paris, and get the first train. Each pair will pretend not to know the others, but we'll try to sit close together on the train. We regroup in Paris: you have the address." They were going to a flophouse called Hôtel de la Chapelle, where the proprietress, though not actually in the Resistance, could be relied upon not to ask questions. If they arrived in time, they would go on to Reims immediately; if not, they could stay overnight at the flophouse. Flick was not pleased to be going to Paris—it was crawling with Gestapo men and their collaborators, the "Kollabos"—but there was no way around it by train.

Only Flick and Greta knew the real mission of the Jackdaws. The others still thought they were going to blow up a railway tunnel.

"Diana and Maude first, off you go, quick! Jelly and Greta next, more slowly." They went off, looking scared. Chevalier shook their hands, wished them luck, and drove away, heading back to the field to fetch the rest of the containers. Flick and Ruby walked out of the alley.

The first few steps in a French town were always the worst. Flick felt that everyone she saw must know who she was, as if she had a sign on her back saying British Agent! Shoot Her Down! But people walked by as if she were nobody special, and after she had safely passed a gendarme and a couple of German officers her pulse began to return to normal.

She still felt very strange. All her life she had been respectable, and she had been taught to regard policemen as her friends. "I hate being on the wrong side of the law," she murmured to Ruby in French. "As if I've done something wicked."

Ruby gave a low laugh. "I'm used to it," she said. "The police have always been my enemies."

Flick remembered with a start that Ruby had been in jail for murder last Tuesday. It seemed a long four days.

They reached the cathedral, at the top of the hill, and Flick felt a thrill at the sight of it, the summit of French medieval culture, a church like none other. She suffered a sharp pang of regret for the peaceful times when she might have spent a couple of hours looking around the cathedral.

They walked down the hill to the station, a modern stone building the same color as the cathedral. They entered a square lobby in tan marble. There was a queue at the ticket window. That was good: it meant local people were optimistic that there would be a train soon. Greta and Jelly were in the queue, but there was no sign of Diana and Maude, who must already be on the platform.

They stood in line in front of an anti-Resistance poster showing a thug with a gun and Stalin behind him. It read:

THEY MURDER!
wrapped in the folds of
OUR FLAG

That's supposed to be me, Flick thought.

They bought their tickets without incident. On the way to the platform they had to pass a Gestapo checkpoint, and Flick's pulse beat faster. Greta and Jelly were ahead of them in line. This would be their first encounter with the enemy. Flick prayed they would be able to keep their nerve. Diana and Maude must have already passed through.

Greta spoke to the Gestapo men in German. Flick could clearly hear her giving her cover story. "I know a Major Remmer," said one of the men, a sergeant. "Is he an engineer?"

"No, he's in Intelligence," Greta replied. She seemed remarkably calm, and Flick reflected that pretending to be something she was not must be second nature to her.

"You must like cathedrals," he said conversationally. "There's nothing else to see in this dump."

"Yes."

He turned to Jelly's papers and began to speak French, "You travel everywhere with Frau Remmer?"

"Yes, she's very kind to me," Jelly replied. Flick heard the tremor in her voice and knew that she was terrified. The sergeant said, "Did you see the bishop's palace? That's quite a sight."

Greta replied in French. "We did—very impressive."

The sergeant was looking at Jelly, waiting for her response. She looked dumbstruck for a moment, then she said, "The bishop's wife was very gracious."

Flick's heart sank into her boots. Jelly could speak perfect French, but she knew nothing about any foreign country. She did not realize that it was only in the Church of England that bishops could have wives. France was Catholic, and priests were celibate. Jelly had given herself away at the first check.

What would happen now? Flick's Sten gun, with the skeleton butt and the silencer, was in her suitcase, disassembled into three parts, but she had her personal Browning automatic in the worn leather shoulder bag she carried. Now she discreetly unzipped the bag for quick access to her gun, and she saw Ruby put her right hand in her raincoat pocket, where her pistol was.

"Wife?" the sergeant said to Jelly. "What wife?"

Jelly just looked nonplussed.

"You are French?" he said.

"Of course."

Greta stepped in quickly. "Not his wife, his housekeeper," she said in French. It was a plausible explanation: in that language, a wife was *une femme* and a housekeeper was *une femme de ménage.*

Jelly realized she had made a mistake, and said, "Yes, of course, his housekeeper, I meant to say."

Flick held her breath.

The sergeant hesitated for a moment longer, then shrugged and handed back their papers. "I hope you won't have to wait too long for a train," he said, reverting to German.

Greta and Jelly walked on, and Flick allowed herself to breathe again.

When she and Ruby got to the head of the line, they were about to hand over their papers when two uniformed French gendarmes jumped the queue. They paused at the checkpoint and gave the Germans a sketchy salute but did not offer their papers. The sergeant nodded and said, "Go ahead."

If I were running security here, Flick thought, I'd tighten up on that point. Anyone could pretend to be a cop. But the Germans were overly deferential to people in uniform: that was part of the reason they had let their country be taken over by psychopaths.

Then it was her turn to tell her story to

the Gestapo. "You're cousins?" the sergeant said, looking from her to Ruby and back again.

"Not much resemblance, is there?" Flick said with a cheerful air she did not feel. There was none at all: Flick had blonde hair, green eyes and fair skin, whereas Ruby had dark hair and black eyes.

"She looks like a gypsy," he said rudely.

Flick pretended to be indignant. "Well, she's not." By way of explanation for Ruby's coloring, she added, "Her mother, my uncle's wife, came from Naples."

He shrugged and addressed Ruby. "How did your parents die?"

"In a train derailed by saboteurs," she said.

"The Resistance?"

"Yes."

"My sympathies, young lady. Those people are animals." He handed the papers back.

"Thank you, sir," said Ruby. Flick just nodded. They walked on.

It had not been an easy checkpoint. I hope they're not all like that, Flick thought; my heart won't stand it.

Diana and Maude had gone to the bar.

Flick looked through the window and saw they were drinking champagne. She felt cross. SOE's thousand-franc notes were not for that purpose. Besides, Diana should realize she needed her wits about her at every second. But there was nothing Flick could do about it now.

Greta and Jelly were sitting on a bench. Jelly looked chastened, no doubt because her life had just been saved by someone she thought of as a foreign pervert. Flick wondered whether her attitude would improve now.

She and Ruby found another bench some distance away, and sat down to wait.

Over the next few hours more and more people crowded onto the platform. There were men in suits who looked as if they might be lawyers or local government officials with business in Paris, some relatively well-dressed French women, and a scattering of Germans in uniform. The Jackdaws, having money and forged ration books, were able to get *pain noir* and ersatz coffee from the bar.

It was eleven o'clock when a train pulled in. The coaches were full, and not many people got off, so Flick and Ruby had to stand. Greta and Jelly did, too, but Diana and Maude managed to get seats in a six-person compartment with two middle-aged women and the two gendarmes.

The gendarmes worried Flick. She managed to squeeze into a place right outside the compartment, from where she could look through the glass and keep an eye on them. Fortunately, the combination of a restless night and the champagne they had drunk at the station put Diana and Maude to sleep as soon as the train pulled out of the station.

They chugged slowly through woods and rolling fields. An hour later the two French women got off the train, and Flick and Ruby quickly slid into the vacated seats. However, Flick regretted the decision almost immediately. The gendarmes, both in their twenties, immediately struck up a conversation, delighted to have some girls to talk to during the long journey.

Their names were Christian and Jean-Marie. Both appeared to be in their twenties. Christian was handsome, with curly black hair and brown eyes; Jean-Marie had a shrewd, foxy face with a fair moustache. Christian, the talkative one, was in the middle seat, and Ruby sat next to him. Flick was on the opposite banquette, with Maude beside her, slumped the other way with her head on Diana's shoulder.

The gendarmes were traveling to Paris to pick up a prisoner, they said. It was nothing to do with the war: he was a local man who had murdered his wife and stepson, then fled to Paris, where he had been caught by the *flics,* the city police, and had confessed. It was their job to bring him back to Chartres to stand trial. Christian reached into his tunic pocket and pulled out the handcuffs they would put on him, as if to prove to Flick that he was not boasting.

In the next hour Flick learned everything there was to know about Christian. She was expected to reciprocate, so she had to elaborate her cover story far beyond the basic facts she had figured out beforehand. It strained her imagination, but she told herself this was good practice for a more hostile interrogation.

They passed Versailles and crawled through bomb-ravaged train yards at St. Quentin. Maude woke up. She remembered to speak French, but she forgot that she was not supposed to know Flick, so she said, "Hello, where are we, do you know?"

The gendarmes looked puzzled. Flick had told them she and Ruby had no connection with the two sleeping girls, yet Maude had addressed Flick like a friend.

Flick kept her nerve. Smiling, she said, "You don't know me. I think you have mistaken me for your friend on the other side. You're still half asleep."

Maude gave her a don't-be-so-stupid frown, then caught the eye of Christian. In a pantomime of comprehension she registered surprise, put her hand over her mouth in horror, then said unconvincingly, "Of course, you're quite right, excuse me."

Christian was not a suspicious man, however, and he smiled at Maude and said, "You've been asleep for two hours. We're on the outskirts of Paris. But, as you can see, the train is not moving."

Maude gave him the benefit of her most dazzling smile. "When do you think we will arrive?"

"There, Mademoiselle, you ask too much of me. I am merely human. Only God can tell the future."

Maude laughed as if he had said something deliciously witty, and Flick relaxed.

Then Diana woke up and said loudly, in English, "Good God, my head hurts, what bloody time is it?"

A moment later she saw the gendarmes and realized instantly what she had done—but it was too late.

"She spoke English!" said Christian.

Flick saw Ruby reach for her gun.

"You're British!" he said to Diana. He looked at Maude. "You too!" As his gaze went around the compartment he realized the truth. "All of you!"

Flick reached across and grabbed Ruby's wrist as her gun was halfway out of her raincoat pocket.

Christian saw the gesture, looked down at what Ruby had in her hand, and said, "And armed!" His astonishment would have been comical if they had not been in danger of their lives.

Diana said, "Oh, Christ, that's torn it."

The train jerked and moved forward.

Christian lowered his voice. "You're all agents of the Allies!"

Flick waited on tenterhooks to see what he would do. If he drew his gun, Ruby would shoot him. Then they would all have to jump from the train. With luck, they might disappear into the slums beside the railway tracks before the Gestapo was alerted. The train picked up speed. She wondered whether they should jump now, before they were moving too fast.

Several frozen seconds passed. Then Christian smiled. "Good luck!" he said, lowering his voice to a whisper. "Your secret is safe with us!"

They were sympathizers—thank God. Flick slumped with relief. "Thank you," she said.

Christian said, "When will the invasion come?"

He was naive to think that someone who really knew such a secret would reveal it so casually, but to keep him motivated she said, "Any day now. Maybe Tuesday."

"Truly? This is wonderful. Long live France!"

Flick said, "I'm so glad you are on our side."

"I have always been against the Germans." Christian puffed himself up a little. "In my job, I have been able to render some useful services to the Resistance, in a discreet way." He tapped the side of his nose.

Flick did not believe him for a second. No doubt he was against the Germans: most French people were, after four years of scarce food, old clothes, and curfews. But if he really had worked with the Resistance he would not have told anyone—on the contrary, he would have been terrified of people finding out.

However, that did not matter. The important thing was that he could see which way the wind was blowing, and he was not going to turn Allied agents over to the Gestapo a few days before the invasion. There was too strong a chance he would end up being punished for it.

The train slowed down, and Flick saw that they were coming into the Gare d'Orsay station. She stood up. Christian kissed her hand and said with a tremor in his voice, "You are a brave woman. Good luck!"

She left the carriage first. As she stepped onto the platform, she saw a workman pasting up a poster. Something struck her as familiar. She looked more closely at the poster, and her heart stopped.

It was a picture of her.

She had never seen it before, and she had no recollection of ever having had her photograph taken in a swimsuit. The background was cloudy, as if it had been painted over, so there were no clues there. The poster gave her name, plus one of her old aliases, Françoise Boule, and said she was a murderess.

The workman was just finishing his task. He picked up his bucket of paste and a stack of posters and moved on.

Flick realized her picture must be all over Paris.

This was a terrible blow. She stood frozen on the platform. She was so frightened she wanted to throw up. Then she got hold of herself.

Her first problem was how to get out of the Gare d'Orsay. She looked along the platform and saw a checkpoint at the ticket barrier. She had to assume the Gestapo officers manning it had seen the picture.

How could she get past them? She could not talk her way through. If they recognized her, they would arrest her, and no tall tale would convince German officers to do otherwise. Could the Jackdaws shoot their way out of this? They might kill the men at the checkpoint, but there would be others all over the station, plus French police who would probably shoot first and ask questions later. It was too risky.

There was a way out, she realized. She could hand over command of the operation to one of the others—Ruby, probably—then let them pass through the checkpoint ahead of her, and finally give herself up. That way, the mission would not be doomed.

She turned around. Ruby, Diana, and Maude had got off the train. Christian and Jean-Marie were about to follow. Then Flick remembered the handcuffs Christian had in his pocket, and a wild scheme occurred to her.

She pushed Christian back into the carriage and climbed in after him.

He was not sure if this was some kind of joke, and he smiled anxiously. "What's the matter?"

"Look," she said. "There's a poster of me on the wall."

Both the gendarmes looked out. Christian turned pale. Jean-Marie said, "My God, you really are spies!"

"You have to save me," she said.

Christian said, "How can we? The Gestapo—"

"I must get through the checkpoint."

"But they will arrest you."

"Not if I've already been arrested."

"What do you mean?"

"Put the handcuffs on me. Pretend you have captured me. March me through the checkpoint. If they stop you, say you're taking me to eighty-four avenue Foch." It was the address of Gestapo headquarters.

"What then?"

"Commandeer a taxi. Get in with me. Then, once we are clear of the station, take the cuffs off and let me out in a quiet street. And continue on to your real destination."

Christian looked terrified. Flick could tell that he wanted with all his heart to back out. But he hardly could, after his big talk about the Resistance.

Jean-Marie was calmer. "It will work," he said. "They won't be suspicious of police officers in uniform."

Ruby climbed back into the carriage. "Flick!" she said. "That poster—"

"I know. The gendarmes are going to march me through the checkpoint in handcuffs and release me later. If things go wrong, you're in charge of the mission." She switched to English. "Forget the railway tunnel, that's a cover story. The real target is the telephone exchange at Sainte-Cécile. But don't tell the others until the last minute. Now get them back in here, quickly."

A few moments later they were all crowded into the carriage. Flick told them the plan. Then she said, "If this doesn't work, and I get arrested, *whatever you do, don't shoot.* There will be too many police at the station. If you start a gun battle you'll lose. The mission comes first. Abandon me, get out of the station, regroup at the hotel, and carry on. Ruby will be in command. No discussion, there isn't time." She turned to Christian. "The handcuffs."

He hesitated.

Flick wanted to scream *Get on with it, you big-mouthed coward,* but instead she lowered her voice to an intimate murmur and said: "Thank you for saving my life—I'll never forget you, Christian."

He took out the cuffs.

"The rest of you, get going," Flick said.

Christian handcuffed Flick's right hand to Jean-Marie's left, then they stepped down from the train and marched along the platform three abreast, Christian carrying Flick's suitcase and her shoulder bag with the automatic pistol in it. There was a queue at the checkpoint. Jean-Marie said loudly, "Stand aside, there. Stand aside, please, ladies and gentlemen. Coming through." They went straight to the head of the line, as they had at Chartres. Both gendarmes saluted the Gestapo officers, but they did not stop.

However, the captain in charge of the checkpoint looked up from the identity card he was examining and said quietly, "Wait."

All three stood still. Flick knew she was very near death.

The captain looked hard at Flick. "She's the one on the poster."

Christian seemed too scared to speak. After a moment, Jean-Marie answered the question. "Yes, captain, we arrested her in Chartres."

Flick thanked heaven that one of them had a cool head.

"Well done," said the captain. "But where are you taking her?"

Jean-Marie continued to answer. "Our orders are to deliver her to avenue Foch."

"Do you need transport?"

"There is a police vehicle waiting for us outside the station."

The captain nodded, but still did not dismiss them. He continued to stare at Flick. She began to think there was something about her appearance that had given away her subterfuge, something in her face that told him she was only pretending to be a prisoner. Finally he said, "These British. They send little girls to do their fighting for them." He shook his head in disbelief.

Jean-Marie sensibly kept his mouth shut.

At last the captain said, "Carry on."

Flick and the gendarmes marched through the checkpoint and out into the sunshine.

CHAPTER 33

Paul Chancellor had been angry with Percy Thwaite, violently angry, when he found out about the message from Brian Standish. "You deceived me!" Paul had shouted at Percy. "You deliberately made sure I was out of the way before you showed it to Flick!"

"It's true, but it seemed best—"

"I'm in command—you have no right to withhold information from me!"

"I thought you would have aborted the flight."

"Perhaps I would have—maybe I *should* have."

"But you would have done it for love of Flick, not because it was right operationally."

There Percy had touched Paul's weak

spot, for Paul had compromised his position as leader by sleeping with one of his team. That had made him more angry, but he had been forced to suppress his rage.

They could not contact Flick's plane, for flights over enemy territory had to observe radio silence, so the two men had stayed at the airfield all night, smoking and pacing and worrying about the woman they both, in different ways, loved. Paul had, in his shirt pocket, the wooden French toothbrush he and Flick had shared on Friday morning, after their night together. He was not normally superstitious, but he kept touching it, as if he were touching her, making sure she was okay.

When the plane returned, and the pilot told them how Flick had become suspicious of the reception committee at Chatelle, and had eventually dropped near Chartres, Paul had been so relieved he almost wept.

Minutes later, Percy had taken a call from SOE headquarters in London and had learned of Brian Standish's message demanding to know what had gone wrong. Paul had decided to respond by sending the reply drafted by Flick and brought home by her pilot. In case Brian was still at liberty, it told him that the Jackdaws had landed and would contact him, but it gave no further information, because of the possibility that he was in the hands of the Gestapo.

Still no one was sure what had happened out there. The uncertainty was unbearable for Paul. Flick had to go to Reims, one way or another. He had to know whether she was walking into a Gestapo trap. Surely there must be a way to check whether Brian's transmissions were genuine?

His signals bore the correct security tags: Percy double-checked. But the Gestapo knew about security tags, and they could easily have tortured Brian to learn his. There were subtler methods of checking, Percy said, but they depended on the girls at the listening station. So Paul had decided to go there.

At first Percy had resisted. It was danger-ous for operational people to descend on signals units, he said; they disrupted the smooth running of the service for hundreds of agents. Paul ignored that. Then the head of the station said he would be delighted for Paul to make an appointment to visit in, say, two or three weeks? No, Paul had said, two or three hours is what I had in mind. He had insisted, gently but firmly, using the threat of Monty's wrath as a last resort. And so he had gone to Grendon Underwood.

As a small boy in Sunday school, Paul had been vexed by a theological problem. He had noticed that in Arlington, Virginia, where he was living with his parents, most of the children of his age went to bed at the same time, seven-thirty. That meant they were saying their prayers simultaneously. With all those voices rising to heaven, how could God hear what he, Paul, was saying? He was not satisfied with the answer of the pastor, who just said that God could do anything. Little Paul knew that was an evasion. The question troubled him for years.

If he could have seen Grendon Underwood, he would have understood.

Like God, the Special Operations Executive had to listen to innumerable messages, and it often happened that scores of them came in at the same time. Secret agents in their hideaways were all tapping their Morse keys simultaneously, like the nine-year-olds of Arlington kneeling at their bedsides at half past seven. SOE heard them all.

Grendon Underwood was another grand country house vacated by the owners and taken over by the military. Officially called Station 53a, it was a listening post. In its extensive grounds were radio aerials grouped in great arcs like the ears of God, listening to messages that came from any-where between the arctic north of Norway to the dusty south of Spain. Four hundred wireless operators and coders, most of them young women in the FANYs, worked in the big house and lived in Nissen huts hastily erected on the grounds.

Paul was shown around by a supervisor, Jean Bevins, a heavy woman with specta-cles. At first she was terrified of the visiting bigshot who represented Montgomery him-self, but Paul smiled and talked softly and made her feel at ease. She took him to the transmitting room, where a hundred or so girls sat in rows, each with headphones, notebook, and pencils. A big board showed agents' code names and scheduled times for transmission—known as "skeds" and al-ways pronounced the American way—and the frequencies they would use. There was an atmosphere of intense concentration, the only sound being the tap of Morse code as an operator told an agent she was receiving him loud and clear.

Jean introduced Paul to Lucy Briggs, a pretty blonde girl with a Yorkshire accent so strong that he had to concentrate hard to understand her. "Helicopter?" she said. "Aye, I know Helicopter—he's new. He calls in at twenty hundred hours and receives at twenty-three hundred. No problems, so far."

She never pronounced the letter aitch. Once Paul realized that, he began to find it easier to interpret the accent.

"What do you mean?" he asked her. "What sort of problems do you get?"

"Well, some of them don't tune the transmitter right, so you have to search for the frequency. Then the signal may be weak, so that you can't hear the letters very well, and you worry that you might be mistaking dashes for dots—the letter B is very like D, for instance. And the tone is always bad from those little suitcase radios, because they're so small."

"Would you recognize his 'fist'?"

She looked dubious. "He's only broadcast three times. On Wednesday he was a bit nervous, probably because it was his first, but his pace was steady, as if he knew he had plenty of time. I was pleased—I thought he must feel reasonably safe. We worry about them, you know. We're sitting here nice and warm and they're somewhere behind enemy lines dodging the bloody Gestapo."

"What about his second broadcast?"

"That was Thursday, and he was rushed. When they're in a hurry, it can be difficult to be sure what they mean—you know, was that two dots run together, or a short dash? Wherever he was sending from, he wanted to get out of there fast."

"And then?"

"Friday he didn't broadcast. But I didn't worry. They don't call unless they have to, it's too dangerous. Then he came on the air on Saturday morning, just before dawn. It was an emergency message, but he didn't sound panicky, in fact I remember thinking to myself, He's getting the hang of this. You know, it was a strong signal, the rhythm was steady, all the letters clear."

"Could it have been someone else using his transmitter that time?"

She looked thoughtful. "It sounded like him . . . but yes, it could have been someone else, I suppose. And if it was a German, pretending to be him, they would sound nice and steady, wouldn't they, because they'd have nothing to fear."

Paul felt as if he were wading through gumbo. Every question he asked had two answers. He yearned for something definite. He had to fight down panic every time he recalled to mind the dreadful prospect that he might lose Flick, less than a week after she had come into his life like a gift from the gods.

Jean had disappeared, and returned now with a sheaf of papers in a plump hand. "I've brought the decrypts of the three signals received from Helicopter," she said. Her quiet efficiency pleased him.

He looked at the first sheet.

CALLSIGN HLCP (HELICOPTER)
SECURITY TAG PRESENT
MAY 30 1944
MESSAGE READS:
ARRIVED OK STOP CRYT
RENDEVOUS UNSAFE STOP
NABBED BY GGESTAPO BUT GOT
AWAY STOP IN FUTURE
RENDEZVOUS AT CAFE DE LA
GARE OVER

"He can't spell for nuts," Paul commented.

"It's not his spelling," Jean said. "They always make errors in the Morse. We order the decoders to leave them in the decrypt, rather than tidy them up, in case there's some significance."

Brian's second transmission, giving the strength of the Bollinger circuit, was longer.

CALLSIGN HLCP (HELICOPTER)
SECURITY TAG PRESENT
MAY 31 1944
MESSAGE READS:
ACTIV AGENTS NOMBER FIVE AS
FOLOWS STOP MONET WHO IS
WOUNED STOP COMTESSE OK
STOP CHEVAL HELPS OCASIONLY
STOP BOURGEOISE STILL IM
PLACE STOP PLUS MY RESCUER
CODNAME CHARENTON STOP

Paul looked up. "This is much worse."

Lucy said, "I told you he was in a rush the second time."

There was more of the second message, mainly a detailed account of the incident at the cathedral. Paul went on to the third:

CALLSIGN HLCP (HELICOPTER)
SECURITY TAG PRESENT
JUN 2 1944
MESSAGE READS:
WHAT THE DEVIL HAPPENED QUERY
SEND INSTRUCTIONS STOP REPLY
IMEDIATELY OVER

"He's improving," Paul said. "Only one mistake."

"I thought he was more relaxed on Saturday," Lucy said.

"Either that, or someone else sent the signal." Suddenly, Paul thought he saw a way to test whether "Brian" was himself or a Gestapo impersonator. If it worked, it would at least give him certainty. "Lucy, do you ever make mistakes in transmission?"

"Hardly ever." She threw an anxious glance at her supervisor. "If a new girl is a bit careless, the agent will kick up a hell of a stink. Quite rightly, too. There should never be any mistakes—the agents have enough problems to cope with."

Paul turned to Jean. "If I draft a message, would you encode it exactly as it is? It would be a kind of test."

"Of course."

He looked at his watch. It was seven-thirty p.m. "He should broadcast at eight. Can you send it then?"

The supervisor said, "Yes. When he calls in, we'll just tell him to stand by to receive an emergency message immediately after transmission."

Paul sat down, thought for a moment, then wrote on a pad:

GIVE YOUR ARMS HOW MAN
AUTOMATS HOW MY STENS ALSO
AMMO HOW MNY ROUNDS
ECH PLUS GREDANES REPLY
IMMMEDIATLY

He considered it for a moment. It was an unreasonable request, phrased in a high-handed tone, and it appeared to be carelessly encoded and transmitted. He showed it to Jean. She frowned. "That's a terrible message. I'd be ashamed of it."

"What do you think an agent's reaction would be?"

She gave a humorless laugh. "He would send an angry reply with a few swear words in it."

"Please encode it exactly as it is and send it to Helicopter."

She looked troubled. "If that's what you wish."

"Yes, please."

"Of course." She took it away.

Paul went in search of food. The canteen operated twenty-four hours a day, as the station did, but the coffee was tasteless and there was nothing to eat but some stale sandwiches and dried-up cake.

A few minutes after eight o'clock, the supervisor came into the canteen. "Helicopter called in to say he had had no word yet from Leopardess. We're sending him the emergency message now."

"Thank you." It would take Brian—or his Gestapo impersonator—at least an hour to decode the message, compose a reply, encode it, and transmit it. Paul stared at his plate, wondering how the British had the nerve to call this a sandwich: two pieces of white bread smeared with margarine and one thin slice of ham.

No mustard.

CHAPTER 34

The red-light district of Paris was a neighborhood of narrow, dirty streets on a low hill behind the rue de la Chapelle, not far from the Gare du Nord. At its heart was "La Charbo," the rue de la Charbonnière. On the north side of the street, the convent of la Chapelle stood like a marble statue in a junkyard. The convent consisted of a tiny church and a house where eight nuns dedicated their lives to helping the most wretched of Parisians. They made soup for starving old men, talked depressed women out of suicide, dragged drunk sailors from the gutter, and taught the children of prostitutes to read and write. Next door to the convent stood the Hôtel de la Chapelle.

The hotel was not exactly a brothel, for there were no whores in residence, but when the place was not full the proprietress was willing to rent rooms by the hour to heavily made-up women in cheap evening gowns who arrived with fat French businessmen, furtive German soldiers, or naive young men too drunk to see straight.

Flick walked through the door with a mighty sense of relief. The gendarmes had dropped her off half a mile away. She had seen two copies of her Wanted poster on the way. Christian had given her his handkerchief, a clean cotton square, red with white dots, and she had tied it over her head in an attempt to hide her blonde hair, but she knew that anyone who looked hard at her would recognize her from the poster. There had been nothing she could do but keep her eyes down and her fingers crossed. It had seemed like the longest walk of her life.

The proprietress was a friendly, overweight woman wearing a pink silk bathrobe over a whalebone corset. She had once been voluptuous, Flick guessed. Flick had stayed at the place before, but the proprietress did not appear to remember her. Flick addressed her as "Madame," but she said, "Call me Régine." She took Flick's money and gave her a room key without asking any questions.

Flick was about to go upstairs to her room when she glanced through the window and saw Diana and Maude arriving in a strange kind of taxi, a sofa on wheels attached to a bicycle. Their brush with the gendarmes did not seem to have sobered them, and they were giggling about the vehicle.

"Good God, what a dump," said Diana when she walked in the door. "Perhaps we can eat out."

Paris restaurants had continued to operate during the occupation, but inevitably many of their customers were German officers, and agents avoided them if they could. "Don't even think about it," Flick said crossly. "We're going to lie low here for a few hours, then go to the Gare de l'Est at first light."

Maude looked accusingly at Diana. "You promised to take me to the Ritz."

Flick controlled her temper. "What world are you living in?" she hissed at Maude.

"All right, keep your hair on."

"Nobody leaves! Is that understood?"

"Yes, yes."

"One of us will go out and buy food later.

I have to get out of sight now. Diana, you sit here and wait for the others while Maude checks into your room. Let me know when everyone's arrived."

Climbing the stairs, Flick passed a Negro girl in a tight red dress and noticed that she had a full head of straight black hair. "Wait," Flick said to her. "Will you sell me your wig?"

"You can buy one yourself around the corner, honey." She looked Flick up and down, taking her for an amateur hooker. "But, frankly, I'd say you need more than a wig."

"I'm in a hurry."

The girl pulled it off to reveal black curls cropped close to her scalp. "I can't work without it."

Flick took a thousand-franc note from her jacket pocket. "Buy yourself another."

She looked at Flick with new eyes, realizing she had too much money to be a prostitute. With a shrug, she accepted the money and handed over the wig.

"Thank you," said Flick.

The girl hesitated. No doubt she was wondering how many more of those notes Flick had. "I do girls, too," she said. She reached out and brushed Flick's breast lightly with her fingertips.

"No, thanks."

"Maybe you and your boyfriend—"

"No."

The girl looked at the thousand-franc note. "Well, I guess this is my night off. Good luck, honey."

"Thanks," said Flick. "I need it."

She found her room, put her case on the bed, and took off her jacket. There was a small mirror over a washbasin. Flick washed her hands, then stood looking at her face for a moment.

She combed her short blonde hair back over her ears and pinned it with hair clips. Then she put on the wig and adjusted it. It was a bit big, but it would stay on. The black hair altered her appearance radically. However, her fair eyebrows now looked peculiar. She took the eyebrow pencil from her makeup kit and darkened them. That was much better. Not only did she look like a brunette, she seemed more formidable than the sweet girl in the swimsuit. She had the same straight nose and severe chin, but that seemed like a family resemblance between two otherwise different-looking sisters.

Next she took her identity papers from her jacket pocket. With great care, she re-touched the photograph, using the eyebrow pencil to draw faint lines of dark hair and narrow dark eyebrows. When she was done, she looked hard at the picture. She did not think anyone would be able to tell it had been doctored unless they rubbed it hard enough to smear the pencil marks.

She took off the wig, stepped out of her shoes, and lay on the bed. She had not slept for two nights, because she had spent Thursday night making love to Paul and Friday night on the metal floor of a Hudson bomber. Now she closed her eyes and dropped off within seconds.

She was awakened by a knock at the door. To her surprise, it was getting dark: she had slept for several hours. She went to the door and said, "Who is it?"

"Ruby."

She let her in. "Is everything all right?"

"I'm not sure."

Flick closed the curtains, then switched on the light. "What's happened?"

"Everyone has checked in. But I don't know where Diana and Maude are. They're not in their room."

"Where have you looked?"

"The proprietress's office, the little church next door, the bar across the street."

"Oh, Christ," Flick said in dismay. "The bloody fools, they've gone out."

"Where would they have gone?"

"Maude wanted to go to the Ritz."

Ruby was incredulous. "They can't be that stupid!"

"Maude can."

"But I thought Diana had more sense."

"Diana's in love," Flick said. "I suppose she'll do anything Maude asks. And she wants to impress her paramour, take her to swanky places, show that she knows her way around the world of high society."

"They say love is blind."

"In this case, love is bloody suicidal. I can't believe it—but I bet that's where they've gone. It will serve them right if they end up dead."

"What'll we do?"

"Go to the Ritz and get them out of there—if we're not too late."

Flick put on her wig. Ruby said, "I wondered why your eyebrows had gone dark. It's effective, you look like someone else."

"Good. Get your gun."

In the lobby, Régine handed Flick a note.
It was addressed in Diana's handwriting.
Flick ripped it open and read:

*We're going to a better hotel. We'll
meet you at the Gare de l'Est at 5 a.m.
Don't worry!*

She showed it to Ruby, then ripped it to
shreds. She was most angry with herself.
She had known Diana all her life, it was no
surprise that she was foolish and irresponsible. Why did I bring her? she asked herself. Because I had no one else, was the
answer.

They left the flophouse. Flick did not want
to use the Métro, for she knew there were
Gestapo checkpoints at some stations and
occasional spot checks on the trains. The
Ritz was in the Place Vendôme, a brisk half-
hour walk from La Charbo. The sun had
gone down, and night was falling fast. They
would have to keep an eye on the time:
there was an eleven o'clock curfew.

Flick wondered how long it would take
the Ritz staff to call the Gestapo about Diana and Maude. They would have known
immediately that there was something odd

about them. Their papers said they were secretaries from Reims—what were two such women doing at the Ritz? They were dressed respectably enough, by the standards of occupied France, but they certainly did not look like typical Ritz clients—the wives of diplomats from neutral countries, the girlfriends of black marketers, or the mistresses of German officers. The hotel manager himself might not do anything, especially if he was anti-Nazi, but the Gestapo had informants in every large hotel and restaurant in the city, and strangers with implausible stories were just what they were paid to report. This kind of detail was drummed into people on SOE's training course—but that course lasted three months, and Diana and Maude had been given only two days.

Flick quickened her step.

CHAPTER 35

Dieter was exhausted. To get a thousand posters printed and distributed in half a day had taken all his powers of persuasion and intimidation. He had been patient and persistent when he could and had flown into a mad rage when necessary. In addition, he had not slept the previous night. His nerves were jangled, he had a headache, and his temper was short.

But a feeling of peace descended on him as soon as he entered the grand apartment building at the Porte de la Muette, overlooking the Bois de Boulogne. The job he had been doing for Rommel required him to travel all over northern France, so he needed to be based in Paris, but getting this place had taken a lot of bribery and bullying. It had been worth it. He loved the dark mahogany paneling, the heavy curtains, the high ceilings, the eighteenth-century silver on the sideboard. He walked around the cool, dim apartment, renewing his acquaintance with his favorite possessions: a small Rodin sculpture of a hand, a Degas pastel of a dancer putting on a ballet slipper, a first edition of *The Count of Monte Cristo*. He sat at the Steinway baby grand piano and played a languid version of "Ain't Misbehavin'":

No one to talk with, all by myself . . .

Before the war, the apartment and much of the furniture had belonged to an engineer from Lyon, who had made a fortune manufacturing small electrical goods, vacuum cleaners and radios and doorbells. Dieter had learned this from a neighbor, a rich widow whose husband had been a leading French Fascist in the thirties. The engineer was a vulgarian, she said: he had hired people to choose the right wallpaper and antiques. For him, the only purpose of objects of beauty had been to impress his wife's friends. He had gone to America, where everyone was vulgar, said the widow. She was pleased the apartment now had a tenant who really appreciated it.

Dieter took off his jacket and shirt and washed the Paris grime from his face and neck. Then he put on a clean white shirt, inserted gold links in the French cuffs, and chose a silver-gray tie. While he was tying it, he switched on the radio. The news from Italy was bad. The newscaster said the Germans were fighting a fierce rearguard action. Dieter concluded that Rome must fall in the next few days.

But Italy was not France.

He now had to wait for someone to spot Felicity Clairet. He could not be certain she would pass through Paris, of course, but it was undoubtedly the likeliest place, after Reims, for her to be seen. Anyway, there was nothing more he could do. He wished he had brought Stéphanie with him from Reims. However, he needed her to occupy the house in the rue du Bois. There was a chance that more Allied agents would land and find their way to her door. It was important to draw them gently into the net. He had left instructions that neither Michel nor Dr. Bouler was to be tortured in his absence: he might yet have uses for them.

There was a bottle of Dom Pérignon champagne in the icebox. He opened it and poured some into a crystal flute. Then, with a feeling that life was good, he sat down at his desk to read his mail.

There was a letter from his wife, Waltraud.

My beloved Dieter,
    I am so sorry we will not be together on your fortieth birthday.

Dieter had forgotten his birthday. He looked at the date on his Cartier desk clock. It was June 3. He was forty years old today. He poured another glass of champagne to celebrate.

In the envelope from his wife were two other missives. His seven-year-old daughter, Margarete, known as Mausi, had drawn a picture of him in uniform standing by the Eiffel Tower. In the picture, he was taller than the tower: so children magnified their fathers. His son, Rudi, ten years old, had written a grown-up letter, carefully rounded letters in dark blue ink:

My dear Papa,
    I am doing well in school although

Dr. Richter's classroom has been bombed. Fortunately it was nighttime and the school was empty.

Dieter closed his eyes in pain. He could not bear the thought of bombs falling on the city where his children lived. He cursed the murderers of the RAF, even though he knew German bombs had fallen on British schoolchildren.

He looked at the phone on his desk, contemplating trying to call home. It was difficult to get through: the French phone system was overloaded, and military traffic had priority, so you could wait hours for a personal call to be connected. All the same, he decided to try. He felt a sudden longing to hear the voices of his children and reassure himself that they were still alive.

He reached for the phone. It rang before he touched it. He picked it up. "Major Franck here."

"This is Lieutenant Hesse."

Dieter's pulse quickened. "You have found Felicity Clairet?"

"No. But something almost as good."

CHAPTER 36

Flick had been to the Ritz once, when she was a student in Paris before the war. She and a girlfriend had put on hats and makeup, gloves and stockings, and walked through the door as if they did it every day. They had sauntered along the hotel's internal arcade of shops, giggling at the absurd prices of scarves and fountain pens and perfume. Then they had sat in the lobby, pretending they were meeting someone who was late, and criticized the outfits of the women who came there to tea. They themselves had not dared to order so much as a glass of water. In those days, Flick had saved every spare penny for cheap seats at the Comédie Française.

Since the occupation began, she had heard that the owners were attempting to run the hotel as normally as possible, even though many of the rooms had been taken over permanently by top Nazis. She had no gloves or stockings today, but she had powdered her face and set her beret at a jaunty angle, and she just had to hope that some of the hotel's wartime patrons would be forced into similar compromises.

Lines of gray military vehicles and black limousines were lined up outside the hotel in the Place Vendôme. On the facade of the building, six blood-red Nazi banners flapped boastfully in the breeze. A commissionaire in top hat and red trousers looked doubtfully at Flick and Ruby. "You can't come in," he said.

Flick was in a light blue suit, very creased, and Ruby in a navy frock and a man's raincoat. They were not dressed to dine at the Ritz. Flick tried to imitate the *hauteur* of a French woman dealing with an irritating inferior. Putting her nose in the air, she said, "What is the matter?"

"This entrance is reserved for the top brass, Madame. Even German colonels can't come in this way. You have to go around to the rue Cambon and use the back door."

"As you wish," Flick said with an air of weary courtesy, but in truth she was pleased he had not told them they were under-dressed. She and Ruby walked quickly around the block and found the rear entrance.

The lobby was bright with light, and the bars on either side were full of men in evening dress or uniform. The buzz of conversation clicked and whirred with German consonants, not the languid vowels of French. Flick felt as though she were walking into the enemy's stronghold.

She went up to the desk. A concierge in a coat with brass buttons looked down his nose at her. Judging her to be neither a German nor a wealthy French woman, he said coldly, "What is it?"

"Check whether Mademoiselle Legrand is in her room," Flick said peremptorily. She assumed that Diana must be using the false name on her papers, Simone Legrand. "I have an appointment."

He backed off. "May I tell her who is inquiring?"

"Madame Martigny. I am her employee."

"Very good. In fact, Mademoiselle is in the rear dining room with her companion.

Perhaps you would speak to the head waiter."

Flick and Ruby crossed the lobby and entered the restaurant. It was a picture of elegant living: white tablecloths, silver cutlery, candles, and waiters in black gliding around the room with dishes of food. No one would have guessed that half Paris was starving. Flick smelled real coffee.

Pausing on the threshold, she immediately saw Diana and Maude. They were at a small table on the far side of the room. As Flick watched, Diana took a bottle of wine out of a gleaming bucket beside the table and poured for Maude and herself. Flick could have throttled her.

She turned to make for the table, but the head waiter stood in her way. Pointedly looking at her cheap suit, he said, "Yes, Madame?"

"Good evening," she said. "I must speak with that lady over there."

He did not move. He was a small man with a worried air, but he was not to be bullied. "Perhaps I can give her a message for you."

"I'm afraid not, it's too personal."

"Then I will tell her that you are here. The name?"

Flick glared in Diana's direction, but Diana did not look up. "I am Madame Martigny," Flick said, giving up. "Tell her I must speak to her immediately."

"Very well. If Madame would care to wait here."

Flick ground her teeth with frustration. As the head waiter walked away, she was tempted just to run past him. Then she noticed a young man in the black uniform of an SS major at a nearby table staring at her. She met his eye and looked away, fear rising in her throat. Had he merely taken an idle interest in her altercation with the head waiter? Was he trying to remember where he had seen her before, having seen the poster but not yet made the connection? Or did he simply find her attractive? In any event, Flick realized, it would be dangerous for her to make a fuss.

Every second she stood here was dangerous. She resisted the temptation to turn and run.

The head waiter spoke to Diana, then turned and beckoned Flick.

Flick said to Ruby, "You'd better wait

here—one is less conspicuous than two." Then she walked quickly across the room to Diana's table.

Neither Diana nor Maude had the grace to look guilty, Flick observed angrily. Maude appeared pleased with herself, Diana haughty. Flick put her hands on the edge of the table and leaned forward to speak in a low voice. "This is terribly dangerous. Get up, now, and leave with me. We'll pay the bill on the way out."

She had been as forceful as she knew how, but they were living in a fantasy world. "Be reasonable, Flick," Diana said.

Flick was outraged. How could Diana be such an arrogant idiot? "You stupid cow," she said. "Don't you realize you'll get killed?"

She saw immediately that it had been a mistake to use abuse. Diana looked superior. "It's my life. I'm entitled to take that risk—"

"You're endangering us too, and the whole mission. Now get up off that chair!"

"Look here—" There was a commotion behind Flick. Diana stopped and looked past her.

Flick turned around and gasped.

Standing in the entrance was the well-dressed German officer she had last seen in the square at Sainte-Cécile. She took him in at a glance: a tall figure in an elegant dark suit with a white handkerchief in the breast pocket.

She quickly turned her back, heart pounding, and prayed that he had not noticed her. With her dark wig, there was a good chance he would not have recognized her at first glance.

His name came back to her: Dieter Franck. She had found his photograph in Percy Thwaite's files. He was a former police detective. She recalled the note on the back of his photo: "A star of Rommel's intelligence staff, this officer is said to be a skilled interrogator and a ruthless torturer."

For the second time in a week, she was close enough to shoot him.

Flick did not believe in coincidence. There was a reason he was here at the same time as she.

She soon found out what it was. She looked again and saw him striding across the restaurant toward her, with four Gestapo types trailing him. The head waiter came after them, a look of panic on his face.

Keeping her face averted, Flick walked away.

Franck went straight to Diana's table.

The whole place suddenly became quiet: customers fell silent in mid-sentence, waiters stopped serving vegetables, the sommelier froze with a decanter of claret in his hand.

Flick reached the doorway, where Ruby stood waiting. Ruby whispered, "He's going to arrest them." Her hand moved toward her gun.

Flick again caught the eye of the SS major. "Leave it in your pocket," she murmured. "There's nothing we can do. We might take on him and four Gestapo men, but we're surrounded by German officers. Even if we killed all those five we'd be mowed down by the others."

Franck was questioning Diana and Maude. Flick could not make out the words. Diana's voice took on the tone of supercilious indifference she used when she was in the wrong. Maude became tearful.

Franck must have asked for their papers, because the two women simultaneously reached for their handbags, on the floor beside their chairs. Franck shifted his position so that he was to one side of Diana and slightly behind her, looking over her shoulder, and suddenly Flick knew what was going to happen next.

Maude took out her identity papers, but Diana pulled a gun. A shot rang out, and one of the uniformed Gestapo men doubled over and fell. The restaurant erupted. Women screamed, men dived for cover. There was a second shot, and another Gestapo man cried out. Some diners ran for the exit.

Diana's gun hand moved toward a third Gestapo man. Flick had a flash of memory: Diana in the woods at Somersholme, sitting on the ground smoking a cigarette with dead rabbits all around her. She remembered what she had said to Diana: "You're a killer." She had been right.

But Diana did not fire the third shot.

Dieter Franck kept a cool head. He seized Diana's right forearm with both his hands and banged her wrist on the edge of the table. She screamed with pain and the gun fell from her grasp. He yanked her out of her chair, threw her facedown on the carpet, and fell on her with both knees in the small of her back. He pulled her hands behind her back and handcuffed her, ignoring the screams of pain she gave as he jerked her injured wrist. He stood up.

Flick said to Ruby, "Let's get out of here."

There was a crush at the doorway, panicky men and women all trying to pass through at the same time. Before Flick could move, the young SS major who had been staring at her earlier sprang to his feet and grabbed her arm. "Wait a moment," he said in French.

Flick fought down panic. "Take your hands off me!"

He tightened his grip. "You seem to know those women over there," he said.

"No, I don't!" She tried to move away.

He pulled her back with a jerk. "You'd better stay here and answer some questions."

There was another shot. Several women screamed, but no one knew where the shot had come from. The SS officer's face twisted in a grimace of agony. As he slumped to the floor, Flick saw Ruby, behind him, slipping her pistol back into her raincoat pocket.

They both forced their way through the crowd at the door, shoving ruthlessly, and burst out into the lobby. They were able to run without drawing attention to themselves, because everyone else was running.

Cars were parked in a line along the curb in the rue Cambon, some of them attended by chauffeurs. Most of the chauffeurs were hurrying toward the hotel to see what was happening. Flick picked a black Mercedes 230 sedan with a spare wheel perched on the running board. She looked into the front: the key was in the dash. "Get in!" she yelled at Ruby. She got behind the wheel and pulled the self-starter. A big engine rumbled into life. She engaged first gear, heaved the steering wheel around, and accelerated away from the Ritz. The car was heavy and sluggish, but stable: at speed, it cornered like a train.

When she was several blocks away she reviewed her position. She had lost a third of her team, including her best marksman. She considered whether to abandon the mission and immediately decided to carry on. It would be awkward: she would have to explain why only four cleaners had come to the château instead of the usual six, but she could make up some excuse. It meant they might be questioned more closely, but she would take that risk.

She dumped the car in the rue de la Chapelle. She and Ruby were out of immediate danger. They walked quickly to the flophouse. Ruby rounded up Greta and Jelly and brought them to Flick's room. She told them what had happened.

"Diana and Maude will be questioned immediately," she said. "Dieter Franck is a capable and ruthless interrogator, so we have to assume they will tell everything they know—including the address of this hotel. That means the Gestapo could be here at any moment. We have to leave right away."

Jelly was crying. "Poor Maude," she said. "She was a silly cow, but she didn't deserve to be tortured."

Greta was more practical. "Where will we go?"

"We'll hide in the convent next door to the flophouse. They'll take anyone in. I've hidden escaped prisoners of war there before now. They'll let us stay until daybreak."

"Then what?"

"We'll go to the station as planned. Diana is going to tell Dieter Franck our real names, our code names, and our false identities. He will put out an alert for anyone traveling under our aliases. Fortunately, I have a spare set of papers for all of us, using the same photographs but different identities. The Gestapo don't have photographs of you three, and I've changed my appearance, so the checkpoint guards will have no way of recognizing us. However, to be safe, we won't go to the station at first light—we'll wait until about ten o'clock when it should be busy."

Ruby said, "Diana will also tell them what our mission is."

"She'll tell them we're going to blow up the railway tunnel at Marles. Fortunately, that's not our real mission. It's a cover story I gave out."

Jelly said admiringly, "Flick, you think of everything."

"Yes," she said grimly. "That's why I'm still alive."

CHAPTER 37

Paul sat in the dismal canteen at Grendon Underwood, brooding anxiously about Flick, for more than an hour. He was beginning to believe that Brian Standish had been compromised. The incident in the cathedral, the fact that Chatelle had been in total darkness, and the unnatural correctness of the third radio message all pointed in the same direction.

In the original plan, Flick would have been met at Chatelle by a reception committee consisting of Michel and the remnants of the Bollinger circuit. Michel would have taken them to a hideaway for a few hours, then arranged transport to Sainte-Cécile. After they entered the château and blew up the telephone exchange he would have driven them back to Chatelle to meet their pickup plane. All that had changed now, but Flick would still need both transport and a hiding place when she got to Reims, and she would be relying on the Bollinger circuit to help. However, if Brian had been compromised, would there be any of the circuit left? Was the safe house safe? Was Michel in Gestapo hands, too?

At last, Lucy Briggs came into the canteen and said, "Jean asked me to tell you that Helicopter's reply is being decrypted now. Would you like to come with me?"

He followed her to the tiny room—formerly a boot cupboard, he guessed—that served as Jean Bevins's office. Jean had a sheet of paper in her hand. She looked annoyed. "I can't understand this," she said.

Paul read it quickly.

CALLSIGN HLCP (HELICOPTER)
SECURITY TAG PRESENT
JUN 3 1944

MESSAGE READS:

TWO STENS WITH SIX MAGAZINES FOR EACH STOP ONE LEE ENFELD RIFLE WITH TEN CLIPS STOP

SIX COLT AUTOMATICS WITH APPROXIMATELY ONE HUNDRED ROUNDS STOP NO GRENADES OVER

Paul stared at the decrypt in dismay, as if hoping the words might change to something less horrifying, but of course they remained the same.

"I expected him to be furious," Jean said "He doesn't complain at all, just answers your questions, as nice as pie."

"Exactly," said Paul. "That's because it's not him." This message did not come from a harassed agent in the field who had been presented with a sudden unreasonable request by his bureaucratic superiors. The reply had been drafted by a Gestapo officer desperate to maintain the smooth appearance of calm normality. The only spelling mistake was "Enfeld" instead of "Enfield," and even that suggested a German, for *"feld"* was German for "field."

There was no longer any doubt. Flick was in terrible danger.

Paul massaged his temples with his right hand. There was now only one thing to do.

The operation was falling apart, and he had to save it—and Flick.

He looked up at Jean, and caught her looking at him with an expression of compassion. "May I use your phone?" he said.

"Of course."

He dialed Baker Street. Percy was at his desk. "This is Paul. I'm convinced Brian has been captured. His radio is being operated by the Gestapo." In the background, Jean Bevins gasped.

"Oh, hell," Percy said. "And without the radio, we have no way to warn Flick."

"Yes, we do," said Paul.

"How?"

"Get me a plane. I'm going to Reims—tonight."

THE EIGHTH DAY

Sunday, June 4, 1944

CHAPTER 38

The Avenue Foch seemed to have been built for the richest people in the world. A wide road running from the Arc de Triomphe to the Bois de Boulogne, it had ornamental gardens on both sides flanked by inner roads giving access to the palatial houses. Number 84 was an elegant residence with a broad staircase leading to five stories of charming rooms. The Gestapo had turned it into a house of torture.

Dieter sat in a perfectly proportioned drawing room, stared at the intricately decorated ceiling for a moment, then closed his eyes, preparing himself for the interrogation. He had to sharpen his wits and at the same time numb his feelings.

Some men enjoyed torturing prisoners. Sergeant Becker in Reims was one. They smiled when their victims screamed, they got erections as they inflicted wounds, and they experienced orgasms during their victims' death throes. But they were not good interrogators, for they focused on pain rather than information. The best torturers were men such as Dieter who loathed the process from the bottom of their hearts.

Now he imagined himself closing doors in his soul, shutting his emotions away in cupboards. He thought of the two women as pieces of machinery that would disgorge information as soon as he figured out how to switch them on. He felt a familiar coldness settle over him like a blanket of snow, and he knew he was ready.

"Bring the older one," he said.

Lieutenant Hesse went to fetch her.

He watched her carefully as she came in and sat in the chair. She had short hair and broad shoulders and wore a man-tailored suit. Her right hand hung limply, and she was supporting the swollen forearm with her left hand: Dieter had broken her wrist. She was obviously in pain, her face pale and gleaming with sweat, but her lips were set in a line of grim determination.

He spoke to her in French. "Everything

that happens in this room is under your control," he said. "The decisions you make, the things you say, will either cause you unbearable pain or bring you relief. It is entirely up to you."

She said nothing. She was scared, but she did not panic. She was going to be difficult to break, he could tell already.

He said, "To begin with, tell me where the London headquarters of the Special Operations Executive is located."

"Eighty-one Regent Street," she said.

He nodded. "Let me explain something. I realize that SOE teaches its agents not to remain silent under questioning but to give false answers that will be difficult to check. Because I know this, I will ask you many questions to which I already know the answers. This way I will know whether you are lying to me. Where is the London headquarters?"

"Carlton House Terrace."

He walked across to her and slapped her face as hard as he could. She cried out in pain. Her cheek turned an angry red. It was often useful to begin with a slap in the face. The pain was minimal, but the blow was a humiliating demonstration of the helplessness of the prisoner, and it quickly sapped their initial bravery.

But she looked defiantly at him. "Is that how German officers treat ladies?"

She had a haughty manner, and she spoke French with the accent of the upper classes. She was some kind of aristocrat, he guessed. "Ladies?" he said scornfully. "You have just shot and killed two policemen who were going about their lawful business. Specht's young wife is now a widow, and Rolfe's parents have lost their only child. You're not a soldier in uniform, you have no excuse. In answer to your question—no, this is not how we treat ladies, it's how we treat murderers."

She looked away. He had scored a hit with that remark. He was beginning to undermine her moral foundation.

"Tell me something else," he said. "How well do you know Flick Clairet?"

Her eyes widened in an involuntary expression of surprise. That told him he had guessed correctly. These two were part of Major Clairet's team. He had shaken her again.

But she recovered her composure and said, "I don't know anyone of that name."

He reached down and knocked her left hand away. She cried out in pain as her broken wrist lost its support and sagged. He took her right hand and jerked it. She screamed.

"Why were you having dinner at the Ritz, for God's sake?" he said. He released her hand.

She stopped screaming. He repeated the question. She caught her breath and said, "I like the food there."

She was even tougher than he had thought. "Take her away," he said. "Bring the other one."

The younger girl was quite pretty. She had put up no resistance when arrested, so she still looked presentable, her dress unruffled and her makeup intact. She appeared much more frightened than her colleague. He asked her the question he had asked the older one: "Why were you having dinner at the Ritz?"

"I've always wanted to go there," she replied.

He could hardly believe his ears. "Weren't you afraid it might be dangerous?"

"I thought Diana would look after me."

So the other one's name was Diana.
"What's your name?"

"Maude."

This was suspiciously easy. "And what
are you doing in France, Maude?"

"We were supposed to blow something
up."

"What?"

"I don't remember. Would it have something to do with railways?"

Dieter began to wonder whether he was
being led up the garden path. "How long
have you known Felicity Clairet?" he tried.

"Do you mean Flick? Only a few days.
She's awfully bossy." A thought crossed her
mind. "She was right, though—we shouldn't
have gone to the Ritz." She began to cry. "I
never meant to do anything wrong. I just
wanted to have a good time and see places,
that's all I've ever wanted."

"What's your team's code name?"

"The Blackbirds," she said in English.

He frowned. The radio message to Helicopter had referred to them as Jackdaws.
"Are you sure?"

"Yes. It's because of some poem, 'The
Blackbird of Reims,' I think. No, 'The Jackdaw of Reims,' that's it."

If she was not completely stupid, she was doing a very good imitation. "Where do you think Flick is now?"

Maude thought for a long moment then said, "I really don't know."

Dieter sighed in frustration. One prisoner was too tough to talk, the other too stupid to know anything useful. This was going to take longer than he had hoped.

There might be a way of shortening the process. He was curious about the relationship between these two. Why had the dominant, mannish older woman risked her life to take the pretty, empty-headed girl to dinner at the Ritz? Perhaps I've got a dirty mind, he said to himself. But still . . .

"Take her away," he said in German. "Put her in with the other one. Make sure the room has a judas."

When they had been locked away, Lieutenant Hesse showed Dieter to a small room in the attic. He looked through a peephole into the room next door. The two women were sitting side by side on the edge of the narrow bed. Maude was crying and Diana was comforting her. Dieter watched carefully. Diana's broken right wrist rested in her lap. With her left hand she stroked Maude's hair. She was talking in a low voice, but Dieter could not hear the words.

How close a relationship was this? Were they comrades in arms, bosom friends . . . or more? Diana leaned forward and kissed Maude's forehead. That did not mean much. Then Diana put a forefinger on Maude's chin, turned the girl's face to her own, and kissed her lips. It was a gesture of comfort, but surely too intimate for a mere friend?

Finally Diana poked out the tip of her tongue and licked Maude's tears. That made up Dieter's mind. It was not foreplay— no one could have sex in such circum- stances—but it was the kind of comfort that would be offered only by a lover, not by a mere friend. Diana and Maude were lesbi- ans. And that solved the problem.

"Bring the older one again," he said, and he returned to the interview room.

When Diana was brought in the second time, he had her tied to the chair. Then he said, "Prepare the electrical machinery." He waited impatiently while the electric shock machine was rolled in on its trolley and plugged to a socket in the wall. Every minute that passed was taking Flick Clairet farther away from him.

When everything was ready, he seized Diana by the hair with his left hand. Holding her head still, he attached two crocodile clips to her lower lip.

He turned the power on. Diana screamed. He left it on for ten seconds, then switched off.

When her sobbing began to ease he said, "That was less than half power." It was true. He had rarely used full power. Only when the torture had gone on a long time, and the prisoner kept passing out, was full power used in an effort to penetrate the subject's fading consciousness. And by then it was generally too late, for madness was setting in.

But Diana did not know that.

"Not again," she begged. "Please, please, not again."

"Are you willing to answer my questions?"

She groaned, but she did not say yes.

Dieter said, "Bring the other one."

Diana gasped.

Lieutenant Hesse brought Maude in and tied her to a chair.

"What do you want?" Maude cried.

Diana said, "Don't say anything—it's better."

Maude was wearing a light summer blouse. She had a neat, trim figure with full breasts. Dieter tore her blouse open, sending the buttons flying.

"Please!" Maude said. "I'll tell you anything!"

Under her blouse she wore a cotton chemise with a lacy trim. He took hold of the neckline and ripped it off. Maude screamed.

He stood back and looked. Maude's breasts were round and firm. A part of his mind noticed how pretty they were. Diana must love them, he thought.

He took the crocodile clips from Diana's mouth and carefully fastened one to each of Maude's small pink nipples. Then he returned to the machine and put his hand on the control.

"All right," Diana said quietly. "I'll tell you everything."

Dieter arranged for the railway tunnel at Marles to be heavily guarded. If the Jackdaws got that far, they would find it almost impossible to enter the tunnel. He felt confident that Flick would not now achieve her objective. But that was secondary. His burning ambition was to capture her and interrogate her.

It was already two o'clock on Sunday morning. Tuesday would be the night of the full moon. The invasion could be hours away. But in those few hours Dieter could break the back of the French Resistance—if he could get Flick in a torture chamber. He only needed the list of names and addresses that she had in her head. The Gestapo in every city in France could be galvanized into action, thousands of trained staff. They were not the brightest of men, but they knew how to arrest people. In a couple of hours they could jail hundreds of Resistance cadres. Instead of the massive uprising that the Allies were no doubt hoping for to aid their invasion, there would be calm and order for the Germans to organize their response and push the invaders back into the sea.

He had sent a Gestapo team to raid the Hôtel de la Chapelle, but that was a matter of form: he was certain Flick and the other three would have left within minutes of the arrest of their comrades. Where was Flick now? Reims was the natural jumping-off point for an attack on Marles, which was why the Jackdaws had originally planned to land near the city. Dieter thought it likely Flick would still pass through Reims. It was on the road and rail routes to Marles, and there was probably some kind of help she needed from the remnants of the Bollinger circuit. He was betting she was now on her way from Paris to Reims.

He arranged for every Gestapo checkpoint between the two cities to be given details of the false identities being used by Flick and her team. However that, too, was something of a formality: either they had alternative identities, or they would find ways to avoid the checkpoints.

He called Reims, got Weber out of bed, and explained the situation. For once Weber was not obstructive. He agreed to send two Gestapo men to keep an eye on Michel's town house, two more to watch Gilberte's building, and two to the house in the rue du Bois to guard Stéphanie.

Finally, as the headache began, Dieter called Stéphanie. "The British terrorists are on their way to Reims," he told her. "I'm sending two men to guard you."

She was as calm as ever. "Thank you."

"But it's important that you continue to go to the rendezvous." With luck, Flick would not suspect the extent to which Dieter had penetrated the Bollinger circuit, and she would walk into his arms. "Remember, we changed the location. It's not the cathedral crypt any more, it's the Café de la Gare. If anyone shows up, just drive them back to the house, the way you did with Helicopter. Then the Gestapo can take over from that point."

"Okay."

"Are you sure? I've minimized the risk to you, but it's still dangerous."

"I'm sure. You sound as if you have a migraine."

"It's just beginning."

"Do you have the medicine?"

"Hans has it."

"I'm sorry I'm not there to give it to you."

He was, too. "I wanted to drive back to Reims tonight, but I don't think I can make it."

"Don't you dare. I'll be fine. Take a shot and go to bed. Come back here tomorrow."

He knew she was right. It was going to be hard enough getting back to his apartment, less than a kilometer away. He could not travel to Reims until he had recovered from the strain of the interrogation. "Okay," he said. "I'll get a few hours' sleep and leave here in the morning."

"Happy birthday."

"You remembered! I forgot it myself."

"I have something for you."

"A gift?"

"More like . . . an action."

He grinned, despite his headache. "Oh, boy."

"I'll give it to you tomorrow."

"I can't wait."

"I love you."

The words *I love you, too,* came to his lips, but he hesitated, reluctant from old habit to say them, and then there was a click as Stéphanie hung up.

CHAPTER 39

In the early hours of Sunday morning, Paul Chancellor parachuted into a potato field near the village of Laroque, west of Reims, without the benefit—or the risk—of a reception committee.

The landing gave him a tremendous jolt of pain in his wounded knee. He grit his teeth and lay motionless on the ground, waiting for it to ease. The knee would probably hurt him every so often for the rest of his life. When he was an old man he would say a twinge meant rain—if he lived to be an old man.

After five minutes, he felt able to struggle to his feet and get out of his parachute harness. He found the road, oriented himself by the stars, and started walking, but he was limping badly, and progress was slow.

His identity, hastily cobbled together by Percy Thwaite, was that of a schoolteacher from Epernay, a few miles west. He was hitchhiking to Reims to visit his father, who was ill. Percy had got him all the necessary papers, some of them hastily forged last night and rushed to Tempsford by motorcycle. The limp fitted quite well with the cover story: a wounded veteran might well be a schoolteacher, whereas an active young man should have been sent to a labor camp in Germany.

Getting here was the simple part. Now he had to find Flick. His only way of contacting her would be via the Bollinger circuit. He had to hope that part of the circuit was left intact, and Brian was the only member in Gestapo custody. Like every new agent dropping in to Reims, he would contact Mademoiselle Lemas. He would just have to be especially cautious.

Soon after first light he heard a vehicle. He stepped off the road into the field alongside and concealed himself behind a row of vines. As the noise came closer, he realized the vehicle was a tractor. That was safe enough: the Gestapo never traveled by tractor. He returned to the road and thumbed a lift.

The tractor was driven by a boy of about fifteen and was pulling a cartload of artichokes. The driver nodded at Paul's leg and said, "War wound?"

"Yes," Paul said. The likeliest moment for a French soldier to have been hurt was during the Battle of France, so he added: "Sedan, nineteen-forty."

"I was too young," the boy said regretfully.

"Lucky you."

"But wait till the Allies come back. Then you'll see some action." He gave Paul a sideways look. "I can't say any more. But you wait and see."

Paul thought hard. Was this lad a member of the Bollinger circuit? He said, "But do our people have the guns and ammunition they need?" If the boy knew anything at all, he would know that the Allies had dropped tons of weaponry in the past few months.

"We'll use whatever weapons come to hand."

Was he being discreet about what he knew? No, Paul thought. The boy looked vague. He was fantasizing. Paul said no more.

The lad dropped him off on the outskirts, and he limped into town. The rendezvous had changed, from the cathedral crypt to the Café de la Gare, but the time was the same, three o'clock in the afternoon. He had hours to kill.

He went into the café to get breakfast and reconnoitre. He asked for black coffee. The elderly waiter raised his eyebrows, and Paul realized he had made a slip. Hastily, he tried to cover up. "No need to say 'black,' I suppose," he said. "You probably don't have any milk anyway."

The waiter smiled, reassured. "Unfortunately not." He went away.

Paul breathed out. It was eight months since he had been undercover in France, and he had forgotten the minute-to-minute strain of pretending to be someone else.

He spent the morning dozing through services in the cathedral, then went back into the café at one-thirty for lunch. The place emptied out around two-thirty, and he stayed drinking ersatz coffee. Two men came in at two forty-five and ordered beer. Paul looked hard at them. They wore old business suits and talked about grapes in colloquial French. They were eruditely discussing the flowering of the vines, a critical period that had just ended. He did not think they could possibly be agents of the Gestapo.

At exactly three o'clock a tall, attractive woman came in, dressed with unobtrusive elegance in a summer frock of plain green cotton and a straw hat. She wore odd shoes: one black, one brown. This must be Bourgeoise.

Paul was a little surprised. He had expected an older woman. However, that was probably an unwarranted assumption: Flick had never actually described her.

All the same, he was not yet ready to trust her. He got up and left the café.

He walked along the pavement to the railway station and stood in the entrance, watching the café. He was not conspicuous: as usual, there were several people hanging around the station waiting to meet friends.

He monitored the café's clientele. A woman walked by with a child who was demanding pastry and, as they reached the café, the mother gave in and took the child inside. The two grape experts left. A gendarme went in and came out immediately with a packet of cigarettes in his hand.

Paul began to believe this was not a Gestapo trap. There was no one in sight who looked remotely dangerous. Changing the location of the rendezvous had shaken them off.

Only one thing puzzled him. When Brian Standish had been caught at the cathedral, he had been rescued by Bourgeoise's friend Charenton. Where was he today? If he had been keeping an eye on her in the cathedral, why not here, too? But the circumstance was not dangerous in itself. And there could be a hundred simple explanations.

The mother and child left the café. Then, at three-thirty, Bourgeoise came out. She walked along the pavement away from the station. Paul followed on the other side of the street. She went up to a small black car of Italian design, the one the French called a Simca Cinq. Paul crossed the street. She got into the car and started the engine.

It was time for Paul to decide. He could not be sure this was safe, but he had gone as far as he could with caution, short of not making the rendezvous at all. At some point, risks had to be taken. Otherwise he might as well have stayed at home.

He went up to the car on the passenger side and opened the door.

She looked coolly at him. "Monsieur?"

"Pray for me," he said.

"I pray for peace."

Paul got into the car. Giving himself a code name, he said, "I am Danton."

She pulled away. "Why didn't you speak to me in the café?" she said. "I saw you as soon as I walked in. You made me wait there half an hour. It's dangerous."

"I wanted to be sure this wasn't a trap."

She glanced over at him. "You heard what happened to Helicopter."

"Yes. Where's your friend who rescued him, Charenton?"

She headed south, driving fast. "He's working today."

"On Sunday? What does he do?"

"Fireman. He's on duty."

That explained that. Paul moved quickly to the real purpose of his visit. "Where's Helicopter?"

She shook her head. "No idea. My house is a cut-out. I meet people, I pass them on

to Monet. I'm not supposed to know anything."

"Is Monet all right?"

"Yes. He phoned me on Thursday afternoon, checking up on Charenton."

"Not since?"

"No. But that's not unusual."

"When did you last see him?"

"In person? I've never seen him."

"Have you heard from Leopardess?"

"No."

Paul brooded as the car threaded through
the suburbs. Bourgeoise really had no information for him. He would have to move to
the next link in the chain.

She pulled into a courtyard alongside a
tall house. "Come inside and get cleaned
up," she said.

He got out of the car. Everything seemed
to be in order: Bourgeoise had been at the
right rendezvous and had given all the correct signals, and there had been no one following her. On the other hand, she had given
him no useful information, and he still had
no notion how deeply the Bollinger circuit
had been penetrated, nor how much danger
Flick was in. As Bourgeoise led him to the
front door and opened it with her key, he

touched the wooden toothbrush in his shirt pocket: it was French-made, so he had been permitted to bring it with him. Now an impulse seized him. As Bourgeoise stepped into the house, he slipped the toothbrush from his pocket and dropped it on the ground just in front of the door.

He followed her inside. "Big place," he said. It had dark, old-fashioned wallpaper and heavy furniture, quite out of character with its owner. "Have you been here long?"

"I inherited it three or four years ago. I'd like to redecorate, but you can't get the materials." She opened a door and stood aside for him to go first. "Come into the kitchen."

He stepped inside and saw two men in uniform. Both held automatic pistols. And both guns were pointed at Paul.

CHAPTER 40

Dieter's car suffered a puncture on the RN3 road between Paris and Meaux. A bent nail was stuck in the tire. The delay irritated him, and he paced the roadside restlessly, but Lieutenant Hesse jacked up the car and changed the wheel with calm efficiency, and they were on their way again within a few minutes.

Dieter had slept late, under the influence of the morphine injection Hans had given him in the early hours, and now he watched with impatience as the ugly industrial landscape east of Paris changed gradually to farming country. He wanted to be in Reims. He had set a trap for Flick Clairet, and he needed to be there when she fell into it.

The big Hispano-Suiza flew along an arrow-straight road lined with poplars—a road probably built by the Romans. At the start of the war, Dieter had thought the Third Reich would be like the Roman Empire, a pan-European hegemony that would bring unprecedented peace and prosperity to all its subjects. Now he was not so sure.

He worried about his mistress. Stéphanie was in danger, and he was responsible. Everyone's life was at risk now, he told himself. Modern warfare put the entire population on the front line. The best way to protect Stéphanie—and himself, and his family in Germany—was to defeat the invasion. But there were moments when he cursed himself for involving his lover so closely in his mission. He was playing a risky game and using her in an exposed position.

Resistance fighters did not take prisoners. Being in constant peril themselves, they had no scruples about killing French people who collaborated with the enemy.

The thought that Stéphanie might be killed made his chest tighten and his breathing difficult. He could hardly contemplate life without her. The prospect seemed dismal, and he realized he must be in love with her. He had always told himself that she was just a beautiful courtesan, and he was using her the way men always used such women. Now he saw that he had been fooling himself. And he wished all the more that he was already in Reims at her side.

It was Sunday afternoon, so there was little traffic on the road, and they made good progress.

The second puncture occurred when they were less than an hour from Reims. Dieter wanted to scream with frustration. It was another bent nail. Were wartime tires poor quality, he wondered? Or did French people deliberately drop their old nails on the road, knowing that nine vehicles out of ten were driven by the occupying forces?

The car did not have a second spare wheel, so the tire had to be mended before they could drive on. They left the car and walked. After a mile or so they came to a farmhouse. A large family was sitting around the remains of a substantial Sunday lunch: on the table were cheese and strawberries and several empty wine bottles. Country folk were the only French people who were well fed. Dieter bullied the farmer into hitching up his horse and cart and driving them to the next town.

In the town square was a single gas pump

on the pavement outside a wheelwright's shop with a Closed sign in the window. They banged on the door and woke a surly *garagiste* from his Sunday-afternoon nap. The mechanic fired up an ancient truck and drove off with Hans beside him.

Dieter sat in the living room of the mechanic's house, stared at by three small children in ragged clothes. The mechanic's wife, a tired woman with dirty hair, bustled about in the kitchen but did not offer him so much as a glass of cold water.

Dieter thought of Stéphanie again. There was a phone in the hallway. He looked into the kitchen. "May I make a call?" he asked politely. "I will pay you, of course."

She gave him a hostile glare. "Where to?"

"Reims."

She nodded and made a note of the time by the clock on the mantelpiece.

Dieter got the operator and gave the number of the house in the rue du Bois. It was answered immediately by a low, gruff voice reciting the number in a provincial accent. Suddenly alert, Dieter said in French, "This is Pierre Charenton."

The voice at the other end changed into Stéphanie's, and she said, "My darling."

He realized she had answered the phone with her imitation of Mademoiselle Lemas, as a precaution. His heart gladdened with relief. "Is everything all right?" he asked her.

"I've captured another enemy agent for you," she said coolly.

His mouth went dry. "My God . . . well done! How did it happen?"

"I picked him up in the Café de la Gare and brought him here."

Dieter closed his eyes. If something had gone wrong—if she had done anything to make the agent suspect her—she could be dead by now. "And then?"

"Your men tied him up."

She had said *him.* That meant the terrorist was not Flick. Dieter was disappointed. All the same, his strategy was working. This man was the second Allied agent to walk into the trap. "What's he like?"

"A young guy with a limp and half his ear shot off."

"What have you done with him?"

"He's here in the kitchen, on the floor. I was about to call Sainte-Cécile and have him picked up."

"Don't do that. Lock him in the cellar. I want to talk to him before Weber does."

"Where are you?"

"Some village. We have a damn puncture."

"Hurry back."

"I should be with you in an hour or two."

"Okay."

"How are you?"

"Fine."

Dieter wanted a serious answer. "But really, how do you feel?"

"How do I *feel?*" She paused. "That's a question you don't usually ask."

Dieter hesitated. "I don't usually involve you in capturing terrorists."

Her voice softened. "I feel fine. Don't worry about me."

He found himself saying something he had not planned. "What will we do after the war?"

There was a surprised silence at the other end of the line.

Dieter said, "Of course, the war could go on for ten years, but on the other hand it might be over in two weeks, and then what would we do?"

She recovered her composure somewhat, but there was an uncharacteristic tremor in her voice as she said, "What would you like to do?"

"I don't know," he said, but that left him dissatisfied, and after a moment he blurted out, "I don't want to lose you."

"Oh."

He waited for her to say something else.

"What are you thinking?" he said.

She said nothing. There was an odd sound at the other end, and he realized she was crying. He felt choked up himself. He caught the eye of the mechanic's wife, still timing his phone call. He swallowed hard and turned away, not wanting a stranger to see that he was upset. "I'll be with you soon," he said. "We'll talk some more."

"I love you," she said.

He glanced at the mechanic's wife. She was staring at him. To hell with her, he thought. "I love you, too," he said. Then he hung up the phone.

CHAPTER 41

It took the Jackdaws most of the day to get from Paris to Reims.

They passed through all the checkpoints without incident. Their new fake identities worked as well as the old, and no one noticed that Flick's photograph had been retouched with eyebrow pencil.

But their train was delayed repeatedly, stopping for an hour at a time in the middle of nowhere. Flick sat in the hot carriage fuming with impatience as the precious minutes leaked away uselessly. She could see the reason for the holdups: half the track had been destroyed by the bombers of the U.S. Air Force and the RAF. When the train chugged into life and moved forward, they looked out of the windows and saw emergency repair crews cutting through twisted

rails, picking up smashed sleepers, and lay-
ing new track. Her only consolation was that
the delays would be even more maddening
for Rommel as he attempted to deploy his
troops to repel the invasion.

There was a feeling in her chest like a
cold, inert lump, and every few minutes her
thoughts returned to Diana and Maude.
They had certainly been interrogated by
now, probably tortured, possibly killed. Flick
had known Diana all her life. She was going
to have to tell Diana's brother, William, what
had happened. Flick's own mother would be
almost as upset as William. Ma had helped
raise Diana.

They began to see vineyards, then champagne warehouses alongside the track, and
at last they arrived in Reims a few minutes
after four on Sunday afternoon. As Flick had
feared, it was too late to carry out their mission the same evening. That meant another
nerve-racking twenty-four hours in occupied territory. It also gave Flick a more specific problem: Where would the Jackdaws
spend the night?

This was not Paris. There was no red-light
district with disreputable flophouses whose
proprietors asked few questions, and Flick

did not know of a convent where the nuns would hide anyone who begged for sanctuary. There were no dark alleys in which down-and-outs slept behind rubbish bins ignored by the police.

Flick knew of three possible hideouts: Michel's town house, Gilberte's apartment, and Mademoiselle Lemas's house in the rue du Bois. Unfortunately, any of them might be under surveillance, depending on how deeply the Gestapo had penetrated the Bollinger circuit. If Dieter Franck was in charge of the investigation, she had to fear the worst.

There was nothing to do but go and look. "We must split up into pairs again," she told the others. "Four women together is too conspicuous. Ruby and I will go first. Greta and Jelly, follow a hundred meters behind us."

They walked to Michel's place, not far from the station. It was Flick's marital home, but she always thought of it as his house. There was plenty of room for four women. But the Gestapo almost certainly knew of the place: it would be astonishing if none of the men taken captive last Sunday had revealed the address under torture.

The house was in a busy street with several shops. Walking along the pavement, Flick surreptitiously looked into each parked car while Ruby checked the houses and shops. Michel's property was a high, narrow building in an elegant eighteenth-century row. It had a small front yard with a magnolia tree. The place was still and quiet, with no movement at the windows. The doorstep was dusty.

On their first pass along the street, they saw nothing suspicious: no workmen digging up the road, no watchful loiterers at the pavement tables outside the bar, Chez Régis, no one leaning on a telegraph pole reading a newspaper.

They returned on the opposite side. Outside the baker's shop was a black Citroën Traction Avant with two men in suits sitting in the front, smoking cigarettes and looking bored.

Flick tensed. She was wearing her dark wig, so she felt sure they would not recognize her as the girl on the Wanted poster, but all the same her pulse beat faster and she hurried past them. All along the pavement she listened for a shout behind her, but it did not come, and at last she turned the corner and breathed easier.

She slowed her pace. Her fears had been justified. Michel's house was no use to her. It did not have a rear entrance, being part of a row with no back alley. The Jackdaws could not enter without being seen by the Gestapo.

She considered the other two possibilities. Michel was presumably still living at Gilberte's apartment, unless he had been captured. The building had a useful back entrance. But it was a tiny place, and four overnight guests at a one-room apartment would not only be uncomfortable but also might be noticed by other people in the building.

The obvious place for them to spend the night was the house in the rue du Bois. Flick had been there twice. It was a big house with lots of bedrooms. Mademoiselle Lemas was completely trustworthy and was more than willing to feed unexpected guests. She had been sheltering British agents, downed airmen, and escaping prisoners of war for years. And she might know what had happened to Brian Standish.

It was a mile or two from the center of town. The four women set out to walk there, still in pairs a hundred meters apart.

They arrived half an hour later. The rue du Bois was a quiet suburban street: a surveillance team would have trouble concealing themselves here. There was only one parked car within sight, an impeccably upright Peugot 201 that was much too slow for the Gestapo. It was empty.

Flick and Ruby took a preliminary walk past Mademoiselle Lemas's house. It looked the same as always. Her Simca Cinq stood in the courtyard, which was unusual only in that she normally parked it in the garage. Flick slowed her pace and surreptitiously looked in at the window. She saw no one. Mademoiselle Lemas used that room only rarely: it was an old-fashioned front parlor, the piano immaculately dusted, the cushions always plumped, the door kept firmly closed except for formal visits. Her secret guests always sat in the kitchen at the back of the house, where there was no chance they would be seen by passersby.

As Flick passed the door, her eye was caught by something on the ground. It was a wooden toothbrush. Without pausing in her stride, she stooped and picked it up.

Ruby said, "Do you need to clean your teeth?"

"This looks like Paul's." She almost

thought it *was* Paul's, although there must be hundreds like it in France, maybe thousands.

"Do you think he might be here?"

"Maybe."

"Why would he have come?"

"I don't know. To warn us of danger, perhaps."

They walked on around the block. Before approaching the house again, she let Greta and Jelly catch up. "This time we'll go together," she said. "Greta and Jelly, knock on the front door."

Jelly said, "Thank gordon, my feet are killing me."

"Ruby and I will go around to the back, just as a precaution. Don't say anything about us, just wait for us to appear."

They walked along the street again, all together this time. Flick and Ruby went into the courtyard and past the Simca Cinq and crept around to the back. The kitchen ran almost the whole width of the house at the rear, with two windows and a door between. Flick waited until she heard the metallic ring of the doorbell, then she risked a peep through a window.

Her heart stopped.

There were three people in the kitchen:

two men in uniform, and a tall woman with luxuriant red hair who was definitely not the middle-aged Mademoiselle Lemas.

In a frozen fraction of a second, Flick noted that all three were looking away from the windows, reflexively turning in the direction of the front door.

Then she ducked down again.

She thought fast. The men were obviously Gestapo officers. The woman must be a French traitor, posing as Mademoiselle Lemas. She had looked vaguely familiar, even from the back: there was something about the stylish drape of her green summer dress that struck a chord in Flick's memory.

It was dismayingly clear to Flick that the safe house had been betrayed. The place was now a trap for Allied agents. Poor Brian Standish must have fallen straight into it. Flick wondered whether he was still alive.

A feeling of cold determination came over her. She drew her pistol. Ruby did the same.

"Three people," she told Ruby in a low voice. "Two men and a woman." She took a deep breath. It was time to be ruthless. "We're going to kill the men," she said. "Okay?"

Ruby nodded.

Flick thanked heaven for Ruby's cool head. "I'd prefer to keep the woman alive for questioning, but we'll shoot her if she seems likely to escape."

"Got it."

"The men are at the left-hand end of the kitchen. The woman will probably go to the door. You take this window, I'll take the far one. Aim at the man nearest to you. Shoot when I shoot."

She crept across the width of the house and crouched under the other window. Her breath was coming fast and her heart was beating like a steam hammer, but she was thinking as clearly as if she were playing chess. She had no experience of firing through glass. She decided to shoot three times in rapid succession: once to shatter the window, a second time to kill her man, and a third time to be sure of him. She thumbed the safety catch on her pistol and held it pointing to the sky. Then she straightened up and looked in through the window.

The two men were standing facing the door to the hall. Both had pistols drawn. Flick leveled her gun at the one nearest her.

The woman had gone, but as Flick looked she returned, holding the kitchen door open.

Greta and Jelly walked in ahead of her, all unsuspecting; then they saw the Gestapo men. Greta gave a small scream of fear. Something was said—Flick could not hear what—then Greta and Jelly raised their hands in the air.

The fake Mademoiselle Lemas walked into the kitchen behind them. Seeing her full-face, Flick felt a shock of recognition. She had seen her before. An instant later she remembered where. The woman had been in the square at Sainte-Cécile last Sunday with Dieter Franck. Flick had thought she was the officer's mistress. Obviously she was something more than that.

A moment later the woman saw Flick's face at the window. Her mouth dropped open, her eyes widened, and she lifted her hand to point at what she had seen. The two men began to turn.

Flick pulled the trigger. The bang of the gun seemed simultaneous with the crash of breaking glass. Holding the gun level and steady, she fired twice more.

A second later, Ruby fired.

Both men fell to the ground.

Flick threw open the back door and stepped inside.

The young woman had already turned away. She was making a dash for the front door. Flick raised her gun, but too late: in a split second the woman was in the hall and out of Flick's line of sight. Then Jelly, moving surprisingly fast, threw herself through the door. There was a crash of falling bodies and breaking furniture.

Flick crossed the kitchen and looked. Jelly had brought the woman down on the tiled floor of the hall. She had also broken the delicate curved legs of a kidney-shaped table, smashed a Chinese vase that had stood on the table, and scattered a spray of dried grasses that had been in the vase. The French woman struggled to get up. Flick aimed her pistol but did not fire. Jelly, showing remarkably quick reactions, grabbed the woman by the hair and banged her head on the tiles until she stopped wriggling.

The woman was wearing odd shoes, one black and one brown.

Flick turned back and looked at the two Gestapo men on the kitchen floor. Both lay still. She picked up their guns and pocketed them. Loose firearms left lying around might be used by the enemy.

For the moment, the four Jackdaws were safe.

Flick was operating on adrenaline. The time would come, she knew, when she would think about the man she had killed. The end of a life was a dreadful moment. Its solemnity might be postponed but would return. Hours or days from now, Flick would wonder if the young man in uniform had left behind a wife who was now alone, and children fatherless. But for the present, she was able to put that aside and think only of her mission.

She said, "Jelly, keep the woman covered. Greta, find some string and tie her to a chair. Ruby, go upstairs and make sure there's no one else in the house. I'll check the basement."

She ran down the stairs to the cellar. There on the dirt floor she saw the figure of a man, tied up and gagged. The gag covered much of his face, but she could see that half his ear had been shot off.

She pulled the gag from his mouth, bent down, and gave him a long, passionate kiss. "Welcome to France."

He grinned. "Best welcome I ever had."

"I've got your toothbrush."

"It was a last-second thing, because I wasn't perfectly sure of the redhead."

"It made me just that little bit more suspicious."

"Thank God."

She took the sharp little knife from its sheath under her lapel and began to cut the cords that bound him. "How did you get here?"

"Parachuted in last night."

"What the hell for?"

"Brian's radio is definitely being operated by the Gestapo. I wanted to warn you."

She threw her arms around him in a burst of affection. "I'm so glad you're here!"

He hugged and kissed her. "In that case I'm glad I came."

They went upstairs. "Look who I found in the cellar," Flick said.

They were all waiting for instructions. She thought for a moment. Five minutes had passed since the shooting. The neighbors must have heard gunfire, but few French citizens were quick to call the police nowadays: they were afraid they would end up answering questions at the Gestapo office. However, she would not take needless risks. They had to be out of here as soon as possible.

She turned her attention to the fake Mademoiselle Lemas, now tied to a kitchen chair. She knew what had to be done, and her heart sank at the prospect. "What is your name?" she asked her.

"Stéphanie Vinson."

"You're the mistress of Dieter Franck."

She was as pale as a sheet but looked defiant, and Flick thought how beautiful she was. "He saved my life."

So that was how Franck had won her loyalty, Flick thought. It made no difference: a traitor was a traitor, whatever the motive. "You brought Helicopter to this house to be captured."

She said nothing.

"Is Helicopter alive or dead?"

"I don't know."

Flick pointed to Paul. "You brought him here, too. You would have helped the Gestapo capture us all." The anger sounded in her voice as she thought of the danger to Paul.

Stéphanie lowered her gaze.

Flick walked behind the chair and drew her gun. "You're French, yet you collaborated with the Gestapo. You might have killed us all."

The others, seeing what was coming, stood aside, out of the line of fire.

Stéphanie could not see the gun, but she sensed what was happening. She whispered, "What are you going to do with me?"

Flick said, "If we leave you here now, you will tell Dieter Franck how many we are, and describe us to him, and help him to capture us so that we can be tortured and killed . . . won't you?"

She did not answer.

Flick pointed the gun at the back of Stéphanie's head. "Do you have any excuse for helping the enemy?"

"I did what I had to. Doesn't everyone?"

"Exactly," Flick said, and she pulled the trigger twice.

The gun boomed in the confined space. Blood and something else spurted from the woman's face and splashed on the skirt of her elegant green dress, and she slumped forward soundlessly.

Jelly flinched and Greta turned away. Even Paul went white. Only Ruby remained expressionless.

They were all silent for a moment. Then Flick said, "Let's get out of here."

CHAPTER 42

It was six o'clock in the evening when Dieter parked outside the house in the rue du Bois. His sky-blue car was covered with dust and dead insects after the long journey. As he got out, the evening sun slipped behind a cloud, and the suburban street was thrown into shadow. He shivered.

He took off his motoring goggles—he had been driving with the top down—and ran his fingers through his hair to flatten it. "Wait for me here, please, Hans," he said. He wanted to be alone with Stéphanie.

Opening the gate and entering the front garden, he noticed that Mademoiselle Lemas's Simca Cinq was gone. The garage door was open and the garage was empty. Was Stéphanie using the car? But where would she have gone? She should be waiting here for him, guarded by two Gestapo men.

He strode up the garden path and pulled the bell rope. The ring of the bell died away, leaving the house strangely silent. He looked through the window into the front parlor, but that room was always empty. He rang again. There was no response. He bent down to look through the letter box, but he could not see much: part of the staircase, a painting of a Swiss mountain scene, and the door to the kitchen, half open. There was no movement.

He glanced at the house next door and saw a face hastily withdraw from a window, and a curtain fall back into place.

He walked around the side of the house and through the courtyard to the rear garden. Two windows were broken and the back door stood open. Fear grew in his heart. What had happened here?

"Stéphanie?" he called. There was no answer.

He stepped into the kitchen.

At first he did not understand what he was looking at. A bundle was tied to a kitchen chair with ordinary household string. It looked like a woman's body with a disgusting mess on top. After a moment, his police experience told him that the disgusting thing was a human head that had been shot. Then he saw that the dead woman was wearing odd shoes, one black and one brown, and he understood she was Stéphanie. He let out a howl of anguish, covered his eyes with his hands, and sank slowly to his knees, sobbing.

After a minute, he dragged his hands from his eyes and forced himself to look again. The detective in him noted the blood on the skirt of her dress and concluded that she had been shot from behind. Perhaps that was merciful; she might not have suffered the terror of knowing she was about to die. There had been two shots, he thought. It was the large exit wounds that had made her lovely face look so dreadful, destroying her eyes and nose, leaving her sensual lips bloodstained but intact. Had it not been for the shoes, he would not have known her. His eyes filled with tears until she became a blur.

The sense of loss was like a wound. He had never known a shock like this sudden knowledge that she was gone. She would not throw him that proud glance again; she would no longer turn heads walking through restaurants; he would never again see her pull silk stockings over her perfect calves. Her style and her wit, her fears and her desires, were all canceled, wiped out, ended. He felt as if *he* had been shot, and had lost part of himself. He whispered her name: at least he had that.

Then he heard a voice behind him.

He cried out, startled.

It came again: a wordless grunt, but human. He leaped to his feet, turning around and wiping the moisture from his eyes. For the first time he noticed two men on the floor. Both wore uniform. They were Stéphanie's Gestapo bodyguards. They had failed to protect her, but at least they had given their lives trying.

Or one of them had.

One lay still, but the other was trying to speak. He was a young chap, nineteen or twenty, with black hair and a small moustache. His uniform cap lay on the linoleum floor beside his head.

Dieter stepped across the room and knelt beside him. He noted exit wounds in the chest: the man had been shot from behind. He was lying in a pool of blood. His head jerked and his lips were moving. Dieter put his ear to the man's mouth.

"Water," the man whispered.

He was bleeding to death. They always asked for water near the end, Dieter knew—he had seen it in the desert. He found a cup, filled it at the tap, and held it to the man's lips. He drank it all, the water dribbling down his chin onto his blood-soaked tunic.

Dieter knew he should phone for a doctor, but he had to find out what had happened here. If he delayed, the man might expire without telling what he knew. Dieter hesitated only a moment over the decision. The man was dispensable. Dieter would question him first, then call the doctor. "Who was it?" he said, and he bent his head again to hear the dying man's whispers.

"Four women," the man said hoarsely.

"The Jackdaws," Dieter said bitterly.

"Two at the front . . . two at the back."

Dieter nodded. He could visualize the course of events. Stéphanie had gone to the front door to answer the knock. The Gestapo men had stood ready, looking toward the hall. The terrorists had sneaked up to the kitchen windows and shot them from behind. And then . . .

"Who killed Stéphanie?"

"Water . . ."

Dieter controlled his sense of urgency with an effort of will. He went to the sink, refilled the cup, and put it to the man's mouth again. Once again he drank it all, and sighed with relief, a sigh that turned into a dreadful groan.

"Who killed Stéphanie?" Dieter repeated.

"The small one," said the Gestapo man.

"Flick," said Dieter, and his heart filled with a raging desire for revenge.

The man whispered: "I'm sorry, Major . . ."

"How did it happen?"

"Quick . . . it was very quick."

"Tell me."

"They tied her up . . . said she was a traitor . . . gun to the back of the head . . . then they went away."

"Traitor?" Dieter said.

The man nodded.

Dieter choked back a sob. "She never shot anyone in the back of the head," he said in a grief-stricken whisper.

The Gestapo man did not hear him. His lips were still and his breathing had stopped.

Dieter reached out with his right hand and closed the man's eyelids gently with his fingertips. "Rest in peace," he said.

Then, keeping his back to the body of the woman he loved, he went to the phone.

CHAPTER 43

It was a struggle to fit five people into the Simca Cinq. Ruby and Jelly sat on the rudimentary backseat. Paul drove. Greta took the front passenger seat, and Flick sat on Greta's lap.

Ordinarily they would have giggled about it, but they were in a somber mood. They had killed three people, and they had come close to being captured by the Gestapo. Now they were watchful, hyperalert, ready to react fast to anything that happened. They had nothing on their minds but survival.

Flick guided Paul to the street parallel with Gilberte's. Flick remembered coming here with her wounded husband exactly seven days ago. She directed Paul to park near the end of the alley. "Wait here," Flick said. "I'll check the place."

Jelly said, "Be quick, for God's sake."

"Quick as I can." Flick got out and ran down the alley, past the back of the factory to the door in the wall. She crossed the garden quickly and slipped through the back entrance into the building. The hallway was empty and the place was quiet. She went softly up the stairs to the attic floor.

She stopped outside Gilberte's apartment. What she saw filled her with dismay. The door stood open. It had been broken in and was leaning drunkenly from one hinge. She listened but heard nothing, and something told her the break-in had happened days ago. Cautiously, she stepped inside.

There had been a perfunctory search. In the little living room, the cushions on the seats were disarranged, and in the kitchen corner the cupboard doors stood open. Flick looked into the bedroom and saw a similar scene. The drawers had been pulled out of the chest, the wardrobe was open, and someone had stood on the bed with dirty boots.

She went to the window and looked down into the street. Parked opposite the building was a black Citroën Traction Avant with two men sitting in the front.

This was all bad news, Flick thought despairingly. Someone had talked, and Dieter Franck had made the most of it. He had painstakingly followed a trail that had led him first to Mademoiselle Lemas, then to Brian Standish, and finally to Gilberte. And Michel? Was he in custody? It seemed all too probable.

She thought about Dieter Franck. She had felt a shiver of fear the first time she had looked at the short MI6 biography of him on the back of his file photo. She had not been scared enough, she now knew. He was clever and persistent. He had almost caught her at La Chatelle, he had scattered posters of her face all over Paris, he had captured and interrogated her comrades one after another.

She had set eyes on him just twice, both times for a few moments only. She brought his face to mind. There was intelligence and energy in his look, she thought, plus a determination that could easily become ruthlessness. She was quite sure that he was still on her trail. She resolved to be ever more vigilant.

She looked at the sky. She had about three hours until dark.

She hurried down the stairs and out through the garden back to the Simca Cinq parked in the next street. "No good," she said as she squeezed into the car. "The place has been searched and the Gestapo are watching the front."

"Hell," Paul said. "Where do we go now?"

"I know of one more place to try," said Flick. "Drive into town."

She wondered how long they could continue to use the Simca Cinq, as the tiny 500cc engine struggled to power the overloaded car. Assuming the bodies at the house in the rue du Bois had been discovered within an hour, how long would it be before police and Gestapo men in Reims were alerted to look out for Mademoiselle Lemas's car? Dieter had no way of contacting men who were already out on the streets, but at the next change of shift they would all be briefed. And Flick did not know when the night crews came on duty. She concluded that she had almost no time left. "Drive to the station," she said. "We'll dump the car there."

"Good idea," Paul said. "Maybe they'll think we've left town."

Flick scanned the streets for military Mercedes cars or black Gestapo Citroëns. She held her breath as they passed a pair of gendarmes patrolling. But they reached the center of the city without incident. Paul parked near the railway station, and they all got out and hurried away from the incriminating vehicle.

"I'll have to do this alone," Flick said. "The rest of you had better go to the cathedral and wait for me there."

"All my sins have been forgiven several times over, I've spent so much time in church today," Paul said.

"You can pray for a place to spend the night," Flick told him, and she hurried away.

She returned to the street where Michel lived. A hundred meters from his house was the bar Chez Régis. Flick went in. The proprietor, Alexandre Régis, sat behind the counter smoking. He gave her a nod of recognition but said nothing.

She went through the door marked Toilettes. She walked along a short passage, then opened what looked like a cupboard door. It led to a steep staircase going up. At the top of the stairs was a heavy door with a peephole. Flick banged on it and stood where her face could be seen through the judas. A moment later the door was opened by Mémé Régis, the mother of the proprietor.

Flick entered a large room whose windows were blacked out. It was crudely decorated with matting on the floor, brown-painted walls, and several naked bulbs hanging from the ceiling. At one end of the room was a roulette wheel. Around a large circular table a group of men were playing cards. There was a bar in one corner. This was an illegal gambling club.

Michel liked to play poker for high stakes, and he enjoyed louche company, so he occasionally came here for an evening. Flick never played, but she sometimes sat and watched the game for an hour. Michel said she brought him luck. It was a good place to hide from the Gestapo, and Flick had been hoping she might find him here, but as she looked from face to face around the room she was disappointed.

"Thank you, Mémé," she said to Alexandre's mother.

"It's good to see you. How are you?"

"Fine, have you seen my husband?"

"Ah, the charming Michel. Not tonight, I regret." The people here did not know Michel was in the Resistance.

Flick went to the bar and sat on a stool, smiling at the barmaid, a middle-aged woman with bright red lipstick. She was Yvette Régis, the wife of Alexandre. "Have you any scotch?"

"Of course," said Yvette. "For those who can afford it." She produced a bottle of Dewar's White Label and poured a measure.

Flick said, "I'm looking for Michel."

"I haven't seen him for a week or so," Yvette said.

"Damn." Flick sipped her drink. "I'll wait awhile, in case he shows up."

CHAPTER 44

Dieter was desperate. Flick had proved too clever. She had evaded his trap. She was somewhere in the city of Reims, but he had no way of finding her.

He could no longer have members of the Reims Resistance followed, in the hope that she would contact one of them, for they were all now in custody. Dieter had Michel's house and Gilberte's flat under surveillance, but he felt sure that Flick was too wily to let herself be seen by the average Gestapo flatfoot. There were posters of her all over town, but she must have changed her appearance by now, dyed her hair or something, for no one had reported seeing her. She had outwitted him at every stop.

He needed a stroke of genius.

And he had come up with one—he thought.

He sat on the seat of a bicycle at the roadside. He was in the center of town, just outside the theater. He wore a beret, goggles, and a rough cotton sweater, and his trousers were tucked into his socks. He was unrecognizable. No one would suspect him. The Gestapo never went by bicycle.

He stared west along the street, narrowing his eyes to look into the setting sun. He was waiting for a black Citroën. He checked his watch: any minute now.

On the other side of the road, Hans was at the wheel of a wheezy old Peugeot, which had almost come to the end of its useful life. The engine was running: Dieter did not want to take the risk that it might not start when it was needed. Hans was also disguised, in sunglasses and a cap, and wore a shabby suit and down-at-the-heel shoes, like a French citizen. He had never done anything like this before, but he had accepted his orders with unflappable stoicism.

Dieter, too, had never done this before. He had no idea whether it would work. All kinds of things could go wrong and anything could happen.

What Dieter had planned was desperate, but what did he have to lose? Tuesday was the night of the full moon. He felt sure the Allies were about to invade. Flick was the grand prize. She was worth a great deal of risk.

But winning the war was no longer what most occupied his mind. His future had been wrecked; he hardly cared who ruled Europe. He thought constantly of Flick Clairet. She had ruined his life; she had murdered Stéphanie. He wanted to find Flick, and capture her, and take her to the basement of the château. There he would taste the satisfaction of revenge. He fantasized constantly about how he would torture her: the iron rods that would smash her small bones, the electric shock machine turned up to maximum, the injections that would render her helpless with great wrenching spasms of nausea, the ice bath that would give her shivering convulsions and freeze the blood in her fingers. Destroying the Resistance, and repelling the invaders, had become merely part of his punishment of Flick.

But first he had to find her.

In the distance he saw a black Citroën.

He stared at it. Was this the one? It was

a two-door model, the kind always used when transporting a prisoner. He tried to see inside. He thought there were four people all together. This had to be the car he was waiting for. It drew nearer, and he recognized the handsome face of Michel in the back, guarded by a uniformed Gestapo man. He tensed.

He was glad now that he had given orders that Michel was not to be tortured while Dieter was away. This scheme would not have been possible otherwise.

As the Citroën came level with Dieter, Hans suddenly pulled away from the curb in the old Peugeot. The car swung out into the road, leaped forward, and smashed straight into the front of the Citroën.

There was a clatter of crumpling metal and a medley of breaking glass. The two Gestapo men leaped out of the front of the Citroën and began yelling at Hans in bad French—seeming not to notice that their colleague in the back appeared to have banged his head and was slumped, apparently unconscious, beside his prisoner.

This was the critical moment, Dieter thought, his nerves strung like wire. Would

Michel take the bait? He stared at the tableau in the middle of the street.

It took Michel a long moment to realize his opportunity. Dieter almost thought he would fail to seize it. Then he seemed to come to. He reached over the front seats, fumbled at the door catch with bound hands, succeeded in getting the door open, pushed down the seat, and scrambled out.

He glanced at the two Gestapo men still arguing with Hans. They had their backs to him. He turned and walked quickly away. His expression said he could hardly believe his good luck.

Dieter's heart leaped with triumph. His plan was working.

He followed Michel.

Hans followed Dieter on foot.

Dieter rode the bicycle for a few yards, then he found himself catching up with Michel, so he got off and pushed it along the pavement. Michel turned the first corner, limping slightly from his bullet wound but walking fast, holding his bound hands low in front of him to make them less conspicuous. Dieter followed discreetly, sometimes walking, sometimes riding, dropping back out of Michel's sight whenever he could, taking cover behind high-sided vehicles if he got the chance. Michel occasionally glanced back but made no systematic attempt to shake off a tail. He had no notion that he was being tricked.

After a few minutes, Hans overtook Dieter, by arrangement, and Dieter dropped back to follow Hans. Then they switched again.

Where would Michel go? It was essential to Dieter's plan that Michel should lead him to other Resistance members, so that he could once again pick up Flick's trail.

To Dieter's surprise, Michel headed for his house near the cathedral. Surely he must suspect that his home was under surveillance? Nevertheless, he turned into the street. However, he did not go to his own place but entered a bar across the street called Chez Régis.

Dieter leaned his bicycle against the wall of the next building, a vacant store with a faded *Charcuterie* sign. He waited a few minutes, just in case Michel should come out again immediately. When it was clear Michel was staying a while, Dieter went in.

He intended simply to make sure Michel was still there—relying on his goggles and beret to conceal his identity from Michel. He would buy a pack of cigarettes as an excuse and go back outside. But Michel was nowhere in sight. Puzzled, Dieter hesitated.

The barman said, "Yes, sir?"

"Beer," said Dieter. "Draft." He hoped that if he kept his conversation to a minimum the barman would not notice his slight German accent and accept him as a cyclist who had stopped to quench his thirst.

"Coming up."

"Where's the toilet?"

The barman pointed to a door in the corner. Dieter went through it. Michel was not in the men's room. Dieter risked a glance into the ladies': it was empty. He opened what looked like a cupboard door and saw that it led to a staircase. He went up the stairs. At the top was a heavy door with a peephole. He knocked on the door, but there was no answer. He listened for a moment. He could hear nothing, but the door was thick. He felt sure there was someone on the other side, looking at him through the peephole, realizing he was not a regular customer. He tried to act as if he had taken a wrong turn on the way to the toilet. He scratched his head, shrugged, and went back down the stairs.

There was no sign of a back entrance to the place. Michel was here, Dieter felt sure, in the locked room upstairs. But what should Dieter do about it?

He took his glass to a table so that the barman would not try to engage him in small talk. The beer was watery and tasteless. Even in Germany, the quality of beer had declined during the war. He forced himself to finish it, then went out.

Hans was on the other side of the street, looking in the window of a bookshop. Dieter went across. "He's in some kind of private room upstairs," he told Hans. "He may be meeting with other Resistance cadres. On the other hand, it may be a brothel, or something, and I don't want to bust in on him before he's led us to anyone worthwhile."

Hans nodded, understanding the dilemma.

Dieter made a decision. It was too soon to rearrest Michel. "When he comes out, I'll follow him. As soon as we're out of sight, you can raid the place."

"On my own?"

Dieter pointed to two Gestapo men in a

Citroën keeping watch on Michel's house. "Get them to help you."

"Okay."

"Try to make it look like a vice thing—arrest the whores, if there are any. Don't mention the Resistance."

"Okay."

"Until then, we wait."

CHAPTER 45

Until the moment when Michel walked in, Flick was feeling pessimistic.

She sat at the bar in the little makeshift casino, making desultory conversation with Yvette, indifferently watching the intent faces of the men as they concentrated on their cards, their dice, and the spinning roulette wheel. No one took much notice of her: they were serious gamblers, not to be distracted by a pretty face.

If she did not find Michel, she was in trouble. The other Jackdaws were in the cathedral, but they could not stay there all night. They could sleep in the open—they would survive the weather, in June—but they could so easily be caught.

They also needed transport. If they could not get a car or van from the Bollinger circuit, they would have to steal one. But then they would be forced to carry out the mission using a vehicle for which the police were searching. It added more dangers to an already perilous enterprise.

There was another reason for her gloom: the image of Stéphanie Vinson kept coming back to her. It was the first time Flick had killed a bound, helpless captive, and the first time she had shot a woman.

Any killing disturbed her profoundly. The Gestapo man she had shot a few minutes before Stéphanie had been a combatant with a gun in his hand, but still it seemed dreadful to her that she had brought his life to an end. So it had been with the other men she had killed: two Milice cops in Paris, a Gestapo colonel in Lille, and a French traitor in Rouen. But Stéphanie was worse. Flick had put a gun to the back of her head and executed her. It was exactly how she had taught trainees to do it in the SOE course. Stéphanie had deserved it, of course—Flick had no doubt about that. But she wondered about herself. What kind of person was capable of the cold-blooded killing of a helpless prisoner? Had she become some kind of brutish executioner?

She drained her whisky but declined a refill for fear of becoming maudlin. Then Michel came through the door.

Overwhelming relief flooded her. Michel knew everyone in town. He would be able to help her. Suddenly the mission seemed possible again.

She felt a wry affection as she took in the lanky figure in a rumpled jacket, the handsome face with the smiling eyes. She would always be fond of him, she imagined. She suffered a painful stab of regret as she thought of the passionate love she had once had for him. That would never come back, she was sure.

As he came closer, she saw that he was not looking so good. His face seemed to have new lines. Her heart filled with compassion for him. Exhaustion and fear showed in his expression, and he might have been fifty rather than thirty-five, she thought anxiously.

But her greatest anxiety came from the thought of telling him that their marriage was over. She was afraid. It struck her as ironic: she had just shot and killed a Gestapo man and a French traitress, and she was undercover in occupied territory, yet her worst fear was of hurting her husband's feelings.

He was visibly delighted to see her. "Flick!" he cried. "I knew you would get here!" He crossed the room to her, still limping from his bullet wound.

She said quietly, "I was afraid the Gestapo had captured you."

"They did!" He turned so that his back was to the room and no one could see, and showed her his hands, bound at the wrists with stout rope.

She drew the little knife from its sheath under her lapel and discreetly cut through his bonds. The gamblers saw nothing. She put the knife away.

Mémé Régis spotted him just as he was stuffing the ropes into his trousers pockets. She embraced and kissed him on both cheeks. Flick watched him flirt with the older woman, talking to her in his come-to-bed voice, giving her the benefit of his sexy grin. Then Mémé resumed her work, serving drinks to the gamblers, and Michel told Flick how he had escaped. She had been afraid he would want to kiss her passionately, and she had not known how she would deal with that but, in the event, he was too full of his own adventures to get romantic with her.

"I was so lucky!" he finished. He sat on a bar stool, rubbing his wrists, and asked for a beer.

Flick nodded. "Too lucky, perhaps," she said.

"What do you mean?"

"It could be some kind of trick."

He was indignant, no doubt resenting the implication that he was gullible. "I don't think so."

"Could you have been followed here?"

"No," he said firmly. "I checked, of course."

She was uneasy, but she let it go. "So Brian Standish is dead, and three others are in custody—Mademoiselle Lemas, Gilberte, and Dr. Bouler."

"The rest are dead. The Germans released the bodies of those killed in the skirmish. And the survivors, Gaston, Geneviéve, and Bertrand, were shot by a firing squad in the square at Sainte-Cécile."

"Dear God."

They were silent for a moment. Flick was weighed down by the thought of the lives lost, and the suffering endured, for the sake of this mission.

Michel's beer came. He drank half in a single draft and wiped his lips. "I presume you've come back for another attempt on the château."

She nodded. "But the cover story is that we're going to blow up the railway tunnel at Marles."

"It's a good idea, we should do it anyway."

"Not now. Two of my team were taken in Paris, and they must have talked. They will have told the cover story—they had no idea of the real mission—and the Germans are sure to have doubled the guard on the railway tunnel. We'll leave that to the RAF and concentrate on Sainte-Cécile."

"What can I do?"

"We need somewhere to stay the night."

He thought for a moment. "Joseph Laperrière's cellar."

Laperrière was a champagne maker. Michel's aunt Antoinette had once been his secretary. "Is he one of us?"

"A sympathizer." He gave a sour grin. "Everyone is a sympathizer now. They all think the invasion is coming any day." He looked inquiringly at her. "I imagine they're right about that . . ."

"Yes," she said. She did not elaborate. "How big is the cellar? There are five of us."

"It's big, he could hide fifty people down there."

"Fine. The other thing I need is a vehicle for tomorrow."

"To drive to Sainte-Cécile?"

"And afterwards, to meet our pickup plane, if we're still alive."

"You realize that you can't use the usual drop zone at Chatelle, don't you? The Gestapo know about it—it's where I was picked up."

"Yes. The plane is coming to the other one at Laroque. I gave instructions."

"The potato field. Good."

"And the vehicle?"

"Philippe Moulier has a van. He delivers meat to all the German bases. Monday is his day off."

"I remember him, he's pro-Nazi."

"He was. And he's been making money out of them for four years. So now he's terrified that the invasion is going to succeed, and after the Germans have gone he'll be strung up as a collaborator. He's desperate to do something to help us, to prove he's not a traitor. He'll lend us his van."

"Bring it to the cellar tomorrow at ten o'clock in the morning."

He touched her cheek. "Can't we spend the night together?" He smiled his old smile and looked as roguishly handsome as ever.

She felt a familiar stirring inside, but it was not as strong as it had been in the old days. Once, that smile would have made her wet. Now, it was like the memory of a desire.

She wanted to tell him the truth, for she hated to be anything less than honest. But it might jeopardize the mission. She needed his cooperation. Or was that just an excuse? Perhaps she just did not have the nerve.

"No," she said. "We can't spend the night together."

He looked crestfallen. "Is it because of Gilberte?"

She nodded, but she could not lie, and she found herself saying, "Well, partly."

"What's the other part?"

"I don't really want to have this discussion in the middle of an important mission."

He looked vulnerable, almost scared. "Have you got someone else?"

She could not bring herself to hurt him. "No," she lied.

He looked hard at her. "Good," he said at last. "I'm glad."

Flick hated herself.

Michel finished his beer and got off his stool. "Laperrière's place is in the chemin de la Carrière. It will take you thirty minutes to walk there."

"I know the street."

"I'd better go and see Moulier about the van." He put his arms around Flick and kissed her lips.

She felt dreadful. She could hardly refuse the kiss, having denied that she had someone else, but kissing Michel seemed so disloyal to Paul. She closed her eyes and waited passively until he broke the clinch.

He could not fail to notice her lack of enthusiasm. He looked thoughtfully at her for a moment. "I'll see you at ten," he said, and he left.

She decided to give him five minutes to get clear before she followed him out. She asked Yvette for another scotch.

While she was sipping it, a red light began to flash over the door.

No one spoke, but everyone in the room

moved at once. The croupier stopped the roulette wheel and turned it upside down so that it looked like a normal tabletop. The card players swept up their stakes and put on their jackets. Yvette picked up the glasses from the bar and dumped them in the sink. Mémé Régis turned out the lights, leaving the room illuminated only by the flashing red bulb over the door.

Flick picked up her bag from the floor and put her hand on her gun. "What's happening?" she asked Yvette.

"Police raid," she said.

Flick cursed. What hellish luck it would be to get arrested for illegal gambling.

"Alexandre downstairs has given us the warning," Yvette explained. "Get going, quickly!" She pointed across the room.

Flick looked in the direction Yvette indicated and saw Mémé Régis stepping into what looked like a cupboard. As she watched, Mémé shoved aside a couple of old coats hanging from a rail to reveal, at the back of the cupboard, a door, which she hurriedly opened. The gamblers began to leave by the hidden door. Maybe, Flick thought, she could get away.

The flashing red light went out, and a

banging began on the main door. Flick crossed the room in the dark and joined the men pushing through the cupboard. She followed the crowd into a bare room. The floor was about a foot lower than she expected, and she guessed this was the apartment over the shop next door. They all ran down the stairs and, sure enough, she found herself in the disused charcuterie, with a stained marble counter and dusty glass cases. The blind in the front window was drawn down so that no one could see in from the street.

They all went out through the back door. There was a dirty yard surrounded by a high wall. A door in the wall led to an alley, and the alley led to the next street. When they reached the street, the men went in different directions.

Flick walked quickly away and soon found herself alone. Breathing hard, she reoriented herself and headed for the cathedral, where the other Jackdaws were waiting. "My God," she whispered to herself, "that was close."

As she got her breath back, she began to see the raid on the gambling club in a different light. It had happened just minutes after Michel had left. Flick did not believe in coincidence.

The more she thought about it, the more

convinced she became that whoever was banging on the door had been looking for her. She knew that a small group of men had been playing for high stakes in that room since before the war. The local police certainly knew about the place. Why would they suddenly decide to close it down? If not the police, it must have been the Gestapo. And they were not really interested in gamblers. They went after communists, Jews, homosexuals—and spies.

The story of Michel's escape had aroused her suspicions from the start, but she had been partly reassured by his insistence that he had not been followed. Now she thought otherwise. His escape must have been faked, like the "rescue" of Brian Standish. She saw the sly brain of Dieter Franck behind this. Someone had followed Michel to the café, guessed at the existence of the secret upstairs room, and hoped to find her there.

In that case, Michel was still under surveillance. If he continued to be careless, he would be trailed to Philippe Moulier's house tonight, and in the morning, driving the van, he would be followed to the champagne cellar where the Jackdaws were hiding.

And what the hell, Flick thought, am I going to do about that?

THE NINTH DAY

Monday, June 5, 1944

CHAPTER 46

Dieter's migraine began shortly after midnight, as he stood in his room at the Hotel Frankfort, looking at the bed he would never again share with Stéphanie. He felt that if he could weep, the pain would fade, but no tears came, and he injected himself with morphine and collapsed on the counterpane.

The phone woke him before daylight. It was Walter Goedel, Rommel's aide. Groggily, Dieter said, "Has the invasion begun?"

"Not today," Goedel replied. "The weather is bad in the English Channel."

Dieter sat upright and shook his head to clear it. "What, then?"

"The Resistance were clearly *expecting* something. Overnight, there has been an eruption of sabotage throughout northern

France." Goedel's voice, already cool, descended to an arctic chill. "It was supposed to be your job to prevent that. What are you doing in bed?"

Caught off guard, Dieter struggled to regain his usual poise. "I'm right on the tail of the most important of all Resistance leaders," he said, trying hard not to sound as if he was making excuses for failure. "I almost caught her last night. I'll arrest her today. Don't worry—by tomorrow morning we'll be rounding up terrorists by the hundreds. I promise you." He immediately regretted the pleading tone of the last three words.

Goedel was unmoved. "After tomorrow, it will probably be too late."

"I know—" Dieter stopped. The line was dead. Goedel had hung up.

Dieter cradled the phone and looked at his wristwatch. It was four o'clock. He got up.

His migraine had gone, but he felt queasy, either from the morphine or the unpleasant phone call. He drank a glass of water and swallowed three aspirins, then began to shave. As he lathered his face, he nervously ran over the events of the previous evening, asking himself if he had done everything possible.

Leaving Lieutenant Hesse outside Chez Régis, he had followed Michel Clairet to the premises of Philippe Moulier, a supplier of fresh meat to restaurants and military kitchens. It was a storefront property with living quarters above and a yard at the side. Dieter had watched the place for an hour, but no one had come out.

Deciding that Michel intended to spend the night there, Dieter had found a bar and phoned Hans Hesse. Hans had got on a motorcycle and joined him outside the Moulier place at ten. The lieutenant told Dieter the story of the inexplicably empty room above Chez Régis. "There's some early-warning system," Dieter speculated. "The barman downstairs is ready to sound the alarm if anyone comes looking."

"You think the Resistance were using the place?"

"Probably. I'd guess the Communist Party used to hold meetings there, and the Resistance took over the system."

"But how did they get away last night?"

"A trapdoor under the carpet, something like that—the communists would have been prepared for trouble. Did you arrest the barman?"

"I arrested everyone in the place. They're at the château now."

Dieter had left Hans watching the Moulier property and had driven to Sainte-Cécile. There he questioned the terrified proprietor, Alexandre Régis, and learned within minutes that his speculation had been off target. The place was neither a Resistance hideout nor a communist meeting place, but an illegal gambling club. Nevertheless, Alexandre confirmed that Michel Clairet had gone there last night. And, he said, Michel had met his wife there.

It was another maddeningly near miss for Dieter. He had captured one Resistance member after another, but Flick always eluded him.

Now he finished shaving, wiped his face, and phoned the château to order a car with a driver and two Gestapo men to pick him up. He got dressed and went to the hotel kitchen to beg half a dozen warm croissants, which he wrapped in a linen napkin. Then he went out into the cool of the early morning. The towers of the cathedral were silvered by the breaking dawn. One of the fast Citroëns favored by the Gestapo was waiting.

He gave the driver the address of the Moulier place. He found Hans lurking in a warehouse doorway fifty meters along the street. No one had come or gone all night, Hans said, so Michel must still be inside. Dieter told his driver to wait around the next corner, then stood with Hans, sharing the croissants and watching the sun come up over the roofs of the city.

They had a long wait. Dieter fought to control his impatience as the minutes and hours ticked away uselessly. The loss of Stéphanie weighed on his heart, but he had recovered from the immediate shock, and he had regained his interest in the war. He thought of the Allied forces massing somewhere in the south or east of England, shiploads of men and tanks eager to turn the quiet seaside towns of northern France into battlefields. He thought of the French saboteurs—armed to the teeth thanks to parachute drops of guns, ammunition, and explosives—ready to attack the German defenders from behind, to stab them in the back and fatally cramp Rommel's ability to maneuver. He felt foolish and impotent, standing in a doorway in Reims, waiting for an amateur terrorist to finish his breakfast. Today, perhaps, he would be led into the very heart of the Resistance—but all he had was hope.

It was after nine o'clock when the front door opened.

"At last," Dieter breathed. He moved back from the sidewalk, making himself inconspicuous. Hans put out his cigarette.

Michel came out of the building accompanied by a boy of about seventeen who, Dieter guessed, might be a son of Moulier. The lad keyed a padlock and opened the gates of the yard. In the yard was a clean black van with white lettering on the side that read *Moulier & Fils—Viandes.* Michel got in.

Dieter was electrified. Michel was borrowing a meat delivery van. It had to be for the Jackdaws. "Let's go!" he said.

Hans hurried to his motorcycle, which was parked at the curb, and stood with his back to the road, pretending to fiddle with the engine. Dieter ran to the corner, signaled the Gestapo driver to start the car, then watched Michel.

Michel drove out of the yard and headed away.

Hans started his motorcycle and followed. Dieter jumped into the car and ordered the driver to follow Hans.

They headed east. Dieter, in the front passenger seat of the Gestapo's black Citroën, looked ahead anxiously. Moulier's van was easy to follow, having a high roof with a vent on top like a chimney. That little vent will lead me to Flick, Dieter thought optimistically.

The van slowed in the chemin de la Carrière and pulled into the yard of a champagne house called Laperrière. Hans drove past and turned the next corner, and Dieter's driver followed. They pulled up and Dieter leaped out.

"I think the Jackdaws hid out there overnight," Dieter said.

"Shall we raid the place?" Hans said eagerly.

Dieter pondered. This was the dilemma he had faced yesterday, outside the café. Flick might be in there. But if he moved too quickly, he might prematurely end Michel's usefulness as a stalking horse.

"Not yet," he said. Michel was the only

hope he had left. It was too soon to risk losing that weapon. "We'll wait."

Dieter and Hans walked to the end of the street and watched the Laperrière place from the corner. There was a tall, elegant house, a courtyard full of empty barrels, and a low industrial building with a flat roof. Dieter guessed the cellars ran beneath the flat-roofed building. Moulier's van was parked in the yard.

Dieter's pulse was racing. Any moment now, Michel would reappear with Flick and the other Jackdaws, he guessed. They would get into the van, ready to drive to their target—and Dieter and the Gestapo would move in and arrest them.

As they watched, Michel came out of the low building. He wore a frown and he stood indecisively in the yard, looking around him in a perplexed fashion. Hans said, "What's the matter with him?"

Dieter's heart sank. "Something he didn't expect." Surely Flick had not evaded him again?

After a minute, Michel climbed the short flight of steps to the door of the house and knocked. A maid in a little white cap let him in.

He came out again a few minutes later. He still looked puzzled, but he was no longer indecisive. He walked to the van, got in, and turned it around.

Dieter cursed. It seemed the Jackdaws were not here. Michel appeared just as surprised as Dieter was, but that was small consolation.

Dieter had to find out what had happened here. He said to Hans, "We'll do the same as last night, only this time *you* follow Michel and I'll raid the place."

Hans started his motorcycle.

Dieter watched Michel drive away in Moulier's van, followed at a discreet distance by Hans Hesse on his motorcycle. When they were out of sight, he summoned the three Gestapo men with a wave and walked quickly to the Laperrière house.

He pointed at two of the men. "Check the house. Make sure no one leaves." Nodding at the third man, he said, "You and I will search the winery." He led the way into the low building.

On the ground floor there was a large grape press and three enormous vats. The press was pristine: the harvest was three or four months away. There was no one present but an old man sweeping the floor. Dieter found the stairs and ran down. In the cool underground chamber there was more activity: racked bottles were being turned by a handful of blue-coated workers. They stopped and stared at the intruders.

Dieter and the Gestapo man searched room after room of bottles of champagne, thousands of them, some stacked against the walls, others racked slantwise with the necks down in special A-shaped frames. But there were no women anywhere.

In an alcove at the far end of the last tunnel, Dieter found crumbs of bread, cigarette ends, and a hair clip. His worst fears were dismally confirmed. The Jackdaws had spent the night here. But they had escaped.

He cast about for a focus for his anger. The workers would probably know nothing about the Jackdaws, but the owner must have given permission for them to hide here. He would suffer for it. Dieter returned to the ground floor, crossed the yard, and went to the house. A Gestapo man opened the door. "They're all in the front room," he said.

Dieter entered a large, gracious room

with elegant but shabby furnishings: heavy curtains that had not been cleaned for years, a worn carpet, a long dining table and a matching set of twelve chairs. The terrified household staff were standing at the near end of the room: the maid who opened the door, an elderly man who looked like a butler in his threadbare black suit, and a plump woman wearing an apron who must have been the cook. A Gestapo man held a pistol pointed at them. At the far end of the table sat a thin woman of about fifty, with red hair threaded with silver, dressed in a summer frock of pale yellow silk. She had an air of calm superiority.

Dieter turned to the Gestapo man and said in a low voice, "Where's the husband?"

"He left the house at eight. They don't know where he went. He's expected home for lunch."

Dieter gave the woman a hard look. "Madame Laperrière?"

She nodded gravely but did not deign to speak.

Dieter decided to puncture her dignity. Some German officers behaved with deference to upper-class French people, but

Dieter thought they were fools. He would not pander to her by walking the length of the room to speak to her. "Bring her to me," he said.

One of the men spoke to her. Slowly, she got up from her chair and approached Dieter. "What do you want?" she said.

"A group of terrorists from England escaped from me yesterday after killing two German officers and a French woman civilian."

"I'm sorry to hear that," said Madame Laperrière.

"They tied the woman up and shot her in the back of the head at point-blank range," he went on. "Her brains spilled out onto her dress."

She closed her eyes and turned her head aside.

Dieter went on, "Last night your husband sheltered those terrorists in your cellar. Can you think of any reason why he should not be hanged?"

Behind him, the maid began to cry.

Madame Laperrière was shaken. Her face turned pale and she sat down suddenly. "No, please," she whispered.

Dieter said, "You can help your husband by telling me what you know."

"I don't know anything," she said in a low voice. "They came after dinner, and they left before dawn. I never saw them."

"How did they leave? Did your husband provide them with a car?"

She shook her head. "We have no gas."

"Then how do you deliver the champagne you make?"

"Our customers have to come to us."

Dieter did not believe her. He felt sure Flick needed transportation. That was why Michel had borrowed a van from Philippe Moulier and brought it here. Yet, when Michel got here, Flick and the Jackdaws had gone. They *must* have found alternative means of transport and decided to go on ahead. No doubt Flick had left a message explaining the situation and telling Michel to catch up with her.

Dieter said, "Are you asking me to believe they left here on foot?"

"No," she replied. "I'm telling you that I don't know. When I woke up, they had gone."

Dieter still thought she was lying, but to get the truth out of her would take time and patience, and he was running out of both. "Arrest them all," he said, and his angry frustration injected a petulant note into his voice.

The phone rang in the hall. Dieter stepped out of the dining room and picked it up.

A voice with a German accent said, "Let me speak to Major Franck."

"This is he."

"Lieutenant Hesse here, Major."

"Hans, what happened?"

"I'm at the station. Michel parked the van and bought a ticket to Marles. The train is about to leave."

It was as Dieter had thought. The Jackdaws had gone ahead and left instructions for Michel to join them. They were still planning to blow up the railway tunnel. He felt frustrated that Flick was continuing to stay one step ahead of him. However, she had not been able to escape him completely. He was still on her tail. He would catch her soon. "Get on the train, quickly," he said to Hans. "Stay with him. I'll meet you at Marles."

"Very good," said Hans, and he hung up.

Dieter returned to the dining room. "Call the château and have them send transportation," he said to the Gestapo men. "Turn all the prisoners over to Sergeant Becker for interrogation. Tell him to start with Madame." He pointed to the driver. "You can drive me to Marles."

CHAPTER 47

In the café de la Gare, near the railway station, Flick and Paul had a breakfast of ersatz coffee, black bread, and sausage with little or no meat in it. Ruby, Jelly, and Greta sat at a separate table, not acknowledging them. Flick kept an eye on the street outside.

She knew that Michel was in terrible danger. She had contemplated going to warn him. She could have gone to the Moulier place—but that would have played into the hands of the Gestapo, who must be following Michel in the hope that he would lead them to her. Even to phone the Moulier place would have risked betraying her hideout to a Gestapo eavesdropper at the telephone exchange. In fact, she had decided, the best thing she could do to help Michel was *not* to contact him directly. If her theory was right, Dieter Franck would let Michel remain at large until Flick was caught.

So she had left a message for Michel with Madame Laperrière. It read:

> *Michel—*
> *I am sure you are under surveillance. The place we were at last night was raided after you left. You have probably been followed this morning.*
> *We will leave before you get here and make ourselves inconspicuous in the town center. Park the van near the railway station and leave the key under the driver's seat. Get a train to Marles. Shake off your shadow and come back.*
> *Be careful—please!*
> *—Flick.*
> *Now burn this.*

It seemed good in theory, but she waited all morning in a fever of tension to see whether it would work.

Then, at eleven o'clock, she saw a high van draw up and park near the station entrance. Flick held her breath. On the side, in white lettering, she read *Moulier & Fils— Viandes.*

Michel got out, and she breathed again.

He walked into the station. He was carrying out her plan.

She looked to see who might be following him, but it was impossible. People arrived at the station constantly, on foot, on bicycles, and in cars, and any of them might have been shadowing Michel.

She remained in the café, pretending to drink the bitter, unsatisfying coffee substitute, keeping an eye on the van, trying to discover whether it was under surveillance. She studied the people and vehicles coming and going outside the station, but she did not spot anyone who might have been watching the van. After fifteen minutes, she nodded to Paul. They got up, picked up their cases, and walked out.

Flick opened the van door and got into the driving seat. Paul got in the other side. Flick's heart was in her mouth. If this was a Gestapo trap, now would be the moment when they arrested her. She fumbled beneath her seat and found a key. She started the van.

She looked around. No one seemed to have noticed her.

Ruby, Jelly, and Greta came out of the café. Flick jerked her head to indicate that they should get in the back.

She looked over her shoulder. The van was fitted out with shelves and cupboards, and trays for ice to keep the temperature down. Everything looked as if it had been well scrubbed, but there remained a faint, unpleasant odor of raw meat.

The rear doors opened. The other three women threw their suitcases into the van and clambered in after them. Ruby pulled the doors shut.

Flick put the gearshift into first and drove away.

"We did it!" Jelly said. "Thank gordon."

Flick smiled thinly. The hard part was still ahead.

She drove out of town on the road to Sainte-Cécile. She watched for police cars and Gestapo Citroëns, but she felt fairly safe for the moment. The van's lettering announced its legitimacy. And it was not unusual for a woman to be driving such a vehicle, when so many French men were in labor camps in Germany—or had fled to the hills and joined the Maquis to avoid being sent to the camps.

Soon after midday they reached Sainte-Cécile. Flick noted the sudden miraculous quiet that always fell on French streets at the stroke of noon, as the people turned their attention to the first serious meal of the day. She drove to Antoinette's building. A pair of tall wooden doors, half-open, led to the inner courtyard. Paul leaped out of the van and opened the doors, Flick drove in, and Paul closed the doors behind her. Now the van, with its distinctive legend, could not be seen from the street.

"Come when I whistle," Flick said, and she jumped out.

She went to Antoinette's door while the others waited in the van. Last time she had knocked on this door, eight days and a lifetime ago, Michel's aunt Antoinette had hesitated to answer, jumpy on account of the gunfire from the square, but today she came right away. She opened the door, a slim middle-aged woman in a stylish but faded yellow cotton dress. She looked blankly at Flick for a moment: Flick still had on the dark wig. Then recognition dawned. "You!" she said.

A look of panic came over her face. "What do you want?"

Flick whistled to the others, then pushed Antoinette back inside. "Don't worry," she said. "We're going to tie you up so the Germans will think we forced you."

"What is this?" Antoinette said shakily.

"I'll explain in a moment. Are you alone?"

"Yes."

"Good."

The others came in and Ruby closed the apartment door. They went into Antoinette's kitchen. A meal was laid out on the table: black bread, a salad of shredded carrots, a heel of cheese, a wine bottle without a label. Antoinette said again, "What is this?"

"Sit down," Flick said. "Finish your lunch."

She sat down, but she said, "I can't eat."

"It's very simple," Flick said. "You and your ladies are not going to clean the château tonight . . . we are."

She looked baffled. "How will that happen?"

"We're going to send notes to each of the women on duty tonight, telling them to come here and see you before they go to work. When they arrive, we will tie them up.

Then we will go to the château instead of them."

"You can't, you don't have passes."

"Yes, we do."

"How . . . ?" Antoinette gasped. "You stole my pass! Last Sunday. I thought I had lost it. I got into the most terrible trouble with the Germans!"

"I'm sorry you got into trouble."

"But this will be worse—you're going to blow the place up!" Antoinette began to moan and rock. "They'll blame me, you know what they're like, we'll all be tortured."

Flick gritted her teeth. She knew that Antoinette could be right. The Gestapo might easily kill the real cleaners just in case they had had something to do with the deception. "We're going to do everything we can to make you look innocent," she said. "You will be our victims, the same as the Germans." All the same, there remained a risk, Flick knew.

"They won't believe us," Antoinette moaned. "We might be killed."

Flick hardened her heart. "Yes," she said. "That's why it's called a war."

CHAPTER 48

Marles was a small town to the east of Reims, where the railway line began its long climb into the mountains on its way to Frankfurt, Stuttgart, and Nuremberg. The tunnel just beyond the town carried a constant stream of supplies from the home country to the German forces occupying France. The destruction of the tunnel would starve Rommel of ammunition.

The town itself looked Bavarian, with half-timbered houses painted in bright colors. The town hall stood on the leafy square opposite the railway station. The local Gestapo chief had taken over the mayor's grand office and now stood poring over a map with Dieter Franck and a Captain Bern, who was in charge of the military guard on the tunnel.

"I have twenty men at each end of the

tunnel and another group constantly patrolling the mountain," said Bern. "The Resistance would need a large force to overcome them."

Dieter frowned. According to the confession of the lesbian he had interrogated, Diana Colefield, Flick had started with a team of six women, including herself, and must now be down to four. However, she might have joined up with another group, or made contact with more French Resistance cadres in and around Marles. "They have plenty of people," he said. "The French think the invasion is coming."

"But a large force is hard to conceal. So far we have seen nothing suspicious."

Bern was short and slight and wore spectacles with thick lenses, which was presumably why he was stationed in this backwater rather than with a fighting unit, but he struck Dieter as an intelligent and efficient young officer. Dieter was inclined to take what he said at face value.

Dieter said, "How vulnerable is the tunnel to explosives?"

"It goes through solid rock. Of course it can be destroyed, but they will need a truckload of dynamite."

"They have plenty of dynamite."

"But they need to get it here—again, without our seeing it."

"Indeed." Dieter turned to the Gestapo chief. "Have you received any reports of strange vehicles, or a group of people arriving in the town?"

"None at all. There is only one hotel in town, and at present it has no guests. My men visited the bars and restaurants at lunchtime, as they do every day, and saw nothing unusual."

Captain Bern said hesitantly, "Is it conceivable, Major, that the report you received, of an attack on the tunnel, was some kind of deception? A diversion, as it were, to draw your attention away from the real target?"

That infuriating possibility had already begun to dawn on Dieter. He knew from bitter experience that Flick Clairet was a master of deception. Had she fooled him again? The thought was too humiliating to contemplate. "I interrogated the informant myself, and I'm sure she was being honest," Dieter replied, trying hard to keep the rage out of his voice. "But you could still be right. It's possible *she* had been misinformed, deliberately, as a precaution."

Bern cocked his head and said, "A train is coming."

Dieter frowned. He could hear nothing.

"My hearing is very good," the man said with a smile. "No doubt to compensate for my eyesight."

Dieter had established that the only train to have left Reims for Marles today had been the eleven o'clock, so Michel and Lieutenant Hesse should be on the next one in.

The Gestapo chief went to the window. "This is a westbound train," he said. "Your man is eastbound, I think you said."

Dieter nodded.

Bern said, "In fact there are two trains approaching, one from either direction."

The Gestapo chief looked the other way. "You're right, so there are."

The three men went out into the square. Dieter's driver, leaning on the hood of the Citroën, stood upright and put out his cigarette. Beside him was a Gestapo motorcyclist, ready to resume surveillance of Michel.

They walked to the station entrance. "Is there another way out?" Dieter asked the Gestapo man.

"No."

They stood waiting. Captain Bern said, "Have you heard the news?"

"No, what?" Dieter replied.

"Rome has fallen."

"My God."

"The U.S. army reached the Piazza Venezia yesterday at seven o'clock in the evening."

As the senior officer, Dieter felt it was his duty to maintain morale. "That's bad news, but not unexpected," he said. "However, Italy is not France. If they try to invade us, they'll get a nasty surprise." He hoped he was right.

The westbound train came in first. While its passengers were still unloading their bags and stepping onto the platform, the eastbound train chugged in. There was a little knot of people waiting at the station entrance. Dieter studied them surreptitiously, wondering if the local Resistance was meeting Michel at the train. He saw nothing suspicious.

A Gestapo checkpoint stood next to the ticket barrier. The Gestapo chief joined his underling at the table. Captain Bern leaned on a pillar to one side, making himself less conspicuous. Dieter returned to his car and sat in the back, watching the station.

What would he do if Captain Bern were right, and the tunnel was a diversion? The prospect was dismal. He would have to consider alternatives. What other military targets were within reach of Reims? The château at Sainte-Cécile was an obvious one, but the Resistance had failed to destroy that only a week ago—surely they would not try again so soon? There was a military camp to the north of the town, some railway-marshaling yards between Reims and Paris . . .

That was not the way to go. Guesswork might lead anywhere. He needed information.

He could interrogate Michel right now, as soon as he got off the train, pull out his fingernails one by one until he talked—but would Michel know the truth? He might tell some cover story, believing it to be genuine, as Diana had. Dieter would do better just to follow him until he met up with Flick. She knew the real target. She was the only one worth interrogating now.

Dieter waited impatiently while papers were carefully checked and passengers trickled through. A whistle blew, and the westbound train pulled out. More passengers came out: ten, twenty, thirty. The eastbound train left.

Then Hans Hesse emerged from the station.

Dieter said, "What the hell . . . ?"

Hans looked around the square, saw the Citroën, and ran toward it.

Dieter jumped out of the car.

Hans said, "What happened? Where is he?"

"What do you mean?" Dieter shouted angrily. "You're following him!"

"I did! He got off the train. I lost sight of him in the queue for the checkpoint. After a while I got worried and jumped the queue, but he had already gone."

"Could he have got back on the train?"

"No—I followed him all the way off the platform."

"Could he have got on the other train?"

Hans's mouth dropped open. "I lost sight of him about the time we were passing the end of the Reims platform. . . ."

"That's it," said Dieter. "Hell! He's on his way back to Reims. He's a decoy. This whole trip was a diversion." He was furious that he had fallen for it.

"What do we do?"

"We'll catch up with the train and you can follow him again. I still think he will lead us to Flick Clairet. Get in the car, let's go!"

CHAPTER 49

Flick could hardly believe she had got this far. Four of the original six Jackdaws had evaded capture, despite a brilliant adversary and some mixed luck, and now they were in Antoinette's kitchen, a few steps away from the square at Sainte-Cécile, right under the noses of the Gestapo. In ten minutes time they would walk up to the gates of the château.

Antoinette and four of the other five cleaners were firmly tied to kitchen chairs. Paul had gagged all but Antoinette. Each cleaner had arrived carrying a little shopping basket or canvas bag containing food and drink—bread, cold potatoes, fruit, and a flask of wine or ersatz coffee—which they would normally have during their 9:30 break, not being allowed to use the German can-

teen. Now the Jackdaws were hastily emptying the bags and reloading them with the
things they needed to carry into the
château: electric torches, guns, ammunition, and yellow plastic explosive in 250-
gram sticks. The Jackdaws' own suitcases,
which had held the stuff until now, would
have looked odd in the hands of cleaners
going to work.

Flick quickly realized that the cleaners'
own bags were not big enough. She herself
had a Sten submachine gun with a silencer,
each of its three parts about a foot long.
Jelly had sixteen detonators in a shockproof
can, an incendiary thermite bomb, and a
chemical block that produced oxygen, for
setting fires in enclosed spaces such as
bunkers. After loading their ordnance into
the bags, they had to conceal it with the
cleaners' packets of food. There was not
enough room.

"Damn," Flick said edgily. "Antoinette, do
you have any big bags?"

"What do you mean?"

"Bags, big bags, like shopping bags, you
must have some."

"There's one in the pantry that I use for
buying vegetables."

Flick found the bag, a cheap rectangular basket made of woven reeds. "It's perfect," she said. "Have you any more like it?"

"No, why would I have two?"

Flick needed four.

There was a knock. Flick went to the door. A woman in a flowered overall and a hair net stood there: the last of the cleaners. "Good evening," Flick said.

The woman hesitated, surprised to see a stranger. "Is Antoinette here? I received a note . . ."

Flick smiled reassuringly. "In the kitchen. Please come in."

The woman walked through the apartment, evidently familiar with the place, and entered the kitchen, where she stopped dead and gave a little scream. Antoinette said, "Don't worry, Françoise—they're tying us up so that the Germans will know we didn't help them."

Flick relieved the woman of her bag. It was made of knotted string—fine for carrying a loaf and a bottle but no good to Flick.

This infuriatingly petty detail had Flick stymied just minutes before the climax of the mission. She could not go on until she solved the problem. She forced herself to think calmly, then said to Antoinette, "Where did you get your basket?"

"At the little shop across the street. You can see it from the window."

The windows were open, as it was a warm evening, but the shutters were closed for shade. Flick pushed a shutter open a couple of inches and looked out onto the rue du Château. On the other side of the street was a store selling candles, firewood, brooms, and clothes pins. She turned to Ruby. "Go and buy three more bags, quickly."

Ruby went to the door.

"If you can, get different shapes and colors." Flick was afraid the bags might attract attention if they were all the same.

"Right."

Paul tied the last of the cleaners to a chair and gagged her. He was apologetic and charming, and she did not resist.

Flick gave cleaner's passes to Jelly and Greta. She had held them back until the last minute because they would have given away the mission if found on the person of a captured Jackdaw. With Ruby's pass in her hand, she went to the window.

Ruby was coming out of the store carrying three shopping baskets of different kinds. Flick was relieved. She checked her watch: it was two minutes to seven.

Then disaster struck.

As Ruby was about to cross the road, she was accosted by a man in military-style clothes. He wore a blue denim shirt with buttoned pockets, a dark blue tie, a beret, and dark trousers tucked into high boots. Flick recognized the uniform of the Milice, the security militia that did the dirty work of the regime. "Oh, no!" she said.

Like the Gestapo, the Milice was made up of men too stupid and thuggish to get into the normal police. Their officers were upper-class versions of the same type, snobbish patriots who talked of the glory of France and sent their underlings to arrest Jewish children hiding in cellars.

Paul came and looked over Flick's shoulder. "Hell, it's a frigging Militian," he said.

Flick's mind raced. Was this a chance encounter, or part of an organized security sweep directed at the Jackdaws? The Milice were infamous busybodies, reveling in their power to harass their fellow citizens. They would stop people they did not like the look of, examine their papers minutely, and seek

a pretext to arrest them. Was the questioning of Ruby such an incident? Flick hoped
so. If the police were stopping everyone on
the streets of Sainte-Cécile, the Jackdaws
might never reach the gates of the château.

The cop started to question Ruby aggressively. Flick could not hear clearly, but she
picked up the words "mongrel" and "black,"
and she wondered if the man was accusing
the dark-skinned Ruby of being a gypsy.
Ruby took out her papers. The man examined them, then continued to question her
without handing them back.

Paul drew his pistol.

"Put it away," Flick commanded.

"You're not going to let him arrest her?"

"Yes, I am," Flick said coldly. "If we have
a shootout now, we're finished—the mission
is blown, whatever happens. Ruby's life is
not as important as disabling the telephone
exchange. Put away the damn gun."

Paul tucked it under the waistband of his
trousers.

The conversation between Ruby and the
Militian became heated. Flick watched with
trepidation as Ruby shifted the three baskets to her left hand and put her right hand
into her raincoat pocket. The man grabbed

Ruby's left shoulder in a decisive way, obviously arresting her.

Ruby moved fast. She dropped the baskets. Her right hand came out of her pocket holding a knife. She took a step forward and swung the knife up from hip level with great force, sticking the blade through his uniform shirt just below the ribs, angled up toward the heart.

Flick said, "Oh, *shit.*"

The man gave a scream that quickly died off into a horrible gurgle. Ruby tugged the knife out and stuck it in again, this time from the side. He threw back his head and opened his mouth in a soundless cry of pain.

Flick was thinking ahead. If she could get the body out of sight quickly, they might get away with this. Had anyone seen the stabbing? Flick's view from the window was restricted by the shutters. She pushed them wide and leaned out. To her left, the rue du Château was deserted except for a parked truck and a dog asleep on a doorstep. Looking the other way she saw, coming along the pavement, three young people in police-style uniforms, two men and a woman. They had to be Gestapo personnel from the château.

The Militian fell to the pavement, blood coming from his mouth.

Before Flick could shout a warning, the two Gestapo men sprang forward and grabbed Ruby by the arms.

Flick quickly pulled her head back in and drew the shutters together. Ruby was lost.

She continued to watch through a narrow gap between the shutters. One of the Gestapo men banged Ruby's right hand against the shop wall until she dropped the knife. The girl bent over the bleeding Militian. She lifted his head and spoke to him, then said something to the two men. There was a short exchange of barked words. The girl ran into the shop and came out with a storekeeper in a white apron. He bent over the Militian, then stood up again, his face showing distaste—whether for the man's ugly wounds or for the hated uniform, Flick could not tell. The girl ran off, back in the direction of the château, presumably to get help; and the two men frog-marched Ruby in the same direction.

Flick said, "Paul—go and get the baskets Ruby dropped."

Paul did not hesitate. "Yes, ma'am." He went out.

Flick watched him emerge onto the street and cross the road. What would the storekeeper say? The man looked at Paul and said something. Paul did not reply but bent down, swiftly picked up the three baskets, and came back.

The storekeeper stared at Paul, and Flick could read his thoughts on his face: at first shocked by Paul's apparent callousness, then puzzled and searching for possible reasons, then beginning to understand.

"Let's move quickly," Flick said as Paul came into the kitchen. "Load the bags and out, now! I want us to pass through that checkpoint while the guards are still excited about Ruby." She quickly stuffed one of the baskets with a powerful flashlight, her disassembled Sten gun, six 32-round magazines, and her share of the plastic explosive. Her pistol and knife were in her pockets. She covered the weapons in the basket with a cloth and put in a slice of vegetable terrine wrapped in baking paper.

Jelly said, "What if the guards at the gate search the baskets?"

"Then we're dead," Flick said. "We'll just

try to take as many of the enemy with us as we can. Don't let the Nazis capture you alive."

"Oh, my gordon," said Jelly, but she checked the magazine in her automatic pistol professionally and pushed it home with a decisive click.

The church bell in the town square struck seven.

They were ready.

Flick said to Paul, "Someone is sure to notice there are only three cleaners instead of the usual six. Antoinette is the supervisor, so they may decide to ask her what's gone wrong. If anyone shows up here, you'll just have to shoot him."

"Okay."

Flick kissed Paul on the mouth, briefly but hard, then went out, with Jelly and Greta following.

On the other side of the street, the storekeeper was staring down at the Militian dying on the pavement. He glanced up at the three women, then looked away again. Flick guessed he was already rehearsing his answers to questions: "I saw nothing. No one else was there."

The three remaining Jackdaws turned toward the square. Flick set a brisk pace, wanting to get to the château as quickly as possible. She could see the gates directly ahead of her, on the far side of the square. Ruby and her two captors were just passing through. Well, Flick thought, at least Ruby is inside.

The Jackdaws reached the end of the street and started across the square. The window of the Café des Sports, smashed in last week's shootout, was boarded over. Two guards from the château came across the square at a run, carrying their rifles, their boots clattering on the cobblestones, no doubt heading for the wounded Militian. They took no notice of the little group of cleaning women, who scuttled out of the way.

Flick reached the gate. This was the first really dangerous moment.

One guard was left. He kept looking past Flick at his comrades running across the square. He glanced at Flick's pass and waved her in. She stepped through the gate, then turned to wait for the others.

Greta came next, and the guard did the same. He was more interested in what was going on in the rue du Château.

Flick thought they were home and dry, but when he had checked Jelly's pass he glanced into her basket. "Something smells good," he said.

Flick held her breath.

"It's some sausage for my supper," Jelly said. "You can smell the garlic."

He waved her on and looked across the square again.

The three Jackdaws walked up the short drive, mounted the steps, and at last entered the château.

CHAPTER 50

Dieter spent the afternoon shadowing Michel's train, stopping at every sleepy country halt in case Michel got off. He felt sure he was wasting his time, and that Michel was a decoy, but he had no alternative. Michel was his only lead. He was desperate.

Michel rode the train all the way back to Reims.

A doomy sense of impending failure and disgrace overwhelmed Dieter as he sat in a car beside a bombed building near the Reims station waiting for Michel to emerge. Where had he gone wrong? It seemed to him that he had done everything he could—but nothing had worked.

What if following Michel led nowhere? At some point, Dieter would have to cut his losses and interrogate the man. But how much time did he have? Tonight was the night of the full moon, but the English Channel was stormy again. The Allies might postpone the invasion—or they might decide to take their chances with the weather. In a few hours it might be too late.

Michel had come to the station this morning in a van borrowed from Philippe Moulier, the meat supplier, and Dieter looked around for it, but could not see it. He guessed the van had been left here for Flick Clairet to pick up. By now she might be anywhere within a radius of a hundred miles. He cursed himself for not setting someone to watch the van.

He diverted himself by considering how to interrogate Michel. The man's weak point was probably Gilberte. Right now she was in a cell at the château, wondering what was going to happen to her. She would stay there until Dieter was quite sure he had finished with her, then she would be executed or sent to a camp in Germany. How could she be used to make Michel talk—and fast?

The thought of the camps in Germany gave Dieter an idea. Leaning forward, he said to his driver, "When the Gestapo send prisoners to Germany, they go by train, don't they?"

"Yes, sir."

"Is it true that you put them in the kind of railway cars normally used for transporting livestock?"

"Cattle trucks, yes, sir, it's good enough for those scum, communists and Jews and the like."

"Where do they board?"

"Right here in Reims. The train from Paris stops here."

"And how often do those trains run?"

"There's one most days. It leaves Paris late in the afternoon and stops here around eight in the evening, if it's on time."

Before he could progress his idea further, Dieter saw Michel emerge from the station. Ten yards behind him in the crowd was Hans Hesse. They approached Dieter on the other side of the street.

Dieter's driver started the engine.

Dieter turned in his seat to watch Michel and Hans.

They passed Dieter. Then, to Dieter's surprise, Michel turned into the alley alongside the Café de la Gare.

Hans quickened his pace and turned the same corner less than a minute later.

Dieter frowned. Was Michel trying to shake off his tail?

Hans reemerged from the alley and looked up and down the street with a worried frown. There were not many people on the pavements, just a few travelers walking to and from the station and the last of the city-center workers heading for home. Hans mouthed a curse and turned back into the alley.

Dieter groaned aloud. Hans had lost Michel.

This was the worst foul-up Dieter had been involved in since the battle of Alam Halfa, when wrong intelligence had led Rommel to defeat. That had been the turning point of the North African war. Dieter prayed this was not to be the turning point in Europe.

As he stared despondently at the mouth of the alley, Michel emerged from the front entrance of the café.

Dieter's spirits leaped. Michel had shaken off Hans but did not realize he had a second shadow. All was not yet lost.

Michel crossed the road, breaking into a

run, and headed back the way he had come—toward Dieter in the car.

Dieter thought fast. If he tried to follow Michel, maintaining the surveillance, then he, too, would have to run, and that would make it obvious that he was tailing the man. It was no good: the surveillance was over. It was time to seize Michel.

Michel pounded along the pavement, shoving other pedestrians aside. He ran awkwardly, because of his bullet wound, but he moved fast and rapidly approached Dieter's car.

Dieter made a decision.

He opened the car door.

As Michel drew level, Dieter got out, narrowing the available pavement by holding the door wide. Michel swerved to dodge around the obstacle. Dieter stuck out his leg. Michel tripped over his outstretched foot and went flying. A big man, he fell heavily on the paved sidewalk.

Dieter drew his pistol and thumbed the safety catch.

Michel lay prone for a second, stunned. Then, groggily, he tried to get to his knees.

Dieter touched the barrel of the gun to

Michel's temple. "Don't get up," he said in French.

The driver got a pair of handcuffs from the trunk, secured Michel's wrists, and bundled him into the back of the car.

Hans reappeared, looking dismayed. "What happened?"

"He went in through the back door of the Café de la Gare and came out of the front," Dieter explained.

Hans was relieved. "What now?"

"Come with me to the station." Dieter turned to the driver. "Do you have a gun?"

"Yes, sir."

"Keep a close watch on this man. If he tries to escape, shoot him in the legs."

"Yes, sir."

Dieter and Hans walked briskly into the station. Dieter buttonholed a uniformed railwayman and said, "I want to see the stationmaster right away."

The man looked surly, but he said, "I'll take you to his office."

The stationmaster was dressed in a black jacket and waistcoat with striped trousers, an elegant old-fashioned uniform, worn thin at the elbows and knees. He kept his bowler hat on even in his office. He was frightened by this visit from a high-powered German. "What can I do for you?" he said with a nervous smile.

"Are you expecting a train from Paris with prisoners tonight?"

"Yes, at eight o'clock, as usual."

"When it comes, hold it here until you hear from me. I have a special prisoner I want to board."

"Very good. If I could have written authorization . . ."

"Of course. I will arrange it. Do you do anything with the prisoners while the train is here?"

"Sometimes we hose out the cars. Cattle trucks are used, you see, so there are no lavatory facilities, and frankly it becomes extremely unpleasant, without wishing to criticize—"

"Do not clean the trucks tonight, you understand?"

"Of course."

"Do you do anything else?"

The man hesitated. "Not really."

He was guilty about something, Dieter could tell. "Come on, man, out with it, I'm not going to punish you."

"Sometimes the railwaymen take pity on

the prisoners, and give them water. It's not allowed, strictly speaking, but—"

"No water will be given tonight."

"Understood."

Dieter turned to Hans. "I want you to take Michel Clairet to the police station and lock him in a cell, then return here to the station and make sure my orders are carried out."

"Of course, Major."

Dieter picked up the phone on the stationmaster's desk. "Get me the château of Sainte-Cécile." When he got through he asked for Weber. "There's a woman in the cells called Gilberte."

"I know," said Weber. "Pretty girl."

Dieter wondered why Weber sounded so pleased with himself. "Would you please send her in a car to the railway station in Reims. Lieutenant Hesse is here, he will take charge of her."

"Very well," said Weber. "Hold the line a moment, will you?" He moved the phone away from his mouth and spoke to someone in the room, giving orders for Gilberte to be moved. Dieter waited impatiently. Weber came back on the line. "I've arranged that."

"Thank you—"

"Don't hang up. I have some news for you."

This would be why he was sounding pleased. "Go on," Dieter said.

"I have captured an Allied agent myself."

"What?" Dieter said. This was a lucky break. "When?"

"A few minutes ago."

"Where, for God's sake?"

"Right here in Sainte-Cécile."

"How did that happen?"

"She attacked a Militian, and three of my bright young people happened to witness it. They had the presence of mind to capture the culprit, who was armed with a Colt automatic."

"Did you say 'she'? The agent is a woman?"

"Yes."

That settled it. The Jackdaws were in Sainte-Cécile. The château was their target.

Dieter said, "Weber, listen to me. I think she is part of a team of saboteurs intending to attack the château."

"They tried that before," Weber said. "We gave them a hiding."

Dieter controlled his impatience with an effort. "Indeed you did, so they may be more sly this time. May I suggest a security alert? Double the guards, search the château, and question all non-German personnel in the building."

"I have given orders to that effect."

Dieter was not sure he believed that Weber had already thought of a security alert, but it did not matter, so long as he did so now.

Dieter briefly considered rescinding his instructions about Gilberte and Michel but decided not to. He might well need to interrogate Michel before the night was over.

"I will return to Sainte-Cécile immediately," he told Weber.

"As you wish," Weber said casually, implying he could manage perfectly well without Dieter's assistance.

"I need to interrogate the new prisoner."

"I have already begun. Sergeant Becker is softening her up."

"For God's sake! I want her sane and able to speak."

"Of course."

"Please, Weber, this is too important for mistakes. I beg you to keep Becker under control until I get there."

"Very well, Franck. I will make sure he doesn't overdo it."

"Thank you. I'll be there as fast as I can." Dieter hung up.

CHAPTER 51

Flick paused at the entrance to the great hall of the château. Her pulse was racing and there was a cold sensation of fear in her chest. She was in the lions' den. If she were captured, nothing could save her.

She surveyed the room rapidly. Telephone switchboards had been installed in precise parade-ground rows, incongruously modern against the faded grandeur of the pink-and-green walls and the pudgy cherubs painted on the ceiling. Bundled cables twisted across the checkerboard marble floor like uncoiled ropes on the deck of a ship.

There was a hubbub of chatter from forty operators. Those nearest glanced at the new arrivals. Flick saw one girl speak to her neighbor and point to them. The operators were all from Reims and the surrounding district, many from Sainte-Cécile itself, so they would know the regular cleaners and would realize the Jackdaws were strangers. But Flick was gambling that they would say nothing to the Germans.

She oriented herself quickly, bringing to mind the plan Antoinette had drawn. The bombed west wing, to her left, was disused. She turned right and led Greta and Jelly through a pair of tall paneled doors into the east wing.

One room led to another, all palatial reception rooms full of switchboards and equipment racks that buzzed and clicked as numbers were dialed. Flick did not know whether the cleaners normally greeted the operators or passed them in silence: the French were great people for saying good morning, but this place was run by the German military. She contented herself with smiling vaguely and avoiding eye contact.

In the third room, a supervisor in German uniform sat at a desk. Flick ignored her, but the woman called out, "Where is Antoinette?"

Flick answered without pausing in her stride. "She's coming." She heard the tremor of fear in her own voice and hoped the supervisor had not noticed.

The woman glanced up at the clock, which said five past seven. "You're late."

"Very sorry, madame, we'll get started right away." Flick hurried into the next room. For a moment she listened, heart in her mouth, for an angry shout calling her back, but none came, and she breathed easier and walked on, with Greta and Jelly close behind.

At the end of the east wing was a stairwell, leading up to the offices or down to the basement. The Jackdaws were headed for the basement, eventually, but first they had preparations to make.

They turned left and moved into the service wing. Following Antoinette's directions, they found a small room where cleaning materials were stored: mops, buckets, brooms, and garbage bins, plus the brown cotton overall coats the cleaners had to wear on duty. Flick closed the door.

"So far, so good," said Jelly.

Greta said, "I'm so scared!" She was pale and trembling. "I don't think I can go on."

Flick gave her a reassuring smile. "You'll

be fine," she said. "Let's get on with it. Put your ordnance into these cleaning buckets."

Jelly began to transfer her explosives into a bucket, and after a moment's hesitation Greta followed suit. Flick assembled her submachine gun without its rifle butt, reducing the length by a foot, to make it easier to conceal. She fitted the noise suppressor and flicked the switch for single-shot firing. When using the silencer, the chamber had to be reloaded manually before each shot.

She pushed the weapon under her leather belt. Then she put on an overall coat. It covered the gun. She left the buttons undone for quick access. The other two also put on overalls, concealing the guns and ammunition stuffed into their pockets.

They were almost ready for the basement. However, it was a high-security area, with a guard at the door, and French personnel were not allowed down there—the Germans cleaned it themselves. Before entering, the Jackdaws were going to create a little confusion.

They were about to leave the room when the door opened and a German officer looked in. "Passes!" he barked.

Flick tensed. She had been expecting

some kind of security alert. The Gestapo must have guessed that Ruby was an Allied agent—no one else would be carrying an automatic pistol and a lethal knife—and it made sense for them to take extra precautions at the château. However, she had hoped that the Gestapo would move too slowly to interfere with her mission. That wish had not been granted. Probably they were double-checking all French personnel in the building.

"Quickly!" the man said impatiently. He was a Gestapo lieutenant, Flick saw from the badge on his uniform shirt. She took out her pass. He looked at it carefully, comparing the picture with her face, and handed it back. He did the same with Jelly and Greta. "I must search you," he said. He looked into Jelly's bucket.

Behind his back, Flick drew the Sten gun from under her overall.

The officer frowned in puzzlement and took from Jelly's bucket the shockproof canister.

Flick disengaged the cocking lever of her gun from the safety slot.

The officer unscrewed the lid of the canister. Amazement dawned on his face as he saw the detonators.

Flick shot him in the back.

The gun was not really silent—the noise suppressor was not perfectly effective—and the shot made a soft bang like a book being dropped on the floor.

The Gestapo lieutenant jerked and fell.

Flick ejected the cartridge and pulled back the bolt, then shot him again in the head to make sure of him.

She reloaded the chamber and put the gun back under her overall.

Jelly dragged the body to the wall and shoved it behind the door, where it would not be seen by anyone glancing casually into the room.

"Let's get out of here," said Flick.

Jelly went out. Greta stood frozen and pale, staring at the dead officer.

Flick said, "Greta. We have a job to do. Let's go."

At last Greta nodded, picked up her mop and bucket, and walked through the door, moving like a robot.

They went from the cleaning store into the canteen. It was empty but for two girls in uniform drinking coffee and smoking.

Speaking French in a low voice, Flick said, "You know what you have to do."

Jelly began to sweep the floor.

Greta hesitated.

Flick said, "Don't let me down."

Greta nodded. She took a deep breath, straightened her back, and said, "I'm ready."

Flick entered the kitchen, and Greta followed.

The fuse boxes for the building were in a cupboard off the kitchen, beside the large electric oven, according to Antoinette. There was a young German man at the kitchen stove. Flick gave him a sexy smile and said, "What have you got to offer a hungry girl?"

He grinned at her.

Behind his back, Greta took out a stout pair of pliers with rubberized handles, then opened the cupboard door.

The sky was partly cloudy, and the sun disappeared as Dieter Franck drove into the picturesque square of Sainte-Cécile. The clouds were the same shade of dark gray as the slate roof of the church.

He noticed four guards at the château

gate, instead of the usual two. Although he was in a Gestapo car, the sergeant carefully examined his pass and his driver's before opening the wrought-iron gates and waving the car in. Dieter was pleased: Weber had taken seriously the need for extra security.

A cool breeze blew as he walked from the car to the steps of the grand entrance. Passing into the hall and seeing the rows of women at their switchboards, he thought about the female secret agent Weber had arrested. The Jackdaws were an all-woman team. It occurred to him that they might try to enter the château disguised as telephonists. Was it possible? As he passed through the east wing he spoke to the German woman supervisor. "Have any of these women joined in the last few days?"

"No, Major," she said. "One new girl was taken on three weeks ago, and she was the last."

That put paid to his theory. He nodded and walked on. At the end of the east wing he took the staircase down. The door to the basement stood open, as usual, but there were two soldiers instead of the usual one standing inside. Weber had doubled the guard. The corporal saluted and the sergeant asked for his pass.

Dieter noticed that the corporal stood behind the sergeant while the sergeant checked the pass. He said, "The way you are now, it's too easy for someone to overpower you both. Corporal, you should stand to the side, and two meters away, so that you have a clear shot if the sergeant is attacked."

"Yes, sir."

Dieter entered the basement corridor. He could hear the rumble of the diesel-fueled generator that supplied electricity to the phone system. He passed the doors of the equipment rooms and entered the interview room. He hoped to find the new prisoner here, but the room was empty.

Puzzled, he stepped inside and closed the door. Then his question was answered. From the inner chamber came a long scream of utter agony.

Dieter threw open the door.

Becker stood at the electric shock machine. Weber sat on a chair nearby. A young woman lay on the operating table with her wrists and ankles strapped and her head clamped in the head restraint. She wore a blue dress, and wires from the electric shock machine ran between her feet and up her dress.

Weber said, "Hello, Franck. Join us, please. Becker here has come up with an innovation. Show him, Sergeant."

Becker reached beneath the woman's dress and drew out an ebonite cylinder about fifteen centimeters long and two or three in diameter. The cylinder was ringed by two metal bands a couple of centimeters apart. Two wires from the electric shock machine were attached to the bands.

Dieter was accustomed to torture, but this hellish caricature of the sexual act filled him with loathing, and he shuddered with disgust.

"She hasn't said anything yet, but we've only just started," Weber said. "Give her another shock, Sergeant."

Becker pushed up the woman's dress and inserted the cylinder in her vagina. He picked up a roll of electrician's tape, tore off a strip, and secured the cylinder so that it would not fall out.

Weber said, "Turn the voltage up this time."

Becker returned to the machine.
Then the lights went out.

There was a blue flash and a bang from
behind the oven. The lights went out, and
the kitchen was filled with the smell of
scorched insulation. The motor of the refrig-
erator ran down with a groan as the power
was cut off. The young cook said in German,
"What's going on?"

Flick ran out of the door and through the
canteen with Jelly and Greta hard on her
heels. They followed a short corridor past
the cleaning cupboard. At the top of the
stairs Flick paused. She drew her submachine gun and held it concealed under the
flap of her coat.

"The basement will be in total darkness?"
she said.

"I cut all the cables, including the wires
to the emergency lighting system," Greta
assured her.

"Let's go."

They ran down the stairs. The daylight
coming from the ground-floor windows
faded rapidly as they descended, and the
entrance to the basement was half-dark.

There were two soldiers standing just inside the door. One of them, a young corporal with a rifle, smiled and said, "Don't worry, ladies, it's only a power cut."

Flick shot him in the chest, then swung her weapon and shot the sergeant.

The three Jackdaws stepped through the doorway. Flick held her gun in her right hand and the flashlight in her left. She could hear a low rumble of machinery and several voices shouting questions in German from distant rooms.

She turned on an electric torch for a second. She was in a broad corridor with a low ceiling. Farther along, doors were opening. She switched off the flashlight. A moment later she saw the flicker of a match at the far end. About thirty seconds had passed since Greta cut off the power. It would not be long before the Germans recovered from the shock and found flashlights. She had only a minute, maybe less, to get out of sight.

She tried the nearest door. It was open. She shone her flashlight inside. This was a photo lab, with prints hanging to dry and a man in a white coat fumbling his way across the room.

She slammed the door, crossed the corridor in two strides, and tried a door on the opposite side. It was locked. She guessed, from the position of the room at the front of the château under a corner of the parking lot, that the room beyond contained the fuel tanks.

She moved along the corridor and opened the next door. The rumble of machinery became louder. She shone her flashlight once more, just for a split second, long enough to see an electricity generator—the independent power supply to the phone system, she assumed—then she hissed, "Drag the bodies in here!"

Jelly and Greta pulled the dead guards across the floor. Flick returned to the basement entrance and slammed the steel door shut. Now the corridor was in total darkness. As an afterthought, she shot the three heavy bolts on the inside. That might give her precious extra seconds.

She returned to the generator room, closed the door, and turned on her flashlight.

Jelly and Greta had pushed the bodies behind the door and stood panting with the effort. "All done," Greta murmured.

There was a mass of pipes and cables in the room, but they were all color-coded with German efficiency, and Flick knew which was which: fresh-air pipes were yellow, fuel lines were brown, water pipes were green, and power lines were striped red-and-black. She directed her torch at the brown fuel line to the generator. "Later, if we have time, I want you to blow a hole in that."

"Easy," said Jelly.

"Now, put your hand on my shoulder and follow me. Greta, you follow Jelly the same way. Okay?"

"Okay."

Flick turned off her flashlight and opened the door. Now they had to explore the basement blind. She put her hand to the wall as a guide and began to walk, heading farther inside. A confused babble of raised voices revealed that several men were blundering about the corridor.

An authoritative voice said in German, "Who closed the main door?"

She heard Greta reply, but in a man's voice, "It seems to be stuck."

The German cursed. A moment later there was the scrape of a bolt.

Flick reached another door. She opened

it and shone her flashlight again. It contained two huge wooden coffers the size and shape of mortuary slabs. Greta whispered, "Battery room. Go to the next door."

The German man's voice said, "Was that a flashlight? Bring it over here!"

"Just coming," said Greta in her Gerhard voice, but the three Jackdaws walked in the opposite direction.

Flick came to the next room, led the other two inside, and closed the door before shining her flashlight. It was a long, narrow chamber with racks of equipment along both walls. At the near end of the room was a cabinet that probably held large sheets of drawings. At the far end, the beam of her flashlight revealed a small table. Three men sat at it holding playing cards. They appeared to have remained sitting during the minute or so since the lights went out. Now they moved.

As they rose to their feet, Flick leveled her gun. Jelly was just as quick. Flick shot one. Jelly's pistol cracked and the man beside him fell. The third man dived for cover, but Flick's flashlight followed him. Both Flick and Jelly fired again, and he fell still.

Flick refused to let herself think about the

dead men as people. There was no time for feelings. She shone her flashlight around. What she saw gladdened her heart. This was almost certainly the room she was looking for.

Standing a meter from one long wall was a pair of floor-to-ceiling racks bristling with thousands of terminals in tidy rows. From the outside world the telephone cables came through the wall in neat bundles to the backs of the terminals on the nearer rack. At the farther end, similar cables led from the backs of the terminals up through the ceiling to the switchboards above. At the front of the frame, a nightmare tangle of loose jumper wires connected the terminals of the near rack to those of the far one. Flick looked at Greta. "Well?"

Greta was examining the equipment by the light of her own flashlight, a fascinated expression on her face. "This is the MDF—the main distribution frame," she said. "But it's a bit different from ours in Britain."

Flick stared at Greta in surprise. Minutes ago she had said she was too frightened to go on. Now she was unmoved by the killing of three men.

Along the far wall more racks of equipment glowed with the light of vacuum tubes. "And on the other side?" Flick asked.

Greta swung her torch. "Those are the amplifiers and carrier circuit equipment for the long-distance lines."

"Good," Flick said briskly. "Show Jelly where to place the charges."

The three of them went to work. Greta unwrapped the wax-paper packets of yellow plastic explosive while Flick cut the fuse cord into lengths. It burned at one centimeter per second. "I'll make all the fuses three meters long," Flick said. "That will give us exactly five minutes to get out." Jelly assembled the fire train: fuse, detonator, and firing cap.

Flick held a flashlight while Greta molded the charges to the frames at the vulnerable places and Jelly stuck the firing cap into the soft explosive.

They worked fast. In five minutes all the equipment was covered with charges like a rash. The fuse cords led to a common source, where they were loosely twisted together, so that one light would serve to ignite them all.

Jelly took out a thermite bomb, a black can about the size and shape of a tin of soup, containing finely powdered aluminum oxide and iron oxide. It would burn with intense heat and fierce flames. She took off the lid to reveal two fuses, then placed it on the ground behind the MDF.

Greta said, "Somewhere in here are thousands of cards showing how the circuits are connected. We should burn them. Then it will take the repair crew two weeks, rather than two days, to reconnect the cables."

Flick opened the cupboard and found four custom-made card holders containing large diagrams, neatly sorted by labeled file dividers. "Is this what we're looking for?"

Greta studied a card by the light of her flashlight. "Yes."

Jelly said, "Scatter them around the thermite bomb. They'll go up in seconds."

Flick threw the cards on the floor in loose piles.

Jelly placed an oxygen-generating pack on the floor at the blind end of the room. "This will make the fire hotter," she said. "Ordinarily, we could only burn the wooden frames and the insulation around the cables, but with this, the copper cables should melt."

Everything was ready.

Flick shone her flashlight around the room. The outer walls were ancient brick, but the inner walls between the rooms were light wooden partitions. The explosion would destroy the partition walls and the fire would spread rapidly to the rest of the basement.

Five minutes had passed since the lights went out.

Jelly took out a cigarette lighter.

Flick said, "You two, make your way outside the building. Jelly, on your way, go into the generating room and blow a hole in the fuel line, where I showed you."

"Got it."

"We meet up at Antoinette's."

Greta said anxiously, "Where are *you* going?"

"To find Ruby."

Jelly warned, "You have five minutes."

Flick nodded.

Jelly lit the fuse.

When Dieter passed from the darkness of the basement into the half-light of the stairwell, he noticed that the guards had gone from the entrance. No doubt they were fetching help, but the ill discipline infuriated him. They should have remained at their post.

Perhaps they had been forcibly removed. Had they been taken away at gunpoint? Was an attack on the château already underway?

He ran up the stairs. On the ground floor, there were no signs of battle. The operators were still working: the phone system was on a separate circuit from the rest of the building's electricity, and there was still enough light coming through the windows for them to see their switchboards. He ran through the canteen, heading for the rear of the building, where the maintenance workshops were located, but on the way he looked into the kitchen and found three soldiers in overalls staring at a fuse box. "There's a power cut in the basement," Dieter said.

"I know," said one of the men. He had a sergeant's stripes on his shirt. "All these wires have been cut."

Dieter raised his voice. "Then get your tools out and reconnect them, you damn fool!" he said. "Don't stand here scratching your stupid head!"

The sergeant was startled. "Yes, sir," he said.

A worried-looking young cook said, "I think it's the electric oven, sir."

"What happened?" Dieter barked.

"Well, Major, they were cleaning behind the oven, and there was a bang—"

"Who? Who was cleaning?"

"I don't know, sir."

"A soldier, someone you recognized?"

"No, sir . . . just a cleaner."

Dieter did not know what to think. Clearly the château was under attack. But where were the enemy? He left the kitchen, went to the stairwell, and ran up toward the offices on the upper floor.

As he turned at the bend in the stairs, something caught his eye, and he looked back. A tall woman in a cleaner's overall was coming up the stairs from the basement, carrying a mop and a bucket.

He froze, staring at her, his mind racing. She should not have been there. Only Germans were allowed into the basement. Of course, anything could have happened in the confusion of a power cut. But the cook had blamed a cleaner for the power cut. He recalled his brief conversation with the supervisor of the switchboard girls. None of them was new to the job—but he had not asked about the French women cleaners.

He came back down the stairs and met her at ground level. "Why were you in the basement?" he asked her in French.

"I went there to clean, but the lights are out."

Dieter frowned. She spoke French with an accent that he could not quite place. He said, "You're not supposed to go there."

"Yes, the soldier told me that, they clean it themselves, I didn't know."

Her accent was not English, Dieter thought. But what was it? "How long have you worked here?"

"Only a week, and I've always done upstairs until today."

Her story was plausible, but Dieter was not satisfied. "Come with me." He took her arm in a firm grip. She did not resist as he led her through to the kitchen.

Dieter spoke to the cook. "Do you recognize this woman?"

"Yes, sir. She's the one who was cleaning behind the oven."

Dieter looked at her. "Is that true?"

"Yes, sir, I'm very sorry if I damaged something."

Dieter recognized her accent. "You're German," he said.

"No, sir."

"You filthy traitor." He looked at the cook. "Grab her and follow me. She's going to tell me everything."

Flick opened the door marked Interview Room, stepped inside, closed the door behind her, and swept the room with her flashlight.

She saw a cheap pine table with ashtrays, several chairs, and a steel desk. The room was empty of people.

She was puzzled. She had located the prison cells on this corridor and had shone her flashlight through the judas in each door. The cells were empty: the prisoners the Gestapo had taken during the last eight days, including Gilberte, must have been moved somewhere else . . . or killed. But Ruby had to be here somewhere.

Then she saw, on her left, a door leading, presumably, to an inner chamber.

She switched off her flashlight, opened

the door, stepped through, closed the door, and switched on her flashlight.

She saw Ruby right away. She was lying on a table like a hospital operating table. Specially designed straps secured her wrists and ankles and made it impossible for her to move her head. A wire from an electrical machine led between her feet and up her skirt. Flick guessed immediately what had been done to Ruby and gasped with horror.

She stepped to the table. "Ruby, can you hear me?"

Ruby groaned. Flick's heart leaped: she was still alive. "I'll free you," she said. She put her Sten gun down on the table.

Ruby was trying to speak, but her words came out as a moan. Swiftly, Flick undid the straps that bound Ruby to the table. "Flick," Ruby said at last.

"What?"

"Behind you."

Flick jumped to one side. Something heavy brushed her ear and thumped her left shoulder hard. She cried out in pain, dropped her flashlight, and fell. Hitting the floor she rolled sideways, moving as far as possible from her original position so that her assailant could not hit her again.

She had been so shocked by the sight of Ruby that she had not shone her flashlight all around the room. Someone else had been lurking in the shadows, waiting for his chance, and had slowly crept up behind her.

Her left arm was momentarily numbed. Using her right hand, she scrabbled on the floor for her flashlight. Before she found it, there was a loud click, and the lights came on.

She blinked and saw two people. One was a squat, stocky man with a round head and close-cropped hair. Behind him stood Ruby. In the dark Ruby had picked up what looked like a steel bar, and she held it above her head in readiness. As soon as the lights came on, Ruby saw the man, turned, and brought the steel bar down on his head with maximum force. It was a crippling blow, and the man slumped to the floor and lay still.

Flick got up. The feeling was rapidly returning to her arm. She picked up the Sten gun.

Ruby was kneeling over the prone body of the man. "Meet Sergeant Becker," she said.

"Are you all right?" Flick said.

"I'm in bloody agony, but I'm going to get my own back on this fucking bastard." Grasping the front of Becker's uniform tunic, Ruby heaved him upright then, with an effort, pushed him onto the operating table.

He groaned.

"He's coming round!" Flick said. "I'll finish him off."

"Give me ten seconds." Ruby straightened the man's limbs and strapped him in by his wrists and ankles, then she tightened the head restraint so that he could not move. Finally, she took the cylindrical terminal from the electric shock machine and stuffed it into his mouth. He choked and gagged but could not move his head. She picked up a roll of electrician's tape, tore off a strip with her teeth, and secured the cylinder so that it would not come out of his mouth. Then she went to the machine and fumbled with the switch.

There was a low hum. The man on the table let out a strangled scream. His strapped-down body shook with convulsions. Ruby looked at him for a moment, then she said, "Let's go."

They went out, leaving Sergeant Becker

writhing on the table, squealing like a pig in the slaughterhouse.

Flick checked her watch. Two minutes had passed since Jelly lit the fuses.

They passed through the Interview Room and stepped out into the corridor. The confusion had died down. There were just three soldiers near the entrance, talking calmly. Flick walked rapidly toward them with Ruby close behind.

Flick's instinct was to walk straight past the soldiers, relying on a confident air to get her through, but then she glimpsed, through the door, the tall figure of Dieter Franck approaching, followed by two or three other people she could not clearly see. She stopped abruptly. Ruby bumped into her back. Flick turned to the nearest door. It was marked Wireless Room. She opened it. The room was empty. They stepped inside.

She left the door an inch open. She heard Major Franck bark in German, "Captain, where are the two men who should be guarding this entrance?"

"I don't know, Major, I was just asking."

Flick took the silencer off her Sten gun and flicked the switch for rapid fire. She had used only four bullets so far, leaving twenty-eight in the magazine.

"Sergeant, you and this corporal stand guard. Captain, you go up to Major Weber's office and tell him Major Franck strongly recommends he conduct a search of the basement immediately. Off you go, on the double!"

A moment later, Franck's footsteps passed the Wireless Room. Flick waited, listening. A door slammed. She peeped out. Franck had disappeared.

"Let's go," she said to Ruby. They left the Wireless Room and walked to the main door.

The corporal said in French, "What are you doing here?"

Flick had an answer ready. "My friend Valérie is new to the job, and she came to the wrong place in the confusion of the blackout."

The corporal looked dubious. "It's still light upstairs, how could she get lost?"

Ruby said, "I'm very sorry, sir, I thought I was supposed to clean here, and no one stopped me."

The sergeant said in German, "We're supposed to keep them out, not keep them in, Corporal." He laughed and waved them on.

Dieter tied the prisoner to a chair, then dismissed the cook who had escorted her from the kitchen. He looked at the woman for a moment, wondering how much time he had. One agent had been arrested in the street outside the château. Another, if she was an agent, had been caught coming up the stairs from the basement. Had the others come and gone? Were they waiting somewhere to be let in? Or were they here in the building right now? It was maddening not to know what was happening. But he had ordered the basement searched. The only other thing he could do was interrogate the prisoner.

Dieter began with the traditional slap in the face, sudden and demoralizing. The woman gasped with shock and pain.

"Where are your friends?" he asked her.

The woman's cheek reddened. He studied her expression. What he saw mystified him.

She looked happy.

"You're in the basement of the château,"

he told her. "Through that door is the torture chamber. On the other side, beyond that partition wall, is the telephone switchgear. We are at the end of a tunnel, the bottom of the sack, as the French say. If your friends plan to blow up the building, you and I will surely die here in this room."

Her expression did not change.

Perhaps the château was not about to blow up, Dieter thought. But then what was the mission? "You're German," he said. "Why are you helping your country's enemies?"

At last she spoke. "I'll tell you," she said. She spoke German with a Hamburg accent. "Many years ago, I had a lover. His name was Manfred." She looked away, remembering. "Your Nazis arrested him and sent him to a camp. I think he died there—I never heard." She paused, swallowing. Dieter waited. After a moment she went on. "When they took him away from me, I swore I would have my revenge—and this is it." She smiled happily. "Your foul regime is almost finished. And I've helped to destroy it."

There was something wrong here. She spoke as if the deed was already done. Furthermore, the power cut had come and gone. Had the blackout already served its purpose? This woman showed no fear. But could it be that she did not mind dying?

"Why was your lover arrested?"

"They called him a pervert."

"What kind?"

"He was homosexual."

"But he was your lover?"

"Yes."

Dieter frowned. Then he looked harder at the woman. She was tall and broad-shouldered, and underneath the makeup she had a masculine nose and chin . . .

"Are you a man?" he said in astonishment.

She just smiled.

A dreadful suspicion dawned on Dieter. "Why are you telling me this?" he said. "Are you trying to keep me occupied while your friends get away? Are you sacrificing your life to ensure the success of the mission—"

His train of thought was broken by a faint noise. It sounded like a strangled scream. Now that he noticed it, he realized he had heard it two or three times before and ignored it. The sound seemed to come from the next room.

Dieter sprang up and went into the torture chamber.

He expected to see the other woman agent on the table and was shocked to find someone else there. It was a man, he saw immediately, but at first he did not know who, because the face was distorted—the jaw dislocated, the teeth broken, the cheeks stained with blood and vomit. Then he recognized the squat figure of Sergeant Becker. The wires from the electric shock machine led to Becker's mouth. Dieter realized that the terminal from the machine was in Becker's mouth, secured there by electrician's tape. Becker was still alive, twitching and emitting a dreadful squealing sound. Dieter was horrified.

He swiftly turned off the machine. Becker stopped twitching. Dieter grasped the electric wire and jerked hard. The terminal came out of Becker's mouth. He threw it to the floor.

He bent over the table. "Becker!" he said. "Can you hear me? What happened here?"

There was no reply.

Upstairs, all was normal. Flick and Ruby walked quickly through the ranks of telephone operators, all busy at their switchboards, murmuring into their headsets in low voices as they plugged jacks into sockets, connecting decision-makers in Berlin, Paris, and Normandy. Flick checked her watch. In exactly two minutes all those connections would be destroyed, and the military machine would fall apart, leaving a scatter of isolated components, unable to work together. Now, Flick thought, if only we can get out . . .

They passed out of the building without incident. In seconds they would be in the town square. They had almost made it. But, in the courtyard, they met Jelly—coming back.

"Where's Greta?" she said.

"She left with you!" Flick replied.

"I stopped to set a charge on the diesel fuel line in the generator room, like you said. Greta went on ahead of me. But she never reached Antoinette's place. I've just met Paul, he hasn't seen her. I came back to look for her." Jelly had a paper packet in her hand. "I told the guard at the gate that I just went out to fetch my supper."

Flick was dismayed. "Greta must be inside—hell!"

"I'm going back for her," Jelly said determinedly. "She saved me from the Gestapo, back in Chartres, so I owe her."

Flick looked at her watch. "We have less than two minutes. Let's go!"

They ran back inside. The switchboard girls stared at them as they raced through the rooms. Flick was already having second thoughts. In attempting to save one of her team, was she about to sacrifice two more—and herself?

When they reached the stairwell, Flick paused. The two soldiers who had let them out of the basement with a joke would not let them in again so easily. "As before," she said quietly to the others. "Approach the guards innocently and shoot at the last moment."

A voice from above said, "What's going on here?"

Flick froze.

She looked back over her shoulder. On the staircase coming down from the top floor stood four men. One, in major's uniform, was pointing a pistol at her. She recognized Major Weber.

This was the search party Dieter Franck

had asked for. It had appeared at precisely the wrong moment.

Flick cursed herself for a bad decision. Now four would be lost instead of one.

Weber said, "You women have a conspiratorial air."

"What do you want with us?" Flick said. "We're the cleaners."

"Perhaps you are," he said. "But there is a team of female enemy agents in the district."

Flick pretended to be relieved. "Oh, good," she said. "If you're looking for enemy agents, we're safe. I was afraid you might be dissatisfied with the cleaning." She forced a laugh. Ruby joined in. Both sounded false.

Weber said, "Raise your hands in the air."

As she lifted her wrist past her face, Flick checked her watch.

Thirty seconds left.

"Down the stairs," said Weber.

Reluctantly, Flick went down. Ruby and Jelly went with her, and the four men followed. She went as slowly as she could, counting seconds.

She stopped at the foot of the stairs. Twenty seconds.

"You again?" said one of the guards.

Flick said, "Speak to your major."

"Keep moving," said Weber.

"I thought we weren't supposed to go into the basement."

"Just keep going!"

Five seconds.

They passed through the basement door.

There was a tremendous bang.

At the far end of the corridor, the partition walls of the equipment chamber exploded outwards. There was a series of crashing sounds. Flames billowed over the debris. Flick was knocked down.

She got up on one knee, pulled the submachine gun out from under her overall, and spun around. Jelly and Ruby were on either side of her. The basement guards, Weber, and the other three men had also fallen. Flick pulled the trigger.

Of the six Germans, only Weber had kept his presence of mind. As Flick sprayed bullets, Weber fired his pistol. Beside Flick Jelly, struggling to her feet, cried out and fell. Then Flick hit Weber in the chest and he went down.

Flick emptied her gun into the six bodies

on the floor. She ejected the magazine, took a fresh one from her pocket, and reloaded.

Ruby bent over Jelly, feeling for a pulse. After a moment she looked up. "Dead," she said.

Flick looked toward the far end of the corridor, where Greta was. Flames were billowing out from the equipment chamber, but the wall of the Interview Room seemed intact.

She ran toward the inferno.

Dieter found himself lying on the floor without knowing how he had got there. He heard the roaring of flames and smelled smoke. He struggled to his feet and looked into the Interview Room.

He realized immediately that the brick walls of the torture chamber had saved his life. The partition between the Interview Room and the equipment chamber had disappeared. The few pieces of furniture in the Interview Room had been thrown up against the wall. The prisoner had suffered the same fate and lay on the ground, still tied to the chair, neck at the horrid angle that indicated it was broken and she—or he—was dead.

The equipment chamber was aflame and the fire was spreading rapidly.

Dieter realized he had only seconds to get away.

The door to the Interview Room opened and Flick Clairet stood there holding a submachine gun.

She wore a dark wig that had fallen askew to reveal her own blonde hair beneath. Flushed, breathing hard, a wild look in her eyes, she was beautiful.

If he had had a gun in his hand at that moment, he would have mowed her down in blind rage. She would be an incomparable prize if captured alive, but he was so enraged and humiliated by her success and his own failure that he could not have controlled himself.

But she had the gun.

At first she did not see Dieter but stared at the dead body of her comrade. Dieter's hand moved inside his jacket. Then she lifted her gaze and met his eyes. He saw recognition dawn on her face. She knew who he was. She knew whom she had been fighting for the past nine days. There was a light of triumph in her eyes. But he also saw the thirst for revenge in the twist of her mouth, and she raised the Sten gun and fired.

Dieter ducked back into the torture chamber as her bullets chipped fragments of brick off the wall. He drew his Walther P38 automatic pistol, thumbed the safety lever to the fire position, and pointed it at the doorway, waiting for Flick to come through.

She did not appear.

He waited a few seconds, then risked a look.

Flick had gone.

He dashed across the burning Interview Room, threw open the door, and stepped into the corridor. Flick and another woman were running toward the far end. As he raised his gun, they jumped over a group of uniformed bodies on the floor. He aimed at Flick, then a hot pain burned his arm. He cried out and dropped his gun. He saw that his sleeve was on fire. He tore off his jacket.

When he looked up again, the women had gone.

Dieter picked up his pistol and went after them.

As he ran, he smelled fuel. There was a

leak—or perhaps the saboteurs had holed a pipe. Any second now, the basement would explode like a giant bomb.

But he might still catch Flick.

He ran out and started up the stairs.

In the torture chamber, Sergeant Becker's uniform started to smolder.

The heat and the smoke brought him back to consciousness and he cried for help, but no one heard.

He struggled against the leather straps that bound him, as so many of his victims had struggled in the past, but, like them, he was helpless.

A few moments later, his clothes burst into flame, and he began to scream.

Flick saw Dieter coming up the stairs after her with his gun in his hand. She was afraid that if she stopped and turned to take aim at him, he would be able to shoot first. She decided to run rather than stand and fight.

Someone had activated the fire alarm, and a klaxon blared throughout the château as she and Ruby raced through the switch-board rooms. All the operators left their stations and crowded to the doors, so that Flick found herself in a crush. The crowd would be making it difficult for Dieter to get a shot at her or Ruby, but the other women were slowing them down. Flick punched and kicked ruthlessly to get people out of her way.

They reached the front entrance and ran down the steps. In the square, Flick could see Moulier's meat van, backed up to the château gates with its engine running and its rear doors open. Paul stood beside it, staring anxiously through the iron railings. Flick thought he was the best thing she had ever seen.

However, as the women poured out of the building, two guards were directing them into the vineyard on the west side of the courtyard, away from the parked cars. Flick and Ruby ignored their waved instructions and ran for the gates. When the soldiers saw Flick's submachine gun, they reached for their weapons.

A rifle appeared in Paul's hands. He aimed through the railings. Two shots rang out, and both guards fell.

Paul threw open the gates.

As Flick dashed through the gateway, shots whistled over her head and hit the van: Dieter was firing.

Paul jumped into the front of the van.

Flick and Ruby threw themselves into the back.

As the van pulled away, Flick saw Dieter turn toward the parking lot, where his sky-blue car stood waiting.

At that moment, down in the basement, the fire reached the fuel tanks.

There was a deep underground boom like an earthquake. The parking lot erupted, gravel and earth and slabs of concrete flying into the air. Half the cars parked around the old fountain were overturned. Huge stones and chunks of brickwork rained down on the rest. Dieter was thrown back across the steps. The gas pump soared into the air, and a gout of flame spurted from the ground where it had stood. Several cars caught fire, and their gas tanks began to explode, one by one. Then the van left the square, and Flick could see no more.

Paul drove at top speed out of the village. Flick and Ruby bounced on the metal floor of the van. It dawned slowly on Flick that they had accomplished their mission. She could hardly believe it. She thought of Greta and Jelly, both dead, and of Diana and Maude, dead or dying in some concentration camp, and she could not feel happy. But she felt a savage satisfaction as she saw again in her mind the blazing equipment chamber and the exploding parking lot.

She looked at Ruby.

Ruby grinned at her. "We did it," she said.

Flick nodded.

Ruby put her arms around Flick and hugged her hard.

"Yes," Flick said. "We did it."

Dieter picked himself up off the ground. He felt bruised all over, but he could walk. The château was ablaze, and the parking lot was a shambles. The women were screaming and panicking.

He stared at the carnage all around. The Jackdaws had succeeded in their mission. But it was not over yet. They were still in France. And if he could capture and interrogate Flick Clairet, he could yet turn defeat into victory. Sometime tonight, she must be planning to meet a small plane, in a field not far from Reims. He had to find out where and when.

And he knew who would tell him.

Her husband.

THE LAST DAY

Tuesday, June 6, 1944

CHAPTER 52

Dieter sat on the platform at the Reims railway station. French railwaymen and German troops watched with him, standing patiently under the harsh lights. The prison train was late, hours late, but it was coming, he had been assured of that. He had to wait for it. He had no other cards to play.

His heart was full of rage. He had been humiliated and defeated by a girl. Had she been a German girl, he would have been proud of her. He would have called her brilliant and brave. He might even have fallen in love with her. But she belonged to the enemy, and she had outwitted him at every turn. She had killed Stéphanie, she had destroyed the château, and she had escaped. But he would catch her yet. And when he did, she would suffer tortures worse than her most terrifying imaginings—then she would talk.

Everyone talked.

The train rolled in a few minutes after midnight.

He noticed the stink even before it came to a halt. It was like the smell of a farmyard but disgustingly human.

There was an assortment of rail cars, none of them designed for passengers: goods wagons, cattle trucks, even a mail car with its narrow windows broken. Each was crammed with people.

The livestock wagons had high wooden sides pierced by slats to permit observation of the animals. The prisoners nearest put their arms through the slats, hands open with palms upward, begging. They asked to be let out, they pleaded for something to eat, but most of all they begged for water. The guards looked on impassively: Dieter had given instructions that the prisoners were to have no relief at Reims tonight.

He had two Waffen SS corporals with him, guards from the château, both good marksmen. He had extracted them from the shambles at Sainte-Cécile, trading on his authority as a major. He turned to them now and said, "Bring Michel Clairet."

Michel was locked in the windowless room where the stationmaster kept the cash. The corporals went away and reappeared with Michel between them. His hands were tied behind his back and his ankles were hobbled so that he could not run. He had not been told what had happened at Sainte-Cécile. All he knew was that he had been captured for the second time in a week. There was little left of his buccaneering persona. He was trying to maintain an air of bravado, to keep his spirits up, but the attempt was a failure. His limp was worse, his clothes were dirty, and his face grim. He looked defeated.

Dieter took Michel's arm and walked him closer to the train. At first, Michel did not understand what he was looking at, and his face showed only mystification and fear. Then, when he made out the begging hands and understood the piteous voices, he staggered, as if he had been struck, and Dieter had to hold him upright.

Dieter said, "I need some information."

Michel shook his head. "Put me on the

train," he said. "I'd rather be with them than with you."

Dieter was shocked by the insult and surprised by Michel's courage. He said, "Tell me where the Jackdaws' plane will land—and when."

Michel stared at him. "You haven't caught them," he said, and hope came back into his face. "They've blown up the château, haven't they? They succeeded." He threw back his head and gave a whoop of joy. "Well done, Flick!"

Dieter made Michel walk the length of the train, slowly, showing him the numbers of prisoners and the scale of their suffering. "The plane," he said again.

Michel said, "The field outside La Chatelle, at three a.m."

Dieter was almost certain that was false. Flick had been scheduled to arrive at La Chatelle seventy-two hours ago but had aborted the landing, presumably because she suspected a Gestapo trap. Dieter knew there was a backup landing place, because Gaston had told him so; but Gaston had known only its code name, Champ d'Or, not its location. Michel, however, would know the exact place. "You're lying," Dieter said.

"Then put me on the train," Michel replied.

Dieter shook his head. "That's not the choice—nothing so easy."

He saw puzzlement and the shadow of fear in Michel's eyes.

Dieter walked him back and stopped at the women's car. Their feminine voices begged in French and German, some invoking the pity of God, others asking the men to think of their mothers and sisters, a few offering sexual favors. Michel bowed his head, refusing to look.

Dieter beckoned to two figures standing in the shadows.

Michel looked up, and a terrible dread came over his face.

Hans Hesse walked out of the shadows, escorting a young woman. She might have been beautiful, but her face was ghastly white, her hair lay in greasy strands, and she had sores on her lips. She seemed weak, walking with difficulty.

It was Gilberte.

Michel gasped.

Dieter repeated his question. "Where will the plane land, and when?"

Michel said nothing.

Dieter said, "Put her on the train."

Michel moaned.

A guard opened the gate of a cattle car. While two others kept the women in with bayonets, the guard pushed Gilberte into the car. "No," she cried. "No, please!"

The guard was about to close the gate, but Dieter said, "Wait." He looked at Michel. Tears were pouring down the man's face.

Gilberte said, "Please, Michel, I beg you."

Michel nodded. "All right," he said.

"Don't lie again," Dieter warned.

"Let her out."

"The time and place."

"The potato field east of Laroque, at two a.m."

Dieter looked at his watch. It was twelve-fifteen. "Show me," he said.

Five kilometers from Laroque, the village of L'Epine was asleep. Bright moonlight silvered the big church. Behind the church, Moulier's meat van was parked inconspicuously next to a barn. In the deep moon shadow thrown by a buttress, the surviving Jackdaws sat waiting.

"What are you looking forward to?" said Ruby.

Paul said, "A steak."

Flick said, "A soft bed with clean sheets. How about you?"

"Seeing Jim."

Flick recalled that Ruby had had a fling with the firearms instructor. "I thought . . ." She stopped.

"You thought it was just a casual shag?" Ruby said.

Flick nodded, embarrassed.

"So did Jim," Ruby said. "But I've got other plans."

Paul laughed softly. "I'll bet you get what you want."

"What about you two?" Ruby asked.

Paul said, "I'm single." He looked at Flick.

She shook her head. "I intended to ask Michel for a divorce . . . but how could I, in the middle of an operation?"

"So we'll wait until after the war to get married," Paul said. "I'm patient."

Typical man, Flick thought. He slips marriage into the conversation like a minor detail, on a level with buying a dog license. So much for romance.

But in truth she was pleased. It was the

second time he had mentioned marriage. Who needs romance? she thought.

She looked at her watch. It was one-thirty. "Time to go," she said.

Dieter had commandeered a Mercedes limousine that had been outside the château grounds and so had survived the explosion. The car was now parked at the edge of the vineyard next to the potato field at Laroque, camouflaged with leafy vines torn from the ground. Michel and Gilberte were in the backseat, bound hand and foot, guarded by Hans.

Dieter also had with him the two corporals, each armed with a rifle. Dieter and the riflemen looked into the potato field. They could see clearly in the moonlight.

Dieter said, "The terrorists will be here in the next few minutes. We have the advantage of surprise. They have no idea that we're here. But remember, I must have them alive—especially the leader, the small woman. You have to shoot to wound, not kill."

One of the marksmen said, "We can't guarantee that. This field must be three hundred meters wide. Let's say the enemy is a hundred and fifty meters away. At that distance, no one could be sure of hitting the legs of a running man."

"They won't be running," Dieter said. "They're meeting a plane. They have to form a line, pointing electric torches at the aircraft to guide the pilot down. That means they'll be standing still for several minutes."

"In the middle of the field?"

"Yes."

The man nodded. "Then we can do it." He looked up. "Unless the moon goes behind a cloud."

"In that event, we'll turn on the headlights of the car at the crucial moment." The Mercedes had huge dinner-plate lamps.

The other marksman said, "Listen."

They fell silent. A motor vehicle was approaching. They all knelt. Despite the moonlight, they would not be visible against the dark mass of the vines, provided they kept their heads down.

A van came along the road from the village with its lights off. It pulled up by the gate to the potato field. A female figure jumped out and swung the gate wide. The van pulled in and its engine was silenced.

Two more people got out, another woman and a man.

"Quiet, now," Dieter whispered.

Suddenly the hush was shattered by the blare of a car horn, incredibly loud.

Dieter jumped and cursed. It came from immediately behind him. "Jesus!" he exploded. It was the Mercedes. He leaped to his feet and ran to the open window of the driver's door. He saw immediately what had happened.

Michel had sprung forward, leaning across the front seat, and before Hans could stop him he had pressed on the horn with his bound hands. Hans, in the front passenger seat, was now trying to aim his gun, but Gilberte had joined in, and she was lying half over Hans, hampering his movements so that he kept having to push her away.

Dieter reached in and shoved Michel, but Michel resisted, and Dieter's position, with his arms extended through the car window, was too awkward for him to exert much force. The horn continued to sound a deafening warning that the Resistance agents could not fail to hear.

Dieter fumbled for his gun.

Michel found the light switch, and the

car's headlights came on. Dieter looked up. The riflemen were hideously exposed in the glare of the lights. They both got up off their knees, but before they could throw themselves out of the beam there was a rattle of machine-gun fire from the field. One rifleman cried out, dropped his gun, clutched his belly, and fell across the hood of the Mercedes; then the other was shot in the head. A sharp pain stung Dieter's left arm, and he let out a yell of shock.

Then there was a shot from within the car, and Michel cried out. Hans had at last flung Gilberte off himself and got his pistol out. He fired again, and Michel slumped, but Michel's hand was still on the horn, and his body now lay over his hand, pressing it down, so the horn continued to blare. Hans fired a third time, uselessly, for his bullet thudded into the body of a dead man. Gilberte screamed and threw herself at Hans again, grabbing at his gun arm with her manacled hands. Dieter had his gun out but could not shoot at Gilberte for fear of hitting Hans.

There was a fourth shot. It was Hans's gun again, but now it was somehow pointing upwards, and he shot himself, the bullet hitting him under the chin. He gave a horrid gurgle, blood came out of his mouth, and he slumped back against the door, his eyes staring lifelessly.

Dieter took careful aim and shot Gilberte in the head.

He reached through the window with his right arm and shoved the corpse of Michel away from the steering wheel.

The horn was silenced.

He found the light switch and killed the headlights.

He looked across the field.

The van was still there, but the Jackdaws had disappeared.

He listened. Nothing moved.

He was alone.

Flick crawled through the vineyard on her hands and knees, heading for Dieter Franck's car. The moonlight, so necessary for clandestine flights across occupied territory, was now her enemy. She wished for a cloud to shade the moon, but for the moment the sky was clear. She kept close to the row of vines, but she threw a conspicuous moon shadow.

She had firmly instructed Paul and Ruby to stay behind, hiding at the edge of the field near the van. Three people made three times the noise, and she did not want a companion to betray her presence.

As she crawled, she listened for the incoming plane. She had to locate any remaining enemy and kill them before the plane arrived. The Jackdaws could not stand in the middle of the field with flashlights while there were armed troops aiming at them from the vineyard. And if they did not hold flashlights, the plane would return to England without touching down. The thought was unbearable.

She was deeper into the vineyard than Dieter Franck's car, which was parked at the edge. She was five rows of vines back. She would approach the enemy from behind. She kept the submachine gun in her right hand, ready to fire, as she crawled.

She drew level with the car. Franck had camouflaged it with vegetation, but when she peeped over the rows of vines she saw moonlight glint off the rear window.

The shoots of the vines were espaliered crosswise, but she was able to crawl beneath the lowest strand. She pushed her head through and looked up and down the next alley. It was clear. She crawled across the open space and repeated the exercise. She grew ultracautious as she approached the car, but she saw no one.

When she was two rows away, she was able to see the wheels of the car and the ground around it. She thought she could make out two motionless bodies in uniform. How many were there in total? It was a long Mercedes limousine and could easily carry six.

She crept closer. Nothing moved. Were they all dead? Or had one or two survived, and concealed themselves nearby, waiting to pounce?

Eventually she crawled right up to the car.

The doors were wide open, and the interior seemed full of bodies. She looked in the front and recognized Michel. She choked back a sob. He was a bad husband, but he had been her choice, and now he was lifeless, with three red-ringed bullet holes in his blue chambray shirt. She guessed he had been the one to sound the horn. If so, he had died saving her life. There was no time to think of such things now: she would ponder them later, if she lived long enough.

Next to Michel lay a man she did not recognize who had been shot in the throat. He
wore the uniform of a lieutenant. There were
more bodies in the back. She looked
through the open rear door. One was that
of a woman. She leaned into the car for a
better view. She gasped: the woman was
Gilberte, and she seemed to be staring at
Flick. A ghastly moment later, Flick realized
that the eyes saw nothing, and Gilberte was
dead, shot in the head.

She leaned over Gilberte to look at the
fourth corpse. It rose up from the floor in a
swift motion. Before she had time to
scream, it grabbed her by the hair and thrust
the barrel of a gun into the soft flesh of her
throat.

It was Dieter Franck.

"Drop the gun," he said in French.

She was holding the submachine gun in
her right hand, but it was pointing up and,
before she could aim it, he would be able
to shoot her. She had no choice: she
dropped it. The safety catch was disengaged, and she half-hoped the impact of its
fall would fire the gun, but it landed harm-
lessly on the earth.

"Back away."

As she stepped back, he followed her, getting out of the car, keeping the gun at her throat. He drew himself upright. "You're so small," he said, looking her up and down. "And you've done so much damage."

She saw blood on the sleeve of his suit and guessed she had winged him with her Sten gun.

"Not just to me," he said. "That telephone exchange is every bit as important as you obviously believe."

She found her voice. "Good."

"Don't look pleased. Now you're going to damage the Resistance."

She wished she had not been so fierce in ordering Paul and Ruby to wait in hiding. There was now no chance they would come to her rescue.

Dieter shifted the gun from her throat to her shoulder. "I don't want to kill you, but I'd be happy to give you a crippling wound. I need you able to talk, of course. You're going to give me all the names and addresses in your head."

She thought of the suicide pill concealed in the hollow cap of her fountain pen. Would she have a chance to take it?

"It's a pity you've destroyed the interrogation facility at Sainte-Cécile," he went on. "I'll have to drive you to Paris. I've got all the same equipment there."

She thought with horror of the hospital operating table and the electric shock machine.

"I wonder what will break you?" he said. "Sheer pain breaks everyone eventually, of course, but I feel that you might bear pain for an inconveniently long time." He raised his left arm. The wound seemed to give him a twinge, and he winced, but he bore it. He touched her face. "The loss of your looks, perhaps. Imagine this pretty face disfigured: the nose broken, the lips slashed, one eye put out, the ears cut off."

Flick felt sick, but she maintained a stony expression.

"No?" His hand moved down, stroking her neck, then he touched her breast. "Sexual humiliation, then. To be naked in front of many people, fondled by a group of drunk men, forced to perform acts of grossness with animals . . ."

"And which of us would be most humiliated by that?" she said defiantly. "Me, the helpless victim . . . or you, the real perpetrator of obscenity?"

He took his hand away. "Then again, we have tortures which destroy forever a woman's ability to bear children."

Flick thought of Paul and flinched involuntarily.

"Ah," he said with satisfaction. "I believe I have found the key to unlock you."

She realized she had been foolish to speak to him. Now she had given him information which he could use to break her will.

"We'll drive straight to Paris," he said. "We'll be there by dawn. By midday, you will be begging me to stop the torture and listen to you pour out all the secrets you know. Tomorrow night we will arrest every member of the Resistance in northern France."

Flick was cold with dread. Franck was not bragging. He could do it.

"I think you can travel in the trunk of the car," he said. "It's not airtight, you won't suffocate. But I'll put the corpses of your husband and his lover in with you. A few hours bumping around with dead people will put you in the right frame of mind, I think."

Flick shuddered with loathing. She could not help it.

Keeping the pistol pressed to her shoulder, he reached into his pocket with his other hand. He moved his arm cautiously: the bullet wound hurt but did not incapacitate him. He drew out a pair of handcuffs. "Give me your hands," he said.

She remained motionless.

"I can either handcuff you, or render your arms useless by shooting you in both shoulders."

Helpless, she raised her hands.

He closed one cuff over her left wrist. She moved her right toward him. Then she made her last desperate move.

She struck sideways with her handcuffed left hand, knocking his gun away from her shoulder. At the same time she used her right hand to draw the small knife from its hidden sheath behind the lapel of her jacket.

He flinched back, but not fast enough.

She lunged forward and thrust the knife directly into his left eye. He turned his head, but the knife was already in, and Flick moved farther forward, pressing her body up against his, ramming the knife home. Blood and fluid spurted from the wound. Franck screamed in agony and fired his gun, but the shots went into the air.

He staggered back, but she followed him, still pushing the knife with the heel of her hand. The weapon had no hilt, and she continued to shove until its entire three inches had sunk into his head. He fell backwards and hit the ground.

She fell on him, knees on his chest, and she felt ribs crack. He dropped his gun and clawed at his eye with both hands, trying to get at the knife, but it was sunk too deep. Flick grabbed the gun. It was a Walther P38. She stood upright, held it two-handed, and aimed it at Franck.

Then he fell still.

She heard pounding footsteps. Paul rushed up. "Flick! Are you all right?"

She nodded.

She was still pointing the Walther at Dieter Franck. "I don't think that will be necessary," Paul said softly. After a moment, he moved her hands, then gently took the gun from her and engaged the safety catch.

Ruby appeared. "Listen!" she cried. "Listen!"

Flick heard the drone of a Hudson.

"Let's get moving," Paul said.

They ran out into the field to signal the plane that would take them home.

* * *

They crossed the English Channel in strong winds and intermittent rain. During a quiet spell, the navigator came back into the passenger compartment and said, "You might want to take a look outside."

Flick, Ruby, and Paul were dozing. The floor was hard, but they were exhausted. Flick was wrapped in Paul's arms, and she did not want to move.

The navigator pressed them. "You'd better be quick, before it clouds over again. You'll never see anything like this again if you live to be a hundred."

Curiosity overcame Flick's tiredness. She got up and staggered to the small rectangular window. Ruby did the same. Obligingly, the pilot dipped a wing.

The English Channel was choppy, and a stiff wind blew, but the moon was full and she could see clearly. At first she could hardly believe her eyes. Immediately below the plane was a gray-painted warship bristling with guns. Alongside it was a small ocean liner, its paintwork gleaming white in the moonlight. Behind them, a rusty old steamer pitched into the swell. Beyond them and behind were cargo boats, troop transports, battered old tankers, and great shallow-draft landing ships. There were ships as far as Flick could see, hundreds of them.

The pilot dipped the other wing, and she looked out the other side. It was the same.

"Paul, look at this!" she cried.

He came and stood beside her. "Jeepers!" he said. "I've never seen so many ships in all my life!"

"It's the invasion!" she said.

"Take a look out the front," said the navigator.

Flick went forward and looked over the pilot's shoulder. The ships were spread out over the sea like a carpet, stretching for miles and miles, as far as she could see. She heard Paul's incredulous voice say, "I didn't know there were this many ships in the damn world!"

"How many do you think it is?" Ruby said.

The navigator said, "I heard five thousand."

"Amazing," Flick said.

The navigator said, "I'd give a lot to be part of that, wouldn't you?"

Flick looked at Paul and Ruby, and they all smiled. "Oh, we are," she said. "We're part of it, all right."

ONE YEAR LATER

Wednesday, June 6, 1945

CHAPTER 53

The London street called Whitehall was lined on both sides with grandiose buildings that embodied the magnificence of the British empire as it had once been, a hundred years earlier. Inside those fine buildings, many of the high rooms with their long windows had been subdivided by cheap partitions to form offices for lesser officials and meeting rooms for unimportant groups. As a subcommittee of a subcommittee, the Medals (Clandestine Actions) Working Party met in a windowless room fifteen feet square with a vast, cold fireplace that occupied half of one wall.

Simon Fortescue from MI6 was in the chair, wearing a striped suit, striped shirt, and striped tie. The Special Operations Executive was represented by John Graves from the Ministry of Economic Warfare, which had theoretically supervised SOE throughout the war. Like the other civil servants on the committee, Graves wore the Whitehall uniform of black jacket and gray striped trousers. The Bishop of Marlborough was there in a purple clerical shirt, no doubt to give the moral dimension to the business of honoring men for killing other men. Colonel Algernon "Nobby" Clarke, an intelligence officer, was the only member of the committee who had seen action in the war.

Tea was served by the committee's secretary, and a plate of biscuits was passed around while the men deliberated.

It was mid-morning when they came to the case of the Jackdaws of Reims.

John Graves said, "There were six women on this team, and only two came back. But they destroyed the telephone exchange at Sainte-Cécile, which was also the local Gestapo headquarters."

"Women?" said the bishop. "Did you say six women?"

"Yes."

"My goodness me." His tone was disapproving. "Why women?"

"The telephone exchange was heavily

guarded, but they got in by posing as cleaners."

"I see."

Nobby Clarke, who had spent most of the morning chain-smoking in silence, now said, "After the liberation of Paris, I interrogated a Major Goedel, who had been aide to Rommel. He told me they had been virtually paralyzed by the breakdown in communications on D day. It was a significant factor in the success of the invasion, he thought. I had no idea a handful of girls were responsible. I should think we're talking about the Military Cross, aren't we?"

"Perhaps," said Fortescue, and his manner became prissy. "However, there were discipline problems with this group. An official complaint was entered against the leader, Major Clairet, after she insulted a Guards officer."

"Insulted?" said the bishop. "How?"

"There was a row in a bar, and I'm afraid she told him to fuck off, saving your presence, Bishop."

"My goodness me. She doesn't sound like the kind of person who should be held up as a hero to the next generation."

"Exactly. A lesser decoration than the Military Cross, then—the MBE, perhaps."

Nobby Clarke spoke again. "I disagree," he said mildly. "After all, if this woman had been a milksop she probably wouldn't have been able to blow up a telephone exchange under the noses of the Gestapo."

Fortescue was irritated. It was unusual for him to encounter opposition. He hated people who were not intimidated by him. He looked around the table. "The consensus of the meeting seems to be against you."

Clarke frowned. "I presume I can put in a minority recommendation," he said with stubborn patience.

"Indeed," said Fortescue. "Though I doubt if there's much point."

Clarke drew on his cigarette thoughtfully. "Why not?"

"The Minister will have some knowledge of one or two of the individuals on our list. In those cases he will follow his own inclinations, regardless of our recommendations. In all other cases he will do as we suggest, having himself no interest. If the committee is not unanimous, he will accept the recommendation of the majority."

"I see," said Clarke. "All the same, I

should like the record to show that I dissented from the committee and recommended the Military Cross for Major Clairet."

Fortescue looked at the secretary, the only woman in the room. "Make sure of that, please, Miss Gregory."

"Very good," she said quietly.

Clarke stubbed out his cigarette and lit another.

And that was the end of that.

Frau Waltraud Franck came home happy. She had managed to buy a neck of mutton. It was the first meat she had seen for a month. She had walked from her suburban home into the bombed city center of Cologne and had stood in line outside the butcher shop all morning. She had also forced herself to smile when the butcher, Herr Beckmann, fondled her behind; for if she had objected, he would have been "sold out" to her ever afterwards. But she could put up with Beckmann's wandering hands. She would get three days of meals out of a neck of mutton.

"I'm back!" she sang out as she entered

the house. The children were at school, but Dieter was at home. She put the precious meat in the pantry. She would save it for tonight, when the children would be here to share it. For lunch, she and Dieter would have cabbage soup and black bread.

She went into the living room. "Hello, darling!" she said brightly.

Her husband sat at the window, motionless. A piratical black patch covered one eye. He had on one of his beautiful old suits, but it hung loosely on his skinny frame, and he wore no tie. She tried to dress him nicely every morning, but she had never mastered the tying of a man's tie. His face wore a vacant expression, and a dribble of saliva hung from his open mouth. He did not reply to her greeting.

She was used to this. "Guess what?" she said. "I got a neck of mutton!"

He stared at her with his good eye. "Who are you?" he said.

She bent and kissed him. "We'll have a meaty stew for supper tonight. Aren't we lucky!"

* * *

That afternoon, Flick and Paul got married in a little church in Chelsea.

It was a simple ceremony. The war in Europe was over, and Hitler was dead, but the Japanese were fiercely defending Okinawa, and wartime austerity continued to cramp the style of Londoners. Flick and Paul both wore their uniforms: wedding dress material was very hard to find, and Flick as a widow did not want to wear white.

Percy Thwaite gave Flick away. Ruby was matron of honor. She could not be bridesmaid because she was already married—to Jim, the firearms instructor from the Finishing School, who was sitting in the second row of pews.

Paul's father, General Chancellor, was best man. He was still stationed in London, and Flick had got to know him quite well. He had the reputation of an ogre in the U.S. military, but to Flick he was a sweetheart.

Also in the church was Mademoiselle Jeanne Lemas. She had been taken to Ravensbrueck concentration camp, with young Marie; and Marie had died there, but somehow Jeanne Lemas had survived, and Percy Thwaite had pulled a hundred strings to get her to London for the wedding. She sat in the third row, wearing a cloche hat.

Dr. Claude Bouler had also survived, but Diana and Maude had both died in Ravensbrueck. Before she died, Diana had become a leader in the camp, according to Mademoiselle Lemas. Trading on the German weakness of showing deference to aristocracy, she had fearlessly confronted the camp commandant to complain about conditions and demand better treatment for all. She had not achieved much, but her nerve and optimism had raised the spirits of the starving inmates, and several survivors credited her with giving them the will to live.

The wedding service was short. When it was over, and Flick and Paul were husband and wife, they simply turned around and stood at the front of the church to receive congratulations.

Paul's mother was there, too. Somehow the general had managed to get his wife on a transatlantic flying boat. She had arrived late last night, and now Flick met her for the first time. She looked Flick up and down, obviously wondering whether this girl was good enough to be the wife of her wonderful son. Flick felt mildly put out. But she told herself this was natural in a proud mother and kissed Mrs. Chancellor's cheek with warmth.

They were going to live in Boston. Paul would take up the reins of his educational-records business. Flick planned to finish her doctorate, then teach American youngsters about French culture. The five-day voyage across the Atlantic would be their honeymoon.

Flick's ma was there in a hat she had bought in 1938. She cried, even though it was the second time she had seen her daughter married.

The last person in the small congregation to kiss Flick was her brother, Mark.

There was one more thing Flick needed to make her happiness perfect. With her arm still around Mark, she turned to her mother, who had not spoken to him for five years. "Look, Ma," she said. "Here's Mark."

Mark looked terrified.

Ma hesitated for a long moment. Then she opened her arms and said, "Hello, Mark."

"Oh, Ma," he said, and he hugged her.

After that, they all walked out into the sunshine.

FROM THE OFFICIAL HISTORY

"Women did not normally organize sabotage; but Pearl Witherington, a trained British courier, took over and ran an active Maquis of some two thousand men in Berry with gallantry and distinction after the Gestapo arrested her organizer. She was strongly recommended for an MC [Military Cross], for which women were held ineligible; and received instead a civil MBE, which she returned, observing she had done nothing civil."
—M. R. D. Foot, SOE in France (HMSO, London, 1966)

ACKNOWLEDGMENTS

For information and guidance about the Special Operations Executive, I'm grateful to M. R. D. Foot; on the Third Reich, Richard Overy; on the history of telephone systems, Bernard Green; on weapons, Candice De-Long and David Raymond. For help with research in general, I am grateful, as always, to Dan Starer of Research for Writers in New York City, Dstarer@bellatlantic.net; and to Rachel Flagg. I received much invaluable help from my editors: Phyllis Grann and Neil Nyren in New York, Imogen Tate in London, Jean Rosenthal in Paris, and Helmut Pesch in Cologne; and my agents Al Zuckerman and Amy Berkower. Several family members read the drafts and made helpful criticisms, especially John Evans, Barbara Follett, Emanuele Follett, Jann Turner, and Kim Turner.